The Traitor's Heir

THE TRAITOR'S HEIR

Every man has a destiny.
His is to betray.

THE KNIGHT OF ELDARAN
—— BOOK 1 ——

ANNA THAYER

LION FICTION

The three who were there from the beginning:
Esther, a faithful bookkeeper; Jonathan, a tireless consigliere; and
Thea, a first-rate "guinea pig".
For your friendship, enthusiasm, and words of courage, my thanks!

Published by Lion Fiction
an imprint of
Lion Hudson plc
Wilkinson House, Jordan Hill Road
Oxford OX2 8DR, England
www.lionhudson.com/fiction

ISBN 978 1 78264 075 2
e-ISBN 978 1 78264 076 9

This edition 2014

A catalogue record for this book is available from the British Library

Printed and bound in the UK, April 2014, LH26

Cover illustration by Jacey: www.jacey.com

CONTENTS

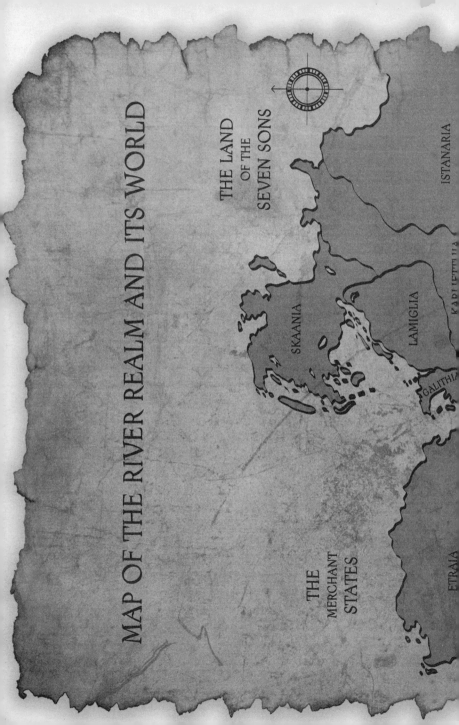

MAP OF THE RIVER REALM AND ITS WORLD

THE LAND
OF THE
SEVEN SONS

ISTANARIA

SKAANIA

LAMIGLIA

KADLETTHA

GALITHIA

THE
MERCHANT
STATES

ETRAIA

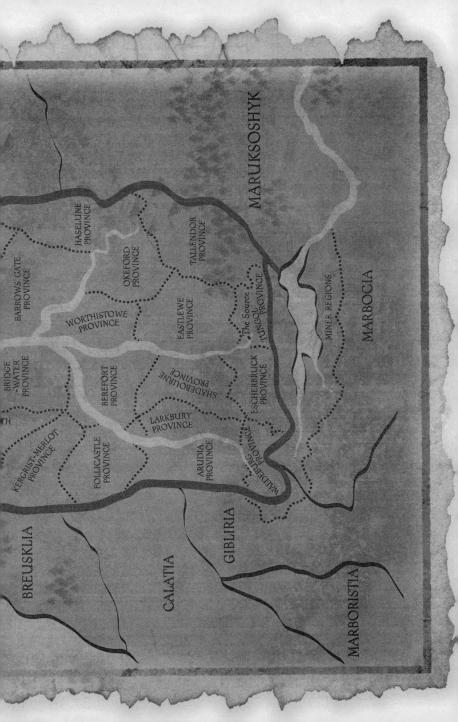

ACKNOWLEDGMENTS

Sir Philip Sidney once wrote, "Look in your heart, and write." There are many without whom I never would have done so.

First and foremost, I heartily thank my family: my mother, Costanza, who never tired in feeding me with books (even when they weighed a tonne in holiday suitcases); my father, Andy, who insisted on reading to his children every night and who piqued my curiosity with references to obscure facts and ancient stories; my sister, Giulia, whose fascination with a badge-making kit one rainy afternoon first drove me to take up the pen for myself, and who was the hearer of my earliest tales; my brother, Nicolas, and my great aunt, Giulia – whose obstinate affection and encouraging lunches upheld me during the writing of a tale that soon grew more complex than I had envisioned – and my grandfather, Leopoldo, whose gracious gift to me was the space and time I needed to write it.

Many friends and colleagues were the first purveyors of Eamon's misadventures; in weekly instalments Esther, Jonathan, and Thea acted as my first soundboards, continuity checkers, and "guinea pigs"; they helped me to flesh out and refine the world that grew up around Eamon as he journeyed into the dark heart of Dunthruik. There were many others who read and commented on early drafts; of these "beta testers", Matthew Davison and Tony Prior deserve special mention – the first for unbridled enthusiasm, and the latter for his exquisite, fine-toothed comb!

My thanks also go to my many students, all of whom, upon learning that I was writing a book, unabashedly and delightedly encouraged me to persevere with it.

I am indebted to all at Lion Hudson, for working so tirelessly and dedicatedly with me to see my novel come to fruition – and for giving me the chance to do so!

Lastly, I thank my amazing and loving husband, Justin, whose heart for story and eucatastrophe beats in time with mine.

Leith: Two ways you see, each from the other parts.
            The one with broken stones is packed, and briars
            That rend and grots that swift devour a man;
            The other upward leads. Though toilsome steps
            They be at first its region is the sun.
            This is no choice! These cannot mingled go.
            Perhaps before this day you might plead blind
            But the dread wheel has turned, and choose you must.

Tobias: O cursed all-cleaving soul!
            If I but knew I would not tarry more.

The Standard Won,
The River Poet

PROLOGUE

PROLOGUE

Darkness smothered the valleys and lurked in the curves of the River, shrouding the light of every star.

The slopes around Edesfield were marked with trees that surrendered their leaves to the wind in weeping moans. Beyond them, what had once been a mighty tower lay impotent in ruins. The trees spread blackly up towards it.

Groups of torches moved through the tower copses, combing fiercely back and forth across the muddy woodland. But the lights did not mark every man in the valley that night.

One felt the wind pulling at his face as he moved through the treeline. Branches clawed his face; roots and weeds clutched at his ankles like snakes. The glint of torches was behind him, casting an eerie glow across the trunks of the trees: pillars of harsh, reddened stone.

His hand slipped on the grizzled bark; he drew his fingers up to his face and tasted blood.

He spat it out. "Light!" he called softly.

A torchbearer came across the dell towards him, struggling not to sink in the mud. A second man came with him, with dark, tousled hair and eyes that glinted keenly under the torchlight. Both wore the Gauntlet's red uniform and had cloaks thrown over them to ward off the September chill.

The second man gave him a small smile. "I bring you light, Mr Goodman."

"Thank you, Mr Kentigern, sir."

"Report."

Cadet Goodman held forward his bloodied hand. The dark-haired lieutenant gestured and at his command the light was directed towards the tree. Goodman winced as the heat of the torch passed his face.

The light showed what he had known it would; blood on the bark, smeared in part by his hand and in part by the flight of the hunted man who had left it there.

The lieutenant turned to the torchbearer. "Fan along this treeline. Concentrate on the north ridge."

The torchbearer swept off; the dell receded into tombed blackness.

The cadet turned to his lieutenant. "He's making for the River?"

A flash of moonlight illuminated the lieutenant's face for a moment, showing a smile. "That he is. Our fleeing friend will be distraught when he finds that we know it!"

Together they moved to the eaves of the treeline. Goodman heard shouts farther up the hillside and saw the flicker of torches fanning out across the stretches of woods. In the heart of the valley below, torchlight sharply figured a rider in black: Lord Penrith. Even with the distance between them, the sight of the Hand chilled Goodman to his marrow. A man in Gauntlet uniform rode beside the Hand; lord and captain surveyed fields and woodland with grim faces.

Goodman swallowed in a constricted throat and glanced at the lieutenant. "What kind of man are we hunting, Ladomer?"

"Concentrate on the matter in hand, Eamon," the lieutenant answered. "You can ask Lord Penrith in person tomorrow, if the mood takes you."

Goodman did not know whether to shiver or laugh. "Do you think me mad?"

"I have known you for far too long, Eamon Goodman, to think otherwise." Suddenly the lieutenant gestured to the trees where another Gauntlet man stood. "Move into the line here with Spencing." His voice had taken on a tone of crisp command. "Barns and Ilwaine will be to your right and left. I want this bastard found, Mr Goodman; so do Captain Belaal and Lord Penrith."

"Yes, sir." Goodman did not hesitate a moment before going into the trees.

Ensign Spencing looked him over with distaste.

"You're with me?"

"Lieutenant's orders, Mr Spencing," Goodman returned sharply.

"Just don't make an idiot of yourself, Goodman," Spencing growled.

Goodman didn't answer him; they were already moving. Briars snatched at him as they passed into the line of men trying to force their quarry to surface. There were torches to his left and right, but light was poor; his best sense of direction came from the sounds of Spencing's movement.

Suddenly he heard a heavy thud somewhere to his left. He stopped; Spencing glowered back at him.

"The line is moving, Goodman!"

"I heard something." Goodman pinned all his sense on the dark.

"You heard nothing," Spencing spat. "We have orders to search the ridge. The done thing with orders, Mr Goodman, is to carry them out!"

The noise again. What good would it be to follow orders and lose the fugitive?

Impulse shot through his limbs.

"Goodman –!"

He didn't hear the rest but plunged into the thorny thickness of the trees, pushing on through ankle-deep mud and stinging branches. He knew what he had heard.

He came suddenly through the trees into a clearing and stopped. The torchlight was distant.

He heard someone drawing breath.

The wind swept through the trees and a stroke of moonlight illuminated the mud. It showed deep footprints and the shape of a man caved in the roots of a tree. The man clutched at his arm; blood flowed about his fingertips, weaving dark threads in torn clothes.

For a moment Goodman simply stared. Was this bloody wretch the man they had been hunting for so many hours?

It did not matter. He surged towards the fugitive, hand flying to his dagger. As the cadet crossed the clearing the fugitive seemed to see him for the first time; his face went white.

"No –"

Goodman seized the man's throat and hauled him bodily to his feet.

Goodman smiled. "The hunt is up," he said. But it wasn't.

Someone rushed at him from behind; the unexpected force of the impact shocked through him. A sudden arm latched about his throat.

With a cry he struck at it with his dagger. He drew blood. But before he could follow up the blow, his arm was seized and wrenched harshly backwards.

The fugitive fell from his grip. Goodman spun back and to one side, trying to free himself. He was too slow; both his arms were caught and driven up behind him, wresting his dagger from his hand. He saw the glint of his blade, a shrinking shard of the moon as it disappeared into the trees.

A blow forced him to his knees and he was thrown to the ground; mud plastered his ears and mouth.

He heard men speaking softly to the wounded man. He knew there was torchlight nearby and would have struggled wildly to make a noise – but it was as much as he could do to breathe. Some of his captors disappeared into the woods; they were moving south.

South!

The hiss of a blade being unsheathed. He stiffened. His heart lay in his throat.

Strong hands seized his. He lay still, fearing the worst; but the new hands violently bound his own together.

"Lucky little Glove!" laughed a snide voice. Its keeper delivered him a belittling pat on the shoulder before shoving his face down.

Goodman heard the last of the men vanish as he writhed and gasped in the mud. He did not think about how nearly he had lost his life, nor did he wonder how it had been spared; all he could think was how easily the men would slip through the Gauntlet's northward-roaming line.

Driving his hands into the mud he slipped and slid them together, trying to escape the ropes. He lost both gloves in the process but eventually drew them free. Shivering with cold and rage he tore his hands across his face, peeling mud from his eyes.

The fugitives were gone.

Staggering to his feet, not stopping to recover gloves or dagger, or to wonder where Spencing was or whether he should return to him, he turned and hurtled through the trees.

His feet brought him swiftly back to the fields. The lines still combed the hillside, moving north towards the River. With a cry of immense frustration, he ran on.

His lieutenant, Ladomer Kentigern, stood with Captain Belaal and Lord Penrith. He could not imagine how he looked to them, a mud-spattered cadet racing madly across the field, but he knew only too well how they would look on him when he delivered his news.

He tripped to a slipping halt before them, only just remembering to bow before Lord Penrith, the Master's chosen Hand over the town and province of Edesfield.

"His glory," Goodman panted. At least while he bowed he did not have to meet their eyes.

"Mr Goodman." Captain Belaal's voice was icy as the biting wind.

"The fugitive, sir," he spluttered, gesturing wildly behind him. "He's aided, he's gone south."

"South?" Belaal repeated harshly, incredulous. The faces of both Hand and lieutenant echoed it.

"I swear it, sir!"

"Leave your swearing until tomorrow, Goodman," the captain retorted. "That's if any of you will merit the swearing." Sensing his displeasure, his horse fretted unevenly. The captain drew his reins tightly into his hand. "By your leave, Lord Penrith, I will redirect search parties immediately."

The Hand nodded silently. With an angry grunt Belaal wheeled his horse to the side and spurred it towards the northward-roving torches.

Goodman's chest was still heaving as the Hand's gaze settled darkly on him.

"You let him escape."

Goodman blinked hard. "My lord, I was taken by surprise and –"

"Taken by surprise?" the Hand replied contemptuously. "How could that be so, when you were searching in pairs? Unless you disobeyed an order."

Goodman stopped. He had – and with good reason. But he could hardly say that to the Hand.

"Did you disobey an order?" The Hand's tone had grown as pitch as the night about him.

"My lord –"

Ladomer flashed him a warning look.

Goodman quailed. He swallowed hard. "Yes, my lord."

There was an agonizing silence.

"Name, cadet," Penrith commanded.

"Eamon Goodman, my lord." He did not meet the Hand's gaze; he did not dare.

The Hand raised a mocking eyebrow. "The bookbinder's boy?"

Goodman felt Ladomer Kentigern's gaze on him, commanding him not to speak out of turn; he obeyed it. "Yes, my lord."

"So, after three years of cadet training, you are woefully vulnerable to surprise and are incapable of obeying orders? You are a disgrace to your dead father, to yourself, and to your captain, Cadet Goodman," the Hand spat. "You'll be lucky to swear tomorrow."

"Yes, my lord," the cadet answered. It took all his will to keep insolence from his voice. They could not take his swearing from him! He had worked so hard…

"Where's your dagger?"

Goodman looked up. The Hand's gaze pierced him; he knew how condemning his reply would be.

"I don't know, my lord," he said at last.

"I can see that Gauntlet work is best left to the Gauntlet," he hissed. His ire was crushing. "You're of no further use here, cadet. You will not present yourself at college until you've found your dagger."

Goodman gaped. Quivering in every limb, he bowed low. "Yes, my lord."

The Hand turned to follow Captain Belaal. Goodman remained bowed until the sound and feel of hoof-beats receded. He was reeling as he straightened; breath fled from him in ragged bursts.

A firm, kind touch alighted on his shoulder. "Are you hurt, Eamon?" Ladomer asked.

Eamon turned his stinging eyes out over the fields and hills. "No," he answered as the lights passed by.

CHAPTER I

It was a September morning in the 532nd year of the Master's throne. In distant fields the sun was rising, stirring all the world to gold, the sky so clear and crisp that an upward glance might yet catch sight of hidden stars.

But Eamon had eyes for none of it; all his look and thought was bent fastidiously on the filthy dagger in his hands. With a grim sigh he tried to scrape more mud from the details of the small hilt; he had not yet dared to assess the state of his boots or uniform. As he scrubbed furiously at the weapon, fatigue sapped his limbs.

For over five hundred years the River Realm had lain in the charge of the Master and, from Dunthruik – the city that had always guarded the river-mouth – the Master's power had kept the land strong against its enemies. To the north, south, and, across the sea, the west lived merchant-lords with whom a grudging peace was sometimes granted by trade; to the east in the land of the Seven Sons roamed strange lordlings who were little more than inbred, misfit chieftains. The Master had held against them and their like and, since the River Realm had been bathed in the glory that emanated from the Master's throne, none had dared to come across the mountains from Istanaria.

The strength and endurance of that power was seen in the Master's Hands and in the Gauntlet, the ancient and noble legion of soldiers that kept his law. To bear their uniform was to be marked as the Master's own, and to serve him was the greatest honour that the River Realm could afford. Though there were regional militia forces across the land it was to the Gauntlet that men aspired: this was the Master's eyes and ears, his blade and blood. To run them was a dangerous business indeed.

There were few young men who did not dream of setting their hands in the Master's Gauntlet. Training was long, arduous, and fierce; it was not uncommon for cadets to be killed in their extensive preparation, but the families of such men were well honoured. Men who glorified the Master in the Gauntlet guaranteed honour for themselves and for their heirs; the exceptional were promoted and made draybants and captains, and some were taken from the Gauntlet's ranks to join the Hands.

For most, dreams of the Gauntlet were enough. Many young men sought to realize them, and Cadet Eamon Goodman of Edesfield was no exception. He had joined the Gauntlet later than most others, and at twenty-three he was one of the oldest cadets that hoped to take their oath that day in Edesfield province.

But as he sat in the yard of the smithy where he lived, Eamon despaired of it. He had sold his hope in a futile act the night before. He had lost everything with it. How could he have been such a fool?

"Eamon?"

A young woman was passing the yard. She had auburn hair, pulled back in loose tresses. As he met her gaze her look grew worried. He realized that his pale face was stained with tears.

"Good morning," he tried, hoping that his tone might mask what his face could not, but his voice sounded frail and hopeless even to himself. He rubbed a dirty hand across aching eyes.

"I've been looking for you since last night." His friend sat down on the wall beside him. As she cocked her head at him her hair flashed like gold in the light. "Have you slept at all?"

"No." He fell silent, staring angrily at his dagger.

"Eamon?" she prompted. "What happened?"

"What happened?" He looked at her, unable to form words. "I ruined everything, Aeryn!" he spat at last. "That's what happened!" He flung the dagger aside, willing it to disintegrate.

Aeryn didn't flinch. "I don't believe that."

Eamon looked at her incredulously. "They're not going to let me swear!"

His words hung in the air. "That's not the drying of the River," Aeryn replied gently.

"Not the drying of the River?" Eamon could only stare at her. "How can you say that? You know how much this means to me!" he cried, pointing to his uniform, its distinctive Gauntlet red barely visible between rips and mud. Eamon let out a cry of disgust.

"I know what you think joining the Gauntlet means," Aeryn told him.

"Do you? Put yourself in my place for a moment, Aeryn!"

"Eamon –"

"You know this is all I've ever wanted!"

Aeryn pursed her lips. "That's not true, Eamon. I've lost count of the number of times that you told me your mother wanted you to go to the university."

"Don't bring *her* into this, Aeryn!" Eamon snapped. "She's been dead for more than a decade; if she was alive I'd still be in Dunthruik, not this forsaken backwater!"

"I'm just saying that it hasn't always been your dream," Aeryn placated.

Eamon glared at her. "How would *you* know? How could I go to the Gauntlet when my father was alone? How could I even talk about it?" He gripped his dagger hard. "He needed me. He wanted me to learn his trade. And we got by without dreams."

Aeryn laughed. "You more than got by, Eamon! You loved it. The smell and the feel of the books, the taste of story on your tongue? Your father practically had to force you to come and play with other children; all you ever wanted to do was read! That was how I first met you – sobbing, because he had taken your books away and sent you outside." Her eyes shone. "Don't you remember?"

Eamon did not answer her. He remembered. The books had seemed his only comfort in a world that had shorn him of home and mother in a night. He had loved them. He had loved sharing them with his father.

"Yes, I loved it. I loved being the bookbinder's son – even after my father died. I was still a boy, but I scraped by. Perhaps I would have been happy binding books all my days, despite my struggle to buy bread. But the fire finished it all."

She looked at him sadly. "I know –"

"No, Aeryn," he retorted. "You don't. My father and his books were all that I had left. Everything I loved, everything I had worked for, my home and my livelihood…"

Aeryn touched his hand. "You still had hope."

Eamon scoffed angrily. "Being taken in by a kind-hearted smith and given work isn't hope, Aeryn. The Gauntlet was my hope – a chance to do something better, be someone better. A chance to start again. It's been taken from me, just like everything else." He could not meet her gaze. "I've been forbidden to swear."

Aeryn watched him hard for a moment. "What happened last night?"

He paused, and suddenly he was pushing through the trees, the smell of blood and fire in his nostrils.

"You want to know what happened to me?" he said. "I was sent to hunt for a man in the woods and I disobeyed an order to search in groups. I found the fugitive and I lost him. He got away from me and nobody caught him. And because I brought the news of his escape to Captain Belaal and Lord Penrith, and lost my dagger in the process – thus making an idiot of myself – *they won't let me swear*." His hands began to shake. "I've made a fool of myself and I've lost everything," he said bitterly, "as I always do."

Gently, Aeryn reached across and touched his arm. "You're not a fool, Eamon," she said. "If Hughan were here, he'd say the same."

"How do you know what he would say?" Eamon retorted.

"You used to listen to him," Aeryn answered.

"Yes," Eamon said, and fresh, wrathful tears leapt into his eyes.

"But Hughan's been dead for eight years! For Master's sake, Aeryn!"

Aeryn looked at him strangely. "Don't swear by him."

"Don't start with that," Eamon snapped.

"Hughan never thought the Gauntlet was where you should be," Aeryn said quietly.

"Hughan's *dead!*" Eamon cried, and then fell silent. The memory of Hughan stung at him in the long quiet. He pressed his hands into his eyes. "Ladomer thought I could do it," he whispered. "He told me I could do it…"

"Ladomer is a Gauntlet officer," Aeryn pointed out. "Isn't it possible that his opinion is biased?"

"He was my friend long before he was my officer," Eamon answered. It had been Ladomer who had finally convinced him that it was not too late to try for the Gauntlet, and Ladomer who had encouraged him, guiding him through every part of his difficult training. "Ladomer knows me, Aeryn."

"So do I."

As Eamon looked across at her injured face, some of his anger ebbed away.

"I'm sorry, Aeryn," he said at last. "I didn't mean to get so angry with you. It's just…"

There was a pause. "I know what you've been through, Eamon," Aeryn told him, "and I know how much you have longed for this day, and how much of your hope you've set on it. But I don't believe for a moment that you are lost if you don't swear. Something greater might come of it."

"Like what?"

Aeryn shrugged. "I don't know," she said, "but something will come. It always has before."

Eamon drew a deep breath. He looked down at the patches of black beneath the caked layers of mud on his boots, then back to Aeryn. He wondered whether she might be right.

"I expect I look like a beast," he exhaled miserably, though not quite as miserably as before.

Aeryn brushed some of the dirt from his sleeves. "Red isn't your colour," she said with a smile.

"Maybe," Eamon murmured.

They sat together in silence, the sun just peeking over the walls of the yard. The air chimed with the sound of the smith at work.

Eamon heard approaching footsteps. He blinked against the light. It wasn't until the man stopped right in front of him that Eamon recognized him.

"I wasn't sure whether you'd be here or still playing at wraith in the woods," the man said.

"I'm here," Eamon answered, somewhat wistfully.

"To judge by the colour of you, I reckon that you'd make a good wraith."

"Thank you, sir," he said sarcastically.

"You found it?"

Eamon nodded and pointed to the muddy thing on the ground. With a laugh, Ladomer picked up the discarded blade.

"I'm impressed," he said, flicking it pensively back and forth across his hands. He smiled. "Very impressed, and glad, too; I won't have to lend you mine."

"Lend me yours?" Eamon looked at him, confused. "Why would you want to do that?"

"Because I wouldn't want you to go and see the captain without one."

Eamon glanced at Aeryn; she shook her head blankly.

"You know far too well that I'm not going to see the captain," Eamon told him.

Ladomer sighed and shook his head. "Eamon, Eamon! When are you going to learn that I know a good many more things than you do?" With a small grin Ladomer came and perched on the wall at Eamon's other side. "Captain Belaal has asked to see you."

"Asked to see me?" Eamon snorted bitterly. "And why might that be? So that he can dress me down a little more?"

"Whence all this discouragement?" Ladomer laughed, laying his hand grandly on Eamon's shoulder. "Anyone would think that you weren't going to swear today!"

Eamon shook Ladomer's hand away. "Were you even listening when Lord Penrith raked me?" he asked belligerently.

"Yes."

"Then you already know that I'm not going to swear!"

"Were you even listening when your lieutenant said that he knows more than you do?"

"Yes –"

"Captain Belaal wants to see you," Ladomer told him, "and he's going to ask you if you're prepared to swear."

Eamon gaped. "*What?*"

"Wake up, Ratbag!" Ladomer laughed, tapping Eamon's forehead like a door. "They want you to swear!"

"But –" Eamon stared at him. "But Lord Penrith –"

"– has clearly changed his mind."

"I don't understand –"

"Nothing new there! Do you honestly think you're the only cadet who has ever been threatened with revoked swearing?" Ladomer asked. "You're just the kind of man the Gauntlet wants: able and keen to serve! At least that is what I, biased as I am, think. Captain Belaal seems to think so, too, because he said that he wanted to see you in an hour. Of course," he added, pressing the dagger into Eamon's hands, "it *has* taken me a quarter of an hour to find you, which doesn't leave you much time to get cleaned up."

The thought snapped Eamon out of his trance like a thunderclap. "It doesn't!" he yelped, and leapt to his feet.

CHAPTER II

With Ladomer's help, enthusiasm, and a spare jacket filched on the quiet from the college vestry, Eamon found himself walking into the college on the stroke of Belaal's hour. Edesfield's Gauntlet college was small in comparison to those in other regions but, being the province's key college, merited a captain of its own. Eamon had heard it said that the captaincy of Edesfield was thought of as an ornamental one, but Captain Belaal was by no means an ornamental man. He was harsh and blunt, quicker to condemn than to praise.

The captain's offices were in the central part of the college. Eamon's pulse raced as he went quickly through the corridors. There were a lot of other cadets going to and fro, and some ensigns, too. The single flame pinned to their jackets distinguished them as the men who had already proven that they were worthy of the Gauntlet and taken their oaths to the Master.

Would he be counted among their number by the end of the day?

A fierce lieutenant guarded Belaal's office, greeting Eamon with a crushing look.

"Oh, it's *you*."

Eamon wondered what rumours about him had flown through the college during the night. Not that it would have made much difference; the captain's lieutenant had never liked him.

"Captain Belaal sent for me, sir," Eamon answered, saluting before discreetly straightening his jacket. The lieutenant snorted as if no amount of tidying or straightening could redeem so hopeless a case.

"Yes," he said. "Wait here."

Eamon waited anxiously while the lieutenant disappeared into Belaal's door. He tried to distract himself by listening to the cadets and ensigns going about their business, and watching the central courtyard through the window. Dozens of Gauntlet were busily arranging a platform for the swearing ceremony; behind the tall stage a couple of young cadets were struggling to hang Edesfield's red banner, showing four golden lions, on a wall. They japed merrily about how lopsided it was until their officer came and chastened them.

The lieutenant returned. "The captain will see you now, Mr Goodman."

"Thank you, sir," Eamon answered. Drawing a tense breath he went as crisply and smartly as he could into Belaal's office. The lieutenant followed him, papers in hand.

The office was small but primly kept; a smaller version of Edesfield's banner hung within, a great crown stitched into one corner. Belaal was standing near it, his large hands clasped behind his back, admiring the courtyard preparations through his own window.

"Cadet Goodman, sir," Eamon said, drawing himself to formal attention.

"Ah yes," Belaal laughed. He turned from the window, a broad smile on his face. "Quite an adventure we had yesterday evening, Mr Goodman."

"Yes, sir."

"You in particular."

"Yes, sir." Eamon tried not to sound nervous as Belaal's dark eyes assessed him.

"I have had a formal report from Ensign Spencing. His opinion of your actions is, needless to say, not altogether agreeable."

Eamon quelled a feeling of growing alarm. "Sir."

"Report, Mr Goodman."

Eamon swallowed once to clear his throat; he noticed that the lieutenant had sat down at a small side desk and was already making swift, fluid notes of the conversation.

Eamon looked back to Belaal. "Your orders were to capture the fugitive. Lieutenant Kentigern assigned me to go with Spencing, sir," he said. "Passing through the trees I heard movement. Mr Spencing was neither of my ear nor my opinion. I went to investigate the noise without him, sir, and I found the fugitive, badly injured in the left arm, hiding in a clearing. I went to take him and was then attacked myself by the fugitive's allies; I injured one before they overpowered and bound me. They left, moving south, and I took a few minutes to escape and come back to you and Lord Penrith to report."

Belaal watched him with a sharp expression somewhere between interest and annoyance. "You are aware, Mr Goodman, that we did not catch our man last night?"

"Yes, sir."

"Would you say that that was your doing, Mr Goodman?"

Eamon tried hard to match the captain's gaze without flinching. Belaal had always frightened him; it was the kind of disquieting fear that could raise his whole skin to gooseflesh with a glance.

"I did everything in my power to apprehend the man, sir," he managed. Surely it was obvious that the aided fugitive would have slipped through the search lines regardless of whether or not he had seen them? But Eamon did not express those thoughts to his captain.

"Lord Penrith is more than a little disappointed in last night's performance," Belaal said, leaning against the front edge of his desk so as to fix Eamon in a firm gaze. "He had it in mind that the escape could be pinned on you."

Eamon's blood started to race. If he was scapegoated then he might never swear: it would become a permanent mark on his Gauntlet record.

Belaal was still watching him. "Lord Penrith, however, is a reasonable man. He has retracted his objection to your swearing, in acknowledgment of your courageous attempt to take the man. It was, after all, your primary objective, and courage is prized highly in the Gauntlet." A smile flickered on his face. "Mr Goodman, you will be delighted to know that your name, which had been stricken from it, has been marked again on the swearing list."

Joy flooded through him. "Thank you, sir."

"You have no duties this morning," Belaal continued. "You will present yourself at the eighth hour for the ceremony. In the meantime," he added, "try and resolve yourself to do nothing that might change Lord Penrith's mind."

Eamon nodded firmly. "Yes, sir."

Captain Belaal dismissed him and Eamon left the office, feeling lightheaded. The noises of the busy college seemed faint in his ears but the great red banner, which now hung proudly (and straight) in the courtyard, seemed bold and bright. That very day he would stand beneath it and take the Gauntlet's oath.

He left the college, and as he went into the street he felt a friendly hand land on his shoulder.

"So?" Ladomer asked. The lieutenant's eyes twinkled with anticipation of good news.

Eamon grinned. "I'm going to swear."

Ladomer flung his arms about Eamon in an overjoyed embrace. For a moment his friend's jubilance reminded him, sharply and suddenly, of just how close he had come to not swearing; then Eamon was laughing too, and only a little less loudly.

"Well done!" Ladomer cried, laying an almighty slap of congratulation on his shoulder.

"Thank you. Really," Eamon added more seriously, "thank you, Ladomer. I would never have become a cadet if it wasn't for you; my oath today is your doing."

Ladomer smiled. "My *dear* Ratbag," he said, treating Eamon to a contortedly elegant bow. "You are most welcome."

They took a deep breath, inhaling the precious moment. Ladomer looked at him again.

"Aeryn asked whether you and I wanted to join her at the Star to eat something," he said. "I said that we would."

"You mean that?" Eamon asked. "You don't have to go running

off on some errand, or to some other unit in a far-flung corner of the Realm?" In his role as a lieutenant, and a gifted one at that, Ladomer was away from Edesfield more often than he was home. "You actually have time to sit and eat with us?" Eamon couldn't remember when they had last had that chance.

Ladomer smiled and clapped him about the shoulders again. "My dear Eamon," he said, "today of all days, my time is for you."

Eamon beamed. "Sounds perfect."

Edesfield, capital of Edesfield province, stood south of the Great Bend. It was the last bridgeable point on the River, which from there ran west to the city of Dunthruik and the sea. Edesfield's bustling riverside was filled with docks where holks – river-faring vessels more shallowly drafted than the great merchant cogs that crossed the seas, used to carry men and wares all over the River Realm – frequently halted to do business or resupply. This high turnover of traders ensured that Edesfield was well provisioned with inns and taverns.

The Morning Star was one those inns. It was only a few streets away from the Gauntlet college and, with a swearing just around the corner, was hosting the families of men from all over the province who had come to Edesfield to take their oaths.

The imminent swearing made the town busier than usual. As Eamon and Ladomer threaded their way through the crowded streets Ladomer talked and joked, as he always did, but Eamon scarcely heard him; the return of his lost hopes had made his heart light and his steps vague.

"Watch where you're going, Ratbag!" Ladomer laughed, tugging him to keep him from strolling straight into some passers-by.

Together they turned on to Bury's Hill, one of the oldest parts of Edesfield. The houses there stood hunched against one another as though the whole line relied on the buildings at the bottom and a single, well-judged gust of wind might send them tumbling down in a pile of wood and brick and thatch. Eamon tried to cross the cobbles without marking his boots but soon found that even after more than a decade of walking the street, he had not mastered it. At least, he thought to himself as they reached the inn, he had not made any of his usual encounters with animal excrement.

Two ornamental spears stood to either side of the Morning Star's door, homage to an old wives' tale which claimed that Edesfield had been built over the ruins of an ancient fort. The inn had offered ale, food, and lodgings more or less as long as Edesfield had stood.

The establishment was owned by Aeryn's father, Telo, and was a place where the three friends had been meeting for years. Eamon remembered the long afternoons that he had spent there in his youth. It had always been like a second home to him, and Aeryn's father had been kind to him in the days after his own had died.

A worn wooden sign hung over the doorway. Telo had been saying for years that he would carve a new one, though he never had. The man's wife had made the sign shortly before her death, and it had not been touched since she had set it there. Even so, it did not take a sign to tell Edesfield's Morning Star; it was always the first to light its windows and the last to douse them.

Eamon and Ladomer went in together. The inn buzzed with men, women, and children who were preparing to attend the swearing.

Telo was behind the bar, wiping tankards, while his serving-hands whizzed between the tables. Eamon thought that Telo looked tired, though cheerful even so. He supposed that was only natural when the inn was so busy. Aeryn was with him.

Ladomer took the room in at a gaze and then moved to one of the few unoccupied tables. He drew out a chair and sat.

"I thought I would make myself useful for a change, and save us a table – and quickly, too!" Ladomer grandly put his feet up on the chair opposite him, presumably as part of his table-reserving scheme.

"What would we do without you, Ladomer?" Aeryn asked, passing by with a laugh.

Ladomer paused, as though deeply considering the question. "I really don't know," he said at last. "But I'll tell you what you *can* do – swipe a couple of drinks and bring yourselves over here, the pair of you!"

"Is that an order?" Eamon asked wryly.

"It most certainly is!" Ladomer tilted his head back and laughed. Eamon laughed with him, but thought that he saw an odd look pass across Aeryn's face. Looking again, he saw only a smile.

Eamon turned to carry out Ladomer's playful command, but before he could, a tray of mugs was set in his hands.

"Big day today?" Telo asked.

"Yes."

Telo smiled warmly. "Then you may need the drink! It's on the house, my lad."

"It always is." Eamon was struck, as so many times before, by the innkeeper's kindness. "Thank you," he said earnestly.

Telo smiled.

Eamon courteously waited for Aeryn to go across to the table then followed her, bearing his precious cargo. He saw that Ladomer's feet were still firmly planted on the remaining chair.

"Might I sit, sir?" Eamon asked playfully. He had once made the mistake of not only sitting on Ladomer, but also of comparing him favourably to upholstery in the process. He had meant both things in jest; the same could be said for the crushing kick with which Ladomer had rewarded him for his impudence. Ladomer had, of course, apologized profusely, and Eamon had done the same, but it had still taken some weeks for the bruise to heal completely.

Eamon knew, from this and other experience, that Ladomer Kentigern was one of the strongest and most agile men that he had ever met. Ladomer had always bested him, often painfully, in training. Long years of that same Gauntlet training had also taught him that Ladomer was an extremely capable soldier. Eamon knew that he would never want to be on the wrong side of his friend or stand against his lieutenant in a real fight.

At Eamon's grandiloquent request an enormous grin rolled

across Ladomer's face. "You wish me to remove my feet?" he asked innocently. They were both remembering the same incident.

"I would be greatly obliged," Eamon answered.

The smile grew broader. "Anything for you, Eamon!" Ladomer told him.

The lieutenant moved his feet and Eamon sat. He passed the mugs round, and Ladomer raised one high.

"A toast!" he said. "To Eamon! May he be the finest Glove the River Realm has ever seen!"

The mugs chinked together, chiming their terracotta accord and drawing the attention of bystanders, who cheered. With an embarrassed smile Eamon took a sip of his drink. Like him, Ladomer had come to Edesfield in the years following the culls in the city and, like Eamon, Ladomer had lost both his parents in the upheaval that had followed. Ladomer was a few years older than him and had always seemed to bear his misfortune as equally as his fortune. He was a fine lieutenant, and Eamon wondered whether the man sitting opposite him would one day become one of the Master's Hands. The thought of his friend winning such an accolade made him smile.

Ladomer set his mug down. "Did Belaal tell you where you're to be assigned?" he asked, leaning forward with deep interest. Before Eamon could answer he ploughed on: "I hope you're not staying in Edesfield!"

Aeryn gave him a strange look. "Come on, Aeryn!" Ladomer laughed. "Edesfield is a fine place, but there're no prospects here for young men like Eamon and me."

"You're hardly ever in Edesfield," Aeryn commented. "I'm not sure you're qualified to speak about what it's like here!"

"But I know what it's like out there, Aeryn," Ladomer told her, gesturing broadly with his mug. "And that's where we should be, doing our bit for the Master — especially now that the Easters are arming."

"Arming?" Eamon asked.

"They've severed diplomatic relations with Dunthruik."

Eamon nodded slowly; it explained the fretted movement of so many of the Hands back and forth between their regions and the capital.

"I've heard," Ladomer began, lowering his voice and head conspiratorially, "that the Easters are feeding information and support to the wayfarers. You know; urging them on."

Eamon laughed. "Nobody can stand against the Master!" he said confidently. "These 'wayfarers' least of all. I mean, the might of the whole Gauntlet and the Master is against them. They don't stand a chance, Easters or not."

"I know that," Ladomer growled grimly, "but that doesn't stop the roads being marred and the valleys being filled with the bodies of unsworn cadets! It doesn't stop the snakes taking the border towns, murdering the women and children, and burning the fields!"

Eamon drew a deep breath. He had seen such towns in the time he had spent as a cadet on active service in the provinces of Sablemar and Wakebairn – both on the borders to the north-east of Edesfield – during his Gauntlet training.

"I know," he answered.

"What we know doesn't stop them evading us." Ladomer exhaled loudly and with frustration.

Eamon glanced at him in surprise. "The man last night…?"

"He was a wayfarer, Eamon – a snake, just like the men who killed Hughan."

The name drew across Eamon like a blade.

"We don't know that wayfarers killed him, Ladomer," Aeryn said quietly.

"Yes we bloody do!" Ladomer retorted, slamming his fist on the table. "It was wayfarers, and they had no reason to kill him, or anybody else, who died that day. No reason, Aeryn! The snakes did it, and they would do it to any one of us without a second thought. That is what their 'glorious leader', the Serpent, instils in them."

"I don't understand why they do it," Eamon said.

"They have no reason," Ladomer answered bitterly. He looked across at Eamon with a returning smile. "But they will be stopped; they cannot outlast the Master and his Gauntlet."

There was a pause. Chatter bubbled on about them. Telo came past, his arms filled with steaming bowls which he laid, one by one, on the table before them. Eamon looked gratefully at the food; after a night spent crawling about in the mud and a morning lurching between hope and despair, he was ravenous, despite the first singing of nerves in his flesh.

"What's a Glove without his meat in him, eh?" Telo said kindly. "Eat up, lad."

"Thank you, Telo," Eamon replied, looking up at the innkeeper. He suddenly caught sight of a bloody mark on the man's rolled-down sleeves. He leapt to his feet in alarm.

"Telo, you're hurt!" The outcry drew the attention of nearby tables.

"What?" Telo looked down at his sleeves and then laughed. "Oh no, no lad," he said, brushing aside Eamon's concern, "no, that's not mine. I've just been preparing some meat in the kitchen, that's all." He laid a hand over his arm to hide the stain. "I'm sorry it bothered you."

Eamon wasn't convinced. "You're sure you're not hurt?"

"I'm sure."

Eamon reluctantly sat down again.

"Now, eat well!" Telo said.

The innkeeper went quietly back to the bar and out into the back parts of the inn.

Aeryn raised her mug. "To Eamon," she said, and smiled at him.

The lunch was pleasant, and although his swearing was on all their minds it was not mentioned again. They whiled away an hour or so, reminiscing over the long years that they had known each other and wondering about the future. As they talked, Eamon felt that his own future had never seemed as bright as it did then.

At last the lunch ended and Eamon left, anxious to be punctual. Aeryn and Ladomer both walked with him down to the crossroads at the foot of Bury's Hill.

"I should go and get ready for the ceremony myself," Ladomer said.

Eamon laughed. "You're always impeccably turned out," he answered, looking his friend's pristine uniform up and down.

"Comes of being a lieutenant, Mr Goodman!" Ladomer returned. "I'll see you later. Don't dally too long!"

"I won't. I'm so glad you can be here today, Ladomer. It means a lot to me."

His friend smiled. "And to me, Eamon."

Ladomer began moving back through the roads towards the college. Eamon turned to Aeryn. "I should go too," he said, and he meant to, but the look on her face stopped him. "Is something the matter?" he asked. "You've been very quiet today."

"That's hardly usual, is it?" Aeryn offered him a smile, but fell silent. Carts and people passed by, many heading to the river docks. Eamon watched his friend with concern; she seemed distant, guarded.

"Aeryn?"

"Eamon," she whispered, looking up at last, "are you sure that you want –?"

"To swear? Aeryn!" he cried. "I've never been so sure of anything *in my life*."

"Things will change, Eamon." The look on her face had grown serious.

"Don't be ridiculous. They won't change at all," Eamon answered lightly. "Most likely they'll station me here in Edesfield. It will be just the same, and *I'll* be just the same." Aeryn's frown did not relent; she did not meet his gaze. He caught her hand and gave it an encouraging squeeze. "We'll still be here: you, Ladomer, and I. Well, you and I, anyway. Together, as we've always been."

"You had best go and smarten up," Aeryn answered softly, taking her hand from his.

"Yes."

"Good luck with the ceremony," she added, turning away.

"Wait. Will you be there?"

Aeryn surprised him with a smile that seemed sad. She leaned forward and kissed his cheek.

"Yes."

The college courtyard glittered in the afternoon sunlight. In the faraway valleys the first trees were beginning to turn gold and red with the autumn; it was as though the whole of nature rejoiced to wear the Master's colours, just as the young men would who were to swear that day.

Eamon waited nervously in the shaded walkways. There were perhaps four dozen other young men with him. Blood, anticipation, anxiety, and elation pounded through him; he could barely keep still.

Some younger cadets were moving through the lines of men to be sworn in, straightening their jackets and taking the accidental scuffs off their boots. Except for the noise of that work things were silent. Eamon understood the dense quiet; the feelings churning inside him impeded speech.

One of the young cadets passed him, then paused to rub a buffing cloth over the toe of his boot. He offered Eamon a brilliant smile of good fortune.

"Good luck!"

Eamon nodded and straightened back into his place in line. He could hear voices in the courtyard beyond – officers, and families of the men to be sworn, all expectantly waiting for the ceremony to begin.

At that moment Captain Belaal came in. He was followed by Edesfield's first lieutenant, and by another lieutenant who bore a covered object in his hands. With a start Eamon realized that the second man was Ladomer. He hadn't known that Ladomer would be the pommel bearer, but he supposed that he should have suspected it; the honour usually fell to one of the college lieutenants.

Belaal swept down the line of cadets, assessing every man with a swift gaze, then nodded with what approached satisfaction. "You know what to do, gentlemen."

"Yes, sir," came a quiet chorus. They did. They had been through a practice ceremony the previous week. For more than most of them the practice had been the enacting of a dream that had been rehearsed far longer.

At the trumpet's call the line of cadets to be sworn began to move. His heart beating like a drum, Eamon wondered whether he could stand at all. But his feet took the lead, and he walked in line with the others, caught up in the immutable ritual of the ceremony.

The line filed out into the courtyard. The sun ran over his face and into his eyes. Those gathered in the courtyard to watch recognized their entry: the cadets, ensigns, and officers drew their swords up to their faces in formal salute. Eamon was dazzled by the light of the flashing blades. Behind them the men and women of Edesfield province were watching with pride; their sons were to be sworn.

The swearing-line drew up solemnly before the platform where Belaal stood, First Lieutenant Ellis at his right and Ladomer at his left. Lord Penrith loomed behind them, his presence lending further authority. Eamon gazed at them for a second before he found his voice, in unison with the voices of the other cadets.

"His glory!" they cried. The words rang victoriously in the air.

"Today, these men formally make known their allegiance to the Master." Belaal surveyed the line with a smile. "May their service be to his pleasure and his glory."

The captain turned to Ladomer, who graciously uncovered what he carried: a long golden staff with a broad pommel at its head. It was Edesfield's swearing staff, and had been given from the Master's own hand years before. Every cadet would lay his right hand on it to make his oath. At the sight of it Eamon's heart leapt in excitement.

Belaal took the staff and looked back to the line of cadets.

"Offley Barns of Edesfield."

Eamon watched as the first cadet in the line went steadily up onto the platform and knelt down before Belaal.

"What do you seek?" Belaal asked.

"Service with the Gauntlet, captain." Barns's voice was less steady than his walk had been; Eamon could see his jaw quivering.

"What is your pledge?"

"I, Offley Barns, do hereby pledge my allegiance to the Master. My blood, my blade, and my body are all given in his service."

"And do you swear this most solemnly to the Master, such an oath as may not be broken?"

"I do swear it."

"Then receive the mark of your allegiance." Belaal held forth the staff, tilting the glinting pommel towards the cadet. Barns reached his right hand to it. He bowed his head for a moment, then looked up with wide, ecstatic eyes. The first lieutenant stepped forward to pin a single flame on his red jacket.

Belaal spoke in a loud voice. "Rise, Ensign Offley Barns. You belong to the Master."

Barns stood and left the platform. Belaal called the next cadet: "Geraint Ilwaine of Edesfield."

Eamon risked a glance along the line; there were at least two dozen men in it before him. It frustrated and terrified him.

With ever-increasing nervousness he watched as man after man went forward and did what Barns had done, what he himself would do… He wondered if, somewhere in the crowd, Aeryn was watching him. He remembered the strange look on her face. What was it that had worried her so much?

"Eamon Goodman of Edesfield."

For a second he couldn't move. His name, *his* name! He had been called by name. Belaal's eyes were fixed upon him.

He went forward giddily. The steps leading up to the bannered platform seemed steeper than mountains. Pressing his lips together, he drew a deep breath. Then, like so many men before him, he knelt down before Belaal.

"What do you seek?" Belaal's words seemed both grossly loud and horribly intimate in his ear; the sensation disquieted him.

"Service with the Gauntlet, captain." Out of the corner of his eye he saw Ladomer smiling. He tried to latch on to his face for encouragement, but it slipped away from him.

"And what is your pledge?"

"I-I, Eamon Goodman, d-do hereby pledge my allegiance to the M-Master." A series of paralysing chills ran down his spine. He pressed his quaking lips together.

Had he not long dreamt of this? But something seemed wrong. "My blood, my blade, and my body are all given in his service."

"And do you swear this most solemnly to the Master, such an oath as may not be broken?" Belaal continued.

Looking up, Eamon frowned. The words that he had so long sought to say – that he had fought and bled to say – stuck in his throat. What was the matter with him?

He took a deep, shuddering breath to force down his strange misgivings. Surely it was simply a surfeit of emotion? "I do swear it."

"Then receive the mark of your allegiance," the captain intoned. So saying he brought forward the staff, inclining the gilded pommel towards Eamon.

As it came closer Eamon saw that an eagle was marked upon it. Its wings were spread wide and its head bowed down as it devoured a serpent. It was the mark of the Master; it was the mark Eamon would take as his own.

Eamon watched the staff hanging in the air before him and slowly reached out towards it. The crown stitched on his jacket felt heavy on him; the emblem of the Gauntlet seemed then like an empty cage.

He faltered. The eagle stared back at him, beckoning him to touch it; but something in his very soul railed against it.

To serve in the Gauntlet was to protect the River Realm and its people. That had been his desire since his earliest childhood. He had always wanted this; why should a moment undo him?

He mastered himself. "I swear," he said, and laid his bare hand over the eagle.

Suddenly the metal became hot and seared his skin. Eamon gasped in alarm and wanted to cry out, but something greater thralled him to silence. He felt something – unknown, but swift and terrible – flowing into his throbbing veins; his whole blood seemed on fire with its consuming poison. What was happening to him?

Though he strained to tear his hand away he found that he could not move; yet to all outward eyes he would appear a feeling man sensing a moment of deep devotion to the Master.

Suddenly the pommel was shorn from his hand. Eamon nearly recoiled but Belaal laid a firm hand on his shoulder, holding him immobile as if by some other will. The captain smiled as First Lieutenant Ellis set the pin at Eamon's throat.

"Thus are you sworn," Belaal said. "Rise, Ensign Eamon Goodman; you belong to the Master."

Belaal removed his hand, and strength returned to Eamon's limbs. Quickly he got to his feet and stared at the captain. His eyes felt dry and sore, yet he thought that he could see too sharply; things seemed unnaturally bright. He looked across at Ladomer, but his friend smiled – a broad, encompassing smile that showed no knowledge of what had happened.

What *had* happened?

Slowly, uncertain and driven by Belaal's gaze, he saluted and turned to leave the platform. As he passed the next cadet who was to kneel he almost reached out to stop him, but the cry of his heart was not matched by the will of his limbs. He simply kept on walking to join the line of new ensigns.

During the following hour he stood and watched young men that he had trained with kneel and touch the pommel. Outwardly he rejoiced – but inwardly he writhed.

When at last the ceremony was over he endured the congratulations of the townsfolk as long as could be deemed reasonably polite. Though he searched the crowd for Aeryn, he did not find her, and Ladomer, evidently having business to attend to, was nowhere to be seen. Not knowing what else he could do, he left as soon as he was able.

Night was beginning to fall when he found himself beyond the college walls. Sounds of merriment emanated from taverns filled to the brim with new ensigns drinking to their achievement.

It seemed an alien celebration to Eamon; his hand ached still, his veins throbbed, and the pin at his collar seemed like a hangman's noose about his neck.

He had joined the Gauntlet. He should have been rejoicing, but his heart was empty. And still his palm burned.

Angrily he stopped under a lantern and stared at his right hand. It was difficult to see in the swinging light but as his eyes adjusted his palm came gradually into focus. Suddenly he staggered, sick to the stomach.

It was faint, and perhaps no man apart from him would ever be able to see it, but on his palm he bore the shape of the eagle. It glared back at him with mocking, dreadful jubilance.

Eamon reeled. He bore the mark of the Master in his flesh.

He didn't know how long he stood there trying to grasp the fullness of what was on his hand; certainly it was long enough for his fingers to grow numb and pale with the increasing cold.

At the sound of footsteps coming towards him, he quickly tucked his hands away.

"Goodman!" It was Ensign Offley Barns.

"Mr Barns?"

"Duty calls," Barns told him. "The captain wants us for an arrest."

Nodding, Eamon hurried to the young man and matched pace with him. He tried to steal a glance at his companion's hands, but they were gloved. He wondered if they had both been given the same mark.

As he was about to try to draw Barns on the subject they turned up Bury's Hill. The windows of the Morning Star were all but obscured by a dozen men, all in Gauntlet uniform, standing outside it.

Eamon froze. "The inn?"

"Wayfarer trouble, the captain said. Maybe even something to do with last night."

"Wayfarer?"

The word was dead on Eamon's lips as they reached the inn. A crowd of evicted men and women stood huddled to one side, some still nursing mugs of beer in their hands and sullen looks on their faces. Eamon saw curious eyes peering from every window and door along the street.

"Move along, move along!" yelled an officer. The man emerged from the empty inn and cleared a path before the door. More soldiers followed him. Two dragged between them a man whom Eamon did not recognize at first. He seemed middle-aged; his dishevelled hair was turning grey at the roots and his jaw was thick with untidy stubble. His shirt was torn and his left arm was bound tightly in a clean bandage.

Eamon gaped. Suddenly he saw again the bleeding man huddled among the tree roots, felt the impact of the man who had attacked him, remembered drawing his blade across the arm that had seized him…

Then he remembered the blood he had seen on Telo's arm that morning, and understood.

Two more soldiers emerged from the besieged inn. The innkeeper himself, bound, strode defiantly between them. Belaal came after them, a dark, satisfied smile on his face.

"Telo, Telo!" The now captured fugitive called in desperation, as though blinded.

"I'm here, Wystan," Telo answered, his voice bewitchingly confident. "I'm right here with you."

"These men are traitors to the Master," Belaal called, addressing the gathered onlookers. "They will be paid in the coin by which they pay."

He turned to his officers and ensigns, barking orders to them that were swiftly obeyed. Eamon did not hear them. Aeryn's father and the man called Wystan were dragged roughly down the hill.

Stunned, Eamon watched them. Telo... a traitor?

"Goodman!"

Eamon looked up. Belaal stood not a pace away from him.

"Sir, I think there must be some mistake," Eamon began. "I know this man –"

Belaal's eyes flashed in the torchlight. "I will not hear excuses for a snake from the mouth of a sworn man," he hissed, stabbing at him viciously with a gloved finger. "You're Gauntlet, Goodman; *act* like it."

Eamon felt his throat constricting. "Yes, sir."

Belaal held his gaze. "Go down to the square. We'll light them both before the moon rises."

Eamon remained rooted to the spot, wishing that he could misunderstand the command. Belaal raised an irate eyebrow, then turned to the man next to him. "Mr Barns," he snarled.

Barns had none of Eamon's qualms. "Sir."

"Take your friend Goodman to the square and see to it that he does his job. You both know where the necessary tools are."

"Yes, sir." Barns gave Eamon a shove. "Let's go, Goodman."

Numbly, Eamon walked down the hill in the wake of the arrested men. He knew full well what tools Belaal meant. He swallowed down his horror.

The innkeeper might not even be guilty; what proof was there against Telo? A cut on his arm, a man who knew his name... But the more Eamon thought about it, the more certain the innkeeper's crime became.

Before Eamon knew it, he was in the square with a dozen other new ensigns, his hands helping to build the place where Aeryn's father would be burned alive.

CHAPTER III

The kindling swiftly piled high, and men and women from the town began to gather in the shadowy corners of the square. They could not come too close; the Gauntlet needed room to work.

Eamon felt the weight of the wood in his hands as he and a dozen other ensigns built the pyre. They worked in silence, and for a moment he was able to pretend that it was just an exercise, that the dry wood would not be lit.

But torches lit up the square and two tall stakes had been set at the centre of the pyre. The Gauntlet's work that evening was precise, diligent. All the grim totems lacked were their offerings.

As the kindling went higher Eamon felt a churning sickness deep in his gut. He had been to public burnings and executions before but he had never felt as he did now: wretched, trapped, desperate. It was Telo whom they meant to burn, and Telo was a wayfarer.

Death to the snakes! His mind was filled with cries from long ago. *Death to the snakes!*

His mind's eye opened in the cold, grey streets of Dunthruik, and though the streets seemed faint and dim to his memory the cries were not, and neither was the feel of his mother's hands on his own. He vividly remembered the group of men that had been jeered towards the city's heart. The crowd had called them snakes and wayfarers, enemies of the Master deserving of death. The condemned men had been pelted with stones as they were taken through the streets until they bled and staggered. Eamon remembered the crowd's rage and the man falling in a swamp of hail and blood.

Ceremonial pyres, much like the ones he now had a hand in building, stood high that day. The men had been bound and the kindling set alight while the whole city exulted in the flames that snatched about the Master's enemies.

His mother's hands turned his face towards her so that he could not watch; he had heard her heart beating fast. He could still recall the soft touch of his father, smoothing his hair and caressing his brow as he had trembled with fear. And the smell: the charred, gruesome smell of burning flesh. The men and women of the city baying for blood and rejoicing in the screams. His ear burned with that moaning, stifled only slightly by the great knots of his mother's cloak that he forced into his ears. It had been the time of the great culls. He had been nine years old.

Death to the snakes!

Tears stung at his eyes but still his hands moved. They moved until his task was done.

"Good work, Goodman." Barns's voice struck him; looking up he saw that a ring of Gauntlet ensigns was forming up about the central part of the square. These soldiers had the double task of keeping back the onlookers and keeping the prisoners from fleeing should they somehow escape the flames.

Eamon did not form part of that line; he followed Barns as more experienced ensigns hustled them out of the ring and into the crowd. Eamon knew the drill: Gauntlet men were always stationed among the masses to keep them calm in what followed. In a daze, Eamon took his place in the pressing throng. Barns moved farther on.

Belaal and a group of lieutenants and ensigns came through the square in procession. Belaal marched proudly at the head of the line, leading his bedraggled, grim-faced prisoners as though he had won them by noble endeavour. A drummer, one of the college's youngest cadets, marched by the captain's side. With each stroke that he beat, the crowds of men and women lurched forward eagerly; some beat their hands along with it. Some spat at the passing prisoners. All jeered them.

"Death to the snakes!" cried one. The whole square filled with the cry.

The procession drew closer and came within the guarding ring; Eamon could clearly see Telo and the other prisoner as they were marched past him. He could only stare.

What could he do?

His mind raced as ensigns began fastening the two men to the stakes with irons. The Gauntlet knew how to use bands, and Eamon saw Wystan wince as the chains came tight about his injured arm. His pain was mocked.

Eamon's breath quickened; the chains were fastened and the fasteners withdrew, leaving the wayfarers open to the crowd's jeers.

He bit his lip hard. Even if he could release the men – a task that seemed altogether impossible… he had no right to. His duty was to the Gauntlet, and he was bound to that service now in ways more powerful than he ever had been tied to Aeryn's father. What call had he to interfere in a matter of the Master's glory? Snakes were snakes, and traitors deserved death.

As the drum beat into his brain Eamon tried to pull himself together. He had known Telo since he was a child; the man was the closest thing to family that he had. Besides which, Telo was the beloved father of a friend. It was true that Eamon didn't know the stranger, but it seemed unthinkable to him that a friend of Telo's might be an evil man.

Captain Belaal went to the centre of the execution space and turned to address the heckling onlookers.

"Enemies of the Master are enemies of the River and enemies of the people!" he called crisply. "These men were taken whilst plotting against the Master and against his glory. Their crime is against you and against him."

Eamon barely registered what Belaal was saying; his heart was in his mouth and a gagged feeling lay slick all along his throat. It was no enemy bound to the pyre; it was Telo… Couldn't he speak for the innkeeper?

Guilty instinct told him that to speak out would be to barter for a place in the pyre. Belaal had declared them enemies, and both men appeared to be enemies, bound and wretched on the stakes... Could he give his life for such men?

He looked desperately at them and saw Telo raise his head. Their gazes met and locked; it stole Eamon's breath.

"The men before you, people of Edesfield, are snakes: thieves, murderers, and traitors," Belaal boomed.

"They are thieves that serve a thief."

All eyes turned suddenly to the innkeeper as his voice resounded: "We do not serve the throned," Telo called. "We serve the King."

He spoke out with dignity that surpassed him, shattering in a single moment everything that Eamon had ever believed about him.

A terrible silence fell. Eamon gasped and stared. The innkeeper's eyes were still on his and Eamon could not fathom what he saw there.

"Snakes! Snakes, by their own admission!" Belaal howled, his words stirring fury in the crowd. "Traitors and defilers! They will be put to death as they deserve, to the Master's glory!"

The crowd erupted into hot-blooded yells: "Death to the snakes!"

Stones began flying. The innkeeper received the blows in silence; he had said all that he meant to say. Telo's companion wept and struggled, drawing breath for a cry that was neither defiant nor desperate: "The King!"

King. Eamon's heart beat fast as the strange word washed through him. The River Realm had a master, not a king. He remembered his mother once telling him that the Master had taken the realm from a king in a great battle long years past – an argument late at night when his father had told her not to speak of it to their son. It had been long ago, if it had even happened, and what mattered was that the Master was sovereign in glory over the River. That was what his father had told him.

As his thoughts churned in him he felt the strength of Telo's gaze; the whole of time from the beginning to the end of days was distilled into the innkeeper's eyes, in some knowledge or hope that Eamon could not understand.

Telo smiled at him. "The King!" he said, and though there were hundreds of men and women around them Eamon knew that the words were spoken to him.

"Light the pyre!" Belaal commanded.

A lieutenant bearing a torch walked between Eamon and the condemned men, releasing him from the innkeeper's gaze. Suddenly Eamon felt scores of people pressing around him, carried ecstatically forward by the moving torch. The Gauntlet kept them distant from the pyres. The yells were deafening. It was as he took in those around him that Eamon realized that scarcely a pace away was a face he knew.

Breaking from where he stood he pushed roughly through the crowd, reaching Aeryn's side just as the first crack of kindling marked the air.

The crowd pulsed with a screeching cry. At the same moment his friend started forward. Eamon reached her just in time to jerk her back.

"No!" he cried. Those around were oblivious to him as he hauled her backwards.

"Let go of me!" Aeryn retorted. She seemed to neither see nor recognize him.

"Aeryn –"

"Filthy Glove, *let go!*"

With a yell she twisted and turned hard to the side, nearly wrenching away from him; he strengthened his grip and tried to pull her farther back from the execution ring. Aeryn's normally gentle hands clawed at him.

"Let me go!"

"You don't know what you're doing –"

A victorious squeal rent the air. The next scream that Eamon heard was Aeryn's.

"*Father!*"

It was the worst possible time for her to advertise her kinship. There was no alternative. Eamon threw his arm about his friend's neck, stunning her, and jammed his other hand over her mouth. Shouts of primal violence rose from the crowd like flames. Eamon felt bile in his throat as he hauled Aeryn another pace backwards. There was another scream from the ring – long, high, agonized. Eamon found a sob on his own lips.

It was that sound which stopped Aeryn from struggling. At last she saw him clearly.

She tensed in his grip, as though she wasn't sure whether to strike him or collapse in his arms. Her face was haggard in the horrid light.

"Let go of me." Her voice shook and rage smouldered in fierce eyes. Though the scream and roar of the spectacle went on all around them, nothing was as clear to him then as her face and words, and nothing seemed more terrible than what she might do.

"You can't go to him!" He shook her, so hard that he was afraid he would hurt her – she *had* to listen to him. "*Aeryn!*"

There was a crack as a pile of kindling crumbled in the heat. The smoke in the square grew dense. Ash was cast through the crowd and the air filled with the horrendous smell that Eamon knew so vividly.

His stomach turned. He staggered and turned to one side, retching.

"Death to the snakes!"

Aeryn darted away from him into the crowd. He could not follow her: his throat was racked with bile, his eyes ran with the acrid sting of the smoke, and his ears boomed with the shouts of the crowd.

A hand grasped his wheeling shoulder. "You all right, lad?"

Eamon looked up dully to see a kind, weathered face above his: the smith's. In that hideous moment it was a comfort to him.

Coughing and spluttering, he wondered if he was going to vomit up his lungs as well as everything else. He staggered on to the support of the smith's willingly offered arm. The man helped him to move some distance from the crowd.

They reached the steps of the college and Eamon sat there, shivering. Away from the fire the air seemed clammy. He could see the crowd of men and women beating about the ring, creatures of shadow and smoke about a flaming heart.

The smith sat down by him. "Quite a first day," he commented. Eamon couldn't answer; the flames still held his eyes.

"Who would have thought it: Telo, one of *them*. Time was when Edesfield was safe from snakes, more or less."

Eamon could feel grief working into the dark marks about his eyes. Black smoke tunnelled off the stakes. He didn't dare look to see how much remained. How long had he staggered in the square, disgorging his stomach? A moan left his lips.

"Telo seemed such a good man." Smithy's voice was steady as he pressed Eamon's shoulder in comfort. "Appearances can be deceptive, I suppose. A snake is a snake, lad, and the Gauntlet are just in dealing with them."

Just? The vulturous word hovered in Eamon's mind. What justice was this?

The wind blew ash into his face. People danced around the fires under the watchful eye of the Gauntlet, under his eyes. He heard Telo's voice in his mind again and drove it away in terror.

But Aeryn. Where was Aeryn?

The smith briskly rubbed his hands and patted Eamon fondly on the back. "Go home and rest, lad."

Eamon rose. Some of the Gauntlet had begun to disperse back towards the college and the barracks. Belaal and a few others remained in the square, encouraging the patriotic celebration.

Eamon was entitled to stay in the college barracks, but he knew that he could not that night. He would go back to the smith's, to the small rented room that had been home since his own had burned down.

He looked once more at the dying pyres; the grim glint of the flames grinned back at him.

The smith disappeared back into the crowd to join the celebrations. With a dreadful shudder, Eamon turned for home.

Smoke permeated the streets, clinging with leech-like intensity to his lungs. His mind tossed over the day's events, trying to force them to a logical conclusion, but there was none to be reached.

His steps wound towards the smith's forge, past the wall where he had sat that morning picking mud from his dagger. Though not even a day had passed, he felt a year older.

He stopped at the building's side door. The forge was cramped up against the wall of a fishmonger's, and the smell of fish and smoke mingled uncomfortably. Scales and innards were mashed in among the cobbles in the yard. They would not be removed until rain came, and the smell would linger for some time thereafter.

Eamon fumbled in the small pouch at his side, searching for his key. Even if he could find it he expected that it would be difficult to locate the keyhole; then again, the door was a feeble thing and he knew it could be convinced to open without one. His father's house had been warm and dry, with broad rooms of books which Eamon had read while his father worked at binding. Eamon sighed; it had been a long time since he had read a book, and longer still since he had bound one.

The lodging that the smith had offered him was made up of an old, disused storeroom that let out the warmth in the winter and did not keep cool in the summer. Eamon's hands had gone from binding books to stoking the forge and polishing blades until he had joined the Gauntlet; then he had paid the smith rent from his slim wages.

His fingers found the stalks of his keys; they chinked as he grasped them in his aching hand. He stood, keys suspended uncertainly by the door, for a few moments. His hands shook. Everything had happened so fast...

Why Telo? The thought hounded him. Why? There had to be an answer.

He could not sleep, not like this. He shoved his key back into his pouch and returned to the streets.

Soon he neared the shattered windows of the Morning Star. No lights burned there that evening; the Gauntlet had doused them and smoke clung to the walls. As he approached, Eamon saw several figures with barrels and bottles fleeing from the doorway; rats that sensed the coming of a feline adversary.

Feeling oddly bruised Eamon watched them go. A smoke-clogged wind pushed the inn's sign on mournful hinges; the doorway yawned blackly before him.

He went forward to the threshold and stopped for a long time there, peering inwards.

Why had he come? Staring at the unfamiliar black he wondered whether he should leave.

Tugging his jacket closer over his shoulders, he stepped inside.

A shred of moonlight followed him through the doorway, glancing off the remains of the inn. Night lay like iron sheets over the tables and chairs, which lay strewn over the floor amid pools of cracked ceramic made slippery by spilt food and drink.

As he passed the bar Eamon saw Telo's wiping cloth laid carefully over three tankards; the struggle had not come from the innkeeper. He stopped and took the rag in his hands. It was the tool of a diligent man.

Swallowing, Eamon laid it back.

He followed the bar to the doors in the wall behind it. Some led into the kitchen; he smelt the fire burning itself to ashes in the grate and saw an open sack of flour spilt over the floor.

A slim corridor led to the stairs, which creaked beneath him. The Star had upstairs rooms for guests – he had sometimes played in them as a child – but the innkeeper and his family had also slept there.

Eamon's curiosity led him to Telo's room. Though small and sparse, it was comfortable enough to receive a weary man at the end of each day. The bed, Eamon knew, had been one of Telo's prized possessions, handcrafted years before by a carpenter who worked in the city. Not many people in Edesfield slept in a real bed, rather than a motley assortment of hay and blankets, but Telo had been one of them.

Shredded linen lay everywhere, pitchers and basins had been cracked on the floor, and the great bed was out of place, wrenched to one side. Eamon was not the first from the Gauntlet to have been there that night. The room had been ransacked.

But he knew something they did not: as a child Aeryn had often boasted that her father's bed could be used to hold secrets. After he had repeatedly refused to believe her angry assertions she had triumphantly shown him the secret compartment that her father had had built into the bed. If Telo really had something to hide, it would be there.

What could Telo have had to hide?

The bedposts were thick and sturdy, the grain majestic in the moonlight. He leaned over to look at the base of the bed and accidentally banged his elbow, hard, against one of the posts. In the split second before he leapt away to nurse a numb bone he heard the reverberation of a hollow.

Shaking his arm to coax it to forget its hurt, he knelt by the post and ran his hands over the smooth wood. In the back of the fourth leg there was a small groove about the size of his thumb. Just as Aeryn had shown him a decade before, Eamon pressed it hard and listened to the answering click. A portion of the bedpost swung open against his hand.

He had to crawl under the frame and peer awkwardly up into the gap to see, but, straining his eyes, he made out the slim shape of a piece of parchment in the hidden hole.

Getting his hands into the compartment was difficult; the bed was only about a foot off the ground, and he had to slide under it on his back before he could take his prize. After several awkward attempts, parchment touched his fingers. He groped at it in the dark before threading it out.

It was as he seized the parchment that he heard a step on the landing.

He stilled his breathing to almost nothing and tuned every sense to the noise. His Gauntlet uniform would protect him from looters and other Gauntlet, but if there were more snakes about…

CHAPTER III

He held himself still. Another step. His arms were heavy where he held them suspended; he could not risk resting them. A step came closer. He hoped that he might pass unnoticed by the pile of blankets.

The pressure of a bladepoint rested sharply on his unguarded midriff.

"Up," a voice demanded. It was thickly muffled. He didn't move. "Up, *now*; keep your eyes closed."

For a few seconds Eamon stayed very still, trying to think of a way to hide the paper. He realized at once that it would be impossible. He was caught.

He edged out from under the bed, his eyes held firmly and obligingly shut.

"Sit up. Not a word or I will kill you."

Eamon sat in silence as rope was put about his hands. The skin that brushed past his own surprised him; it seemed too soft for a man's. As the knot was tied he pulled curiously against it. It was by no means tight enough.

"You bind very poorly," he commented.

The paper was snatched out of his fingers. From the silence that followed, he inferred that his captor was reading it.

"Clearly, I mean you no offence," he added. The silence continued.

He heard a sigh and a rustle of cloth as his captor knelt next to him.

"I have half a mind to leave you here, Eamon!" Eamon recognized the now undisguised voice with a start.

"Aeryn?" Angry words bubbled up in him – he had had too many surprises for one evening. "River's sake! What are you doing here?"

"I live here," she replied curtly. "What are *you* doing here?"

"You threatened to kill me!"

"You could have been anyone."

Eamon opened his eyes and fixed her in a steely glare. He noted uncertainly that his friend still held a small, sharp knife in her hand.

"Someone is going to get hurt if you don't put that down," he told her, eyeing the blade. He refrained from adding, "Most likely you."

"I know how to use a knife, thank you," Aeryn snapped.

"You wouldn't be holding it like that if you did." He thought he saw a look of embarrassment cross her face but her grip on the knife didn't lessen in the slightest. "You're not going to put it down?"

"Answer my question," Aeryn rejoined, prodding none-too-gently at him with the blade. "What are you doing in my house?"

Eamon rolled his eyes. "I saw everyone else helping themselves and thought it a fine idea!"

She glared at him. "There's no need to be sarcastic."

"Who said I was being sarcastic?" Eamon's voice quivered on the verge of violence. "Damn it, Aeryn! What did you think you were doing?"

"What did *I* think *I* was doing?" Aeryn stared at him. "*You* swore to the Gauntlet; *you* built that pyre; *you* put my father in it; if anyone is doing anything today, it's you!"

The words were keener against Eamon's heart than the knife that she held there. "I didn't kill him, Aeryn," he tried.

"You're such a Glove," she told him viciously. "No, Gloves only ever follow orders. Accountability wasn't in your training, I suppose?"

"Do you have any idea what they did to me?" Eamon yelled. Tears stung at his eyes; flames danced before them and fire was in his palm once more.

For a moment the moon became free of cloud; its beams showed two tear-marked faces watching each other wrathfully in the dark.

Aeryn held his gaze for a moment. "I tried to warn you –"

"'Red isn't your colour'? You call *that* a warning?"

He glared at her. With a deep sigh, Aeryn lowered her blade then unbound his wrists, carefully bringing his hands out where she could see them. Snuffling with tears, she turned his right hand over between her own.

CHAPTER III

The mark of the eagle was still there; in the dark it seemed to glow embers.

Aeryn traced it with delicate fingers; the gesture caused excruciating pain to run up Eamon's arm. Agonized, he snatched his hand away.

Aeryn looked at him with alarm. "I'm sorry," she whispered. Her eyes were fixed on his palm. Eamon saw that the glow there filled the whole flesh of his hand.

He looked at her with horror. "What have I done, Aeryn?"

"You have sworn a powerful oath." Eamon recoiled; the words seemed to spell an inescapable doom over him. "The throned does not give up his sworn," Aeryn added quietly.

Eamon glanced at her. "You mean the Master," he whispered uneasily.

Aeryn matched his gaze. "He is no master, Eamon; he took what was not his to take and sits where it was never given to him to sit. I mean the throned."

Eamon began to shake. "You're a wayfarer… a snake…"

Aeryn sat very still before him. "It is as you say," she answered. A sad smile crossed over her face. "Will you execute me, too?"

For a long moment, Eamon said nothing. "Why didn't you ever tell me?" he breathed at last.

"Why didn't I ever…?" Her mouth hung open incredulously. "You were set on that uniform!" she cried, gesturing to his jacket in disgust. "The Gauntlet would have found out or you would have had to kill me. Even if you didn't, one of the others might have killed you for fear that you might betray me."

"Others… other wayfarers?" Eamon's glance flicked to the shadows, as though he expected strange creatures to leap out from them. "How many of you are there?" He shook his head. "No, a better question – and for River's sake, Aeryn, you had better answer me this one – who are these wayfarers? No stories: I want the truth."

Aeryn watched him closely, carefully assessing every aspect of his face. He wondered whether she might be weighing up every second of the years they had known each other, to judge whether the signs of their friendship pointed to him as meriting her trust. Eamon matched her scrutiny steadily.

She reached her decision. "What is this town called, Eamon?"

Eamon stared. Was she mad? "Edesfield," he said.

"It should be pronounced Ede's Field, not Ed-es-field," Aeryn told him.

"Ede's Field?" Eamon repeated the new pronunciation dumbly. "Why should it be pronounced like that?"

"Because Ede was the King who fell in battle here. The battle is remembered, even though he is not. He was of the house of Brenuin, the house of kings."

Eamon felt a weight in his stomach. His mother had talked of kings; his father had tried to drive such thoughts from him. "There has never been a house of kings over the River, except perhaps in the dreams of small boys."

Aeryn watched him for a moment. Then she began to recite something. As Eamon listened he felt something old and deep, like distant music, hidden in her words.

> *"Silver the glint as the midnight hills*
> *Of the King's spear.*
> *Dark, dark the foes of the throne,*
> *Sly in the mere."*

Eamon gazed at her. "What is that?" he whispered.

Aeryn smiled at him sadly. "A poem not read by bookbinders' sons. It tells how Ede was betrayed and how the throned unlawfully took the River Realm from him."

"What happened?" Eamon breathed.

"The throned moved both people and land against their rightful king, Ede, promising power to those who went to war with him. The land had to swallow the swollen corpses of many of its own before the last battle was joined. At Edesfield, King Ede and the throned met for the last time." She paused. "Ede was killed, and the throned marched down the River to take the city that you call Dunthruik."

"Ede can't have been much of a king if he lost," Eamon ventured. "Power changes hands, Aeryn; it's natural, and the fact that it is sometimes done in battle isn't 'unlawful'. Besides which," he added, "Dunthruik is a great city and the throned is a good master of this land."

"A good master?" Aeryn shook her head with an angry laugh. "Look at your hand, Eamon. What kind of master gave you that?"

Eamon looked uncomfortably at his palm.

"The throned has done much that is evil, Eamon," Aeryn continued, "and in more ways than I can explain to you now – probably in more ways than I understand. The mark on your hand is just a reflection of it. Dunthruik is a darkened city, built on suffering and founded in blood."

"Freedom is bought by blood."

"I suppose you'll be telling me that that's why your uniform is red, next!"

Eamon fell silent. It was taught in the Gauntlet colleges that red, the Master's colour, was one of sacrifice and glory.

Aeryn reached out and touched his shoulder, drawing his eyes back to her. "Believe me when I tell you that the throned works evil in Dunthruik, as do his Hands and his Gauntlet."

"So what about Ede?" Eamon was struggling to grasp what she was saying.

"Ede died in battle against the throned but Ede's line was not destroyed. His sister survived the fighting and escaped the siege of her city, carrying an unborn son who was the last child of royal blood…" Aeryn paused, as though wondering what to say next. "The throned, with his Hands and his Gauntlet, had – and have – great power. But after Ede's death some of the King's men began to show new courage of their own."

"These 'King's men'," Eamon asked uncertainly, "are they the wayfarers?"

"The King's men – wayfarers or 'snakes', as the throned and his own call us – believe that your 'master' has wrongfully taken rule of this land and that we suffer for it."

Eamon sat silent and pensive. His eyes drifted to his palm and to the eagle etched upon it. Part of him wondered what this, his own mark, would bring him. Part of him did not dare to entertain the thought.

Aeryn seemed to read his troubled mind. "The mark of the throned is not easily cast aside," she said. "I can't tell you exactly what it does or doesn't do, except that by it you have given yourself to him. Some say that the Gauntlet are his possessions in more ways than one and that his mark grants strange strengths."

Eamon's flesh crawled. "But… it's just a uniform. I serve the people of the River Realm and –"

"No, Eamon; you are bound to him. You serve *him*."

Eamon took a deep breath, hoping that his heart might be kind and return to a steady pace. It did not.

Aeryn looked once more at the parchment in her hand and then tucked it into her cloak. Silently, she rose.

"I have to go. My father died for these papers and I cannot let you take them."

He blinked at her in astonishment. "What are they?"

She hesitated. "I can't tell you, Eamon." She turned to go.

"Is that it?" Eamon asked angrily. "You're just going to leave me here?"

"Eamon –"

He leapt to his feet, his bonds falling easily from him; Aeryn shied back from him as he grabbed her arm. He was angry with her – for not warning him before he swore and for leaving him now in impossible turmoil. His anger rose in him like a thing alive, tightening his grip on her.

"After everything you've said?" he cried, laughing bitterly. "You're just going to go!" What right had she to tie him up, feed him a wild collection of lies, question his allegiance, doubt his integrity, and, to top it all, take what he had found by his own initiative – with no explanation as to what it was and where it came from! More than any of that, she meant to go… If he let her go he would never see her again.

And he would never learn what she knew.

The answer, then, was simple: he would not let her go. He would take what he wanted from her, by force if he had to. She was making him; it was her own fault.

"*Eamon!*"

Aeryn's words seemed far away but something in him heard them. He blinked hard and a terrible veil was lifted from his sight.

His friend's face was wracked with pain as he gripped her about the neck. His other hand had somehow wrested the knife from her and held it fast, ready to use it.

With a cry of horror Eamon dropped the blade and let go of her. His chest heaving, he stared at her. She clutched her arm to her breast. A dark trail ran from her fingers to her elbow.

She bled.

"Aeryn?" he whispered dumbly, trembling.

She stared at him, corpse-pale. Eamon reached out to her.

"Aeryn, I'm sorry, I didn't –"

Before he could finish she was gone. He was left numb and alone.

With a shuddering breath Eamon looked down. The mark of the throned pulsed thickly in his hand.

He wasn't sure how long he stood amidst the crumpled sheets gazing vacantly at the doorway. He tried to recapture what Aeryn had said, but his thoughts always turned to her betrayal and her hatred of everything that he was. She had disavowed him. There was a ridge between them that he could not cross. His duty forbade it.

What was he thinking? Aeryn had not betrayed him, even if she had not warned him of what she knew...

But wasn't that exactly how she had betrayed him?

He shook his head. There were thoughts within his thought, thoughts that did not seem to be his own – could never have been his own. Why had he hurt her?

Her talk of marks was nothing but the talk of disaffected traitors. There had probably never been a king over the River. His father had told him they were just stories. Why should he disbelieve his father?

And yet...

And yet the town of Edesfield was all about him; in the cool midnight he could almost hear the stones speaking.

He left. However many ruthless opportunists had been on the prowl that night he saw no trace of them as he walked back down Bury's Hill.

He needed rest in his own bed. He would need to report to the captain in the morning, to get news of his posting if nothing else. Would he report what he had seen and heard that night?

He did not know if, when he faced Belaal's dark eyes, he would have a choice.

For the second time that night he reached his door and fumbled for his keys. He was just slotting them into the lock when he became aware of a figure in the shadow of the lane. He looked up warily.

"Who's there?"

A sequence of strange moaning noises came from somewhere in the dark. "The Beast of Mirewell!" came the theatrical answer.

As Eamon peered, Ladomer stepped up beside him. "It's only me, Ratbag!" he said, playfully doffing his shoulder. But Eamon could not smile.

"What's the matter with you?" Ladomer asked, assessing Eamon's face with concern. "You look as though death himself had been and shaken your hand as preliminary to his day's business!" Drawing himself up in a spectral fashion, Ladomer reached out and did exactly that.

At last, Eamon laughed faintly. "It's been a long night, Ladomer."

"Telo?" Mournfully, Ladomer shook his head. "I wasn't there. Belaal sent me to run some messages to the post as soon as the swearing had finished. I'm glad I didn't have to see it," he added, his face growing grim. "I don't know what I would have done."

"No," Eamon murmured. Guilt twisted its long knife another wrenching turn in his gut.

"Have you seen Aeryn?" Ladomer asked, his look a worried one. "I saw her briefly at the swearing, but with what has happened perhaps we ought to –"

The compulsion to lie was overwhelming. "I haven't seen her."

"Well, she's a tough one," Ladomer mused. "I dare say she'll bear it."

"Assuming that they don't arrest her, too."

"Eamon!" Ladomer laughed. "The Gauntlet wouldn't arrest someone unless they had reason to, and they won't arrest someone for family connections. Aeryn's record is spotless."

"Yes." Eamon blinked distractedly. "Ladomer, I need some rest," he said, his strength seeping from his limbs like water from a cracked jug. "I'll see you tomorrow?"

Ladomer nodded encouragingly. "Of course. Sleep well. Oh," he added, "congratulations, Ensign Goodman!"

"Thank you."

Eamon watched as Ladomer left, then took himself inside his ramshackle room to his bed. He was exhausted and collapsed gratefully onto it.

Despite the weariness in all his veins, he could not sleep. When he did at last trespass into the realm of dream it was to the thick of a battle of long ago, where a shining king took arms against an eagle with a burning crown.

CHAPTER IV

Morning came, the sun stumbling weary and cold to the horizon. The smell and sound of the fishmonger woke him. With a groan he dug his head deep under the blankets, pulling them tight about his ears. The fibres tickled his nose; he sneezed and moaned as he tried to clear his head. Dreams and visions faded from his mind; others returned to him in their place: Aeryn, the paper, the inn…

Sleep drained from his veins. He passed his hands through his hair and glanced about his small room. His uniform lay draped over a chair, casting long shadows.

"Fresh fish! Fresh fish!" The fishmonger's cry rent the morning air.

Squinting, Eamon made a move to cover his sore eyes, pausing as his hands passed before his face. He stopped. He turned them over, comparing and examining them as well as he could in the sullen light. The mark on his palm seemed to have lessened; indeed, he spent so long searching for it that he wondered if he had not imagined the whole grisly affair.

Perhaps he had not sworn at all.

Tricked, he smiled with relief. But when he looked up, he saw the pin on his uniform. His heart sank.

"Fresh fish!"

He wondered idly whether the fishmonger's assertion was true.

He dressed slowly, unsteady hands slipping on the fastenings of shirt and jacket, then strapped his sword to his side. As he left, locking the rickety door behind him, he fondly reached out and patted the threshold. Pulling his jacket more closely about his neck to dull the morning chill, he began to make his way to the college.

A throng of new ensigns were standing on the college steps by the time he arrived. Built from great slabs of stone, the college was bedecked with columns and graceless statues gesturing ever upwards to where the Master's emblem, encased in gold, lay on the uppermost wall. The glint of light over the courtyard was like gold leaf, glinting austerely over the open iron gates.

He passed without hindrance, greeting a few of his colleagues on the way. Here he was, Ensign Eamon Goodman, ready to hear what service he was to give the Master. Perhaps he would be sent out to one of the more distant garrisons, or up the River, or maybe even to Dunthruik itself...

And in the city? The thought rolled before him like an awesome dawn. In the city he might be assigned to the ports, the streets, or one of the four quarters. He might even take his turn at the palace gates and, were he bold and fortunate, he might prove himself extraordinary and be sent on to become a Hand...

He shivered. Those who became Hands largely began by serving in the Gauntlet, but by exceptionally proving their Master's glory were taken from those ranks and given black to wear. Others might be drawn from the gentry, but rarely and only after outstanding service. Whatever their provenance, the Hands performed the Master's highest bidding and were deep in his confidences.

Sometimes Eamon had dared to picture himself in black, and for the briefest moment he did so again. But if what Aeryn had said was true... if Dunthruik was founded in blood, then Eamon was sure that the Hands had shed it.

He blinked hard. How could he think such things? It was as if there was a voice inside him, questioning his questions.

He shook himself. Did he not have the right to query the things he swore to? No, the voice told him. He had already sworn. Service questioned was no service at all.

"Watch out!"

Eamon looked up just in time to have his nose hit by the mane of a passing horse. A Gauntlet messenger cast a dark look down from the saddle as he rode by, muttering curses.

Eamon folded his arms deeply into his jacket and carried on up the steps. He forwent the liberty of aiming a well-kicked stone at man and horse.

"You look particularly dapper and grippingly miserable this morning, Eamon!" called a cheerful voice.

Raising his head Eamon saw Ladomer leaning on one of the columns. The lieutenant was already sweaty and dishevelled from a couple of hours of swordplay. Eamon smiled. He had borne enthusiasm like Ladomer's once, though hardly so well.

"Ladies like a young man in uniform," he replied. "Why else do you think I joined but to look dapper?"

"You joined because you knew it was the right thing to do," Ladomer answered. "I bet that they already have you marked out for the Hands," he added, sheathing his sword and bowing with a courtier's finesse. "Your record is exemplary."

"Have you already forgotten the other night? Don't be daft, Ladomer," Eamon replied, giving him a none-too-gentle whack on the arm. "They'll look at you for a Hand before ever they look at me – and if they set us side by side then I think I would fare far the worse for standing next to you." He continued walking; Ladomer bounded up to his side with a delighted grin.

"Me, join the Hands?" he laughed loudly. "Oh, I would like to, Eamon, but do you really think black would suit me?"

Eamon looked at him. Notwithstanding the ridiculous and arrogant pose that Ladomer had adopted for his Handiness to be judged, Eamon nodded. "I think it would," he answered. "You are a better man than I."

"I shall never be noticed in Edesfield," Ladomer said sadly. "That's why I try to get out of it as often as I can. But you!" He took hold of Eamon's shoulder with a smile. "You are going to Dunthruik. Black would suit you."

"I don't think it would." Suddenly he grasped what Ladomer

had said. "Going to Dunthruik? Where did you hear –?"

Ladomer's face creased with mirth. "There's some interesting talk in the officers' mess."

"There is?" Eamon gaped.

"You know the officers, Eamon. We hear about things, like *placements*," Ladomer put peculiar emphasis on the word, "before they are officially announced – sometimes our opinions are sought on the matter. Not that we're supposed to discuss it. We're not supposed to discuss impending promotions, either," he added with an ever-increasing grin.

Even if Ladomer hadn't been smiling, the oddly delighted shift in his tone would have alerted Eamon to some hidden message. His jaw dropped. "Promotions?" he stammered.

"Seems that Captain Belaal might be thinking of elevating a couple of ensigns to lieutenants."

Eamon frowned. "Isn't that supposed to happen at the same time as the swearing-in?" he asked haltingly.

"Yes. But there are a few protocols in place for elevating men outside of swearing ceremonies."

"You mean, Belaal just pins an extra badge on someone's throat?"

"And says something meaningful while he's doing it," Ladomer grinned. "That's more or less it, yes."

"So who are these lucky men?"

The lieutenant's grin grew broader. "Interesting talk is never as precise as that, Mr Goodman."

Their footfalls echoed in the college hall. The ornate floor was a stone mosaic with the Master's eagle at its centre. The hall itself was circular with gilded arches running round it like coronal summits. Each keystone glistened red.

"You should go and see Captain Belaal," Ladomer told him. "He's been looking for you this morning."

Eamon nodded, remembering all too well the stern, dark eyes that had commanded him the night before. "Is he in his office?"

Chapter IV

"I imagine so; he's just finished inspecting some of the new recruits. They always come in in droves just after a swearing. Like bees to a hive. And what a hive!" Ladomer turned his grinning face upwards and Eamon saw it illuminated by the glow of the hall. Following his gaze Eamon noticed for the first time the shadowy spaces between the arches of the crown.

"I'll see you later, Ladomer," he said.

His friend smiled. "Of course. I look forward to hearing all about your posting, Ensign Goodman!" Ladomer added, and waved as he departed.

Left alone in the middle of the hall, Eamon tried to compose himself. With all the talk of Hands and wearing black and Dunthruik and lieutenantships, he found that he wasn't thinking straight. He had only just become an ensign; it was far too soon to be thinking about anything else.

Besides which, he would need all of his wits when it came to dealing with Captain Belaal.

With Belaal's lieutenant nowhere to be found, Eamon decided to venture on to the captain's office. As he passed down the corridor he tried to smarten himself up.

The door to the office stood open and he could hear voices inside. A young-faced cadet was leaving so swiftly as Eamon approached that they collided in the doorway. The young man was pale and seemed shaken; he tripped and fell over Eamon's foot with a yell. There was a thud as the young man – whom Eamon recognized as the one who had wished him luck before the swearing the previous day – hit the floor and narrowly escaped driving his head into the wall as he rolled to a stop.

Filled with sympathy, Eamon went to help him up.

"I'm sorry, sir," the boy managed.

"It's my fault – I tripped you! I'm sorry," Eamon added, helping him to his feet. The boy – for it was a boy and not really a man at all – turned his face away in shame as Eamon steadied him.

Suddenly Belaal's voice barked from the office: "For Crown's sake don't apologize to him, and don't help him, either! A whingeing maggot like him doesn't deserve the place he has been given here, whoever's blood he has. Kick him down the corridor, Goodman, and get in here."

The cadet tore away and disappeared down the hallway. Eamon watched him go for a few moments before stepping inside. A curt gesture of Belaal's hand indicated that he should shut the door.

"Sir," Eamon began.

"It's none of your business," Belaal answered. "Your salute, man! Is all decorum to go out the window?" The captain gestured irately to the large pane of glass behind him; it obligingly cast his formidable shadow forward. As Eamon drew his hand flat over his heart in the Gauntlet's swordless salute, he suspected that the whole room had been designed with the sole function of casting formidable shadows.

"That's better," Belaal told him, laying aside a quill. He drew a breath and seemed to put whatever the cadet had done behind him. "Very fine work at the pyre last night, Goodman; showed your determination in service. I appreciate that the circumstance was not an easy one for you."

Eamon wasn't sure what to say. There was an odd glint to the man's eyes. "Thank you, sir."

"It is in recognition of that service that I've called you here this morning."

A thread of lightning anticipation ran through him. He watched as Belaal picked something up from the desk and came forward. Eamon caught the glimpse of a pin in the captain's hand.

"Ensign Goodman," Belaal said, "your blood, blade, and body speak of the Master's glory; will you command men for that glory?"

"His glory," Eamon answered.

"Then for his glory it is given to you to command men."

Eamon's breath was short in his throat as Belaal lodged a pin there. Its heaviness surprised him.

The captain stepped back and smiled. "You show some promise,

Lieutenant Goodman," he said. "The Gauntlet rewards promising men."

"Thank you, sir." He did not know what else he could say. Whatever "promise" he had shown, he did not think he warranted promotion – far from it.

"Fortunately for aspiring ensigns, we do not seem to have exhausted the number of insurgents in this miserable town," Belaal said bitterly. "I had a few teams root a couple more of them out of hiding during the night; Spencing distinguished himself and will be duly rewarded, just as you have been."

Eamon swallowed. So Spencing was to be made a lieutenant, too. He did not know which disquieted him the more: Spencing's promotion or wondering how exactly the man had earned it.

Belaal proceeded to make a very careful study of his face. "You're to be stationed in Dunthruik, lieutenant."

Eamon steadied his nerve and kept his eyes on the window.

"To his glory, sir," he whispered.

"You'll board one of the holks going down the River tonight. They need men like you in Master's city."

"Yes, sir."

"Your assignment will be made clear to you when you arrive. Before all that, I have another job for you."

"Yes, sir."

"Mr Spencing, among others, brought me some vile specimens of snakes during the night. We pressed many, but most died rather than answer very simple questions. One of the remaining prisoners persists in withholding information." Belaal laughed oddly. "Very resistant to our measures, this one, and feisty with it, which makes for some entertainment." He looked at Eamon with a disturbing smile. "Extraction of such information was one of the many talents you exhibited during training, Mr Goodman – so you will try it."

Eamon frowned. He got the feeling that something was being withheld from him. He tried to gauge that hidden knowledge in the captain's dark eyes – but dark they remained.

"Come with me, lieutenant."

"Yes, sir."

Belaal walked with the stride of a man who had earned his position through intimidation and the will to carry through his threats. A tall, gaunt figure, his heels clicked at every pace, sending those in his path scuttling for cover. The captain didn't speak but seemed to be singing something just under his breath and somewhat out of tune. Some old patriotic hymn or other, if Eamon was any judge of tone. He followed in Belaal's steps, trying not to mind the eyes that gazed after them or gaped at the new emblem at his throat.

The captain led the way back across the central courtyard, ignoring each and every salute with which he was greeted along the way. Moving briskly out of the hall's light into one of the darker arches of the colonnade, they came to a door at which stood two guards, who promptly stepped aside for them.

Eamon paused briefly at the doorway, knowing full well that it led to the college holding cells. He had been down many times during the course of his training and, since he had been weaned from heroic story, he had come to know that prisons were barren, sordid affairs, plagued with disease, rats, and a hanging darkness more severe than any sentence. In the prison below him, Eamon had learned of the arts of interrogation.

He knew that it was rare for ordinary men to withstand even the threat of torment. He had learned to threaten, to lie to, and intimidate a man until he would reveal his secrets without ever having to resort to torture. He had been good at it. That skill – and the feeling of power over another that it brought with it – disquieted him.

These dark thoughts loomed threateningly inside the doorway. He could not disobey the captain; he was sworn.

"Goodman!" Belaal bellowed.

Eamon dashed down the stairs.

The stairwell was damp and muggy. A couple of torches lit the curve of the steps. Belaal had taken up one of these and bore it before him, striking with it from side to side to frighten away the occasional large spider. Sounds of scurrying creatures, their spindly legs scraping stone, made Eamon shiver. Thick cobwebs cast chain-like shadows along the stonework. Etched into some of the stones was the Master's crown, emblem of the Gauntlet.

After what seemed like eternity the steps reached their deep end. The air was heavy with every terrible smell that Eamon thought he could name, and some that he couldn't. Discreetly, he raised his sleeve to his nose and mouth.

Two other ensigns were at the bottom of the stairs; they drew themselves up smartly.

"Where's the snake?" Belaal demanded.

"Last cell, sir. Still not a word."

"We'll soon fix that," Belaal snorted and plunged off. Cautiously, Eamon followed.

As the light passed, faces – wraith-like, pallor-wreathed – crept forward. They wailed, or howled for the light to go. Some stood in silence, and only looked.

Belaal turned a deaf ear to them all and did not pause or blink. Eamon tried to steel his heart to do the same. He wore the uniform of the Gauntlet. He was a lieutenant. Snakes and villains deserved the darkness. The faces slipped away.

At last they came to the far end of the holding tunnel, where the cells were cramped and twisted under the bulk of the earth. It would have been wholly dark were it not for the light that Belaal bore.

Stopping in front of the bars the captain peered mockingly into the last cell. "And how is my scaly traitor this morning?" he asked coolly.

Silence.

"You won't speak to me?" With a smile Belaal rattled his fingers over the bars. "Come, come now! I've brought you a visitor. He'd very much like to talk to you."

Eamon hung back. There was still no reply from inside the cell. The captain's smile remained as he hooked the torch into a ring on the wall. It cast a devilish glow. He stooped down again.

"If you won't play nicely I shall have to play foully, my dear."

Neither word nor breath came in response.

Eamon wasn't sure what happened next. Belaal raised his palm towards the bars and for a second he seemed to see a glowing mark on the captain's hand. It grew red-hot and there was a squeal from the cell.

An instant later a body was hurled with ferocious speed against the bars as though flung across its prison by a winter squall.

Eamon was stunned. The mark – Belaal had it too!

"That's better," Belaal crooned, while the hunched body moaned. "Now we can all see each other and speak properly." He gestured to Eamon. "Come here, Goodman, and see what happens to wayfaring scum in this town."

Eamon's heart caught as he gaped; he already knew who he would see when he reached the bars. He knew the shape of the face, even beneath its ample bruises. He did not dare to think what had been done to her, and could not allow himself to wonder if he might free her.

"I'm sure that this wily sample will be a fine test for Dunthruik," Belaal commented, gesturing callously at Aeryn.

Eamon felt crushing hatred for his captain.

"She knows something about the snakes," Belaal told him. "We know there's a list of names, and the name of a place." There was an iron edge beneath his smile. "One of her companions revealed that much to me, most kindly, before he left us. Lord Penrith is eager to hear more about it."

Eamon saw Aeryn clench hooded eyes.

"I want to know where the list is, Goodman," Belaal growled, "and I want the names. You will get them for me."

For what seemed an unspeakably long time Eamon simply stood still. He looked down at Aeryn and her dulled, knotted hair. Her face was purpled, but her eyes were unmistakably firm. He realized that there was no torture that could ever force her to give up what she had hidden from him the night before. She would die before revealing it.

CHAPTER IV

Belaal was asking him to be an executioner.

There had to be another way…

He forced a mask over his face and bore into his friend's eyes with as merciless a look as he could muster.

"I will deliver them, sir," he said. "Leave it to me."

He waited, hoping that the captain might take that as a cue to leave him. But Belaal did not move.

"I have always enjoyed watching you work, lieutenant."

Eamon bit the inside of his lip and stepped up to the bars.

"Will you not speak?"

Aeryn shook her head.

"Then," he heard himself say, "my resolution shall speak in place of yours."

He lifted his hand and the mark on it became unmistakable. He did not know what he was doing or on what his thought was bent, only that there was power and it was in his hands. He forced his flaming palm against her forehead.

Suddenly he stood on a high plain. A red sky brewed around him; thunder rumbled in the distance. He saw Aeryn before him and found in that instant that he could hear, and almost see, her every thought. He felt her terror, anger, and betrayal.

"Eamon!" she screamed. "What are you doing?"

Thunder swallowed her words. Eamon thought suddenly that the strange place where they stood would allow him to speak to her, to explain that he meant her no harm – that he wanted to help her to escape, not because she was a wayfarer but because she was Aeryn.

But as the thoughts bubbled into his mind they were pushed under by another presence, one that grew steadily more powerful. He had no dominion over the voice that suddenly spoke with his lips.

"Tell me the names!" it demanded. He tried desperately to stop it but could not wrest back his tongue.

"I will not speak to you!" Aeryn yelled.

"Then I will take what I need."

Eamon fought to keep his hand limp at his side but saw himself lifting it. A red glow gathered around his fingers, and with a strike like lightning it burst towards Aeryn's form. The screeching torrent of energy wheeled forwards, shattering the air. Eamon suddenly felt sure that if the light struck her she would be destroyed.

"No!" he screamed.

Only seconds before the blast hit, a sheet of blue-white light fell from the sky, dropping like a cloak around her. Touching it, the flames howled and died; a searing pain cracked through Eamon's skull as the light blinded him.

When he next opened his eyes he was back in the holding tunnel in Edesfield.

Aeryn knelt at the bars, trembling and sobbing. Eamon realized that the pain in his head stemmed from the fact that he had been thrown back against the other wall. He blinked hard and when he closed his eyes he could still see the awful, flashing light in his lids. He stared at Aeryn in horror.

"The King's own are protected from the throned's fire," she whispered.

Eamon gaped. Sure that he had his own voice again, he drew breath to bawl out an apology. Belaal hauled him to his feet.

"I see that you're a breacher," the captain commented with a smile, "a fine gift to be given at swearing. But she's too much for you." Belaal leered at her through the bars. "You will go to Dunthruik, girl. Make no mistake about it: Lord Tramist will get everything from you that the Master desires." He laughed cruelly and took the torch from the wall. "Goodman!"

Trembling, Eamon followed. Aeryn sobbed quietly in the darkness behind him.

He walked unsteadily back into daylight. As he followed Belaal back to the captain's offices he knew that he clung only barely to the ground beneath his feet. Where had he been? What had he done?

Belaal seated himself once more in his little dais.

"You did well, Mr Goodman," he said. "I had another breacher on her during the night, and one or two dreamers, too, to try to trick her into revealing what she knew. None of them even connected to her." He looked up with a serious smile. "Breaching is one of the rarest – and most valuable – gifts that the Master bestows upon his own. Dunthruik will be glad to count you among its number."

Eamon swallowed. "Thank you, sir," was all that would come out of his dry throat.

"I will see you at parade this afternoon, lieutenant. Dismissed."

Sickened, Eamon saluted and left.

It was about lunchtime. Scarcely able to think, Eamon wandered the college in search of Ladomer. He checked at the officers' mess but his friend was not there. Feeling shaken, Eamon continued in his search.

He found Lieutenant Kentigern at last in one of the college courtyards, cleaning his blade. As soon as Eamon approached, Ladomer leapt first to his feet and then straight into detailed descriptions of his morning's activities, which he illustrated by brandishing his half-polished sword energetically. Eamon found it a useful distraction while he tried to settle his own mind.

At last Ladomer finished his telling of the morning's exploits and then fixed critically on his friend. "Mean you to make some contribution to this monologue, Mr Goodman, or would you prefer to persist in impersonating a mouldy lemon?"

Caught off-guard, Eamon stared at him. "What?"

"'I beg your pardon for my inattentiveness, Mr Kentigern' might be a more fitting reply, don't you think?" Eamon opened his mouth but his friend waved his apology aside. "You're somewhat dull this afternoon," Ladomer told him, setting his blade down so as to look at Eamon more closely. "Not that you're ever especially sharp..." Ladomer hung back, awaiting a counter to the insult. Receiving none he proceeded to pierce Eamon with a keen gaze. "What's the matter?" he asked impatiently.

"It's been a... a strange morning, Ladomer."

"It seems to have filled you with undue modesty," Ladomer retorted, laughing. "When are you going to talk about this, lieutenant?" he asked, tapping the pins at Eamon's throat.

Eamon looked at him for a moment, startled. "I..."

"Lieutenant Goodman!" Ladomer laughed. "Master knows how you managed it! It chimes well, you know."

"You knew?" Eamon asked quietly.

"I told you: officers hear things," Ladomer answered. "I was overjoyed for you, Eamon! And I am proud of you."

"They're sending me down River tonight," Eamon told him.

Ladomer laughed. "They didn't waste any time with that!"

A sudden sadness washed over him. "It could be a long time before I see you again," he said quietly. "I don't know if I'll be able to say goodbye later, and so I thought –"

Ladomer had a look of mock-suffering on his face. "Eamon Goodman, as you are a man I charge you: spare me your insatiable sentimentality!"

"I'm not being sentimental but I..." Eamon shook his head. "Things aren't turning out quite as I expected and I'll miss you, Ladomer. You're a good friend. You've always been a good friend to me."

Ladomer smiled. "I will do my utmost, dear Ratbag, to get myself transferred to Dunthruik – and to stay there! I heard from one of the messengers that there are a couple of openings in the West Quarter, and that the captain wants a cross-posting from outside the city. He wants someone with an impeccable record." He smiled wryly. "Mine isn't quite impeccable, but maybe I'll try anyway."

"Try," Eamon told him. "Now that Aeryn's... I'll be a bit lost without you," he finished.

"Two days and you'll have forgotten all about me!" Ladomer chided.

"I couldn't forget you."

They watched each other for a moment. Ladomer's smile grew

softer, and, in a rare moment of open affection, the lieutenant embraced him.

"I wish I was coming with you, Eamon."

For a moment, Eamon clung to his friend's strong embrace. "So do I."

The afternoon wore on and soon they reached the hour of parade, a daily occurrence in Gauntlet life. Eamon sensed men marvelling at his new pin; Barns had fairly fallen over when he had seen it.

Along with all the others in the college Eamon joined in the march, sword drawn high in salute, before Belaal's elevated figure. The captain raised himself up to speak.

"As many of you will already have seen, two ensigns, Mr Spencing and Mr Goodman, have been granted lieutenantships due to exceptional performance," he announced.

"His glory!" the college answered, followed by a brief round of applause. Eamon felt himself turning red. He didn't feel in the least bit exceptional. From the corner of his eye he saw Spencing watching him spitefully.

The parade continued as normal. As it concluded and the cadets began filing out, Belaal gestured to Eamon and then to Spencing. Both men went up to him and saluted formally.

"Sir," they said.

"Along with yourselves and some other ensigns who are being assigned to Dunthruik, there'll be a group of cadets with you," he said. "They've been lax in their training and are an embarrassment to Lord Penrith and to this college. I want them beaten into shape. If they aren't corrected by the time they return to me they will be an embarrassment to both of you as well, gentlemen."

"They won't be a problem, sir," Spencing answered.

"I'm also sending one of the snake prisoners up," Belaal said. "She is to go to Lord Tramist."

Amid the bustle and chatter of the busy college, for a second Eamon was transported back to that terrible plain of fire.

"I'll take charge of her, sir," he volunteered boldly.

Spencing glared, but Belaal smiled. "Very well, lieutenant," he said. "She is in your charge. You may appropriate some of the cadets going with you to form a guard detail that will answer to you. It will be on your head, and your record, if you do not discharge her – and them – well."

Lead settled in Eamon's stomach. "Yes, sir."

Evening drew relentlessly on, the sky drowning in the River's purple pall.

Eamon sat at the head of a small cart that ambled past the bridge and on up to the westernmost docks. The wooden frame rattled from side to side as the driver prodded the mules. In the back of the cart sat Aeryn, surrounded by armed guards. It must have looked ridiculous to the passers-by, Eamon supposed, but how could they know the power the girl possessed? If what he had seen was the protection of the King, it was powerful indeed.

Eamon wondered suddenly why that same power hadn't saved Telo. Hadn't he been a King's man, too?

The cobbles wound to the River. The western docks were restricted almost entirely to Gauntlet use. Several river vessels were moored there and bobbed gently in the broad water, sails hanging loose in the dead wind like drooping leaves. Men on the runners called to one another; behind them other craft passed. The water mostly carried barges and small fishing boats heading out for a catch in the River's even wider stretches. These craft bore lanterns on their prows, and traces of net hung over their sides. Small boys battled with their oars, trying to learn their fathers' trade.

The ship bound for Dunthruik was mid-sized and intended for a small but able crew. Including the Gauntlet cadets, ensigns, and officers, there were to be perhaps thirty men on board. Like most of the River's holks, the ship had a below deck. Traders generally used this lower deck to store their goods, but the holks that served the Gauntlet usually adapted much of the space into low-ceilinged sleeping quarters. Shipwrights in the Dunway and Eastport regions had first pioneered such holks, but hostility on the northern borders had seriously impeded the shipyards there – much to the delight of their competitors in the southern regions.

As the cart drew near to the ship's sides Eamon saw barrels and sacks being taken on board, the gangplank bowing a little under the weight. A flag crowned the mast. It needed none to tell what emblem flew there.

Eamon thanked the cart driver for his services and paid him a small coin. The other ensigns climbed down, jostling Aeryn between them as they marched her up the gangplank and into the belly of the ship.

As Eamon boarded the vessel he heard a voice along the deck laugh sharply.

"I didn't know that we were taking rats on board!" it said.

"Good evening, Mr Spencing," he answered.

"There is a notion that one can have too much of a good thing on board, Goodman."

Eamon glared. "I'd be obliged if you'd address me as Mr Goodman, Mr Spencing."

"I'd be obliged if you would cast yourself off the side, preferably the starboard one, and drown," Spencing retorted, and smiled archly. "Perhaps we should each oblige the other, Mr Goodman?"

Eamon didn't answer him; a call from the ship's captain drew him away from Spencing's baiting.

"Lieutenant Goodman?"

"Yes?"

The man smiled warmly at him. "I'm Captain Farlewe. Welcome aboard."

Eamon thanked him. "Is she a good ship?" he asked. He couldn't help but cast an uncertain look across the deck.

Farlewe smiled. "You don't like River travel, Mr Goodman?"

"My experience with it is rather limited," Eamon confessed.

"You may set your mind at ease," the captain laughed. "My

Lark's a good one; she's been sailing the River for fifteen years, and I've been her captain for ten of those. She was made by the Dunway wrights – none of this Okeford nonsense. They couldn't caulk or pitch if their lives depended on it!"

"I should avoid Okeford holks?" Eamon asked.

"You should – troublesome affairs," the captain added ominously. He paused for a moment, and Eamon wondered what terrible things Okeford holks had done to merit the man's professional cynicism.

"I've already spoken with Mr Spencing," Farlewe told him. "There are quarters below. Ensigns and cadets go in the iron hold." Eamon looked at him in confusion. "We used to do the iron runs from Escherbruck to Dunthruik," the captain explained. "That's where we stored it. It's the biggest quarter. It's tight, but that doesn't bother a sleeping man too much."

"No."

"There's a smaller quarter next to it which you and Mr Spencing can use," Farlewe continued, "and the ship's doctor has a quarter by that. Prisoners are stowed in the narrow hold, so that's where yours is now."

Mention of prisoners made Eamon uncomfortable. "How long will it take us to reach Dunthruik?"

"My *Lark* can do the run from Edesfield in just under four days, on a light load and a good wind," Farlewe told him. "So, with the training stops for your cadets, I imagine we'll make the city in five. Almost a relaxing voyage," he smiled.

Eamon grimaced. He was to spend five days as Aeryn's jailer.

"We'll be leaving just as soon as your cadets are all on board," Farlewe added.

"I had best not detain you from your work. Thank you, Captain Farlewe."

"Mr Goodman."

Aeryn had been stowed in a narrow storage hold among various casks, barrels, and crates which were travelling to the city, and would be kept there for the duration of their journey. Trying to get a sense of his river legs Eamon went down to the hold to check that she had been properly bound and to finish organizing the groups of cadets who would watch her. Parts of the below deck were so low Eamon had to duck, and he found the sound of water moving against the ship's boards all around him disconcerting. The whole lower deck was dark and cold; he was glad that he would only need to sleep there.

When he reached the narrow hold he found that Aeryn sat among the ship's stores and had been clapped hand and foot in irons. Her gaze met his; he was not sure whether disgust, hatred, or ire made up the greatest part of it.

"Rest yourself," he said, gesturing to the sacking provided for her. She remained obstinately upright.

Sighing inwardly, Eamon turned his attention to the first of the groups of cadets that were to watch her in shifts. "She is to be guarded at all times."

A smirk crossed one of the soldier's faces. Eamon rounded on him. "Do you have a problem, cadet?"

The cadet paled. "No, sir," he began.

Eamon stared grimly at them. "No liberties will be taken," he growled. "If so much as one man among you touches her without my leave, two of you will be flogged. Is that understood?"

The cadets affirmed his order. Eamon saw a strange look pass over Aeryn's face but shut it from his mind. "In all matters regarding the prisoner, you answer to me. To your posts, gentlemen."

It was with a heavy heart that Eamon returned above deck. He heard the crew calling to each other and tacking the sails to make best use of the paltry wind. The ship's captain was up on the deck, speaking cheerfully with his boatswain.

Eamon found himself a spot at the stern and listened to the whistles and odd language of the sailors as they worked; he envied them their evident pride. Currents swirled like strange fish about the ship's frame.

Soon the mooring ropes were drawn in and Farlewe's *Lark* left the docks.

As Eamon watched Edesfield slipping away he saw a faint black figure on the dockside. Wondering if it was Lord Penrith, he shivered.

Aeryn had to be delivered to Dunthruik. He could not help her. How could she ever trust him again after what he'd done? She probably hated him – a thought that chilled him.

As the breeze picked up and filled the sails, he drove his hands into his jacket. His fingers felt the shape of the keys to his prisoner's chains in his pouch; it did nothing to improve his spirits.

Later that night he passed below deck to check on his charge. A couple of cadets were there, alert and ready. Aeryn lay curled tightly on the sacking, shivering but asleep. The guards spoke softly among themselves and Eamon watched them for a moment, wondering if any of them asked the questions that he asked. Did they think about the Master, about snakes and wayfarers? Or was it he alone, just as it seemed to be he alone who questioned swearing his service to an eagle?

One of the cadets came quietly to him.

"Trouble finding your river legs, sir?" he asked.

It was the young man whom he had met in Belaal's office earlier that day. Eamon wondered what the boy had done to be labelled an ill-performing cadet, and whether a quick trip down the River and back would really solve the problem.

Nonetheless, the boy's concern brought a small smile to his face. "Only a little, cadet," he said. "I am well."

"Worried about your prisoner, sir?"

"She must go to Lord Tramist," Eamon answered, not because he actually knew who Lord Tramist was, but because he had heard Belaal say it.

The boy smiled. "She's in good hands with us, sir!"

Eamon wanted to tell the rash young fool that he could not possibly be expected to answer for a snake as dangerous as Aeryn. Instead he held his tongue and looked at her. She had begun shaking violently in the cold.

"It wouldn't do to have her dead before we get there," he told the cadet. "See that she's kept warm."

The boy smiled brightly. "Yes, sir," he said. "Goodnight."

Eamon nodded and drifted back to the deck and the evening air.

CHAPTER V

During the river trip Eamon spent much of his time on deck caught in a waterward vigil. In fact he spent so long there that he began to be an accurate interpreter of the jargon used by the holk's crew.

Hierarchy on the vessel was straightforward: the captain had overall charge of the craft, the sailors answering to him, while the Gauntlet lieutenants had charge of the cadets, ensigns, and prisoner on board. The ship's captain often discussed details of the route to Dunthruik with Eamon and Spencing, though the latter was sparingly polite in his attention to the captain.

As the days went on, Eamon found himself disliking Spencing, and the two ensigns who clung especially to him, more and more. The ensigns had been in the swearing line with Eamon in Edesfield what seemed like years before: Ensign Ilwaine (quiet and reserved) and Ensign Hill (wasp-tongued and agitated). Lieutenant Spencing was arrogant and unamiable, and Eamon couldn't understand why the two ensigns had such an attachment to him.

These three men, and Eamon himself, formed a significant part of the group who would disembark at Dunthruik together and who presumably also comprised the finest of Edesfield's new ensigns and officers.

Eamon kept his distance from Aeryn. Was he not a sworn man? And yet, when he lay in his bunk at night, rocking with the swaying of the *Lark*, he thought that he would have braved the road to hell for a good glance – but Aeryn never deigned to grant him so much as a bad one. All he received from her was, at best, fury, and at worst, indifference.

It left him caught between two equally unpleasant desires. The first was to somehow rescue Aeryn and free her before they reached Dunthruik. Once they arrived the Hands would be her escort, and though he could protect her from cadets and ensigns, he could not protect her from them.

His other desire, which grew stronger as the days passed, was to simply do what was asked of him: take Aeryn to Dunthruik and hand her over. Whispers in his mind told him that once in the city he might be made a Hand himself as a reward and come into the confidences of the Master. From there his power would be unlimited. Then Aeryn would beg for his help.

Was that what he wanted?

During his first day on board Eamon had watched the changing landscape and grown increasingly uncomfortable as the hills and valleys that he knew became thick, forbidding forests. The brooding trees huddled darkly along the distant banks, full of ghostly shimmers in the moonless night.

It was those woods and banks that made it an unexpected comfort to share the small quarter with Spencing. Since Eamon had taken responsibility for the prisoner, Spencing had never spoken a kind word to him. Still, in the dead of night with the cold gnawing at him and shadowy fears creeping along the hull, Eamon was glad to hear the breathing of another soul, even one as detestable as Spencing's.

One thing that Eamon did enjoy was drilling the cadets and ensigns. There wasn't much room on the deck, so the *Lark* stopped for several hours every day to allow the Gauntlet to drill on their own turf. Though there was nothing special about most of the lads, Eamon didn't see in them any lack of enthusiasm or any reason why they should have been sent down the River to have their heads cleared. Once he and his charge had been deposited at Dunthruik most of them would be going straight back to Edesfield to continue training, and perhaps some of them would be posted out to the borders. Despite the sour words with which Spencing often treated them, the cadets and ensigns did not hesitate to spar or do one more lap of the banks with a double-weighted pack. They were determined young men and the thought of even one lapel pin struck fire into their eyes.

During the drill on the second morning, while the crew was taking water on board, Eamon observed the cadets finish their exercises. His thoughts were far away – so much so that he didn't see one of the cadets approaching him until the boy was drawing himself up for a smart salute.

"Sir!"

Eamon looked up to see the beaming face of the young man whom he had first met in the swearing line. It made him feel old.

"Cadet," he acknowledged. The cadets and ensigns had been dismissed and were returning to the holk. Eamon was acutely aware of Spencing and his ensign lackeys laughing unpleasantly, most likely at him, just *over* their breath.

The boy did not seem to notice. "I know it isn't really my place, sir." He held out his hand; in it was a small golden fruit, still wet with dew. "But I wanted to give you this."

Eamon looked at it, dumbly. Then, at the cadet's urging, he took it. The fruit gleamed in his palm like cool fire.

He looked back at the young man in astonishment.

"We wondered if you might appreciate a change to the ship's rations, sir."

Eamon resisted the urge to raise his eyebrows in surprise.

He realized that other cadets were watching his exchange with the boy. "Is this gesture on your initiative, cadet?" he asked.

"Mostly mine, sir," the young man confessed. "And I wanted to thank you for offering to help me at Belaal's office the other day. I'm sorry I didn't get to thank you at the time. But I can now. It was good of you, sir."

"It was no trouble," Eamon told him, glancing at the fruit. He was touched by the boy's kindness; kindness he had not felt since he had sworn. Had the throned already taken so much from him?

Service to the Master was worth any price.

"What's your name, cadet?"

"Cadet Mathaiah Grahaven, sir."

"And is this the kind of gesture that granted you a place on this ship, Cadet Grahaven?"

The boy grinned. "Honestly, sir, I think it was tearing the college's divisional banner on swearing day."

"You tore the college banner?" Eamon laughed.

"Only a little, sir," the cadet answered. "It slipped when I was hanging it; came clean off the pole, sir."

"Is it possible for a 'little' tear to bring a banner clean off its pole?"

"Lieutenant Kentigern said something of that ilk, sir. He also assured me that Captain Belaal had no stomach for my breed of carelessness. He was right about that, sir," he added wistfully.

"I trust that you are finding yourself less careless since you began this voyage, Mr Grahaven?"

The boy nodded. "I am, sir," he said eagerly.

Eamon looked at the fruit. "Thank you, Mr Grahaven, to you and your fellows," he said. "I will endeavour to pull no further faces at lunch or, at the very least, to pull them where you and your colleagues cannot see them."

Cadet Grahaven smiled. "Yes, sir."

Saluting again, the boy hurried off to join the watching cadets. He was evidently just in time to catch a good joke; they began roaring with laughter.

"Keep yourselves together!" Spencing barked as the boys boarded.

Eamon watched them leadenly. He realized that he had seen the young man on many other occasions at the college: Cadet Grahaven had joined the Gauntlet a year after Eamon himself, though was perhaps as much as four or five years younger. In a couple of months, Mathaiah Grahaven would be sworn.

Spencing interrupted his thought. The lieutenant slid up to him and snatched the fruit.

"Taking bribes, are we, Mr Goodman? Or maybe," he added with a leer, "accepting favours? Well, each to his own!"

Eamon glared. He was struggling to find a suitable retort and Spencing knew it.

Laughing at his hesitance, the lieutenant held the captured fruit up to the sunlight, admiring it. "As for me," he said, "your charge is a creature much more to my liking…"

"You will not touch her," Eamon growled.

Spencing smiled. "I wouldn't dream of it, Mr Goodman," he said, pressing the fruit back into Eamon's hand. The skin burst and flesh and juice smeared everywhere, including down the front of Eamon's jacket.

"I am so sorry!" Spencing cried in an ingratiating manner. "Let me help you with that, Mr Goodman." Before Eamon could stop him Spencing had mockingly smeared sticky mess across his uniform. Eamon seized his wrist.

"Sir?"

Hill was a few paces away; the ensign watched the two lieutenants uncertainly.

"The captain says we're ready to loose moorings."

Spencing's eyes never left Eamon's face. "Thank you, ensign."

With a smile, Spencing primly pulled his wrist free and then straightened Eamon's jacket.

"One must lead by example, Mr Goodman," he said.

That night, despite the gentle rocking of the holk, Eamon couldn't sleep. It made him irritable and as his irritation grew so, it seemed, did the volume of the creaking beams, the snoring sleepers in the iron hold, and the occasional call over deck. As he tossed over onto his other side with a grimace, he realized that sleeping in a hammock was well when one had spent the morning stringing it between two trees with one's father and all the sleeping that needed to be done was that of a lazy afternoon. Sleeping in holks' hammocks was as far removed from his fond childhood memories as it was possible to be.

Spencing's smug and heavy breathing only served to fuel his frustrations at being the only one on board awake. Goaded, he swung his legs over the edge of his hammock. He resolutely pulled on his boots, tucked in his shirt, and tugged his jacket on over the top, grateful that the dark would hide the stain which neither he nor anyone else had been able to remove completely. Then he escaped into the moving air of the passage.

He welcomed the rush of cold that met him as he left the hold. At the top of the deck stairs he saw stars passing in and out between the clouds, and shadows tilting with the mood of the lanterns.

Slowly, his steps turned towards where his prisoner lay bound.

He approached the two soldiers on duty. One of them was Grahaven. Behind him, in a pile of sacks serving as bedding, lay Aeryn, covered with two thick cloaks. A chain led from her ankle to one of the walls and a discarded bowl of water was not far from her head. Eamon knew that she often refused food from his guards, though she drank readily enough.

Aeryn began to toss and turn violently. Half-uttered cries left her lips and she raised her hands to her head. Eamon was startled.

"Nightmares, maybe," Grahaven whispered to him, clearly shaken by the spectacle.

"Sure proof of treachery," hissed the other cadet.

Eamon stared at him. Did the cadet know Aeryn? Had he grown up with her and laughed with her as Eamon had? Had he studied with her and played with her, shared her myriad joys and sorrows over long years?

"Hold your tongue, Stonebrake," Eamon snapped.

Suddenly Aeryn screamed. Without a moment to consider what he was doing Eamon rushed to kneel beside her.

"Wake up!" he said firmly, remembering just in time not to say her name. He could not give the cadets any reason to question him or his authority. "It's just a dream. Wake up!" Catching her in his arms as she tossed, he shook her hard.

Her eyes snapped open. Her brow was wet.

"Eamon?" she whispered, shaking so that the name was almost lost.

"It was just a dream," he told her.

For a few seconds she allowed herself to be comforted by him. Then, with the suddenness of returning memory, she sat bolt upright and tore herself away.

"Get away from me!" she cried. "All of you!"

Reeling, she grabbed the bowl of water and hurled it at him. He raised his arm to his face in time to shield it. Seconds later he was drenched, and shards of broken earthenware were scattered all around him.

"Sir!" Grahaven called.

Stonebrake drew a slim dagger – the hold's ceiling was too low for his sword – and advanced with menace.

"Vile snake!"

Eamon rose, gesturing the cadets to stand aside. Grahaven stopped at once; his companion took a little more convincing.

"Put it away, Stonebrake," Eamon told him. He concealed the ripple of rage in his voice. "I have not been hurt and she must not be." He turned back to Aeryn. "You slept ill and I sought to wake you," he said coolly. "I bid you goodnight."

With that he turned and left the cabin, conscious of three sets of eyes staring after him.

He returned to his hammock to sleep badly for the rest of the night and was late up in the morning. When he finally appeared on deck, rubbing at sore eyes, the ship's captain greeted him with a grin.

"When the cat's away," he jibed in his thick, kindly accent, one garnered from a lifetime of living on the docks and the water. "What would Captain Belaal say if he caught you sleeping past first drill?"

"Drill's done?" Eamon asked blearily.

"Mr Spencing handled it, so I understand."

Eamon grimaced. At the captain's suggestion he visited the ship's cook for a mug of something warm.

When he had finished the dense, porridge-like drink he was

given, he went ashore to assist in what remained of the morning exercises. Spencing and Hill made their insincere good-mornings. Ilwaine said nothing at all.

Eamon led his cadets through a harsh weapons drill. When Aeryn was brought on deck for her daily walk, he quietly delegated supervision of her and the cadets with her to Ensign Ilwaine; he had no wish to see her.

Later that afternoon, his duties done and the cadets all occupied in cleaning weapons or swabbing decks, Eamon retreated to his haunt at the stern. The cook – a ship's doctor by trade – had distributed an unusually pungent gruel at lunch. This now made its presence felt rather disagreeably in Eamon's miserable insides. With no stomach even for the fresh bread they had brought on board from their call at Greystream that morning, Eamon passed his time in breaking the bread into pieces and hurling it into the churning wake of the ship. Someone should enjoy it, after all. Every now and then a fish, swerving along in the holk's shadow, found its way to a crumbling morsel and swallowed it up with glee.

With the sudden drop in the breeze during the morning, the captain thought that they were going to have to resort to oar-work to keep up a good pace. Eamon welcomed the change. It would be good to do something that might later encourage sleep, even if his mind was not at rest.

As he watched the shining, skipping fish that followed his bread-trail he became aware of someone standing at his elbow – the cadet, Mathaiah Grahaven. The afternoon sun burnished the boy's uniform, reminding Eamon of the wretched state of his own.

"Cadet," he acknowledged. He felt sulky and, much as he liked the young man, had no desire for human contact. He wanted to be left alone to gulp down the dregs of his burdened thoughts. For the first time in the two days since they had left Edesfield he became aware of a dull pain in his hand.

He folded the remains of the loaf into his fist, crushing them.

"Are you well, sir?"

"No." Eamon struggled to keep control of himself. The cadet was not the cause of his anger.

"Do you want me to fetch the doctor, sir?"

"No!" Eamon snapped. "I'm tired, Mr Grahaven, that's all."

"I'm sorry, sir. I'll go, sir."

As the cadet turned to leave, Spencing's jibes burned in Eamon's ears. A thought slyly suggested that the young cadet could easily be a plant sent by Belaal to monitor him.

"Why do you follow me, Mr Grahaven?" Eamon demanded.

The boy halted. "Sir?"

"What kindness have I done you that warrants your constant preoccupation with my welfare?"

Mathaiah Grahaven looked down at his feet, and Eamon wondered again how young the man – boy – was. He guessed that nineteen would be a generous estimate.

The cadet still did not answer. Eamon fixed firmly on him. "I asked you a question, cadet."

"I'm sorry, sir." The young man still did not raise his eyes. "I... you offered to help me up, that day outside the captain's office. It was a small thing, but... and I saw you, at the burning, before we left. At least I think it was you." He looked up plaintively. "In the crowd... you stopped someone from rushing at the pyre."

The memory caught at him unbidden. Eamon stared at the cadet. "I did," he said quietly.

"There is something different – something fearless but kind – about you, sir. At least," the boy added apologetically, "that's how it seems to me. I don't know better words to put to it."

Eamon churned inside. He did not feel either fearless or kind. "They are good words," he managed, "although I am not sure they can be applied to me."

Grahaven smiled. "You remind me of my brother, sir. He was sworn in a long time ago. They sent him north, against Galithia. His unit was lost, two years ago at Tenfell."

"The merchant borders are a dangerous place," Eamon told him.

He had been stationed there himself during the previous year. He had returned home, but a good number of the cadets training with him had not.

"We never found out for certain what happened."

"You're joining the Gauntlet to find your brother?"

The young man smiled sadly. "I can't pretend that my brother is still alive, sir. I joined to remember him and to honour what he likely died for."

There was a pause. Eamon cast his eyes over the River, now wider than he had ever seen it, and sighed. He wondered whether there would be space in the cadet's life for two men's hopes.

"I appreciate your honesty, cadet," Eamon said, "and thank you for your kindness. But you do not need to honour me for my resemblance to a dead man. Save your kindness for those who need it. There is little enough of your like in this land without you spending what you have on men like me... Save your kindness for those who need it," he repeated, lamely.

"The people?" Grahaven supplied. Eamon saw in the cadet's eyes the same desire to serve that had once burned in his own. Then he felt the mark on his hand. He dug his nails into his palm.

"Yes," he grimaced.

"If I may, sir?" Eamon nodded. "A Gauntlet officer is also deserving of kindness. You remind me of that."

Eamon blinked hard and stared at him. The boy smiled back.

"Permission to go to guard duty, sir?"

"Permission granted, cadet."

Mathaiah Grahaven saluted smartly, turned, and left.

At that moment the captain's voice bawled across the deck in search of oarsmen; the sails had fallen limp against the dark mast. Eamon tipped the rest of the bread from his hands into the water and went to offer his arms.

Men gathered quickly to lend their strength to the oars; it took another quarter of an hour to assign benches and rowing partners.

Captain Farlewe oversaw the binding of the sails while the last ensigns and cadets took their places, the latter's faces round with the jolly idea of rowing to the city. Eamon mused that, for many of them, the trip down the River was like some kind of schoolhouse jaunt.

At the captain's order the oars began beating a steady drive into the river currents. It wasn't long before the cadets were singing as they pulled.

Eamon took a place on a bench next to Ilwaine. They rowed together in silence.

"It will take us less than three days to reach Dunthruik, even if we row," Ilwaine murmured in between heaves. "Thank the Master!" The voyage had not been kind to him.

"And with the wind?" Eamon asked.

"Less than two days, Mr Goodman," the passing captain answered. "Mind port side!" he called, moving down the lines.

Less than two days? The thought terrified Eamon as much as it pleased him. He firmed his hands to the oars.

He was just getting into the full swing of the rhythm when Cadet Grahaven dashed wildly onto the deck. Turning this way and that, he met gazes with Eamon and ran full tilt towards him. The boy had the build of a sprinter and was at his officer's side in seconds.

"Problem, Mr Grahaven?" asked Spencing savagely. The lieutenant was in the opposite row.

Ignoring Spencing and all addresses of rank, Grahaven turned to Eamon: "She's gone!"

Everything stopped. They stood in the eye of the storm. Then it was a whirlwind as at Eamon's command a dozen cadets leapt to their feet, leaving oars hanging lamely in the air.

"Search over the sides!" he called. "Look for signs of descent, scan the water and banks." He turned to Grahaven.

The cadet answered his question before he asked it: "She was there just after I left you, sir. I left the hold for a few moments –"

"Where was Stonebrake?"

"He wasn't there yet," the cadet answered after only the slightest possible hesitation.

"And the man he should have relieved?"

"He was tired. I told him that he could go on, then when Stonebrake didn't come…" He bit his lip. "I stepped out for a moment to look for him. I'm sorry, sir."

Eamon gripped his shoulder then rushed to the nearest side, managing to trip a grey-looking Spencing in his haste. Craning his neck over, Eamon began searching the water for signs of Aeryn. She was good at hiding, something he knew far too well from years of children's games, and he found it more likely that she would have gone cautiously and concealed herself than recklessly and run. He peered farther over, turning his attention to the rope-work that hung down the sides of the holk.

He could not see far but he knew that she was there. For a second his vision changed and he saw as though he clung to the hull. The eyes that were not his looked up in terror and then down again at the water.

Grahaven had just reached his side when Eamon dashed towards the prow as suggested to him by his strange intelligence. There he once again threw his head over the side.

Aeryn was there, her eyes on the water, as though judging whether or not to risk the drop yet. Suddenly she looked up and their eyes met. He froze.

A chilling voice was suddenly in his mind.

Coward! What are you waiting for?

He could not answer it.

Grahaven was coming rapidly up behind him. Eamon hesitated. Aeryn's look grew dark. It was the last stroke.

"On the hull!" Eamon yelled.

There was a splash below him. When he next looked Aeryn was gone.

"In the water!" he cried.

Three ensigns dived off the side of the holk. Aeryn was making boldly for the bank. A good swimmer, she might have beaten the soldiers and made her escape, but, fatigued from days of depriving herself of food, she lagged and floundered. The ensigns caught up with her in a dozen strokes and after a brief struggle brought her back to the ship.

Bedraggled, Aeryn was hauled back on board. The ensigns brought her before the ship's captain and the Gauntlet officers, who had gathered on the deck as the outcome of the attempted escape grew clear. Eamon's chest heaved with anger as he glared at her.

"A guarded prisoner escape, in broad daylight?" Spencing sneered.

Eamon did not like his tone.

"Whose fault is this outrage?" Spencing demanded.

There was a pause. "Cadet Grahaven was taking turn, sir," a cadet supplied.

Eamon looked at Grahaven; the boy came formally to attention as Spencing spoke again.

"Was it your turn, Cadet Grahaven?"

"Yes, sir." The boy answered as firmly as he could.

"The prisoner has been watched in pairs – is that not so, Mr Goodman?"

Eamon felt Spencing's stare running over him. "Yes, Mr Spencing."

Spencing turned back to the pallid cadet. "And who was with you, Mr Grahaven?"

"No one, sir."

"No one?" Spencing repeated, flashing a calculating glance at Eamon. "No one, Cadet Grahaven?"

"Stonebrake was to be with me, sir," the cadet faltered. "He wasn't there."

"So Stonebrake was late." Spencing's eyes swept over the deck until they found Stonebrake. "Cadet Stonebrake!"

"I was late, sir," Stonebrake agreed haltingly.

"You were late." Spencing cast a disparaging glance at Eamon. "Stonebrake was late and you, Cadet Grahaven, sent on his predecessor and left your post without leave?"

Grahaven grew paler.

"Who was Stonebrake to relieve, cadet?"

"Cadet Whitbread," he answered slowly.

"You allowed this man to dismiss you, Whitbread?" Spencing demanded, turning furiously on him.

"Yes, sir." The cadet looked terrified.

Spencing turned balefully on Grahaven. "Cadet," he growled, "your insolent carelessness is a disgrace and sullies every man here, not least Mr Goodman."

Grahaven glanced worriedly at Eamon before forcing himself to speak. "I'm sorry, sir. It won't happen again, sir."

Eamon nodded. The boy was clearly sincere; he was willing to accept the apology. But Spencing was not satisfied.

"Apologies do not repair or redeem tarnished men," he snapped. "What is the punishment for carelessness on the River, captain?"

Eamon suppressed a gasp, understanding at last what was coming. The scene was fast becoming a spectacle.

"A word, Mr Spencing?" he barked.

Spencing seemed startled. Eamon turned a little so that none could read his lips as he hissed into the lieutenant's ear: "He has apologized, Mr Spencing, and no harm has been done; call off this nonsense."

Spencing received and held his glare. For a moment Eamon believed the man would see reason.

"The punishment, captain?" Spencing repeated loudly.

"A flogging." Farlewe's answer came through pursed, disapproving lips.

"Cadet Grahaven, you will take twenty lashes." The cadet's face grew ashen and Eamon saw him tremble.

"Cadets Stonebrake and Whitbread will each take ten." Stonebrake, ghostly in his pallor, swallowed; Whitbread began to shake. "Captain, the cat and the bar," Spencing called.

The captain gestured to two sailors. A murmur ran through the gathered men. It was difficult to tell whether the ensigns and cadets on the ship – who had to that point considered the voyage as somewhat of an excursion – approved of or were terrified by the sudden turn of the proceedings.

"You there!" None could gainsay Spencing as he pointed at those standing by the guilty cadets. "Relieve Cadets Grahaven, Stonebrake, and Whitbread of their jackets and shirts."

Two cadets, clearly companions of the humiliated Grahaven, stepped forward to him with hesitant hands, two others to Stonebrake, and two more to Whitbread. Whitbread crumpled, Stonebrake began breathing hard, while Grahaven kept a tightly controlled face. Eamon stared.

The Gauntlet's blood must be honed and shed before it serves.

As the strange thought waxed in him Eamon shuddered. Red jackets were taken and cast to the deck. The watching faces of the frightened cadets filled his eyes.

It is the punishment that they richly deserve.

He shook himself free of the taunting voice. Eamon stepped forward.

"The fault is mine, Mr Spencing." He was surprised to hear no fleck of fear in his own voice, no shake and no anger, just the courage of his conviction that a boy should not suffer the punishment of a man, and certainly should not suffer it at Spencing's whim.

The lieutenant turned to him with surprise. "Yours, Mr Goodman?"

Yours? The strange voice in his mind jeered. *Fool! Take back your childish words.*

Eamon steadied his gaze and matched Spencing's unflinchingly. "These cadets were explicitly under my command," he said, "and it is my duty to see that they perform theirs to a standard that will glorify the Master. If they have not done so then the fault is with my command. I will take the lashes."

Gasps stole the breath of every man, cadet, ensign, and sailor. A quick smile worked across Spencing's face.

"Then we shall relieve you of your shirt, Mr Goodman," he said, so kindly that it could not be kind.

"No." Eamon shook his head. "I will do it myself."

The pins glinted at his throat as he unfastened his jacket. Grahaven, Stonebrake, and Whitbread stood not far from him, looking so pale that they might faint. Grahaven's grey face stared at him with awe and horror. The boy drew breath to protest; Eamon silenced the cadet with a steady gaze. At the back of the lines he saw Aeryn, wet and trembling, still held fast in the hands of the men who had recovered her from the water. She had been completely sidelined by Spencing's theatrics. In a way he was glad of it, but he did not want her to watch him being flogged.

"Gentlemen," he said, as he tugged off his jacket and began with his shirt. "Let us secure the prisoner below deck. She has proven herself cunning and I would not put it beyond her to attempt a further escape." Aeryn stared at him, caught between horror and amazement. He did not meet her gaze. Instead he turned and barked out his orders before anyone, even Spencing, could stop him.

"Ilwaine, Barns, Meadhew: take the prisoner below and stand guard until you are relieved. Do not take your eyes from her."

The ensigns saluted and took Aeryn from the hands of their dripping fellows. As they began hauling her below he saw her face one more time: stupefied.

It was then that Eamon realized that he was doing something out of the ordinary – could it be called heroic? He hadn't expected it to be so sudden or to come with such clear conscience.

It is blind idiocy, quivered the voice in his mind. *It glorifies none.*

But Aeryn's look was on the faces all around him and only grew as the bar was brought out onto the deck. It stood, solitary and solemn, where it was set and prepared by the sailors' practised hands.

Eamon folded his shirt. With compulsive neatness that was perhaps intended to steady his mind, he laid it on the deck with his jacket. Then he stepped up to the bar. He tried to regulate his breathing as he was bound, spread-eagled, between the wooden beams. Spencing took it upon himself to check that the bonds were sufficiently tight. As he came past Eamon's face the lieutenant

Chapter V

leaned close: "An enjoyable way to spend the afternoon, wouldn't you agree, Mr Goodman?" He looked delighted.

"None better, Mr Spencing."

He did not see them bring the cat but he heard the tails jingling as it was given to Captain Farlewe. Swift bindings were run about Eamon's lower back to protect his insides from glancing blows. Spencing stepped forward to act as a counter.

Some foreboding of pain at last reached Eamon's thought. He closed his eyes, gratefully accepted the gag which was stuffed into his mouth, and braced himself for the strikes.

"Lieutenant Eamon Goodman will take thirty lashes for failure in his command," Spencing announced. "We shall commence: one."

A sharp hiss went through the air like a dozen arrows and struck him with astounding, flesh-tearing force. Eamon nearly choked on the gag as pain rocketed through him. He bit down hard.

"Two."

The lash came away from Eamon's back, leaving a raw, burning pain. Before the second blow hit him there were tears on his face and his back already ran with blood. Soon he could not feel even that.

The lash came back with viperous ferocity.

"Three."

Chest heaving, Eamon tightened his grip on the ropes at his hands.

"Four. Five. Six."

He bit down harder and harder on the gag. Blood dripped from his mouth.

"Seven. Eight. Nine. Ten."

Each was worse than the last.

"Eleven. Twelve. Thirteen."

This is payment for your ridiculous folly, Eben's son.

"Fourteen. Fifteen."

Tortured noises began bubbling out of him. He could not see for tears and all the sense in his limbs grew dull and blurred, indistinct except for the blistering lacerations that burned his skin like fire.

"Sixteen. Seventeen. Eighteen."

His tongue seemed bloated with blood and swollen with insensate pain; his whole body roared out the agony that raged through him.

"Twenty. Twenty-one."

He clenched his rolling eyes shut. He had simply to hold on, to hold fast...

"Twenty-two. Twenty-three. Twenty-four."

He heard, and felt, to the count of twenty-seven before he knew no more.

"Easy, lad, easy."

They seemed the first words that he had heard in years; they burned in his ears. He could not be sure how much time had passed.

He was laid on his front on a padded workbench in a darkened, narrow room. Strong hands moved about on his back. As sense and sight returned to him he became aware of his shirt and jacket across a nearby trunk and of various sharp-toothed, long-pronged instruments strewn across a shelf crammed with bottles and vials. For a wonderful moment the clothes on the chair let him believe that he was at home, in his own small, fish-scented room, looking after some odd things of Ladomer's while he was away on one of his many missions.

The hands soon disabused him of his notion. Something that was, if the pain was anything to go by, alcohol was applied to a slash that spanned his back. He screamed.

"What's the point of waking me up only to kill me?" he demanded, groggily and unkindly, as soon as his throat permitted it.

The ship's doctor chuckled. "I can't be held responsible for your waking, lad. You managed that yourself! And impressive it is, too, all considered."

"What time is it?"

"Nearly night. The very cream of the day!"

Eamon ignored the incongruity. As he overcame the pain from the alcohol dose he became aware of the motion of the ship and the beating of a steady drum to keep time. They were on the move once more towards Dunthruik... How close were they now?

"Your prisoner is safe, in case you're wondering," the doctor continued. Eamon heard the man pouring something into a bowl and dipping a cloth into it. He suspected that it was more alcohol, destined for his back; he tried not to grow too tense. "You'll be all right too, by the way. That is to say," the jolly doctor added, "there's a couple of pieces of you missing, but they'll more or less grow back, and you'll get some pretty scars into the bargain. Always a winner with the ladies."

"Thank you," Eamon replied. He tried to keep quiet during the next fiery application of alcohol, failed miserably, and then lay still, panting, for a few minutes.

"Will it always hurt like this?" he gasped.

"A little rest and you'll be right as the River. Oh, but do avoid heavy lifting and excessive weapons drills for a while. Don't want to reopen these nice, clean wounds once they're healing."

The doctor stepped away and began wiping his bloodied hands down on an apron before taking up a swathe of bandage.

"I can go?" Eamon asked, surprised.

"It's no excuse from duty, a flogging, you know," the doctor chided. "You'll be straight back to it in the morning."

"Oh."

Eamon allowed the doctor to wrap a strip of fabric about his torso. The man took Eamon's shirt and slipped it gently over his shoulders. The cloth snagged at his torn flesh and Eamon grimaced as the doctor settled the garment on him. He then endured the weight of his jacket.

The doctor took his hand and clasped it firmly.

"I'm right glad to be bandaging you, Mr Goodman."

Eamon took his meaning. "Thank you, doctor." He smiled – and then stopped because it hurt too much.

A few minutes later he left the doctor's tiny, bottle-crammed cabin. He limped a little, and keeping his back straight or turning his head was difficult. Pulling the door closed behind him he turned to make his way to his own bunk to rest.

The corridor beyond the doctor's cabin lay quiet. Eamon steadied himself on a timber as the holk swayed to one side. The silence all about him was broken only by a voice above: Spencing, calling orders to some of the cadets on deck. The lieutenant's voice carried the crack of the lash.

Eamon staggered along the passage. It was as he went that he suddenly caught sight of three shapes in the deepening gloom.

Cadets Grahaven, Stonebrake, and Whitbread sat pressed up against the hull wall in sleep, their weary heads nodding as the holk rolled up and down. Their faces were turned towards the doctor's door.

Eamon stopped for a moment. Then he passed on unseen. He followed the passage towards his own cabin and, quite unexpectedly, found himself going past it.

He stepped into the narrow hold. The two cadets on duty formally saluted him as he paused in the doorway. He offered them a smile before looking at Aeryn. She lay, pale but beautiful in her defiance, curled up in the cloaks and sacks that were the walls of her world. He saw that her escape had garnered her an extra chain on each limb.

She grew restless again. He ached to wake her from whatever nightmare she endured.

His hand throbbed. Wearily, like an old man bent with an age of toil, he turned and left the hold.

CHAPTER VI

He woke feeling as though he had lain in fire, and for a while he wondered why. Then his memory returned – as did the pulsing pain across his shoulders.

He dressed quickly and made his way onto the deck. There Ilwaine greeted him before offering him some breakfast. He had saved it specially, and quite against Spencing's wishes. Eamon thanked him and wondered, as he munched the almost fresh bread, at the man's apparent change of heart.

"Don't rush, sir," Ilwaine told him. "Nobody is expecting you at the exercises today."

Eamon raised a curious eyebrow. "Is that so, ensign?"

Ilwaine smiled. "A few of us spoke to the captain, and he spoke with Lieutenant Spencing – we were all agreed, sir."

Eamon blinked, trying to imagine the meeting between lieutenant and captain; the thought was singularly delightful.

"Thank you, ensign."

"Sir." With a salute Ilwaine left, a distinct smile on his face.

As he went through the day Eamon thought that some showed a little more respect, even if it was grudging, towards him than they had before. It was unexpected but not in the least unpleasant. His uniform was at last bringing him what he deserved.

He corrected himself. He had not even been wearing his uniform when they flogged him. He had been moved to act by something he hadn't understood; the Master had had nothing to do with it. Perhaps it was that, more than anything, which brought a smile to his face. The strange voice and the pain in his palm – whatever they were – did not hold him. He was still his own master.

Later that day he crossed paths with Spencing. The lieutenant scowled.

"I suppose you're feeling very clever, Mr Goodman," he muttered. Evidently he had noted the change his actions had unintentionally wrought upon the crew.

Eamon laughed, inclined to indulge even Spencing. "Only a little tired, Mr Spencing," he answered. "But we must lead by example."

Spencing turned on his heels with a huff, yelling spurious commands at cadets.

During the day Eamon noted that his hand had begun to throb dully, but he put it from his mind. At mid-morning he went to see the doctor, who happily changed the bandages – and reapplied whatever stringent alcohol he used – to Eamon's scars and wounds while soliloquizing on an infinite number of comforting nothings. No subject seemed beyond his scope: the weather, history, politics, the exotic habits and temperaments of the east, or the varying kinds of women in the merchant states. Part of the diatribe was doubtless to draw Eamon's attention away from the pain in his back, which burned at each application of alcohol as though liquid fire were being poured upon it. The doctor chuckled as Eamon tried to stop himself from flinching.

"You're a brave man, Mr Goodman. In fact," he added, "you're a *good man!*" The doctor laughed as though it were possible that he was the first man to make this joke, then applied rather too much alcohol. "My apologies, lieutenant," he said. "You'll heal well. Don't worry about the scars too much," he continued. "Some of them are scabbing over nicely already, but I'm afraid you will have fine streaks on your back 'til the day you die – and may that be long from now! You're already too old to fully recover from a whipping like the one you took, my lad."

Late that afternoon the forests that had surrounded them for the last day or so thinned and broke sporadically into grassy plains before the plains were swallowed again by the forest and woodland. Far to the north and the north-east the dim shape of distant mountains marred the horizon. The River was growing broader still and a road had appeared by its north bank, frequented by horses and carts whose curious old men stared at the ship as though it might carry smugglers or secret wealth. Smoke rose from hamlet chimneys and, where the River rolled like a silver ribbon towards its mouth, Eamon sometimes saw a mass. At first it was indistinguishable, sheltered by mists or woods or distance, but in the balmy autumn light his eyes picked out what looked like towers and huge black walls. The sun was before them, and as the light changed, Eamon imagined that the rays caught gilded rooftops or pennants and banners snapping gaily in the wind. It was said that they would reach Dunthruik sometime the following day.

This left much of the crew thoughtful. The captain announced that he had taken the liberty of letting the cook bring salted meats and some Ravensill wines on board when they had stopped that morning so that their final meal together could be an enjoyable one. It surprised Eamon, for it was certainly not something that the Gauntlet would have done or probably even condoned – indeed, Spencing protested the notion – but neither sailors, ensigns, nor cadets shared their irate officer's opinion on the subject. Eamon's flogging seemed to have elevated him above Spencing, and so it was Eamon's view on the matter that was sought. He thought the meal a fine idea and gave permission for it, noting that Spencing watched him vengefully. But the lieutenant did not oppose him. Eamon wondered whether Spencing meant to cause him trouble in Dunthruik.

Where the bar and the cat had been the previous day the captain ordered the setting up of a series of misfit tables. The holk was not really a place for a sit-down banquet but they would do their best.

Anchorage found, the tables were set and the smell of cooking wafted in the rigging. Eamon's stomach rumbled appreciatively.

Eamon had been asked not to help with the meal's preparations and the captain asked whether he would join him at his table when the meal began. Eamon accepted, partially to spite Spencing. He was very much looking forward to not sharing a room with the arrogant prig when they arrived at their harbour the next day. A cautionary voice reminded him that in all likelihood they would be stationed together in Dunthruik, possibly in the same group, but he tried not to think of that. If he performed well, after all, he could be transferred elsewhere, and there would be others to whom he could report the scheming man.

As the preparations continued Eamon discreetly inquired of the captain whether a portion of the doctor's culinary masterpiece might be taken to the prisoner. The captain's nod spoke enough. Eamon hoped that Aeryn would be able to eat at least some of it.

As he stood surveying the logistical nightmare that half a dozen teenage cadets were able to make of setting up some simple tables, he felt Mathaiah Grahaven watching him. When he looked up to meet the by now familiar gaze he found it lowered in shame.

Stretching his sore shoulders with a wince, Eamon walked across to the young man. The cadet shuffled uncomfortably.

"Is everything all right, Mr Grahaven?" Eamon asked, and found that he spoke to the boy as a friend. He smiled sadly, knowing that their paths would part the next day.

"No sir… I mean, yes, sir." The boy faltered. "You shouldn't have done it, sir!" he burst out angrily.

Eamon laughed. "It was my duty," he answered. "And even a Gauntlet cadet is deserving of kindness," he added.

Grahaven looked aghast. Then, recognizing the irony and seeing the smile on Eamon's face, he laughed. Soon both of them were laughing so hard that it hurt the lashes on Eamon's back.

When at last they managed to contain themselves, the cadet gestured to the hazy silhouette that showed on the most distant horizon.

"Is that Dunthruik, sir?"

Eamon looked at the shadowed shape. It was not growing any closer now because the holk had harboured in a sheltered northern bend of the River. The main sway ran past them, swelling and churning around the deep rocks in its bed. Eamon realized that he preferred the water to the impending city.

"That's Dunthruik."

"I wish I was going there, not back to Edesfield," Grahaven sighed, and drummed his fingers on the side. "Maybe in a few years I will. How long did you train, sir, to get this posting?"

Eamon didn't answer. His heart was suddenly heavier, perhaps heavier still because he had found how precious the boy's kindness was. He saw how it would be in but a few months: Mathaiah Grahaven would kneel before Belaal, put his hand to the awful sceptre, writhe with pain that only he could feel, and then languish in the uncertainty of what had happened to him.

The pain in Eamon's hand grew acute and he felt a battle of wills in his own head. He saw the brave and noble officer that the cadet would become: head and shoulders above all other men, feared and obeyed, Hand to the Master himself, stalking the halls of the palace and leaving swathes of wretched obeisance in his wake.

His vision clearing, Eamon turned back to Cadet Grahaven. He looked at the kind face, already imbued with nobility. But it was not the nobility that Dunthruik desired. Grahaven was kind and true – like Telo.

Telo had believed in kings.

His hands began to shake. Whatever Aeryn had told him, he did not and could not believe in kings... could he?

The cadet watched him expectantly. The boy had noticed the way that he held his palm; Eamon had clasped it to dull the pain. He yearned to speak of it.

"Are you well, sir?"

Eamon looked about him. The other ensigns, and Spencing, were far away. Most were distracted by the hilarity dogging every step of the table setting, or busy preparing the holk for the night. His betrayal would not be seen.

It is treachery against your oath. It will be seen.

He shuddered. It was reckless. It was treachery. The Master's revenge would be terrible. But Grahaven had to be warned.

So slowly that he wondered if he moved at all, he held his palm out towards the cadet. He did not even know whether the boy would be able to see what he saw, what he *knew* to be there, but he had to try.

"Do you see my palm, cadet?" he asked. Grahaven frowned, seeking guidance as to the relevance of the question, then looked carefully down at Eamon's hand.

"Yes?" he offered.

"What do you see?"

The cadet searched for a horridly long moment, and Eamon suddenly worried that he would be seen. He was leading a cadet astray and if Spencing saw... Every noise became a threat to him and he struggled to remain calm.

What seemed like years later, Grahaven looked up. "There's a mark. Did the cat miss?"

Eamon guiltily snatched his hand away, as anxious now to hide it as he had been to show it. Thinking his guess correct, the cadet spoke again.

"I am sorry, sir, and a good hand, too. I should never have let you –"

"This is the mark of the throned, cadet," Eamon whispered. Dunthruik loomed in his sight as though to stop his very voice. He swallowed. "This is what they give you, when you swear."

A disconcerted look passed over the boy's face. Steeling his nerves, Eamon spoke again. "This mark is a violation, Mr Grahaven. You will be commanded to do things in the name of the Master – and you will do them, because you bear this mark..." Seeing the boy's clouded face, Eamon faltered. "It is infinitely noble of you to want to honour your brother by following him in his service. I do not and will not ask you to promise anything to me, cadet, because that would be to set myself on a throne before you, just as he seeks to do." Eamon wondered where his words sprung from. "But please... consider not swearing. Drop out of the college when they take you back." Eamon's voice grew urgent. "Do anything but don't… Don't swear."

Grahaven gaped silently. It looked as though the walls of his world were crashing about his ears and the noise was too much for him to bear.

"That's… that's snake talk…"

Eamon was startled. Snake talk? He supposed it was. "Just… please, just think about it."

Weakly and with odd politeness, Grahaven smiled. "I should go and help the others," he said. He turned, returned as he remembered to salute, and then hurried away.

Eamon nervously chewed the inside of his cheek. He didn't know if his words would have any effect but at least he had spoken. He gave one last look at the brooding city then made his way below deck. He felt weak and tired. He decided to take advantage of the preparations, and rest.

It seemed only moments later that disjointed noises shuffled in and out of his sleep: howling, spectral cries, manic footfalls, the clash of steel. He could hear Spencing roaring with a voice like thunder. Was he dreaming?

His eyes snapped open, but rather than disappearing the sounds from his dream grew louder, more real. Stiff from lying down, Eamon lowered himself from his hammock and hurriedly strapped scabbard and sword to his belt. His shoulders were in agony but he choked back the pain and slipped into the passageway.

In the hatchway above him pink and gold laced the clouded twilight; the ship's lanterns were already lit and the smell of cooking had grown even stronger. In the shifting light he saw shouting shadows moving quickly to and fro on the deck above him. The sounds of the struggle were getting louder and more frenzied.

He edged his way up the stairwell and peered up. Then he froze in horror. Many of the ensigns and cadets were being bound and herded into a corner where they were made to kneel. The sailors were in the opposite corner of the broad deck sitting sullenly. The captain brooded at their head with all the defensiveness of a mother hen. Their silence implied that it was not the first time in their careers they had been boarded.

Creeping up a couple more steps Eamon saw bodies strewn across the bloody decks. Ilwaine was one of them; the ensign's eyes stared vacantly out of his face. Spencing and a couple of others were fighting still, swords flashing in furious flurries, but they were swiftly being overcome. Their opponents were masked men, dressed in dark greens and browns. The boarders were about twenty-five in number, almost as many men as there had been on the holk, but evidently skilled in their trade and favoured in their enterprise. Eamon suspected that the holk had been taken just as supper was beginning; spilled gravy lay mixed with blood. Ensign Hill slipped in a puddle of it, fell, and was impaled by his attacker as he went down.

Eamon stared, incapacitated by anger and fear. He could not challenge two dozen men on his own, but what other choice did he have?

Drawing his sword he leapt up the steps onto the deck with a loud cry. His first opponent fell.

"Sir!" called a voice. Though wounded in his left arm, Mathaiah Grahaven was one of the cadets still free and fiercely fighting. Eamon took his bearings; then he clearly saw the face of the man he had killed. The mask had been dragged askance. It was a harsh face, though not unkind. Its lines and shapes reminded him of Telo.

Enraged, Eamon yelled across the deck: "Stay this madness! There is no need for killing here!"

As if by some miracle, everyone stopped. One of the boarders, a giant, muscular man, gestured to his fellows. The men quickly secured those still standing free, all except Eamon. With bloodied sword in hand and chest heaving, Eamon tried to assess the situation. Spencing shot him a look that might have skewered a charging beast but the lieutenant was manhandled aside before he could do more; he was beaten to his knees.

There was no protocol that could have prepared Eamon for that moment, staring over the bloody deck at men who could kill him at a breath. They were overcome, out-manned, and all of them in danger of their lives.

Eamon stepped boldly towards the one he assumed to be the leading man – only boldness could hide the way he trembled. He cleaned his blade on the side of his jacket and offered the pommel to the stranger.

"In return for the lives of every man on this vessel," he said steadily, "accept my surrender."

A broad smile formed underneath the giant's mask. The stranger snatched Eamon's sword away. Two men stepped up to Eamon's sides and pinioned his arms. He grimaced as pain arched up and down his back like lightning.

"Who, pray, are you?" the stranger asked. His voice was rounded with an odd accent, and he pronounced his vowels with an according and peculiar accuracy. Eamon decided he was from the northern provinces or maybe from Galithia, a merchant state just over the border.

Taking a breath, he tried to pronounce his name in a dignified fashion. "Lieutenant Eamon Goodman."

"Lieutenant Goodman." The stranger repeated the name thoughtfully. "Lieutenant Goodman. Tell me, Lieutenant Goodman – where is your cargo?"

Eamon wondered if the men were pirates. He had heard that some still operated on the River, but for the most part the Gauntlet had driven such ruffians to remote coasts and headlands.

"We have no cargo but ourselves," Eamon answered, truthfully enough. "We are bound for Dunthruik."

"Where is your prisoner, Lieutenant Goodman?" the stranger demanded, his tone vengeful. Eamon glanced discreetly at the others. Grahaven, restrained a few feet away, looked grim but determined. Eamon tried to draw assurance from that look. What should he do? While on active service at the borders his orders had somehow always kept him from the worst parts of skirmishes and battle. He had, more often than not, acted as a courier, and his experience in real fights had never involved surrender. Now, he wished they had.

"Will you guarantee me the life of every man on this ship?" He tried to remain confident but the stranger's answering roar of laughter shattered any pretence he might have maintained.

"It seems to me that you have nothing to bargain with!" The man fixed Eamon with a steely glare. "Search below deck," he said. Several of his followers immediately moved away. Eamon tried to contain his nerves for the eternity it took the men to return. The masked face watched him the whole time, enjoying his discomfort.

Suddenly the men were back, with Aeryn walking freely between them. The keys for some of her bindings had been kept below deck but her hands were still in heavy manacles. She took in the situation at a glance.

"Giles," she breathed. Eamon saw that she addressed the burly stranger in front of him. Wisely, he held his tongue. "Giles," Aeryn continued, "what are you –?"

"The key, if you please, lieutenant," Giles intoned, holding out his hand and addressing Eamon as though he were a child.

"I shall need the use of my arms for that, sir," Eamon replied hotly. That Aeryn knew the man deeply angered him.

The men at his sides gave him a little leeway to move; he wrenched his arms free. Withdrawing the keys for Aeryn's cuffs he tossed them to the strange man. Giles passed them straight to somebody else who released her. She rubbed at her wrists, sore and chafed from her confinement.

"You keep poor hospitality on board your ship, Lieutenant Goodman," Giles said with a solemn shake of his head.

"It is all a snake deserves!" Spencing spat. The lieutenant fell silent as a boarder dealt him a crushing blow to the stomach.

"Giles, stop it!" Aeryn cried. But the big man ignored her. He turned back to Eamon with a terrifying glint to his eye. Before such a look Eamon found it hard to hold his ground.

"I am afraid that we have outstayed our welcome, lieutenant," Giles said. "Your young lady will be coming with us."

"You cannot take her," Eamon replied, knowing how stupid it sounded. He wished that she could know he had only ever wanted to help her. If only he had done something sooner. He fixed his gaze on his captor. The man dwarfed him. "I beseech you," he said, "let her go freely."

Giles roared with laughter.

"Now there's a word! Beseech! You make me laugh, Lieutenant Goodman!" he said, wiping an imagined tear from his large eye. "But not enough, I'm afraid, to earn your keep." His voice went cold. "I grant none of your requests," he pronounced, turning his drawn sword and watching how torchlight sparked down the crimson blade. "But, in recognition of the kindness you have shown me, I will kill you before the others. Thus perish the throned's bloody Gloves!" he yelled, and struck.

Aeryn screamed. Eamon clenched his eyes shut and felt every muscle of his body tense in anticipation of the falling blow, knowing it would not shield him.

But the pain never came. What he felt instead was the weight of a warm body staggering onto him. Opening his eyes, he had the sense to catch Grahaven; Giles's blade had punctured the cadet's side. As the boy fell, Giles cruelly twisted the blade, ensuring a devastating wound. He yanked his weapon free.

Horrified, Eamon took the boy's weight. They slid down to the ground and he tried to staunch the bloody rent. How had the cadet found the strength to pull away from his captors in time to take the blow?

All Eamon knew then was hot blood round his fingers and fear that the blade would come back for him. In the awful moment that followed he saw Aeryn grabbing Giles's hand. Her lips moved to words that he could not hear. Time slowed.

Mathaiah was choking in his arms. Desperately Eamon tore off his jacket, crumpled it together in his hands and forced it down hard on the boy's side. Moments later its red was saturated with a brighter one.

"*Murderer!*" Eamon screamed.

"No less than you," Giles replied evenly.

"This isn't the way, Giles!" Aeryn yelled, struggling to hold back the man's hand. Eamon saw that in moments Giles would shake himself free; then the blade would have nothing between it and its helpless goal. Instinct told him that he had to do something, but there was nothing to be done.

Mathaiah began coughing, his lips rimmed with blood. Eamon tried even harder to staunch the wound, but it was beyond any skill. Had the blade not been twisted there might still have been a chance… but the masked man knew his business.

Robbed of strength the boy's head lolled back and his eyes began to assume the vacant stare of death. It was plain that his spirit fought to stay in its house and also that it could not cling much longer to the threshold. Sobbing, Eamon gathered the young man against him.

But as Eamon held the dying boy, his vision changed. He saw a field, strewn with broken bodies, shattered spears, and splintered shields. A mournful wind moved over it; at its heart a man held his hands over a dying woman who was dressed in finery all covered over with a dark cloak, her arms curved protectively over her womb. Eamon knew instantly that he beheld a queen, beautiful beyond compare, from a time of long ago.

As he watched he saw the man drawing breath. Strange light shimmered about his hands – light like the blue bolt that had surrounded Aeryn in the prison. Eamon saw what the light did, and he somehow knew that he could ask it to do for him what it had done for the man he saw.

The vision faded. He saw Mathaiah's chest falling in what he knew to be a final breath. The time was now.

He hurled aside his jacket and pressed his hands to the pulsing wound. He felt raw flesh beneath his fingertips and nearly jerked back, but his nerve held. Shouts rang out around him; he knew the voice was Aeryn's and that Giles's hand was free and swooping down. But he knew, somehow, that he had the time he needed.

Gone was the pain in his back, gone the pain in his hand. It was all swallowed by the calm he had seen in the light on the battlefield. He saw it again but now it was real light, cool as a dawn breeze and with music in it like the song that had created the world. It danced before him in his mind and when he opened his eyes he saw that it danced about his hands, too. For a few seconds, it hovered; then with the surge of an ocean wave it left him and spread over Mathaiah, breaking like water across sand.

Then it was gone.

Suddenly time went at double speed. The voices over him became distinct and all the calm he had felt in the lull vanished.

With a cry Eamon flung himself over the cadet's body.

"Stop!" Aeryn screamed. "He is a King's man!"

This alone of all the powers on the earth could stop Giles's hand. Slowly, the sword sank down to his side and he gazed with contempt at his intended prey. Eamon felt his chest heaving in terror as the man paced to within a foot of him.

"He bears the throned's mark," Giles spat, stabbing at Eamon's hand with the tip of his blade. Eamon didn't even dare to look up; he gripped Mathaiah's body feverishly tight.

"He is a King's man!" Aeryn cried again, angrily. "Don't pretend you didn't see it, Giles!"

"Prove it!" Giles snorted, kicking Eamon once for good measure. Eamon took the blow on his side. It was crushingly painful, leaving him struggling for breath.

Suddenly Aeryn's voice was at his ear. "Eamon," she said. "Eamon, you have to get up."

He did not know if she meant it kindly or not. He slowly lifted his head to look at her.

"I need to look at the cadet," she said softly.

Eamon matched her gaze uncomprehendingly. She nodded once to him. He sat up, pulling ruddy hands from Mathaiah's side. He knew that there was more blood on him than should give cause to hope. But, like Aeryn, he looked.

Then he stared. What had he done? He wrung his hands as hideous uncertainty came over him. The face below him was still pale, but its eyes were open.

"Sir?" the boy whispered.

Fearing the worst, Eamon reached out and took the cadet's hand. "I'm here," he said. "I'm sorry –"

But he could not finish. No sooner had the boy felt the thick blood on the hand that grasped his own than he sat up in terror.

"Sir, you're hurt!" he cried, and it was clear to see that, bar a stain that spelled doom for his jacket, the boy bore no wound. The blood was all on Eamon's hands.

Staggered and speechless, Eamon stared. Mathaiah saw his face, looked at the blood, and seemed suddenly to remember that it was his. He touched his side in amazement.

"Sir?" he breathed, trembling.

Eamon was no less astounded.

Suddenly Spencing screeched a damning howl across the deck: "Traitor! Snake!"

Whatever reprieve they might have won from Giles they lost in that moment.

"Bind the lieutenant and the boy," he barked, "and take them to the boats. Kill the others. Burn the holk."

"No!" Eamon screamed. But his voice was lost in the panic that suddenly smote every man on board. He saw cadets, ensigns, and sailors, bound though they were, leaping to their feet and hurling themselves overboard, determined to face the River rather than Giles. Most were not so lucky and many never even reached their feet.

Eamon struggled forward and reached for his sword before he remembered that he had surrendered it. He heard Mathaiah's voice calling out in warning, but it came too late. The next thing he knew was a blow that forced him to his knees, and the screaming faded away.

CHAPTER VII

He did not know how much time had passed. Unconsciousness clawed at him as he struggled to drag himself back into the world.

A face bore down on him with a vile, empty smile – a face with a burning mark on its brow more threatening than any instrument of torture. A hand reached towards his and to the flaming mark upon it. Eamon writhed to escape his tormentor and suddenly realized that it was a dream.

He shuddered and forced himself awake. Choked with nightmares, his back burnt, he drew a deep breath and opened his eyes. He found the world around him quite different from the place in which he had been held in his sleep.

To begin with he was in a bed. Warm sheets and furs lay about him and sunlight came shyly in through a shuttered window. Outside he could hear the sounds of life in a small village: grocers harping, pigs squealing, and… was there a fishmonger? His heart ached briefly at the familiar smell of scales and dirt.

He was in a small room – there was barely space in it for anything but the bed and a chair – which seemed to be in some kind of wooden lodge. Furs were neatly laid on the floor to provide further insulation. Clean clothes lay on the nearby chair: warm woollen britches and a plain shirt. He did not know where his uniform was, and didn't really care until he realized that he was naked in the bed. He soon chose not to worry about that; his back felt horribly sore and left occasional marks of blood and pus where he leant. As he took in the room he found that his hand still pulsed dully. What had happened to him?

Overwhelmed and exhausted, he sobbed.

Pieces of his memory returned. He clearly remembered the blow. After that his recollection was vague, and he had trouble distinguishing what he might have seen from where he had wandered in his troubled sleep.

He had dim memories of being dragged from the holk, struggling as much as he was able in his semi-conscious state. It was cold as he was walked down the plank to land and thrown roughly into a boat. He remembered the heat as flames licked up around the *Lark*'s mast like an enormous stake, the sails tearing before turning to ash and smoke. And Aeryn's face, covered with tears, watching him as he faded in and out of consciousness. He remembered seeing stars overhead while he lay crammed in the hull of the tiny rowing boat, being periodically knocked by the rower, and a dark figure, standing at the stern of the blazing holk, watching him as the boat in which he lay was rowed into the night. But none had been left alive, not Hill or Spencing or Farlewe, or the doctor...

Grimly, Eamon tried to master himself; tears hardly befitted a grown man who languished in a perfectly furnished bedroom. He slipped carefully out of the sheets, shuddering at the sudden cold, and felt the fur at his feet. It was a luxury he had not known since his family had lived in Dunthruik. His mother had never held with putting good furs on the ground but had conceded it to his father. Eamon remembered the cold night when his mother had died, the feel of the fur about his knees as she had laid her hand over his and kissed his forehead one last time.

He dressed slowly. He was not bound or restrained in any way, though his wrists were cut where ropes had chafed him. The plain clothes felt comfortable, especially compared to the rigidity of the uniform he had lived in over the last few years. He wondered if professional clothes were intentionally tailored to be unbearable.

It was then that his memory of what had happened on the holk fully returned to him. His thoughts turned to the strange light that had filled him, and to Mathaiah whom it had covered. What had happened to the cadet? He knew that they had both been bound and taken from the holk, but what if Giles had done something terrible since then?

Unable to bear the thought he strode to the door and pulled at the handle. He turned it hard, but it would not open. Then he noticed a collection of things on the floor next to it, cast in alternating light and darkness by the window's shutters. Meticulously arranged on a plate were a small beaker, a jug of water, a loaf of bread, and some slices of cold meat and cheese.

Eamon stared at them dumbly, not knowing whether to laugh or cry. In some ways he had preferred the certain terror of his dream to this strange hospitality.

Slowly he sank down onto the furs. Only after staring at the food for long minutes did he reach out to touch it. The first bite of bread reminded him that he did not know how long it had been since he last ate. He gulped ravenously. When nothing but drops and crumbs were left he returned to the bed and wrapped himself in its covers. All he could do was listen to the noises beyond his unconventional cell door, and wait.

He had not even realized that he had fallen asleep again when the sound of the door opening wakened him. He struggled to sit up.

A middle-aged woman stood in the doorway; her thick hair was pulled back and her sleeves were rolled up as though she had just finished a morning of housework. There was a concerned look on her simple face – probably elicited, Eamon realized, by the astonished way in which he stared at her.

"Are you well, sir?" she asked.

"Yes," Eamon replied after an uncertain pause. He supposed that he was, all considered.

"I heard shouting, you see." The woman brushed the thought away. "I expect you were dreaming."

"I…" Eamon frowned. He didn't remember any dreams and did not want to mention the one that he did remember. "I don't know."

The woman bustled in and cleared the ravaged plate and beaker. Then she disappeared through the door. Eamon stared after her, wondering what to do, but a moment later she came back.

"Come," she said. "He's to see you now."

"He?" Eamon asked. Something about the word filled him with fear. "Who is 'he'?"

"Stop your fussing and follow me," the woman repeated. "There're boots under the bed. Put them on. It's too cold now to go about without them."

Eamon quietly did as he was bid. Like all the other strange garments that he had been left, the boots fit well and soon he was following the woman from the door.

He saw that his room was one of several similar rooms in the same building. The three other doors were closed, and all four doors faced onto a small corridor. He followed his guide to the lodge's main entrance, shielding his eyes as bright sunlight blazed down on him. Stepping onto the porch he looked about.

He was in a small village, much as he had first supposed. Other buildings were made of wood and carefully thatched. There was a well and a speaking platform in the centre of the dwellings. To the east were open fields, while circling round from south to north were the eaves of a dense forest.

People in the village were bustling about jovially enough and none took any notice of him as he passed among them, a complete stranger. He could see no sign of Mathaiah, Aeryn, or Giles, though he examined every face that they passed. He gloomily asked himself how he could hope to recognize the brute; the man had worn a mask.

Seeing him staring, his companion laughed. "Have you never seen a village before, sir?"

"Not this one."

"Well, you shall see a little more of it as we go. Come with me."

Chatting the whole way the woman led him to the western edge of the settlement where thick trees stood guard around an old, crumbling building, the only stone one that Eamon had yet seen. The building's roof was missing and so were large parts of the walls. The coloured cobbles that led to its door-less threshold suggested that it had once been a place of regard. Eamon guessed it might have been some lord's abode and that the village had once been more than it was now.

It was into this gaping ruin that he was led. He had to duck to pass through the tumbled lintel and realized that his guide had now moved on to discussing the conflicting values in bodying out stew with this, rather than that, kind of vegetable. He was not really paying attention and paused to take in what would once have been the hall, its walls crowned with ivy and yellow flowers. Dark entrances suggested the remains of downward stairs, maybe to a cellar or servants' quarters, while others might have led to kitchens or storerooms. Some broken stairs led up into the ivy-strewn trees.

The woman turned aside into one of the collapsed doorways. Perhaps it had once led to a great hall but now it led to nothing but a clearing. Eamon hung back and briefly wondered, as his guide pressed resolutely forward, whether she might be mad.

"Come, sir, come."

Uncertainly, Eamon stepped through the door.

There was no clearing on the other side. He stopped and stared.

He stood in a plain hall, its stonework old but well tended. Tall windows allowed light to fan in from outside, and he saw the village through the eastern-facing pane. Several doors led from the hall and over one of them a great banner hung. The banner was of mid-blue rimmed with dark blue and showed an eight-pointed silver star. Before its lowest point was an upright sword. Both sword and star seemed to shine in the light. Guards stood in the hall and many others passed to and from the various doors, carrying trunks or boxes of supplies and weapons. These they seemed to be depositing in large rooms, indicative of some kind of stockpile. The guards spoke loudly to each other, yet Eamon knew, as he glanced back at the doorway, that they could not be seen or heard from beyond it.

He stood agog and laid his hand against the stone. The hall was real. His fingers touched the cool walls and his sight changed: he saw the house as it had been of old. He saw the woman from his vision on the holk. She still wore the same cloak and she was accompanied by the same man as before, as well as by many others. Eamon watched the man lay his hand to the posts of the hall, to the place where Eamon's own palm was set, and suddenly every part of the stonework shivered with ripples of silvered light…

His guide's voice recalled him to where he was. "You may stare at the Hidden Hall later, sir; for now there's business to attend to!"

Eamon started and began to follow her again. Some looked at him as he passed and he found himself staring at the tabards borne by the guards. Whose token was the sword and star?

At the far end of the hall was an antechamber set behind a magnificent oaken door that had been engraved with a motif of trailing leaves. Eamon would not have dared to touch it himself – it was too awesome for the likes of him – but, after knocking sharply, the woman pushed the doors open and led him inside.

The moderately sized chamber beyond was well lit. Within was a slightly raised platform on which stood a table. About a dozen men sat there, each dressed in blues or greens, a few eyeing him with curiosity, a couple with virulence. On the wall above them, where the sunlight fell, hung a simple banner like that in the hallway, showing sword and star. Beneath it, another showed a unicorn.

Eamon stopped in the doorway, staring. His companion spoke to a guard inside the door. The next thing Eamon knew was his name on the air:

"Lieutenant Eamon Goodman, sire," the guard announced.

One of the men at the table pushed back his chair in a fit of rage.

"I won't stand for it!" he yelled as he stood. "You cannot let him in here!"

"Sit down, Giles," said several voices, some more forcefully than others.

"I'll not sit!"

Eamon swallowed nervously as Giles threw down the papers he had been holding and tore down from the table to the door. As he stalked past, his face was drawn in a fierce scowl and Eamon feared that the man might strike him. Instead Giles turned.

"You will regret it, sire! The mark is the mark and this man bears it." Then, glowering at Eamon, he stormed out. The door shuddered behind him.

There was a moment's silence. Then the woman whom Eamon had followed curtseyed.

"Lieutenant Eamon Goodman, sire," she said, gently. She offered Eamon an encouraging smile and then left.

Eamon found himself alone in the great hall. Well, alone with a dozen strange men, which was, he reasoned, not really alone. But the woman had been a support to him and, without her, he felt adrift in a terrifying world. Drawing a deep breath, he resolved to take whatever was to follow like a man if he could.

A man not much older than him rose from the centre seat at the table and came forward. As he rose all the others did the same; every eye followed him. Eamon felt smaller the closer the man came. He was tall, elegant, and lordly. A beautiful sword hung by his side and about the man's face was an aura of something that took Eamon's breath away; he did not know what to call it, but it spoke of justice and of valour.

Eamon stared awkwardly, knowing no words to say. Suddenly a burning pain shot up his arm. He saw again the face from his dreams, watched it writhe and become a crowned eagle; the pain in his hand grew greater.

Clenching his eyes shut Eamon fought away sudden dizziness. Nausea gripped his stomach and his mind flared, demanding that he leap upon the peasant parading before him and choke him without a moment's delay.

Will you trust this Serpent who makes his lair in hidden places of the earth and condones the murder of boys? Strike him, the voice urged. *Strike and kill him swiftly!*

Eamon trembled as his mind assessed; if he moved now, and moved fast, he could likely seize the blade at the man's belt and run him through before anyone could stop him.

The eagle in his palm burnt with blinding fire. Cries of alarm would come from the table as the other men rushed forward, drawing their own swords to stop him. But they would be too late; there was fire in his hand and at any moment he would strike with it, the Master's fire, and there was nothing that the puny, self-styled king before him could do to save himself…

King? There were no kings…

Suddenly, over the din in his ears, thunder in his mind, and fire in his hand, a voice spoke to him: "First Knight, hear me."

The name fell on his ears, unknown yet carved in a hidden place in his heart. It drove the murderous voice and fire far from him, leaving him master of himself once more. As his eyes cleared he saw that the stranger's hand was clasped over his palm, quenching the embers there.

"Eamon," the man said, his voice jubilant.

Eamon looked and at last clearly beheld the face before him. Bright blue eyes gazed back at him, as clear and deep as the sky itself. The hand that was over Eamon's own bore a small scar. Eamon laid his fingers on it in disbelief. He knew the source of that scar far too well: stealing apples from an old lady's tiny orchard more than a decade ago.

Trembling, he searched the face before him. A name he had thought lost forever came to his lips.

"Hughan?" Fearing that what he saw was some spectral vision, he firmly clasped the hands that lay on his, but they did not melt or fade.

The bright-eyed man smiled at him. "You remember me."

"Remember you?" he breathed. "How could I not?"

With a delighted laugh Hughan embraced him. Eamon shook, his tears mixed with laughter, as he returned it.

"All these years! All these years, you were alive and I…" He pulled back and stared at his friend. "But they found your body. How…?"

He shook his head, stunned, then pressed Hughan's hands in his. "Hughan," he whispered, "where have you been?"

"There is hardly a place where the River runs that I have not been," Hughan answered with a wry smile. "I had much to do, and I have not finished yet."

"Much to do?" Eamon frowned at him. "What do you mean?"

"That's hardly a manner in which to address the King," called another voice.

Eamon blinked and remembered that there were a dozen others in the room, all of whom stood nearby watching him suspiciously. The man who had spoken was older than Eamon and had the stride of a horseman.

"The King?" Eamon repeated, hardly able to believe what he heard. "What do you mean, 'the King'?"

"Just that, lieutenant," the man answered.

"No," Eamon breathed, shaking his head. "No; there is no king."

"There was," Hughan answered softly. "He died at the battle of Edesfield, a long time ago."

"Aeryn told me," Eamon whispered. "His name was Ede."

"His name was Ede," Hughan nodded, "and I descend from his sister, Queen Elaina."

Eamon thought at once of the woman in his visions.

"That's who I saw," he murmured. He felt suddenly unsteady. "Then... then you are..."

Hughan looked at him kindly.

"I'm sorry, Eamon," he said. "You are tired and this is not the manner of meeting that I would have chosen. We have much to discuss and there will be much that you want to ask, and much that I must tell you, but perhaps I have called you here too soon: you are not yet enough recovered." Eamon nodded dumbly. He certainly didn't feel recovered; relapsed might be a better description. "I will escort you back to the lodge."

"Please," Eamon said quietly, "can I see the cadet who was brought with me?"

"Of course," Hughan, his lost friend – the King – answered. "He is quite well."

He offered Eamon his arm and Eamon steadied himself, allowing his old, dear friend to lead him from the stares of the hall, under the banner, through the hidden threshold, and back into the dazzling sunlight and the small village, where life continued as though it knew nothing of the wonder hidden in the crumbling stones. There were a million questions in Eamon's mind; none of them could reach his tongue.

Hughan led him back to the lodge and delivered him into the care of the woman who had first brought him to the hall. Eamon turned to him.

"Is this a dream?"

Hughan smiled at him. "It isn't," he answered. "Ma Mendel will look after you," he added, gesturing to the woman. "Take some more rest, Eamon. Then we'll speak."

Eamon nodded. "Thank you."

Hughan left soon after. Eamon watched him cross the village and go back towards the hall. It was as Hughan crossed the small square that Eamon saw a young woman go confidently down the muddy track towards the King. Hughan stopped to wait for her, a broad and loving smile on his face. The young woman reached his friend, warmly kissed him, and then slipped her hand delicately into his.

With a strange feeling, Eamon watched as Hughan and Aeryn made their way back towards the Hidden Hall, hand in hand.

It was a long time before he remembered the woman at his elbow. She had followed his gaze and perhaps guessed some of the tumult of his thought.

"Come and rest, Mr Goodman," Ma Mendel told him. "You'll soon have much to do."

Ma Mendel took him through the narrow corridor of the lodge to the door that was his.

"Madam," Eamon began.

"None of that nonsense!" the woman chided, clicking her tongue. "Not for me. Call me Ma Mendel."

"Mrs Mendel," Eamon tried again, "Hughan said that I could see the cadet who was brought here with me…"

"He also said that you needed rest."

"I would rest better having spoken with him." He had not yet paused to consider everything that had happened to him in the last day; the events of the last hour would terrify him as soon as he faced them. He needed a familiar face.

Ma Mendel relented.

"Well, if the King said so… you're sure you're not tired?" She still sounded hopeful of discharging him safely to bed.

"Yes," Eamon answered. Her tone implied that it might well be a three-day hike traversing rivers of fire to wherever Mathaiah was.

"Very well," Ma Mendel sighed. She turned to the door opposite and knocked. Eamon stared; the ridiculous simplicity of it nearly induced a fit of laughing in him.

A quiet voice granted admission. Ma Mendel grandly allowed Eamon to pass inside.

"You just give me a shout when you're done, Mr Goodman." Eamon was about to interject that he did not think he would lose his way to his room when she smiled at him, stepped outside, and pulled the door to behind her.

The cadet's room was identical to his but inverted. Mathaiah Grahaven sat on his bed dressed in the clothes their hosts had left them. He looked worried; Eamon wondered if the boy had slept at all.

"Sir!" Mathaiah cried. "Thank goodness it's you. I didn't know what to do…"

Eamon came and sat in the chair next to him.

"I'm not sure that there is anything we can do," he answered. From where he sat he could see through the small window; he felt sure there was a burly figure lurking there, whose shape neatly approximated Giles's. It did not comfort him.

Mathaiah looked at him, bemused. "I'm sorry, sir, I don't follow you."

"This is no prison house, cadet," Eamon replied. "We seem to occupy a grey area between prisoner and guest, being neither one nor the other."

"We shouldn't try to escape, sir?"

"At least not for now."

Mathaiah nodded. The young man had clearly decided there and then to go by his officer's judgment.

"I'll follow you, sir. That's how it should be." He paused. "Why are they keeping us at all, sir?"

Eamon faltered.

"I think we're here because of what I did on the holk," he said at last.

Mathaiah rolled up his shirt to peer at his side, as though he had forgotten it. He prodded himself, seemingly concerned that the hale skin might be some parlour trick. He looked at his arm, but his search for a wound there was as ill rewarded as the search at his side. Increasingly confused, he looked back at Eamon.

"Sir?"

Eamon flexed his hand. Despite its fearsome show earlier the mark he bore was now nearly invisible.

"Was it –" Mathaiah began.

"The throned's mark didn't enable me to do what I did," Eamon told him. He wondered that he chose the name "throned" over that of "Master".

"So all those stories about the swearing…?" Mathaiah breathed.

Eamon cast his mind back to his own days as a cadet. The stories had been about the pride of committing to the Gauntlet and how some of those who did became more than what they had been before. He had never heeded such stories himself, feeling that a metaphorical interpretation of them sufficed. The barracks' favourite had always been of one Ensign Davin, who had apparently been able to read men's minds after his swearing-in and, through this knowledge, had captured a deadly insurgent in Dunthruik. It was also told that he had been able to move great distances seemingly at a thought, though quite what that meant Eamon had never understood. The important part of the story was that the ensign had served the Master's glory and had eventually become a Hand.

He looked back at Mathaiah. "They are true, cadet, in the sense that something happens to you. Something happened to me. Something... can influence me," he blurted. "It has a voice that can speak in my mind. It plays on my fears. I can see things that aren't there and now... Now I can heal a wound that should have laid you beneath a headstone."

"That came from the swearing?"

"No. No; it felt different. I was... graced and aided, not contorted."

"Well, that's good," Mathaiah mused.

"Yes," Eamon answered, fairly sure that it was true. "Aeryn was right," he whispered.

"Aeryn?"

Eamon realized that he had finally slipped but it didn't matter; he didn't see how he could ever go back to Edesfield or Dunthruik. Telling the cadet the truth could hardly harm either of them now.

"The prisoner," he explained. "She's a friend of mine – or was, anyway. We grew up together. It was her father that was burned, back in Edesfield." Barely a week had passed since that day.

"I'm sorry, sir."

"It doesn't matter." Eamon waved away his concern. "I'm sure she cares nothing for me now."

"I'm sure you did everything that you could, to do rightly in regard to her and your duty," Mathaiah offered.

Eamon sighed. How often he had told himself that.

During their "imprisonment" Eamon spent a lot of time with Mathaiah. Both of them felt that they were waiting for something, though it was unclear what. Eamon could only assume that at the appropriate time they would be summoned. They were granted permission to walk about outside the lodge, as long as they didn't stray too far. That provided some change – though Eamon often noticed that Giles was not far away. The giant man seemed to keep a constant watch on them and always wore a grimace. Eamon did not think that Mathaiah noticed their grisly guardian, and decided not to draw attention to him.

Unable to sleep late, Eamon walked in the mornings. He told himself that it aided his thinking, even if Giles sat menacingly in the background. Though he tried not to let it show, the lack of clarity over his own status was gnawing at him, and he couldn't understand what relation the villagers were to the wayfarers, either. They were a disparate group of people. On the second day he had seen a group of men leaving the Hidden Hall. They bore the emblem of a green sun against an orange banner and Eamon realized that they had to be Easters, though which of the Seven Sons the men represented he could not be sure. He wondered what they could possibly be doing in a village so far west of the Algorra Peaks – the mountain range that separated the River Realm from the east – and wondered why they should part from Hughan with warm handclasps.

Eamon and Mathaiah spent some time in swordplay. They didn't have swords, of course, but it was not hard to gather together a few long branches. Mathaiah was a fine young swordsman and Eamon felt that the practice did them good.

On the second afternoon of their strange confinement they were engaged in just such a practice. Eamon was particularly pleased with the stick he had managed to find and felt well equipped to give his young friend a thrashing. The only problem was that Mathaiah seemed reluctant to comply with Eamon's victory. Every thrust and jab was thrown back at him, and Eamon had to work hard to even get close to touching the cadet with his impromptu blade.

"Come on, sir, you can do better than that!" Mathaiah quipped, parrying a blow that was feeble, especially by Eamon's standards. "Do I have to go more gently with you?"

"Nonsense! The only one being gentle around here is me!" Eamon lied, though he struck back with renewed vigour. The reward was good; he landed a blow on Mathaiah's arm and disarmed the cadet with a second stroke. The boy's stick landed a few feet away where a crowd of children had gathered. At first they had eyed him discreetly, pretending to be looking elsewhere. But over the last half an hour they had dropped even the pretence and stood watching the duel with fascination. It reminded Eamon of his own childhood, spent sitting on a wall in Dunthruik watching the Gauntlet exercising.

One of the children fetched Mathaiah's stick and enthusiastically offered it back to the cadet.

"Thank you," Mathaiah smiled.

"Can you help me beat him?" the boy asked, pointing at Eamon.

Mathaiah grinned. "He's a right devil with his stick, but I bet we could beat him together. What do you say?"

The boy's face lit up. He ran to fetch a stick of his own and took up a childish stance. Eamon pursed his lips and chuckled at the little swordsman.

"I care not!" he pronounced, as arrogantly as he could muster. In his mind was a childhood of courtyard adventures with his father. "I can fight you both at once. Do your worst, gentlemen!"

The fight took off again. Eamon had forgotten the advantage that the very short gain over their taller opponents, but he always insisted afterwards that his loss in that particular duel was intentional. It was a good match but he was soon overthrown, fiercely jabbed in the knee by the child and disarmed by a fine turn from Mathaiah. That turn also saw Eamon slipping in a swathe of mud and landing hard on his back.

"I yield!" he called in between gasps of pain and laughter – his scars aching from his fall. "I yield, cede, and surrender!"

"Then we shall be generous, sir," Mathaiah answered.

The little boy came over and looked down at him, the fallen foe.

"They say you're one of the Gauntlet," he said seriously, "and that you're a bad man."

Eamon met the child's gaze evenly. "What do you think?"

"I think you're a good loser!" the boy answered, offering his hand.

The boy was welcomed as a hero among his peers. The children hurried off together, laughing and jibing at Eamon's expense. He didn't mind it.

As he watched them go Eamon rubbed at his wood-marked hand. Chuckling, Mathaiah went inside the lodge to get some water, while Eamon gathered the discarded sticks. He was picking up the last when he saw a shadow hanging over him.

It was Giles. The man bore an angry look. Rising, Eamon faced him.

"What do you want?"

The great brute gave out a low rumble. "I want you to know that as soon as the King disavails you of his personal protection, I will kill you. It is his will, and his will alone, which ensures that you wake each morning."

Eamon matched the glare. "Then it is only his will that keeps me from avenging my crew. You are a murderer and will be repaid in the same coin."

Giles smiled a long, bitter smile. Eamon saw Mathaiah standing quite still on the steps of the lodge. Giles nodded gruffly towards him.

"What's your cadet's name?"

"Grahaven," Eamon answered. The smile on Giles's face grew broader.

"Grahaven," he repeated. Then, more softly: "Ah! *Grahaven.*"

The man walked away, no doubt returning to whatever haunt would best serve him. At least he would not be within arm's reach.

Eamon felt tension slipping away from his shoulders and rolled them back; the movement creased his scarred back. Mathaiah came to his side, wiping his hands down his shirt to dry them.

"What did the beast want?"

Eamon shook his head. "I don't know."

He went to bed that night with a heavy heart. He left the shutters ajar so that moonlight could stream in with the autumn breeze. Birds nested in the trees that overhung the lodge and in the arched branches he heard an owl. Folding his arms behind his head he gazed at the ceiling and tried to think.

He had a mark on his hand and some other kind of mark that left no trace. How could he have the fiery mark of the Master and be called a "King's man"? And what would the wayfarers do with him? Plainly he could not stay in the lodge for the rest of his life.

What were the wayfarers doing? Why the Easters, why the stockpiled collection of arms and supplies? What had Hughan meant when he had said the name "First Knight" – and why had that name spoken so deeply to him? How was he supposed to respond to the friend whom he had so long thought dead, now that he appeared to be the long-lost King of the River Realm? Were they even still friends? Where had Hughan been for the last eight years? What would happen to Mathaiah, neither Gauntlet nor King's man? Why did Eamon keep seeing strange visions? Where was Aeryn, and had she known that Hughan was alive? How long would it be before Giles attempted to throttle him in his sleep? What would he do to the man, if he tried?

He didn't know the answer to any of this. It rattled him.

Heaving a deep sigh he closed his eyes.

He was expecting to see accustomed inky darkness scattered with coloured dots. What he felt was a sudden lurch, as though he had fallen a dozen feet, and a burning sensation in his hand.

He saw a long room; its enormous marble floor was like a reddened pool that flamed in the brazier-light. The walls were pale and bare, though heavy red curtains hung behind the dais at one end. On this dais stood a great throne, laden with plush cushions steeped in gems. A crowned eagle was etched in jewels onto the throne's back so as to imbue the sitter with a choking mane.

A man with grey eyes and flaming hair stood before the throne. An arched crown perched on his head, and he bore a dagger and a dark, heavy book.

A group of men dressed in black were there: four standing and one kneeling – Eamon could not make out his face. The young man's hands and brow began to burn as the man who ruled the throne moved towards him.

Suddenly Eamon was there, kneeling on the fiery floor. The flames on hands and brow were on his own and the grey eyes bored into his.

My mark redeems you and your quailing line, son of Eben.

Eamon recognized the voice; he had heard it in his mind. It had stolen his tongue on the strange plain.

Speak.

Eamon didn't answer. The blaze in front of him was overpowering. What could he tell? He knew nothing.

He began to cobble together ideas of resistance but in the same moment pain engulfed every nerve in his body. He did not know how to stop it. The fire grew stronger and suddenly the book in the man's hands flew open. The writing on its pages seared his eyes. The angular script seemed to twist before him, forming words in his mind that he could not understand – he only knew that they were terrible.

In agony Eamon gripped his hands over his ears. "I don't know anything!" he screamed. "Let me go!"

But you are mine, son of Eben! The voice laughed. *Mine by your blood.*

The grey-eyed man pressed his hand to Eamon's brow. He screamed; something was reaching deep into his mind, reaching and searching, and every thought that it touched burned...

"Sir!"

Hands were shaking him and light was near his eyes: soft, sweet candlelight.

Eamon tore his eyes open with a cry. Ma Mendel and Mathaiah peered down at him with anxious faces. He felt tears on his cheeks, and on his hand he saw the burn of the mark. He felt a flaming hand reaching for his mind.

"No!" he cried in terror.

Ma Mendel laid cool fingers over his. Pain and vision subsided. Eamon lay still.

Mathaiah touched his shoulder. "Are you all right, sir?"

"I… Was I asleep?"

"Yes," Mathaiah answered. The hesitance in Ma Mendel's eyes suggested that she might not have given the same reply.

"You should rest, Mr Goodman."

Mine by your blood. The unutterable words broke into his mind again. He looked fearfully up at her. "I can't sleep!"

Ma Mendel smiled. "Of course you can, Mr Goodman. You trot back off to bed, you young thing," she added, gesturing to Mathaiah. "I'll sit here with your lieutenant."

"You'll wake me if there's trouble?"

"I will."

Mathaiah looked reluctant, but acquiesced and went to bed. Eamon steadied his breathing. The wind outside seemed shrill and full of noise.

Ma Mendel pulled the shutters to and rearranged his blankets. "You lay yourself down, and don't worry about a thing."

Her tone relaxed him. Breathing deeply he closed his eyes again. The woman sat beside him; he felt her hand on his. It was cool to the touch, and with each passing moment the droning pain eased. Ma Mendel began to hum quietly: an old lullaby that Eamon's mother had often sung to him when he was young.

He caught one last glimpse of his unlikely guardian before he slept. The song wove through his thought, and Eamon saw that where Ma Mendel's hand held his, a shimmer of sweet, blue light held against the dark.

CHAPTER VIII

Eamon woke from a deep, dreamless sleep. Ma Mendel was gone. Trying to get rid of a terrible itch, he upset one of the scars on his back. The grip of the remembered lash hummed through his flesh and he saw Spencing's face with all its petty vengeance.

Spencing was dead. All that watched him were the crooked eyes of the shutters.

Not long later Ma Mendel returned, still singing. She looked as though she had been up for several hours already and no less cheerful for it.

"How are you feeling, Mr Goodman?"

"A little better." He noted something new in her darkly rimmed eyes. Perhaps wariness?

She opened the shutters, flooding the room with light. He felt like a boy again.

"The King wants to see you this morning." Light poured into his eyes; he raised his hand to shield them. "He's the best man for all your questions," Ma Mendel continued. "Now, come along. Much of the morning is gone already."

Eamon got up and tried to straighten the creases in his clothing. He had no other things to wear apart from those that he had borne on his arrival, and he had no wish to don them again. As Ma Mendel chivvied him along with all the brightness of a lark, his uniform stared at him from the corner. Turning his back on it, he followed his guardian as she bustled out of the door.

Outside, Eamon saw the villagers moving about their morning business. Groups of women stood together near the well, bearing jugs and pitchers of every size, their faces close in secretive laughter as gossip was passed from lip to lip. Old men sat on the porches of their houses, watching while their wives worked and complained about the lack of help. It was a typical picture of small village life. Eamon wondered how many of the menfolk were employed at the Hidden Hall.

As they passed he saw Mathaiah, accompanied by the band of children from the previous day. They dogged his steps. Eamon deduced that the cadet was the flavour of the moment.

Dodging away from his companions, Mathaiah jogged towards him.

"How are you feeling, sir?" The stick in his hand told Eamon that the morning's activity had already included fencing.

"Well."

To judge by Mathaiah's smile, his reply was satisfactory. The cadet looked from Eamon to Ma Mendel and then back again. "You're going to see him?"

Eamon nodded. Mathaiah held his gaze uncertainly.

"All will be well, Mr Grahaven," Eamon told him, offering the young man a smile. "Your division of followers seems to demand your attention," he added, gesturing to the impatient band of children.

"Yes, sir," Mathaiah answered.

The cadet returned to the gaggle and was soon embroiled in a whirlpool of small boys.

"Come along!" Ma Mendel called. "The King has many things to attend to this morning, and you are not the least of them!"

With a swift apology Eamon returned to her side. Much to his bemusement she went on to describe the medicinal properties of the local flora and fauna. The commentary lasted up to the breed of plant that lined the lintels of the ruined building and how, if ground into water in the right quantities, the leaves would produce a thick drink that could aid stiff bowels.

Despite his unsettled mood the Hidden Hall still amazed him.

Once again he was brought through the great panelled doors. He expected himself to be announced, as before, and to find himself facing the same collection of hostile men. But the chamber was empty, quiet. Birdsong hung in distant eaves.

Only Hughan sat at the table. He seemed deep in thought. Eamon glimpsed responsibility that he did not understand on the face of his childhood friend.

"Lieutenant Goodman, sire," said Ma Mendel.

Hughan looked up, rose, and came quickly to greet them. "Good morning!"

"Good morning," Eamon answered hesitantly.

"Shall I go, sire?" Ma Mendel asked.

"Thank you," Hughan nodded. "And thank you, Mrs Mendel, for your kindness to this man."

Ma Mendel beamed. "A pleasure, sire." Curtseying, she left.

As the doors closed Eamon trembled. He stood alone with the King.

He looked uncertainly at Hughan. "What of your counsellors?"

"Not many of them think you trustworthy," Hughan replied with a small smile, "but they know you're here."

"I didn't mean to imply that you would act without their knowledge," he said, embarrassed.

Hughan laughed. "I know you didn't. I wanted to meet with you myself, Eamon. You have a lot of questions and I want you to feel free to ask them. Here," he added, "come and sit with me."

Hughan gestured to the table. Simply fashioned, it glistened in the light.

At Hughan's invitation Eamon sank into one of the high-backed chairs. As the King sat beside him he grew increasingly restless.

A tall jug stood before them. Hughan poured some of its liquid into a cup and then offered it to him – a warm mix of herbs and honey. They might almost have been sitting back at the Star.

As Eamon's fingers closed about the cup the mark on his hand seared all his nerves like lightning. With a startled cry he dropped the mug, his hand shaking before him.

"Eamon?"

"It's… it's nothing…" He tried to drive his hand under the table, to where it could not be seen, but he could not stop it trembling.

The hideous voice crept into his mind, clearer than ever:

You have no need of him to pour witless sympathies about your feet. He cannot help you, and would not if he could. Leave!

Eamon rose to his feet.

Hughan laid his hand on Eamon's arm. "You needn't listen to him, Eamon." His eyes met and held Eamon's own. "Do you want to sit?"

"Yes," Eamon whispered.

"Then put the voice behind you, and be at peace."

At the authority of the King's voice a growl thundered through Eamon's skull. The voice within suddenly relinquished its hold and died away.

Eamon gazed at his friend and sank back down in amazement.

"H-how…" he stammered, blinking away tears. "How did you know?"

"I know what the mark is, and what it does," Hughan answered gravely. Eamon let out a deep breath.

"Ma Mendel came to see me this morning," Hughan said gently. "She told me that you were having nightmares. Can you tell me about them?"

Words twisted in Eamon's throat. "I…" Shaking, he tried again. "Hughan, he'll…"

The King had never once faltered in holding his gaze. "He has no hold over you here, Eamon," Hughan told him firmly. "Speak, and be comforted."

Eamon gasped. On what authority could Hughan possibly think that the voice had no hold? Had it not already prompted him to attempt murder? Did it not fill him with strength and malice that he could not control? How could Hughan put them both at risk by asking him to defy it?

Chapter VIII

The shake in his hand grew as he wrestled with himself; he folded his arms over his breast, trying to quell it. At last he looked at Hughan. The King had not moved and watched him kindly, as though they had at their disposal all the time ever fashioned. His hand was still on Eamon's arm – an encouraging touch that kept the trembling from reaching the rest of Eamon's body.

Eamon looked into Hughan's eyes and seemed to see the flicker of cool light in them. The throned had granted power to Eamon through the mark. But a gift, measured in grace and authority and bestowed by some power far beyond the throned, lay on Hughan. As Eamon watched his friend's eyes he knew that the King bore the greater, truer power.

The voice stabbed at him one last time:

He will not believe you and cannot aid you. Whisper but a word to the Serpent, son of Eben, and you will see what you reap for your insolence!

"Eamon."

"So much has happened to me, Hughan... I can't..."

"You can speak of it."

Eamon let Hughan's gaze enfold him.

Drawing a deep breath, he concentrated on the strange things that had befallen him since he had left Edesfield. Then he began to pour out his story, growing steadily in confidence as Hughan listened. While Eamon spoke to the King the terrible voice remained absent.

When at last he had finished Hughan nodded thoughtfully.

"You must understand, Eamon, that not every new recruit to the Gauntlet is affected by the throned's mark as savagely as you have been."

"Not everyone hears... hears... Is it him I hear?" Eamon asked.

"It is his voice," Hughan answered.

Eamon fell silent. Hughan looked at him firmly.

"I cannot tell you that I fully understand it; I do not. All I can tell you is that you must not fear it. And do not believe it, for this much

I do know: it will speak to you in perversions and half-truths. He is powerful, Eamon. He means to bait you with his voice, crushing your thoughts and aggrandizing your fear. By having you fear him and his power he would have you act according to his purpose. He wants to draw everything from you, and everything that you are, into his hands."

Eamon stared. "Why?" he demanded. "What can I possibly matter to him? I'm a bookbinder's son!"

"The throned enviously cleaves to all those whom he has claimed," Hughan answered. "In that, you are no different to any other man serving him. But you are worth more to him than many others."

Eamon's stare became a horrified gape. His flesh began to crawl with a fear that drove all warmth from him. "I don't understand."

"You have said that when he speaks to you he calls you 'Eben's son' – but Eben was not your father's name."

"No," Eamon whispered. His father's name had been Elior.

"The throned knows something about you that you don't know yourself," Hughan continued quietly. "That is why he is trying to take such a firm hold on you. It is why his voice has tormented your dreams, as well as your waking."

Eamon's breath quickened. Had Ma Mendel seen his dreams while he slept? "What do you know?"

Hughan paused. His gaze gauged Eamon's own.

"The woman whom you have seen in your visions," he began, "is Elaina, sister of Ede and queen after him. From her I descend. This much you know." Eamon nodded. "When you saw her, lying wounded and near death in a place of battle, you saw a man with her. You saw him saving her with light, much as you then saved Mathaiah Grahaven. The man whom you saw was Eben."

"Son of Eben," Eamon murmured dumbly; the name rang in his ears. "Who was Eben?"

"Eben Goodman was Ede's First Knight."

"Goodman?"

"He was the King's friend and confidant, riding to war at Ede's side when there was war and, when war's rumour was distant, he was the King's closest counsellor, first protector, and upholder of the River Realm in the King's name." Hughan watched him steadily. "The house of Goodman had long performed that office for the house of Brenuin, and so did Eben. But he also betrayed the King."

The blood pounding in Eamon's veins turned leaden. "Betrayed?" he stammered. "Why?"

"What drew him to treachery is beyond my knowledge," Hughan answered, "but he was led astray by the throned. It was at the throned's command that Eben weakened Ede in the days leading to the battle of Edesfield. At the battle itself it was Eben who felled the King so that the throned might strike him."

There was a long silence. Visions of the battle and its treacherous stroke flitted at the edge of Eamon's mind. He looked miserably down at his mug, trying to focus on the steam curling up from it.

The blood in his veins was the blood of a traitor.

"Eben was among the first to receive the mark of the throned," Hughan told him, "and that same day was made the throned's Right Hand, in recognition of his service to the Eagle."

Eamon looked at Hughan aghast. "How can you sit here with me?" he cried.

"A child does not bear the guilt of his father's deeds, Eamon," Hughan told him gently. "Even if you share Eben's blood you did not deal the blow."

Eamon nodded weakly. Hughan spoke again. "After Ede was killed, the throned led his army to Allera, his Right Hand at his side. Allera was Ede's capital city and was besieged but it gave staunch resistance, led by the Duke of the West Bank. The duke was Ede's brother-in-law, married to Elaina. It was December and the city was prepared for a long winter, so it held for a long time – much to the throned's anger.

"The duke tried to break the throned's chokehold around the city. Eben was sent against him and the Right Hand seriously injured the duke, who was taken back to the city. The duke was the city's hope and so in its hour of need his wife, Elaina, donned his armour and rode to battle in his place.

"Soon after, the throned breached the city walls and sacked Allera. Her husband lay dying and Elaina had no wish to flee, but men still loyal to her house took her from the city by force. Elaina carried the only child of royal blood.

"When the throned discovered her escape he dispatched Eben and his Hands to find her and kill her. She was wounded in that meeting; but as she lay dying Eben healed her."

Eamon had been listening with a burdened heart and looked up in astonishment.

"*Eben* healed her?"

"Eben Goodman remembered his promises and saved the King's sister and her house. Her healing at his hands was the first time the 'blue light', as you have called it, was seen. After Eben healed Elaina many of the King's followers began to exhibit this same light. Some called it 'the King's grace', for it came to the King's men for their protection and encouragement in their time of need. Exactly what it is we do not know, but it has enabled us to stand against the throned since those days.

"The King's men went into hiding, going about the River Realm by hidden ways – so becoming 'wayfarers'. Eben Goodman restored his broken allegiance but returned to the city in the guise of Right Hand. He was there as the throned tore down Allera and was an overseer as Dunthruik was built in its place, stones over gardens. The city's ancient quarters were awarded to the throned's closest Hands and one of them, a seer, prophesied that Elaina's line would overthrow the throned. Since that day, the throned has sought to extinguish it."

There was a long silence.

"What happened to Eben?" Eamon asked with a dry throat.

"I do not know why he returned to the city, nor what task he meant to perform for the King's house in Dunthruik," Hughan answered. "It is told that his treachery to the throned was discovered and that he was killed by the Hands."

"And now I carry the throned's mark. Why did you permit them to bring me here, Hughan?" Eamon cried at last, terror in his heart. "I will become his tool against you! I have a traitor's blood and the mark of your enemy."

"You do," Hughan agreed, "but, like Eben, you also bear the King's grace." Eamon's objections fell silent before Hughan's quiet assertion. "The throned desires to make you his, Eamon, fully and completely; that is why his voice insists that you already are."

Eamon swallowed, sensing that there was more to come, and yet he did not feel that he could take another blow; his blood sang a song of treachery and discord that he could not quieten.

"There is more, isn't there?"

Hughan looked at him gently. "The tongue that told that the throned would be overthrown by Elaina's seed also declared that a son of Eben would go before Elaina's heir. He would be a First Knight, just as the fathers of his house were of old."

The words took a long time to sink in.

"You think that's *me*?" Eamon whispered incredulously.

"Yes."

Eamon gaped.

"Before you knew that you were descended from Eben, you answered to it," Hughan told him gently.

Eamon fell silent, remembering how the name had felt in him when it had been spoken. *First Knight*.

Shaking, he looked at Hughan again. "There must be hundreds of Goodmans on the River," he whispered. "How can you be so sure that I'm the one?"

Hughan looked at him once more, the depth of his eyes more than Eamon could fathom.

"Eamon, men that bear the throned's mark do not also carry the King's grace. You are a Goodman whom the throned has taken a special interest in – and you bear both mark and grace. That is how I know."

"Even if that's true, what difference does it make?"

"Much."

"How?"

"The house of Goodman is one of courage and compassion. The River Realm is in need of its First Knight now perhaps more than it has ever been."

Another long silence fell between them.

"I'm sorry," Hughan said kindly. "This is a lot to take in at once."

"Did you always know?" Eamon asked suddenly. To Hughan's questioning look he added: "Did you always know that you were Elaina's heir?"

"No," Hughan answered. "That's why I was taken from Edesfield; to be told, taught, and prepared."

Eamon watched him for a long moment. "What will you do with me now?"

"What do you feel about the wayfarers?"

Eamon felt that much rested on his answer.

"Is Giles one of you?"

Hughan smiled sadly, as though he had anticipated the question. "Giles is trustworthy and hates the throned. He comes from one of the cities in Galithia. His family was killed in the border wars some years ago. I am sorry," he added gravely, "for what he did when he took the holk. Though he had my authority to take all necessary steps to rescue Aeryn, and it was likely that men would be lost, he should not have taken the lives of prisoners who had tokened their surrender."

"You took a lot of risks to rescue her."

"She was being taken to Dunthruik for things that she knows," Hughan replied, "about this place and about me. I wrote, asking her and Telo to come here." Guilt passed over his face. "It was foolish of me. I wanted them both to be safe."

Eamon suddenly stared. "You mean… all this time, Aeryn knew that you were alive?"

Hughan matched his gaze. "She knew."

Betrayal sliced through him like a barb. "Hughan, why didn't you…?" Eamon shook his head in disbelief.

"I wanted to," Hughan answered. "But when I could and did send word to Aeryn, I learnt that you had already joined the Gauntlet. You were a cadet. I could not seek you then and was compelled to ask her not to speak of me to you. She did as I asked, despite her own misgivings, and I chose to trust that there would be a time when I could speak to you myself."

"I understand." Years had passed between Hughan's disappearance and the day Eamon had become a Gauntlet cadet; Hughan would have had no way of telling whether his childhood friend could still have been trusted.

"It was no reflection of my heart for you," Hughan told him. "It was a difficult choice to make, Eamon, one that rendered you less faith than you deserved. Of all the choices that I had to make at that time," he added quietly, "none weighed upon me as much as that. It wronged you."

"No. You were right not to risk sending word to me." He paused, his mind awhirl. In the silence that followed he fiddled with his cooling mug. Eventually he looked once more at Hughan.

"If what you say is true," he began, "and King Ede was killed by treachery, then the throned is not the lawful master of the River. In that regard…" He felt a pulse of heat near his palm and pressed it closed. "But I have sworn to serve the throned, Hughan," he whispered, "with body, blade, and blood." He swallowed, hating the words that came from his mouth. "My oath is binding."

"You can be released."

Eamon gaped. A wellspring of hope opened in the rocky places of his heart.

"I know that what I have told you is difficult to take in all at once, and I know the hold of the oath that you have sworn. But I would ask you to think awhile on all these things and then return to me. If, after you have considered them, you would be willing, there is a service I would ask you to render me."

"You mean… become a wayfarer?" Eamon whispered. That was what rendering service to the King would entail, after all. Part of him recoiled from it, and part of him ached to take his stand with this man whom he had known, trusted, and loved in his youth. "Hughan, I…"

"It honours me enough that you consider it. I ask no more."

He held Eamon's gaze, and Eamon saw that his friend, though young and learning still what he had to do, bore an aura of greatness.

At that moment the doors to the chamber opened and the counsellors began to enter, walking and striding according to their stature. Eamon might have started guiltily to his feet but he was caught and stilled by the King's smile.

Giles was among the first of the entering group. His face broke into an ungainly scowl. "Sire!" he cried. "I protest at you closeting yourself with this verminous –"

"Peace, Giles," Hughan answered, raising his hand.

"I will go, sir," Eamon said quietly, "and I will return to you on this matter."

Hughan nodded to him. "Thank you."

Rising, Eamon bowed awkwardly to his friend and then hurried from the chamber. The cold glares of the counsellors rested on his back.

He was escorted from the Hidden Hall by one of its guards, and went back into the village and the sunlight. Nobody seemed to watch him as he passed, his hands driven deep into the folds of his shirt. He walked in silence and his heart pounded as he thought on all that Hughan had said.

Was Hughan truly to dethrone the Master and could it be that he, Eamon Goodman, was to be his help? He shook his head. Surely it could not be true. It was not for him to make a stand over such a thing. Hughan, he reasoned, had chosen the wrong man. Eamon's place was in Dunthruik, the city to which he had been lawfully commissioned. He could not betray his oath to the Master. Who did these wayfarers think they were? They were dogs in the service of a youth scarcely old enough to bear a beard, let alone a sword. Hughan was barely a year older than Eamon himself.

His duty was clear: he had to make the hall known to the Master. It was to be cleared out, swept clean. The wayfarers would be crushed at a single stroke; Hughan had no heir and was the last of the line. There would be no King. Only then would Eamon Goodman redeem the treachery of his blood.

Better still, why not take a double oath and double cross this witless King? There was no release from the Master's mark or from his service. Everything that the Serpent had told him was a lie. His reward in Dunthruik would be great indeed if he brought the Serpent before the Master. There would be public jubilation and a grand, humiliating execution befitting one that dared to wear dethroned colours. There was no King over the River Realm. History had written that story from the books long ago.

Eamon brought himself up sharply. His heart beat like a drum of war and his whole flesh seemed alive with fire. He felt stronger, thinking of such things. It would be so very easy to reach out and snap this self-styled King like a willow wand. He could redeem Eben's betrayal and barter himself favour with the Master. He should redeem it. He would summon the Hands. They would come. The Master would laud and honour him.

He saw with other sight. Before him once more was the gaudy throne – no, not gaudy, for it was a great and glorious symbol of the Eagle's power. A man sat there. As the darkling face smiled at him he found that he knelt before it. His lips were moving but he could not hear the words he spoke; as his voice tumbled out of him the smile of the grey-eyed broadened.

Suddenly a crushing pain went through his jaw, forcing him to open his eyes. He was kneeling in the mud by the well. He saw Aeryn, her hand drawn back. She had struck him. She stared at him with a white face. "What are you doing?" she hissed.

Eamon saw that every pair of eyes in sight was fixed on him. How they hated him. He surged to his feet like an angry tide. As he towered over her his hand darted out and grabbed her chin.

"How dare you!" he roared. She squirmed in his grip as it tightened. "Whoring snake!"

"Eamon!" Aeryn gasped. "Fight this, or I will fight you!"

Eamon could see her face and feel the terrible strength in his hand. Hughan had said he would be safe here, he had *promised* safety.

Hughan was the Serpent: he had lied.

"Eamon." Aeryn pronounced his name as a warning. There were tears in her eyes. "Please stop." Suddenly she grabbed his arm; something about it loosed his voice.

"Aeryn, forgive me!" He struggled to utter any words at all and with each syllable he spoke he felt as though a grip just as strong as his own sought to crush him. A crowd of people surrounded them but none of them moved to do a thing. Time was horribly slow. He was aware of men running from the Hidden Hall towards him and of Mathaiah appearing at the edge of the crowd, his face aghast.

Eamon looked back to Aeryn. There were twisting, cracking arches of fire along his arm. He could not quench it. But though the fire licked angrily about their flesh it could not pass the soft flicker of blue light about her.

"Fight it, Eamon!" Aeryn told him, her voice clumsy from the grip on her jaw. Eamon closed his eyes. Inside his lids he saw a vision of himself in the dark robes of the Hands, kneeling before the throne. Still the pale face that reigned there watched him, applauding, encouraging, enticing his service. Eamon's knees were rooted to the ground in submission and while he knelt, the joins in the marbled floor about him pulsed with fire. The stones cracked like water on the verge of boiling, and the flames reached flickering hands towards him. The smile engulfed him:

You do well, son of Eben: son of mine.

Resistance kindled in his heart. Sickened, Eamon lifted himself to his feet before the throne. The flames hissed and clawed at him as he rose, meaning to drag him swiftly down to their mandrake embraces. But still he rose. He would not serve this man, creature more than master; he would serve the King.

He felt weak but his will grew stronger; he stretched out his hand and saw in it a bolt-bright sword – silver, stern, and true. The flames scattered from it.

Suddenly he felt his whole body being hurled downward. With a gasp he opened his eyes.

He had been thrown to the ground. Strong hands seized his head; the motion of them was to break his neck. Somewhere in the shouting he heard Mathaiah, calling for mercy.

But the fingers on him never administered the fatal twist.

"Giles." Hughan had no need to shout.

Eamon waited for the hands to let him go, but they didn't. Blinking, he saw that Aeryn also lay in the mud near him, likely knocked when Giles had battered him down. She shook with fear, and tears streamed down her face.

"This man is a threat to us all!" Giles yelled. Eamon felt the man's anger pulsing through the hot hands round his neck. He struggled to breathe unobtrusively, lest the motion remind Giles of the thread that he could snap at a moment. "He cannot stay and he cannot go. We all know it. Give me but a word, sire, and the problem is solved."

There was a tense silence; every eye turned to the King. Hughan's face remained calm, unmoved by the man's resolve.

"Let him go, Giles."

Giles gawked. "Let him *go*? Did you not see what he was doing to Aeryn?"

"I trust him," Hughan answered firmly. "Let him go."

With a cry of disgust, Giles hurled Eamon down and stood. He spat at him. Spittle sprayed all over Eamon's face as he lay, gasping, in the mud. Mathaiah rushed forward at once.

"Are you all right, sir?"

Giles glared at them both, then turned on the cadet. "You're no better than the Grahaven my men felled at the borders," he snarled icily. "A bastard servant to a treacherous tyrant." His glare grew grimmer. "Serving this man," he hissed, hurling a condemning finger at Eamon, "or his oath, will buy you death, boy, as it did for the other, and you will have nothing but blood for your wretched accolade."

Colour drained from Mathaiah's face. Eamon sensed vengeance raising the boy's hackles and saw fledgling murder in reddening eyes.

"Mr Grahaven," he croaked. Then, more loudly: "Mathaiah!"

The boy turned, blinking back furious tears. His hands shook. "Sir?"

"Help me up."

He leaned heavily on the cadet as he rose, not so much because he needed support but because he ensured a power of restraint. He looked across at Hughan.

"I thank you for your mercy, sir," he said formally. "I will return to confinement. I ask that you keep me under constant guard. I will not walk abroad again unless summoned."

"Very well, Eamon," Hughan nodded.

Together, lieutenant and cadet hobbled across the square. Eamon heard Mathaiah choking back angry tears.

The lodge was calm and quiet. Eamon welcomed its seclusion after the dreadful exposure at the well.

They sat in silence while the noise outside grew into heated debate and then died away. Eamon watched Mathaiah nervously twist his fingers together, fidget restlessly, twirl threads of the rug round in his hands, and eventually get up and begin pacing the room. Both of them had been shaken that morning.

Eamon closed the shutters to keep them safe from angry eyes.

"Mr Grahaven?"

The cadet continued pacing. When he at last sat down he shook uncontrollably. "Sir."

"I'm sorry about your brother."

"Thank you, sir." The cadet's answer was curt.

Silence fell. As Mathaiah sat, his eyes clenched and his angry face faltered. He laid his head in his hands and wept, calling on the name of his dead brother until the name became a sob. Eamon knew of no way to console him.

Evening drew on and twilight crept between the shades.

Mathaiah slept in the chair, worn out with grief. Eamon had covered him with the blankets from the bed. He knew that he had much to consider but could not hold his thought steady for any length of time. The feel of the silver-blue sword that he had held returned unbidden to his fingers – what would he have done with it? He wondered why, after everything that he had shown himself capable of, Hughan still insisted on trusting him.

The night was deep when he heard footsteps by the door. He turned his head and held himself still.

Aeryn entered. Eamon laid a finger to his lips and gestured to Mathaiah. Nodding, Aeryn came to sit gently on the end of the bed.

"Are you all right?" She wore a penitent look.

Eamon shrugged. "I hardly know what being all right means."

"Is… is he all right?" Her gaze was on Mathaiah. The cadet stirred in his sleep.

"No. But I hope that he is young enough that he will overcome it."

He looked at Aeryn, who was reluctant to match his gaze. Calling on all his courage – he might not have the chance to speak to her again in his right mind – he said: "Aeryn, I'm sorry about what I did, I didn't mean to –"

"No, I'm sorry," she interrupted. "I spoke to Hughan. He told me about… about what's been happening to you." She looked at him. "Eamon, I have hated you ever since we left Edesfield, even though you tried to help me. A lot may happen in the days that are coming. Things are changing. I wanted you to know that I'm sorry."

"I'm sorry, too." Eamon looked at her guiltily. "Aeryn, I didn't want to breach you in the prison, or attack you today. I… I wanted to help your father."

Aeryn reached across and took his hand. "You were in a difficult position," she said. "I do not hold you accountable for his death. To be honest," she added with a small smile, "I think, when you breached me, you were hurt more than I was."

Eamon pressed at the back of his head where he had struck the wall. It was still bruised. "You may be right," he said.

The air between them grew more relaxed. Eamon sighed.

"Giles is right, you know," he told her. "Whatever Hughan says I am dangerous – to him above all. I shouldn't be here."

"Killing you will not answer anything," Aeryn replied, "though it seems to be Giles's answer to everything. I'm sorry," she added, "about what happened on the *Lark*."

Eamon nodded silently.

"How…" Aeryn faltered. "How is your back?" She looked haunted. Eamon wondered how much of the flogging she had heard from her confinement.

"Still painful."

"You did a good thing. It was worthy of the Eamon that I know."

There was a long pause. Eamon let her words sink in. He was unsure what to say and yet profoundly grateful to have her approval and encouragement.

"It was also worthy of a King's man," she added quietly.

"A King's man?" he whispered. He blinked hard. Her words were as treasure to him, a treasure he could not dare to value. "Aeryn, I can't… I'm not…"

"Eamon," Aeryn began, "the throned wouldn't be doing what he is doing unless he feared what you could become. Hughan is right about you."

"What does Hughan say?" he asked suspiciously.

"That you are the First Knight."

First Knight. Again the name called him, piercing his soul deeper than any mark he had known. Could it be true?

"What is it?" Aeryn asked, searching his face.

"I think… I think I could have regained myself today, if Giles

162

hadn't attacked me." He looked at her, waiting for her to concur with him and hoping that she would. "Not that I blame him for doing it," he added. "He was trying to save you."

Aeryn said nothing for a long time. "Have you thought about what Hughan asked?"

Eamon bristled. "How do you know about that?" Was he jealous that tales of his private conversation with Hughan had got abroad so quickly? He reminded himself that he was a prisoner, not a confidant – and not a First Knight.

"He spoke with his generals."

"You're not one of them," Eamon pointed out.

"He told me," Aeryn answered, and she suddenly blushed. "Eamon, I… I couldn't tell you before. I wanted to –"

"Hughan told me."

"I mean, I couldn't tell you before that…" Aeryn, normally boldly spoken, faltered again. Her face reddened. "I couldn't tell you that he was alive, and I couldn't tell you that I am betrothed to him."

For a moment Eamon stared at her in disbelief.

Aeryn looked awkwardly away. He pressed her hand.

"That's wonderful, Aeryn," he said, and he meant it.

"You're not angry?"

"No," Eamon answered with a small laugh. "It does explain a few things, though."

"So you've thought about what he said?"

"I've thought about it." He sighed heavily. "I wish I could, Aeryn, but… how can I serve him? How could I dare? Look at what happened to me today – what happens to me on a daily basis! I can't open Hughan to that kind of risk. And so Giles is right."

"But you would serve him, if you could?"

Eamon gazed through the shutters at the quiet night. He would rather give an oath to Hughan than to a thousand thrones. But was that because Hughan was the King? He didn't know. To love and serve Hughan for friendship's sake could not be as binding as the fealty he had sworn to the throned. He had to believe, truly believe, that Hughan was the King and that the throned was a usurper, or his service would be vain and empty.

In his mind he saw again the shadows and flames about the throne and the grey-eyed man who sat upon it. How could such a man be good? Would he allow the throned to call him "son"? Would a Goodman bow again before that dreadful Master? Surely he had to undo the treachery of his bloodline...

He felt a sudden, strange oppression in the air. Trying to suspend all his senses, he focused his mind on the present. Noticing the change in him, Aeryn leaned forward.

"What is it?" she asked. Her voice told him that she feared he was again being influenced, but he was in his right mind.

He could feel a horrific presence, enveloping him and driving into his skin like relentless needles.

"Something's coming," he said urgently. Words poured out of his mouth as he leapt to his feet. "We have to go to the Hidden Hall."

"Eamon —"

"We have to go now."

He bolted to the door. Aeryn gave a cry that woke Mathaiah. Both shouted after him as he rushed outside. Lights twinkled in the windows of the little houses. Breaking parole and promise, he raced into the heart of the village.

"To the hall!" he yelled, filling his lungs with so much air that he felt they might burst. "To the hall!"

He thought he saw faces moving behind the windows, but none answered him. No doors opened. He cupped his hands to his mouth.

"Something is coming! Get to the hall!" he roared.

Not a soul stirred.

Eamon stared at the shuttered windows and closed doors in disbelief. He pelted to the nearest door and hammered wildly on it.

"Open, open!" he yelled.

The door was opened by a woman; as soon as she saw him she gasped and tried to close it again, but he jammed his foot over the threshold.

"Please, wait."

"Get out of my house!" The woman tried to force the door closed.

"Please," Eamon said, "listen –"

The door closed. Undeterred, Eamon raced to the next house. Its door was already open: a man stood in it.

"Please listen!" Eamon said.

"Set a foot in my house and I will kill you," the man growled. He was old, and probably didn't have the strength to carry through his threat, but Eamon fell back from him.

"Please," Eamon began, trying to keep calm as the pressure in the air mounted. "We all need to get to the Hidden Hall. We need to go now."

"Why?"

But Eamon didn't answer. He turned and yelled at the top of his voice: "Everyone to the Hidden Hall! Your lives depend on it!"

"Eamon!" Aeryn grabbed his arm and pulled him towards her. "Stop," she continued in a low voice. Perhaps she thought he was mad. Perhaps he was.

He tore his arm from her. "Something is coming that means to kill us all," he answered. Could they not feel it?

"Nobody knows we're here," Aeryn began.

"The Hidden Hall!" he yelled. "To the hall, please!" Dozens of faces glared. "Will none of you believe me?" he cried, looking desperately from one face to another.

"What mischief are you up to, Goodman?" asked an all-too-familiar voice.

Eamon turned to see Giles. The big man flexed his fingers. Eamon reflected afterwards that it was the gentlest appearance that the man had yet made before him.

"Please believe me." He hated to beg it of Giles. "These people are in danger. We need to get to the Hidden Hall, and we need to go now." Giles stared at him hard, and Eamon tried hard to match it. He felt that every second they lost would have deadly consequences. "Please!" he cried. "Tell them to go!"

After what seemed an eternity, Giles nodded gruffly.

"All right," he said, though his voice had an unpleasant edge to it. "To the hall!" he bellowed; the whole depth of his chest was behind it. "The hall!"

The people moved. As Giles roared, again and again, doors opened, lights were doused, and bemused but obedient faces emerged into the night air. There was no mistaking Giles's tone and they all did as he commanded. Eamon watched the streams of people moving and looked anxiously up at the dark eaves of the woods. They didn't have much time.

A rough hand seized his arm. "If these people come to harm through your word, Goodman, I will slaughter you."

"I will let you."

Giles stared, completely thrown, then continued gathering those left behind. The very last were moving towards the Hidden Hall and being taken to safety through its walls.

"That's the last." Eamon was surprised to find that Aeryn was still at his side, and that Mathaiah was with her.

"Hadn't we better go, sir?" Mathaiah asked. Despite Giles's proximity the cadet stayed completely focused on the matter in hand; Eamon admired that.

"Yes," he agreed.

They ran towards the ruined building. As they neared the hallway Eamon saw two men standing by the walls. They were covering the tracks that marked the passage of so many people and were evidently skilled; the ground where they had already worked lay as though it had suffered no tread for weeks.

Eamon crossed the threshold and stumbled inside; two hundred people greeted him. Women and children cowered together in silence while their menfolk gathered weapons that might be used in their defence. Hughan walked among them, laying his hands on their arched shoulders and offering words of comfort, asking for calm and silence. Eamon saw Giles approach the King and speak a few words to him, after which Hughan came to the threshold. As he arrived the two track-clearing doormen also withdrew inside.

"Giles thinks that you may know what is happening, Eamon," Hughan said quietly.

Eamon looked through the tumbled archway to the muddy, rubble-strewn grass, and laid his hand on the stones. Rain had begun falling outside and he could hear it pattering into the earth and off taut forest leaves. Under the otherworldly quiet of the rain Eamon still felt something terrible pricking at every sense, something that he could not name. It was just beyond the silence.

"Something has come for you, Hughan," he said, looking back to the King. "At least, it comes seeking you."

"Are you sure it does not also come seeking you?" Hughan asked gently.

Eamon stared at him.

"Then it'll have to come through me, sir!" Mathaiah growled, hand dropping to draw the sword he did not have. Eamon was surprised by the show of loyalty.

"Where is it, then?" Giles demanded. He had a real sword to lay his hand to and watched with growing suspicion.

"There," Eamon answered suddenly, and pointed.

On the ridge beyond the tree line a faint glow could be seen, as of torches. Whinnying horses could be heard under the soft patter of the rain. The sight that followed stilled their hearts.

Suddenly shadows slipped among the trees and the snarl of wolf-like dogs echoed down the dells. Tall figures followed on horseback.

"Who are they?" Aeryn shrank against Hughan's side.

"Hands," Giles growled.

The silence grew grim. Eamon looked out at the shadows again. The men in the darkness moved towards the abandoned village, turning their eyes this way and that. More than once Eamon felt their gazes match his; his heart leapt into his throat.

"Can they see us?" Mathaiah breathed.

"This place was hidden by a grace stronger than their power," Hughan answered. Though his face showed pale in the moonlight it was not the pallor of fear. "They can neither see us nor hear us, and they would not even if every man here held a torch and sang to the fullness of his heart." Hughan glanced back at his people, huddled and trembling in the hall.

"Giles," he said, "move the women and children into the council chamber. They will feel safer there. Augment the door guards."

Giles obeyed him. After laying a last, comforting touch to Aeryn's shoulder, Hughan went to his people, speaking soft words to them and leading some of them by the hand to the great chamber doors. Giles, soon joined in his endeavour by other counsellors and generals, sent men to bolster the guards at each of the hall's doorways. The sound of moving feet joined that of the rain.

As they emerged from the trees the figures outside grew more distinct. A group of five riders, four bearing torches and one without, assembled in the village square, their horses casting looming shadows. Four dogs prowled about the horses' feet, barking eagerly. Their masters bore bows. Eamon anxiously watched the riders surveying what they had found.

One gestured to the village and, at the seeming command, his companions dismounted to begin exploring it. Torches held high, they went to the nearest house and smashed the door down. The torchless rider – who bore a curved blade – raised a dark-clad hand high and a great orb of red light formed above it. With a gesture the Hand sent the light up, where it spread until the whole settlement was lit with a ghastly red glow. The houses spread twisting shadows across the earth.

Whatever or whomever they sought, the Hands did not mean to be disappointed.

Suddenly, Aeryn drew a sharp breath. "Look!" She seized Eamon's arm in terror. "Look there!"

Eamon's stomach filled with lead as he saw what she saw. Crouched, shaking with fear and cold in the undergrowth, was a woman. The red light made her clear to those in the hall though not to the riders. Her hands were drawn over her head as she forced herself low to the ground.

"Ma Mendel," Aeryn breathed.

The more he looked at her the more Eamon could see his guardian's shape in the shadowed form. He bit his lip. She was defenceless. She might escape the riders – she was certainly well hidden, or at least had been until the orb went up – but if the hounds caught her scent…

"Sir?"

Mathaiah's voice pierced his thought. The cadet was awaiting his orders.

"We can't go out there…" Eamon muttered to himself.

"… but we can't leave her," Mathaiah concluded.

"We can't," Eamon agreed.

Aeryn glanced at him fearfully. "You have to wait until Hughan… you can't –"

Outside the hounds bayed and rushed into a house behind the searchers. In that moment, the torchless Hand turned a darkened face towards the ruins.

Eamon glanced behind; neither Hughan nor any of his generals were anywhere to be seen.

"There's no time to wait," he told her. "Have you a dagger?"

"Yes –"

Eamon snatched it from her belt and tucked it into his boot.

"Orders, sir?" Mathaiah asked.

"Join the door guards here, Mr Grahaven," Eamon replied. "Nobody passes the threshold, going in or out, unless the King commands otherwise, or I return."

"Sir." Mathaiah's assent was brusque and wholehearted. The cadet grabbed a sword from one of the collections of arms nearby and took his post by the door. The guards already there could only stare at the young man who joined them. None of them made a move to stop Eamon as he looked once more into the grim night.

"Eamon," Aeryn tried again, "they're Hands. What if they try to –?"

"Pray that they don't." He took her hand from his arm, held it for a moment, then ducked out of the door.

CHAPTER IX

The weight of the dagger was the only comfort he bore out of the hall. His senses were surreally heightened – the chill air biting him sharply, the crumple of grass beneath his feet as loud in his ears as clashing steel. The orb of red light was molten on his living flesh.

Across the village the search party still moved from house to house. The torchless rider followed at some distance. He could not see the Hands' faces: cavernous hoods obscured them. Something about the torchless Hand utterly disquieted him.

He slid through the stony hedges towards the trees. If he could make it there he might be able to work his way to Ma Mendel unseen, though it would be tortuous. Of course he could not be concealed completely, and since his foes were Hands that would not be nearly good enough.

As he went, the hedges and hillocks grew few and far between. He dropped down behind one to assess his situation. There was only one way to go: he would have to risk a flight across the open.

He looked left and right. Behind him lay the ruins, seeming at once ghastly and noble beneath the glare of the red light. Eamon saw the hall's great window but through it not lights or people – only scattered stones, wild grasses, and trunks. He would not have suspected the collapsed structure as the hiding place of snakes, but thought it only a matter of time before the Hands tested it.

If the Hands moved towards the hall, the situation was going to be more urgent than Ma Mendel's life. The Hidden Hall might be invisible but its doors were not impassable. The thought of Mathaiah, or any of Hughan's guards, having to hold against even one Hand chilled him. But what could he do now?

He glanced out at the Hands. They moved near the well, their backs turned to him. The wolfish dogs followed close by the heels of the searchers. Teeth, swords, and bows glistened in the grim light.

He drew himself into a crouching position. It was not that far between his hiding place and the treeline and yet it seemed a hundred miles. His heart was pounding but his blood seemed frozen in his veins.

Suddenly he tensed the whole strength of his limbs together, leapt up and sprinted wildly across the gap. The wind roared in his ears but the distance between him and the trees seemed to grow larger rather than smaller. The orb cast his shadow in front of him, mocking his running.

Then there was bark at his fingertips and roots at his feet. He threw himself behind the tree and dropped beside its earth-bound limbs. He held himself against the cold wood and listened to his lungs plunging for breath. Eyes clenched, waiting for dogs or torches to discover him, his thoughts turned to the man he had hunted in Edesfield just nine days ago…

For what felt his whole lifetime, he waited.

"Not here," called a voice.

He dared to breathe. Had he passed unseen?

He edged his head around the trunk and looked out again. Keeping his front pressed to the tree he slid about it and looked out on his other side. Not fifty paces away from where he hid, Ma Mendel lay in the bushes. Her hands were over her head and she lay perfectly still, barely breathing.

Eamon stared at her intently, willing her to look up and see him. He needed her to know that he was there before he went to her; a scream would be the end of them both.

Still he stared and still she did not move.

Eamon anxiously bit his lip and decided to risk a whisper. Almost silently he spoke her name between the angled trees. Still she stayed.

He crept back into the denser shelter of the trees and passed slowly, circuitously, from trunk to trunk, making always for her hiding place. Time seemed not to move as his limbs, aching with the strain of silence, performed his will.

At last he reached her, coming up on her other side from the trees. The Hands were looking far away and Eamon firmed his resolve to act.

He dropped swiftly down by Ma Mendel and covered her mouth with his hand. She trembled but did not scream; she did not even draw the breath for it.

He whispered her name again, giving her his own. Relief flooded her frightened eyes.

Eamon laid a finger to his lips. He took her hand then drew the dagger, pressing the hilt between her fingers. Ma Mendel glanced at the blade, but by the time she had looked back to him to search his intention he had moved back into the trees.

A foolhardy plan had taken shape in his mind. There was no way to divert the Hands from the ruins – which they would surely search soon – other than to try it. He knew that everyone in the hall could see him and knew how what he had to do would look to them. He only hoped that he would outlive his folly long enough to tell them what he had intended.

He passed through the trailing forest eaves, heart beating in his breast more loudly than he had ever heard or felt it before. When he was a safe distance from Ma Mendel, he let his stealthy manner fall from him like a cloak to the ground. The Hands' backs were to him. Rising to his full height he strode boldly into the open under the terrible light of the orb.

In his mind, hundreds of voices in the Hidden Hall drew horrified breath. The red light deadened his skin so that he wore a living uniform.

The hounds caught his scent. Baying, snarling, and howling they turned with one motion and bounded at him. It took every fibre of every nerve in his body to keep himself walking steadily on towards their slavering jaws.

The torchless rider moved with the dogs. As his chill gaze passed over him Eamon raised his voice. "Call them off!" he yelled. "You will find nothing here, my lord!"

At some unspoken command the hounds slowed and began to circle him. Their eyes flashed red in the orb-light. Not far behind the beasts came the Hands.

"Who are you?" one demanded.

Eamon raised his palm. The orb-light showed the mark of the Master's eagle in his flesh.

"I am Lieutenant Eamon Goodman, sworn to the Master," he answered. "To his glory!" The words were thick on his tongue.

"Ah, Lieutenant Goodman." The Hand who had cast the orb smiled at him. There was a disquieting courtesy to his voice that seemed an odd match to his face. "You are the very man whom we are searching for. We received reports of snakes attacking a holk on the river, and rumours that the Serpent himself was among them. Such reports bear investigating. It was your holk, was it not? And you were transporting a prisoner of some value to the Master."

Eamon swallowed. The other Hands returned with their torches. They watched him. None spoke. All seemed to be at the command of the torchless, and apparently genteel, Hand. Hardly knowing what else to do, he bowed low once more.

"My lords," he began, "it is as you say. My holk was taken and my crew killed. I am one of only two men who were left alive. We were captured by snakes and have been forcibly held for several days. When they found that they had no further use for us they abandoned my companion and myself here to die."

"You have not the look of a man tortured," the Hand answered him, pleasantly enough. "Or perhaps you bear it well?"

Eamon wished he had let Giles give him a thorough beating. "They fed my companion with delusional poisons that confused mind and body, my lord," he answered. "I was permitted neither to eat nor sleep."

"Ah," the Hand soothed sympathetically.

"The snakes were camped here but moved on this morning, towards the south." He gestured south, towards the hall. He tried not to pale as he lowered his hand. "They took my prisoner with them."

"And did these snakes go with the Serpent?"

"I… I do not know, my lord," Eamon replied. "I thought that I had seen him. But now I do not know whether he was not a spectre in my dulled mind."

"You escaped, Mr Goodman?"

"I was left for dead."

"And your fellow?" The Hand was persistently courteous.

"We were separated. Since I regained some strength I have spent much of this day seeking him, my lord. He is the only one who can verify my story of how the holk was taken," he added, allowing a fierce growl to fill his voice. "I would not lose my post in Dunthruik through vicious rumour." He dared to stare straight into the Hand's eyes, glistening bright green beneath the hood.

"You need not fear for your post, or for rumour, lieutenant," the Hand answered. "We ourselves shall be your escort to Dunthruik."

Eamon forced a smile. "Nothing would please me more, my lords," he answered. "If, however, I might be so bold, I would ask that you permit me one more day to search these woods for my young companion. I will gladly ride with you at nightfall tomorrow."

The Hand watched him. Eamon feared that at any moment the dogs might be set on him or – worse – that the voice in his mind would appear. He feared that it might reveal his frenetically formed lies for what they were.

The motionless eyes before him seemed to be holding some inner discourse. In silent agony Eamon awaited the pronouncement of his fate.

At last the rider spoke. "Very well, Mr Goodman."

Eamon had never heard a more beautiful concession. "There is a bridge not four miles east of here; it crosses one of the River's tributaries and is not often troubled by the Master's enemies. We will meet you there at twilight tomorrow. If you have found your companion we will bear you both to Dunthruik. If not, we will bear you alone."

Eamon threw himself into an eager bow. "My lords, you do me much honour."

"As befits a beloved servant, we invest you with trust." The Hand beamed at him, then caught a torch from one of the others and graciously handed it to Eamon. His languid tone drew on a darker edge. "Perhaps you would assist us, Mr Goodman?"

He knew what he had to do. Bowing, Eamon turned and then lifted the flames high, touching them to a thatched roof. The wood was slow to catch but the thatch sparked before blossoming into hungry flame. When he turned back to the Hand he saw that other dwellings were also burning. The Hands were quick.

"We must press on, Mr Goodman," the Hand told him. "There are many rumours of the Serpent in this area and we must cover ground. You may find the torch helpful and so I leave it with you. Perhaps you will see to those hovels that we have not the time to attend to." His heart churned. Eamon bowed. It was not an order that he could disobey.

The Hand smiled. "I wish you good chance in your search."

"Thank you, my lord."

Without a further word the Hands gathered together and began to ride south. The riders and their following dogs passed close to the ruined hall and on into the woodland.

Eamon stepped to one of the few buildings that did not yet burn and raised his torch with trembling hands. He glanced back over his shoulder towards the dark eaves where the Hands had gone, daring to wait until they passed out of hearing as well as out of sight. The smoke from the blazing village filled his face, stinging acridly.

As soon as he could he cast down the torch and hurried back into the forest. Now the roots and branches tore at his legs, hindering his passage. When he reached Ma Mendel he found her shivering, her hand in her mouth to keep her from crying out. Tears poured over her ashen face.

Without a word he helped her to her feet and they returned to the Hidden Hall. It loomed grey before them, shadows dancing over its tumbled walls. As the flames in the village reached high the Hand's orb faded into darkness and vanished, leaving the smoke and grit of the fire in its wake. Still, Eamon kept one ear and eye always to the south.

At last, coughing and spluttering, they staggered back into the hall. Reeling, Eamon passed Ma Mendel to other arms as soon as he had crossed the threshold. Seconds later angry hands grabbed his throat.

"Liar!" Giles yelled. "Murderous gloved bastard!"

"I didn't kill anyone!" Eamon protested, spluttering.

"Let go of him, Giles!" Aeryn cried, slapping his hands away. The big man gave an angry roar and threw him aside. Eamon gratefully gasped for air.

"The fires, sir!" Mathaiah cried.

"No, we mustn't put them out –" Eamon's words were lost as a fit of coughing raked through his grizzled throat.

"What?" Aeryn sounded horrified.

"Eamon's right," said another voice. It was Hughan's. He did not know where the King had come from; all he knew was that it was the King's hands that steadied him as he reeled.

"It is a trap to draw us out," Hughan added. "If we douse the flames the Hands will know we're here. So here we must stay, and our homes must burn. It is not too high a price for our lives."

Eamon remembered little of the next few minutes. His head throbbed, his breast ached, and all his limbs, tensed for so long, suddenly slackened, dangling lifelessly from him. He could not stand and so settled with huddling against a corner of stonework.

He heard Hughan arranging a rota of guards for the night. The next thing he knew he was being hurried to a side chamber where blankets had been strewn to make a dormitory. Once there, a stranger fed him some foul-tasting syrup. As the pain in his throat died, exhaustion overcame him. Fearing to tell what he had done and of how his bartered promise held him, he fell into a brief, troubled sleep.

What felt like hours later, gentle hands shook his shoulder. He stumbled back to consciousness. Things were quiet. Smoke lingered. Far away an owl hooted at the passing moon.

"What time is it?" he asked, shivering.

"Approaching the second watch," Aeryn told him. "I'm sorry to wake you."

"That's all right." Memory came back with sudden force and he bolted upright. "I need to speak to Hughan."

"That's why I've woken you."

Eamon rose. Most of the chamber was still empty and he wondered whether that was because he had been sleeping in it.

"How is Ma Mendel?"

"She's safe."

He followed Aeryn as she made a path through the blankets. Guards stood silently in the hall by the doors and he could hear the sounds of fitful sleep from the open doors of the great chamber. He was therefore not surprised when Aeryn led him on to another, smaller, side-chamber. It had the look of a storeroom. Small lanterns had been strung along the wall to provide light, granting the crowded room a strange look.

Hughan stood at the head of a small table, his counsellors lining the side of the room. Giles stood near the table, with Mathaiah in front of him, looking nervous.

Eamon took everything in at a moment. Aeryn slipped from his side and went to join Ma Mendel, who stood near some of the counsellors and had regained her look of indomitable cheerfulness.

Eamon raised his eyes to Hughan's. There was a long silence.

"Are we prisoners?" he asked at last.

"Eamon," the King began, gently. "Would you give account of what has happened tonight?"

Eamon drew breath. It was not as easy to tell the truth to Hughan as it had been to twist and turn it before the Hands.

"Sir, honourable counsellors," he began. "The Hands came seeking the prisoner they lost when my holk was captured."

He was surrounded by what felt like a tempest of hateful, bitter gazes, but not a sound accompanied them.

Eamon looked to Hughan for direction. The King nodded to him. He had been guaranteed silence for however long it took to tell his story.

"They sought to be led to you, Hughan, and to recapture Aeryn. If they had found this hall then we would soon have been confronted with many more than five Hands. That is why I went to speak to them," he continued, "and that is why I lied to them. I told them that Mr Grahaven and myself had been captured by wayfarers who had tortured us, depriving me of food and sleep and feeding him with substances that bend the mind. I said that I had never seen the Serpent, that my prisoner had been taken, and that I sought my companion in these woods, as proof of what had befallen me on the holk. I was granted permission to continue in this search and commanded to set fire to what remained of your homes. This I did not do in full." He bit his lip. He had disobeyed a Hand.

"So now I am a double-traitor." His voice was a whisper as the truth of it struck indelibly at his heart. "I am pledged to ride with the Hands to Dunthruik tomorrow evening, else they will know that all I said was a lie and they will come here seeking you. And I do not know if I will ride as a disgraced lieutenant or a prisoner, nor how long this hall will remain hidden once I am taken into the circle of the throned's walls. I ask that you would not force Mathaiah to go with me if he does not wish it. That is the full account," he said at last. He looked up and saw that Hughan was watching him steadily. "I am sorry."

There was a long silence. Aeryn fidgeted uncomfortably with a tress of her hair. Eamon began to panic. Would no one speak a word? He would not care whether they praised or despised him – all he longed for was a sound.

Suddenly his wish was granted.

"Eamon Goodman, will you serve me?"

Eamon found his eyes drawn upwards by the command of that voice, both like and unlike that of the Hughan he knew. He looked at the stern, bright face, and saw a king. His aching eyes saw a circlet of silver upon Hughan's brow that glistened like lit stars over a summer sea. The mark on Eamon's hand throbbed with fire and he felt a whisper in his mind as the voice prepared for a fresh assault. But he turned deaf ears to it and, never once losing sight of the stars that beckoned to him out of the darkness, he knelt down before Hughan in the dusty hall.

"How can I not?" His heart beat with passion and loyalty as he bowed his head. The men and women all around him gasped, but he did not lift his head. The fire in his hand spluttered, forced into submission.

A gentle touch rested on his brow. Eamon felt lightheaded beneath it.

"Eamon Goodman, you enter into my service of a free heart," Hughan said. "And so you will find freedom in it. I do not ask for oaths of fealty or the pledge of your lifeblood for the use of my hands; I ask that you would draw your sword to defend the helpless, lift your hands to raise up the needy, use your heart to love the people of the River, and challenge evil where you find it. In these promises, made to me but not bound in me, I ask you to render service."

Eamon heard each word in wonder. His limbs trembled, and his heart felt as though it might burst forth in a joy that walked hand in hand with her neighbour sorrow.

Through the tumble of his thought he heard Hughan's voice again: "Will you serve me, Eamon Goodman?"

His answer was the boundless desire of his heart: "For what time it is permitted to me to walk the River's realms, I will gladly serve you, my King."

"Then rise, First Knight."

Eamon rose steadily to his feet. A great peace was on him. Across Hughan's hands lay a sword. Eamon recognized it as it ran silver in the light: it was the sword that he had drawn against the throned in his vision. Hughan held it out to him, his joyous face lowered.

"You must not bow your head to me," Eamon breathed.

"I too have taken a promise to serve," the King replied softly. Wondrously, Eamon took the sword in his hand. As he raised it before him it sang.

Eamon opened his eyes. He and Hughan stood once more in the small, crowded chamber. There was no sword in his hands, only traces of blue-silver light fading into the stone like water into sand. Everyone around them stood in awe. He did not know what they had seen – indeed, he barely knew what he had witnessed himself. But Hughan held his gaze steadily and from that Eamon drew strength.

"Let it be known," Hughan said, turning to those by them, "that this man is my First Knight and that he serves me. He has my trust and, as a measure of your trust in me, I ask that each of you affords him the chance to be worthy of your trust also." Eamon tried to tease a feel of the onlookers. Many seemed in shock. Giles looked furious.

"Thank you for your witness," Hughan continued, speaking to the chamber at large. "I discharge all of you to your places of duty and of rest. I ask that Alnos, Leon, and Giles remain with me whilst I speak further with Eamon."

There was a shuffling of feet while the chamber emptied itself, apart from these three and the King. A worried-looking Mathaiah was entrusted to Aeryn, who led him away.

Soon Eamon was alone with those he presumed to be highest in Hughan's council. Giles still watched him, like a predator that would leap for his throat. Eamon recognized Alnos but the third man, Leon, was one whom he did not remember seeing before. Perhaps he had not been paying attention.

Hughan stepped forward and his manner became less formal. "Are you all right?" he asked. Eamon nodded, wondering whether his friend had been just as surprised by what had happened as he had been. With a smile, Hughan continued in a louder voice: "You may remember that when I spoke to you yesterday morning I said that there was a service I would ask you to do me, should you be willing."

"I am willing, sire," Eamon answered.

"Then I wish, in the presence of these generals, to explain this service to you so that you can consider it."

Eamon nodded. He felt as though he could do anything for this man; a strange, wondrously strange, new feeling was in him. "I will do whatever I can," he said.

"Eamon, what I would ask is something that perhaps only you, and few other men, could do and live," Hughan told him. "I will not conceal from you my belief that your life would hang perpetually by a thread of your own wit and courage. But I do not want you to feel compelled or betrayed by me into this, or any, task. It may be that I seek to send you where you do not want to go. If that is so then I would have you choose to go, not for my will so much as for your faith."

Eamon's heart pounded. Bereft of words, he nodded.

"The throned has been seeking me and those who follow me for some time," Hughan began. "This is not a new development, nor is it unexpected, but something has changed. He has redoubled his efforts in his search and is striking with more than his accustomed ferocity. We have been harrying his forces here in the north for some time, taking advantage of the trouble with Galithia and Lamiglia. Much of the north bank supports us. There are dozens of hidden places, like this hall, all along the River, each one filled with weapons and with men ready to use them. This he knows, even if he does not know where we are."

"You mean to challenge him?"

"Yes."

Eamon stared at him in awe.

"There is much that we have yet to finalize. As you may imagine," the King added wryly, "the logistics, strategy, and allies that must be arranged before I can even think about moving openly against the throned or taking Dunthruik, have been proving very complex. Plans for getting men, equipment, and supplies to the city will continue to give my generals plenty of headaches in the coming months."

Hughan's eyes met his again and Eamon felt that they were reaching the critical point. "Clearly, it would be of help to us to know what is happening in Dunthruik," he said. "It would also help us greatly to understand, and exploit, any weaknesses that can be found. The throned has sat in tyranny over the River Realm for the five hundred and thirty-two years since Ede's death. I do not know how such a feat is possible," he added. "I merely know that it is true. Since the day that he seized the throne, Edelred has been searching to eradicate my house, and yet his search has grown keener now. I cannot answer why. There is much that we do not know, either about the throned or about his plans."

Eamon looked once more at Hughan. "What would you have me do?" he asked.

"Keep your promise to the Hands. Go with them to Dunthruik and there, First Knight, in the very heart of my enemy's stronghold, I would ask you to serve me."

Eamon came away from the chamber in a daze, his ears ringing. He heard raised voices behind him:

"He will betray us, sire!"

"It is a fool's errand, sending a Glove to do the work of a King's man, and a fool that entrusts it to him!"

"Do not address the King thus!"

Eamon walked away. He did not want to hear any more.

His steps led him to the Hidden Hall's entrance. The guards paid him little heed as they stood at their posts. Slowly he walked towards the great window; the stone eye gazed over the village, smouldering against the darkened sky. Drawing a deep breath he tried to think.

The throned had bound him to serve as Gauntlet in his city. The King had called him to do the same, as First Knight. He had sworn to do both, but could he do either?

Footsteps approached him from behind. Mathaiah stepped up to his side, wrapped in a blanket that he wore about his shoulders like a cloak. His face was pale with lack of sleep but he was focused and alert.

"Is everything all right, sir?"

"I hardly think you need call me 'sir'," Eamon answered. "Didn't you see me today, Mathaiah? I made an oath to the King. I denied any allegiance to the throned when I did that. I am no longer permitted to wear the uniform in which I so diligently came here, and no longer entitled to your 'sir's or service."

"Yes, sir."

Eamon looked at him and realized that he did not know what his young friend – if they were still friends – thought about the whole affair. He sighed, and rubbed one hand awkwardly through his hair. It was greasy and smelled of smoke.

"What will you do?" he asked.

Mathaiah was gazing out of the long window. "I don't know," he said at last. "In theory I have no oath, no mark of any colour. I can go where I please…" His voice was strained and bore no hint of whimsy. Eamon suspected that the boy had spent too long weighing up his choices.

"As a cadet, you have set yourself on a path that leads to an eagled palm," Eamon cast a glance at his own. "If you would hear my advice, I would not in good faith counsel you to continue in it."

"Even if I promised not to, I don't think I would get back to Edesfield," Mathaiah answered. "Giles doesn't trust me, sir, and I can't think that he would trust me not to talk. I cannot go home and tell my father that I have met the man who killed his eldest son and left the Gauntlet. He is old and frail. But I can't stay here either;

I do not think that most of these men, however noble, would ever really trust me."

Eamon felt a rush of compassion. "I am so very sorry, Mathaiah, that I brought you into this with me —"

The cadet laughed. "I'd be dead if you hadn't, sir, and I'm not sure that would be much better! Anyway, for a part I brought myself. Since I saw you at Belaal's office I've felt that there is something different about you. You weren't like him or like any of the other Gauntlet officers that I saw — Kentigern, Spencing, Ellis... You are different to all of them. There is something left underneath your uniform — something bold, something that they say doesn't belong in the Gauntlet. I suppose that drew me to you, because whatever it is you seem so much richer, so much more, with it, than those without it."

The words cut at Eamon's heart. "I wanted to know what made you like that, sir. Now perhaps I do. You may bear his mark but I don't think that you ever truly served the throned. If you had you could not have given any promise to the King."

Stunned, Eamon stared.

"I'm sorry, sir, if I spoke out of turn —"

"I... don't think you did."

"What did they say to you?" Mathaiah added, looking to the hall.

"They've asked if I will spy on the throned in Dunthruik." Eamon tried to make light of it.

"Did they give you a picnic basket, too?" Mathaiah inquired.

Unable to contain a smile, Eamon burst into laughter.

"I'll take that as a no, sir," Mathaiah smiled.

Eamon looked at the cadet. The boy had come with him from Edesfield, saved him from death, pleaded for him against Giles. Now that he had given an oath to the King, the cadet still followed him.

"Mathaiah," he said quietly, "are you with me or against me?"

"Sir?"

"You cannot serve two masters. Perhaps you should not follow a man who has embroiled himself with two."

Mathaiah remained silent. Eamon held his breath. He desperately wanted the boy to throw his lot in with Hughan and be saved from the flesh-devouring eagle. But as desperately as he wanted it, it was a choice that he could neither make nor force.

At last Mathaiah drew breath. "Sir, I have seen what the Gauntlet can do. For many men there is power and renown to be gained from the oaths that they take. The red uniform is admired and feared, and the black is unassailable." A quiver stole into his voice. "But this King, he shows but a little power, and I am awed by him. He shows less than a little kindness and all other kindnesses wither away. I see why he has your service."

Eamon regarded him gently. He saw the cadet's turmoil and he understood it.

"I have seen, Mr Grahaven, the strength of your sword and the courage of your heart," he said. "Your faith is yours to pledge where you choose."

A faint smile appeared on Mathaiah's lips. "Don't knights have squires, sir?"

Eamon was touched to the core. "Mathaiah, you don't have to come with me."

"I know, sir," Mathaiah answered. As he spoke a weight seemed to fall from his shoulders. "But I want to. Seeing you make your choice somehow gives me the courage to make mine. I want to go with you, and serve the one you serve."

"We could both be killed," Eamon said, trying to sound grave – but a great smile had worked its way into every corner of his face.

"It seems to me," the cadet replied, "that I would rather give my life for the King than bind it to the Eagle."

Far over in the east the first traces of light were appearing. Eamon felt his resolve strengthening with them.

Mathaiah yawned. "What day is it tomorrow, sir?"

"You mean today?" Eamon paused, counting. "The seventeenth of September. We should get some sleep," he added.

"Sounds like a good way to start the morning, sir."

Chapter IX

They made their way silently back to the side-chamber where Eamon had been rested before. He tiptoed round dormant figures to reach his blankets and settled down at last between two strangers. Mathaiah found a space a little distance away and did likewise.

Eamon curved his arms over his chest and rolled onto his side. Sleep came with sudden gentleness to his brow, encouraged by the peace that his new oath granted him.

But as he drifted and was borne away by the welcome, drowsy tide he felt fire lingering on his palm.

CHAPTER X

Aeryn sat in the light next to him. Her arms were folded across her breast against the cold. He reached out and touched her hand, pressing her icy fingers between his own. She tried to smile. No word was exchanged.

The day passed quickly. He spent much of it with Hughan, filling his head with all the details and specifics pertinent to his task. Anything that he could learn would be of value, but he had to know how to get it back to the King.

"We do have some people in Dunthruik," Hughan explained. "Most of them won't take a stand against the throned until they see him losing ground. Of those who are bolder none of them are deep enough in the court to have a chance of learning his plans. There is a lady at the court, Alessia Turnholt by name. She hails from one of Dunthruik's most ancient and respected families."

"She is with us?" Eamon asked, surprised.

"No," Hughan said with a small smile, "but her maidservant is. Her name is Lillabeth Hollenwell. Pass anything that you learn on to Lilly, if you can. She will get it to me. I won't burden you with the names of any other wayfarers, in case something goes wrong."

Eamon nodded. It was a wise precaution.

"This next part is very important, Eamon, and I want you to listen carefully." Hughan fixed him with a stern gaze. "Remember that, for whatever reason, the throned has an interest in you. That will hinder you as much as it may help you at times. If you feel that you have been compromised or discovered, or feel yourself to be in desperate danger of your life, don't have a fit of heroics; just leave.

There is an inn on Serpentine Avenue in the South Quarter. Speak to the bartender and he will hide you until we can get you out."

"Is he –?"

"He has no love of the throned and will do all that he can for you." Eamon nodded again. He felt as though his brain could not quite take everything in. "If you are in the city when we decide to make our move, we will tell you what to do," Hughan added, "but it won't be before the spring in any case. Is Mathaiah going with you?"

"Yes," Eamon answered.

"He's a stubborn one," Hughan observed with a laugh. "But if my eyes see at all I think he will be of help to you. If there is too much trouble send him back via the inn. I will put him under my protection."

"Thank you. Hughan," Eamon added after a moment, "I don't think that they believed me."

"The Hands?"

"Yes." Eamon was surprised at the agility with which Hughan followed his thought. "It's been troubling me. If they didn't believe me then I am walking straight into a trap of their design. I don't like that."

"There are none who would," Hughan agreed.

"Supposing…" Eamon ventured, a little more reluctantly. "Supposing I tell them that I lied and then offer them proof of my allegiance…"

"Did you have anything in mind?"

"No," he admitted. "It would have to be something that would be valuable to them but of no loss to you."

Hughan looked at him pensively. "I'll have some dispatches made up. Fake ones, of course," he added with a smile. "A collection of missives giving indication of the existence and location of other Hidden Halls. I'll write the missives myself and include some detail on our movements as a whole that the throned will be hard-pressed to dispute, and too intrigued to ignore. By the time he has combed through the missives and the false halls he'll have expended a lot of resources for very little, which is always of help to us. We may even be able to surprise him and ambush those whom he sends to investigate." The King's smile faded and he grew serious again. "But perhaps we can do more than that, and even play it to our advantage. Have you heard of Ellenswell?"

A memory of his distant youth came to Eamon's mind. He saw his father working upon the binding of an elegant edition of the River Poet's works. He remembered how he had sat, enthralled, by the tale that his father had told of a place called Ellenswell and the many, many books that had been there. More books, his father had insisted, than could be imagined. Books upon books, hundreds upon hundreds, every corner and every nook of every alcove filled with parchment, leather, and scroll. He had seen the delight in his father's eyes at the telling of it – Ellenswell had been the envy of the city. Eamon remembered his father's sadness as he had told what had befallen it.

"There was a quake in the early days of Dunthruik," Eamon recalled. "It started a fire. The library was lost."

Hughan smiled again. "Not quite," he answered. "Ellenswell was once known as 'Elaina's Well'."

"Elaina?" Eamon repeated in surprise.

"Ede's sister was quite a scholar in her days and spent years collecting books from all over the River Realm and from all its allies. It took her a long time to find a place to store her collection, which she had intended to one day make public."

"Where did she put them?"

"Some say that she emptied the palace cellars, including the best years laid down by her father, and distributed the bottles to her brother's court so as to obtain a keeping place. Even in those days the city had a rich wine trade. Though Ede seems to have approved of her actions I do not think that either her husband or the palace kitchens quite concurred with it." Eamon chuckled at the thought. "At any rate," Hughan continued, "the cellars certainly survived the quake – how else would the palace still be standing? It is the same structure now as it was then, if a little modified. The throned wanted to get into Ellenswell but found it blocked. The flames associated with the quake story were of his making."

"Why would he want to go into the library?" The grey-eyed man Eamon had seen in his mind did not seem to be a man of letters.

"Truthfully, I do not know," Hughan answered. "That is probably a question for the bookkeepers."

Eamon's head spun with the deluge of information. "I'm sorry that I keep asking questions. Who are the bookkeepers?"

"Much that was in the library was removed before the throned cemented his grasp on Dunthruik," Hughan answered. "The bookkeepers were close counsellors to Ede and took charge of much of Elaina's collection. They keep it even now, in a Hidden Hall at Stonemead. For men of letters," he added, "the bookkeepers are a fierce bundle."

"Have you met them?"

"Yes. They know and keep record of many things that the people of the River have forgotten. It was the bookkeepers who explained to me much of the history that I have told you. I was taken to them after I left Edesfield."

Eamon wondered at the revelation it must have been when the bookkeepers had explained the nature of his heritage to Hughan. By the look on Hughan's face he imagined that it was still a strong memory.

"Did they manage to get all of the books when they emptied the library?" Eamon asked.

"From what I understand not quite all," Hughan answered. "I have heard it said that there are still some law books and court records from Ede's time down there. I believe that Eben also had some connection to the well before he was killed."

"And the throned couldn't go down?"

"Though Elaina meant for the library to become public it was often kept locked as the realm plunged into war. Her husband and Ede had a special key commissioned and fashioned by an Easter craftsman. The River and Istanaria were once on close terms.

"As Ede had no heir he meant to pass the rights of his line to Elaina and her descendants; the key was to be an heirloom of that line. As it was made for the King's much-loved sister, the one whom he meant to follow him to the throne, the key came to be called 'the heart of the King'. Without it the library could not be opened – not even by the throned."

As he spoke these last words Hughan produced a small leather pouch. He tugged it open and carefully poured its contents onto his hand. Eamon looked in disbelief.

A stone the size of a small fruit lay there, glimmering in the light. It was a deep blue colour but cast out rays of purple and gold. Eamon reached out to touch it and Hughan placed it in his hand. It was smooth and cool.

"The bookkeepers are adamant that nothing of value remained in the library," Hughan said quietly. "But it is clear that the throned believed otherwise. If you can find out what it is that he desires so much then that is for the good; it may help us. If not, delivering the heart of the King to him will be a trophy bespeaking your oath to him."

Nodding dumbly, Eamon felt the weight of the heirloom in his hand. "Are you sure that you want me to take this?"

Hughan nodded. "An unused key is of little value," he smiled.

Eamon placed the stone back in its pouch and then set it securely about his neck by its long leather cord. "Thank you, Hughan."

After Hughan had gone to compose the dispatches, Eamon rehearsed his learning of the morning. His tasks seemed simple enough. He would go to Dunthruik, explain about the capture of the holk, and ask that he be assigned as Belaal had intended. From there, he would do his best to gain as much information as he could. Given the interest that the throned had already shown in him he suspected that he might find himself in higher circles easily enough, and he would act as though he knew nothing of prophecy or history.

He was, however, unsure of what would happen to Mathaiah. The cadet was sincere in his desire to serve Eamon but he wondered whether the boy would be able to have his wish once they reached Dunthruik. Mathaiah had been destined, after all, to return to Edesfield. He wasn't yet sure how, or if, he would be able to get the cadet to stay, although he suspected that, as someone who had escaped the wayfarers, the Hands would be reluctant to let the boy leave – especially if they grew suspicious. That he could send Mathaiah back to Hughan at any time was a comfort to him.

When he studied the dense map of Dunthruik with Giles late that afternoon he imprinted the twists of Serpentine Avenue into his mind. The inn was called the South Wall; Hughan had told him that its sign showed a tumbling collection of stones.

"They say that a great nest of snakes used to live in the South Quarter, which is why the road's named as it is," Giles told him, his gruffness alleviated by his apparent interest in history. He grinned. "This map's an old one, maybe fifty or sixty years out of date, and some of the roads aren't named or simply aren't there. But it's the best we've got, and the Serpentine was certainly right there last time I looked." He stabbed at the road with one finger.

Eamon looked up at him. "How do you know so much about the city?" he asked. "I thought you came from the borders?"

"Oh, no man has lived until he has seen Dunthruik!" Giles bellowed with sarcastic grandeur. "And I am a man who has lived far more than you." Declining to elucidate further he leaned in close to Eamon. "Let me make one thing clear, Lieutenant Goodman." Eamon was rattled by the return to his erstwhile title. "I don't trust this spying business, and I trust you in it less than any other man that the King could send. If it had been left to me I'd have killed you long before your little stunt last night. It is still the King's judgment and goodwill that keeps you safe from me. If you give even a scent of us away," Giles hissed, "I will outlive any torture or death long enough to find you."

Eamon swallowed. He didn't doubt it.

Chapter X

"Thank you for showing me the map, Giles," he answered as amicably as he could, "and for your trust in me. That you are willing to give it on the King's trust, and not your own, is telling."

As he left, Giles watched him with the narrowed eyes of extreme suspicion.

He walked with Aeryn last of all. She did not really look at him, and kept her hands clasped in front of her – gestures of anxiety that he recognized from their many years of friendship. For a long while they said nothing at all.

"Do you remember the time we made Ladomer think that your arm was broken?" she asked.

Eamon cast his mind back. They had done a good job of improvising a blood-like substance out of a collection of berries that Telo had tended in the Star's garden for his summer fruits. As Eamon recalled, he and Aeryn had pretended that a mad dog had broken into the garden and ravaged Eamon so badly that it broke his arm before leaving to terrorize some local population of rabbits.

"The Mad Beast of Burr's Hill," he said fondly. "The part about the rabbits was a bit juvenile! You'd think that we could have thought up something better than that. Poor Ladomer believed us, too. Do you remember the look on his face?"

"I'm sure he was convinced you were bleeding to death – until he spotted you tasting it!" Aeryn agreed.

"That was a poor move on my part," Eamon conceded, laughing. He had never been able to resist strawberries and had been dipping his finger in the mess on his arm with delight when a frantic Ladomer had come rushing into the garden to inspect the damage. Eamon's knowledge that Ladomer was bigger and stronger than him by far had begun more or less on that day: failing to see the humour, Ladomer had proceeded to beat Eamon to within an inch of his life. Eamon's father had scolded Ladomer harshly for it. It had been far more embarrassing for sixteen-year-old Ladomer than twelve-year-old Eamon. Eamon wondered if Ladomer had ever forgiven his father for it.

Both were silent for long moments, lost in the memory. At last Aeryn took his hand and looked at him.

"What you're doing now, Eamon, is not altogether unlike that game we played," she said softly. "Except it isn't Ladomer who's coming to check on you, and he won't be the one to beat you if you get caught. Remember that. Don't taste the fruit this time!"

Eamon smiled, then leaned forward and kissed her cheek. "I won't. I promise. Besides," he added with a reassuring smile, "I don't really like fruit any more. I think Ladomer beat it out of me."

Aeryn laughed. "I know."

"You take care of Hughan," he told her, "and let him take care of you."

Aeryn blushed. "I will."

He let go of her hand and they walked back to the Hidden Hall. As they approached, Eamon saw Mathaiah standing near the doors. His rapt attention was fixed on the one who spoke with him: Hughan.

As they neared, Eamon saw Mathaiah bow his head low. Smiling, Hughan laid his hands on Mathaiah's shoulders and spoke some words of service and benediction over him. Mathaiah's face warmed through with joy. Eamon and Aeryn stood to watch as the cadet raised his head. Hughan turned to Eamon.

"A good man goes with you," he told him, "and much will come of him." Mathaiah basked in the praise. Hughan regarded Eamon for a long moment. The weight of parting fell upon them.

"Have you the stone?"

Nodding, Eamon laid one hand to his breast where it lay. "I have. Have you the dispatches?"

"I have." Hughan plucked a group of papers from his pouch. "I am sorry that I cannot also give you cloaks or food for your journey."

The papers were creased, as though by many hands, and wax seals bound the folded sheets closed. The seals each bore a unicorn with three stars in an arch over its brow. Like the sword and star, it was one of the emblems of the house of Brenuin, the house of kings.

Eamon stored the papers carefully in his pouch.

"I am sorry to lose you again so soon after finding you," he whispered.

"You have not lost me, Eamon," Hughan replied. "And I will not lose you. Be careful."

"I will," Eamon promised.

They clasped hands firmly and Hughan embraced him. When they stepped apart Hughan looked at both lieutenant and cadet.

"The blessing of my house, the protection of my name, and the prayers of my heart go with you both," he said. Eamon caught a glimpse again of the otherworldly crown, sparks of silver over the King's bright brow.

Hughan smiled at him. "Go in strength and peace, First Knight."

Eamon glanced at the threshold of the Hidden Hall where muddied grass lay in the failing day. Beyond that first step there was no returning.

With papers and stone at breast and Mathaiah beside him, Eamon began to walk. Giving one last look over his shoulder he saw a dozen faces watching them leave – some relieved, some angry and suspicious. Some anxious, he hoped, at the thought of the peril that they freely went to for the service of the man they all served.

But before all those faces, one image marked itself indelibly upon him. Hughan and Aeryn stood together. They held hands before the threshold, the King and Queen of a hidden world and a hope placed, against all trusts, in him.

He crossed the threshold. The walls of the ruin gazed back at him, silent.

"Which way, sir?"

Eamon tore his gaze away from what he left, and felt the reassuring weight of the stone over his own heart.

"We go down past the village," he answered, "and strike east."

The sinking sun cast long shadows before them. They passed the smoking remains of the village and went south and east beyond it to another copse of trees on a small ridge. Calling birds jumped from the high branches and as the sun continued to fade, the shadows grew darker and the temperature dropped.

As they pushed silently through the trees Eamon thought suddenly that, should he wish to speak openly to his companion, this might be one of his last chances.

"Did Hughan explain everything to you as he did me?"

"He did, down to your ruse. I think it very clever, sir."

"Thank you," Eamon replied, honoured by the approval. "Listen, I don't know what time we shall have to speak safely once we meet up with…" he faltered. "*Them*. But keep your eyes and ears open for anything that may be helpful. I don't know what they'll do with either of us when we reach Dunthruik. For the sake of this ruse your chief value to me is as the one person who can verify what I say about the ship. Beyond that, I will say that I know little about you."

"Sir," Mathaiah affirmed.

"We mustn't speak of my healing you," Eamon added, "or, indeed, of any injury to you. We were both captured –"

"And my young mind spent the whole time under the influence of the drugs and poisons," Mathaiah continued, "leaving the more complex lies all for you, I'm afraid." There was the trace of a smile to his voice. "All I remember is being left for dead when the snakes left, and spending all of what I assume to be today struggling with the after-effects of the drugs before being found by you early this afternoon. I'm still partially hallucinatory, so I won't speak much for the next few days, and I'll be somewhat incoherent when I do."

Eamon looked at his friend, surprised and pleased. Whether the cadet had concocted parts of the tale with Hughan or not did not matter: it was clear that he was quite ready for what lay ahead.

It took them at least an hour to clear the treeline and cross the shallow, east-facing valley to the next ridge. A slope led down from it towards a dark ribbon that mirrored the early evening stars. The stream was marked by a stretched shadow. By this were grouped dismounted riders, their eyes watching the ridge.

Eamon tallied them. The hounds gathered intently about something, presumably edible, near the foot of the bridge while the horses grazed and drank from the riverbanks. The five Hands stood immovably. Their eyes upon him filled him with dread.

Mathaiah fell quiet. He wondered if the boy had ever really seen a Hand before. Glancing across in the twilight he saw that his friend had grown a little paler. Well, it would help their ruse.

"It's all right," Eamon told him, more bravely than he felt; now that he was faced with the prospect of several days' journey with these men he felt sudden doubt about his purpose. "Just pretend to be scared and confused. I'll do the rest."

"I think I can do that, sir."

Eamon looped one of Mathaiah's arms over his shoulder and gripped the cadet's lower back so as to help him hobble down the ridge.

The long trip down the hill to the bridge was one of the most terrifying things Eamon had ever done. With every pace he took, his whole being warned him that there would be no chance to run once they reached that bridge. The stone at his breast seemed to grow heavy, as if it too had no wish to go towards the enemy. But his nerve held, both for himself and for Mathaiah, drawing them always closer to their rendezvous.

As they came to the last few yards the dogs raised their heads to growl. The Hand to whom Eamon had spoken the night before spread his arms open in welcome, rather like an uncle welcoming a favourite nephew, and strode on as though he purposed to embrace the prodigal returnees. It was a terrifying sight.

"Lieutenant Goodman and cadet. So good to see you both! I am most glad that you recovered your companion, Mr Goodman. What is his name?"

"Grahaven, my lord, and thank you," Eamon answered, bowing as much as he could while supporting the greater part of Mathaiah's weight.

"Where did you find him? We also searched the woods here about, on the off-chance that we should discover him in your stead." The Hand spoke jovially but Eamon realized that his wit was already being tested.

"In the copses a few miles from here."

"He was put under the poisons of which you spoke?"

"Yes —" Eamon was thrown as the Hand threw back his hood, revealing a long face. It was handsome enough and well proportioned, but there was a glassy tint to the green eyes and a pallid sheen to the middle-aged skin. His dark hair was thickly braided. The man had a golden insignia marked on his cloak showing a raven, and he alone of the other Hands bore a curved sword — the blades borne by the others were all as straight as any in the River Realm. Above all else it was the Hand's eyes that held Eamon's attention. Behind the glassy look a deep green fire moved with a flicker that went beyond the jealous execution of duty.

Eamon took all of this in at a moment. He watched as the pale face peered closely at Mathaiah, inspecting for signs of illness. The Hand touched the young man's forehead with a curious air. Eamon waited with bated breath.

Suddenly the cadet began to twist and jerk. After a few seconds he cried out, babbling incoherently before turning his face towards Eamon as though in severe distress. The young man proceeded to swat at unseen things in the air, occasionally yelping as though struck.

His pulse racing, Eamon tried to grip Mathaiah more firmly. He didn't trust himself to speak. Was Mathaiah pretending? Or had the Hand done something to the boy?

"Hmmm," the pallid face crooned, nodding as though sage to the condition. "It would seem that your captors chose a potent blend of shadeweed. Very unpleasant." He looked back to Eamon. "And you are quite recovered from your own treatment?"

Eamon took his courage with both hands. "I must confess, my lord, that I was not entirely frank with you yestereve."

"Oh?" The pale face raised an eyebrow. Eamon became highly aware of the other Hands, who had formed a partial circle around him.

Although their green-eyed leader had an attitude of nonchalance, he understood that there was a system of signals, unseen by him, by which the Hands took the orders of their fellow. He could be cut down at a gesture should the leading Hand desire it.

"My lord, there were snakes nearby last night."

The pale face showed no flicker of emotion, as though it was accustomed to receiving the confessions of inept soldiers and lieutenants. Eamon resolved to persevere.

"These snakes were mere couriers, of little import. I would have revealed them to you and had you wipe them out in a second, but they held this boy. They would have killed him and he is the only one who can prove what happened when my holk was taken. I would not face rumour that would restrict my service. In that, I must be charged with arrogance as well as falsehood." He lowered his head. "I can only beg for your clemency."

"You were under considerable duress," the Hand answered him, in a tone that seemed kindly and comforting, and yet not quite mocking. "These snakes will not long escape the Master, Mr Goodman, whatever the conspiracies of your arrogance."

"I did speak truly when I said that the great mockery of our Master, the Serpent, was not there," Eamon continued, glancing up defensively. "But while I was there they received dispatches from him. These dispatches I obtained in secrecy this morning, before engineering my escape and the liberation of this cadet." The Hand's face broadened in a smile. "The letters contain details of what these vermin call 'hidden halls', places of treachery sown throughout the River Realm."

"Good," the Hand told him. "The Master will be pleased."

"I did have one other opportunity in my flight," Eamon continued, a little more reluctantly. "That is to say, one of the men in the group that took us was what they called a 'bookkeeper'."

Even the Hand could not conceal the surprise in his voice. "Indeed!" It was plain that the Hand knew of the bookkeepers. Maybe he had searched for them himself.

"This one carried something that he was delivering to the Serpent, something I understood to be of great importance," Eamon told his foe. "A stone."

"A stone?" The Hand watched him with astonishment.

"Indeed, my lord. I carry it now." With his free hand he raised the heart of the King from his travelling pouch and held it in the light.

The Hand erupted into long laughter. "For that alone, the lives and livelihoods of a hundred holks and the arrogance of ten hundred officers would have been traded!" he exclaimed. "Ah, Lieutenant Goodman, you will be rewarded well for your initiative!" He looked at the stone with gleaming eyes then gestured for Eamon to put it away.

"Will you not take it, my lord?" Eamon asked, surprised.

"No indeed!" the Hand answered. "You shall bear it and your papers to Dunthruik. They are marks of your endeavour and you will deliver them to the Master. He will be eager to meet with you."

Eamon bowed. "Such grace, my lord –"

"Maybe not," the Hand replied. "All the other officers vying for the Master's attention will despise you for your mark of passage."

At his gesture the other Hands began to gather the horses and hounds together. A horse was brought to the leading Hand. Eamon watched in surprise as the pale-faced servant of the throned leaned his head close to the beast's, speaking to it affectionately – behaviour wholly at odds with a man who bore the mark of the eagle on his hand and was robed in the Master's black. Eamon wondered what the raven emblem on the man's breast signified. The answer fretted at the edge of his memory but he could not grasp it. It had been long since he had been in the city of Dunthruik.

"Your young cadet shall ride," the Hand said. "He is in no fit state to walk the distance to the city."

Between them, Hand and lieutenant manoeuvred the senseless cadet onto the steed. One of the other Hands mounted behind him as a safeguard. Eamon briefly searched Mathaiah's eyes, looking for assurance, but there was none. He could not tell whether Mathaiah acted or was genuinely hurt.

"Come!" the Hand's voice drew him from one worry to another. "Walk with me, lieutenant, and we shall speak further!"

They walked long into the darkening night. The Hand talked the whole way as though they were intimate friends. He discussed the frivolities of court life in Dunthruik, the details of the latest training course for the officers in the city (which sounded gruelling), and the state of security in the provinces – especially on the northern borders. Spurred by the antics of the north many other merchant states were growing restless and pushing for unreasonable terms of trade, while in the east tension grew between the throned and those who lived near the passes; Dunthruik had been fortifying the cities there. Snakes had been found even in the capital, and had proved most resilient to interrogation; rumours of a snake cull, on a scale greater even than the Great Cull of 508, were gathering strength and support. He was a little less talkative on the doings of the Hands but did hint at the additional perks the Hands enjoyed in regards to the favours of ladies. The topic pushed the bounds of modesty.

It was late that night when they stopped, probably much closer to the third watch than to the second. The Hands quickly built and lit a fire. The dogs settled down near it, their limbs akimbo in the dust. Eamon helped to lower a somnambulant Mathaiah down from the horse before the beasts were tethered. He offered to take watch but, much like a dinner host refusing assistance in clearing the table, the Hand instructed him to rest; they would see to watches.

Eamon sat by Mathaiah, shivering. Two of their escort settled to watch and the other three to sleep. Noticing his reluctance to rest, the leading Hand doffed his cloak and offered it to him. The night was, he explained, only to grow colder. Eamon could only watch the man in surprise as he then moved off, humming, to rub down the horses.

So it was that Eamon settled himself down to rest wrapped in the cloak of a Hand. There was a time when such things would have been inconceivable to him. The blood in his palm stirred and in the dark he felt the mark of the eagle on his hand. He curled his fingers shut and clung with his mind to the silver sword given to him by the King.

The Hand's singing filled his thought for a long time.

When he was certain that the Hands were engaged either in sleeping or discussing things among themselves, he turned discreetly to Mathaiah. The cadet was pale and Eamon tried to tell himself it was the pallor of fatigue. He would not have been able to speak to his companion even had the cadet possessed his right mind, but what he would have given for an exchange of intelligent glances! This too was denied him; the cadet breathed the short, shallow breaths of one who walked in dreams.

Eamon turned his face towards the fire and listened to it crack. After a while he too must have passed into realms of sleep, for he saw shadows in the flames that raised their arms and danced a slow and secret dance, summoning ancient words from a place occult for years unnumbered. As he watched he felt himself fall and become entangled in the fires.

He woke too warm. His clothes stuck to him with cooled sweat and his fingers seemed swollen to twice their size. Light shined on him, the grey herald of the coming dawn.

Slowly he examined what lay about him, hoping that he might gain some intelligence before the Hand again set upon him with talk and incisive green eyes. He watched and listened for a few moments and then sat up, alarmed.

The trees were wrong. To begin with they stood in a small copse and not a nearly rigid line. Secondly, the leaves that lay prone to the pre-dawn breeze were thin, threaded leaves, like those of olives. They had been sturdy pines the night before; he had known them from their smell. The sun rose before him where it should have been behind and the River was behind him, to the south. He had lain the night before on ground composed mostly of moss and stone but now grass and wet earth pushed against his hands outside the warm cocoon of the cloak.

He looked this way and that for an explanation but there was none to be had. The fire in the centre of the camp still burned and two Hands paced in a circle about it, masters of the dismal grey. The sight chilled him.

For what felt like hours he wrestled with the bewilderment that had filled him on waking. He watched as the other Hands slowly rose from their rest and waked both dogs and horses. With his enemies intent on their occupations Eamon tried again to reach Mathaiah. But the pale face still slept, as though it had not moved from one stiff posture for the whole night.

The lurid face of the leading Hand dropped down, beaming, before him. "Good morning, lieutenant. You slept well?"

Eamon couldn't bring himself to answer the question. He could only stare. The Hand laughed.

"Ah!" he said. "You are, of course, bemused. Let me try and explain. You are a breacher, yes? That involves the breaking of the boundaries of thought and the defences of the mind."

Eamon nodded dumbly.

"Well," the Hand continued jovially, "there are those who can change the rules which apply to moving long distances." He left it at that, as though it explained everything, and moved off to set a pack on one of the horses. Eamon felt the air about him beginning to move, bringing with it a tang of the sea.

"Breakfast will be a frugal affair, consumed whilst walking," the Hand advised. Behind him the others were gathering their things. "Wake your cadet; he will ride, of course." The gallantry of this statement made Eamon press hard at his temples.

Waking Mathaiah was a lengthy process. Eamon shook him, hard, several times to little avail. Finally, he combined the shaking with a firm utterance of the young man's name, and two groggy eyes came half-open.

"Come on, cadet," Eamon told him. "Time to be moving on." He didn't dare speak other.

The Hands put Mathaiah on one of the horses. The grey hung

all about them like a shroud. Warming only a little as they walked, Eamon longed for the shroud to be torn in two and for the sun to soar up victorious from the veiled horizon.

In silence the Hands led the way along the River. Suddenly the plain dropped down to swoop forward and Eamon saw a great city standing tall against the plain and the sea behind it. To his left, in the south, ran the wide expanse of the River that churned on to the sea mouth where the city sat. From his elevated vantage Eamon could see the far side of the city and the walls of a well-defended port. To the east were the distant mountains and, near the city's northern walls, hills filled with vines. Below them, between the hills and the plain, were masses of woodland and farmsteads that trickled into plain grassland as it drew near the road. The eastern edge of the plain also had a large, burning pyre.

A road led down from where Eamon stood to the city gates. On it, and through them, he could already see the ant-like forms of men and women going about their business and he wondered if he caught voices in the air. Thick walls gloved the city. They were dotted with rounded watchtowers attended by dozens of men in red uniforms. He saw the whole spread of it, saw its heart and the shape of the four quarters marked out before him by the casting shadows of the rising sun. Deep in the West Quarter he saw the gilded pinnacle of the Crown theatre and, beyond it, the grand wings of the palace itself spreading out in shadow and stone. There were sails in the port and pennants shaking in the wind, impaling the sky over every gate and tower with crowns and eagles.

The Hand smiled.

"Welcome to Dunthruik, Mr Goodman," he said.

CHAPTER XI

The Hands led the way to the waking city. As the sun rose higher, shadows shifted and waned, his own growing longer along the road before him. Eamon felt as though the city watched him, hawked him. He wondered if he might bolt – but he also felt an inexorable pull towards something in the heart of the city's towering arches and spires.

Though Dunthruik was a place of terror to him, it had once been his home. As they came closer to the city he began to be able to pick out the details of the stones and timbers. Memories flashed back at him – of early morning strolls with his mother to buy bread in the crowded market streets, of the sound of Gauntlet patrols marching by. Sometimes his father had taken him to the port to watch the merchant ships, laden with grain, as they docked; sometimes they had passed near the theatre to admire it. He remembered the chill, wet squalls that blasted the city in the winter, the rains that swept down from the mountains and washed the thick-paved streets to muddy grey, and the sweltering grip of the summer sun. He remembered the well-sized house, buried in the North Quarter, where his father had plied and been lauded in his trade. It was the same house where, one dark autumn evening, his mother had died.

He had fled Dunthruik in grief and darkness. Now he returned to it, in the blinding light of day, with a double heart.

"This road takes the smoothest route across the plain to the Blind Gate." He was drawn from his thoughts by the green-eyed Hand beside him. The man led the horse that carried Mathaiah. The cadet leaned hard against the beast's neck and bobbed up and down as they went. "It runs east through the regions of Eastport, Wakebairn, and Sablemar, and eventually on to the Algorras. Thus is it called the East Road; a fair name."

"A logical one, my lord."

"As far as names go, Mr Goodman, it lacks poetic adroitness," the Hand said ruefully. "But such is its name. Of course," he added, "it does afford one of the best views of the River's most prized jewel." He threw his arm out towards Dunthruik. The rising sun burnished it, driving morning mist to sea.

"It does, my lord," Eamon agreed.

They continued their approach to the Blind Gate. Eamon remembered his father had once told him that the Master had taken the city by the east gate. The gate's name recalled the ill-kept watch when the throned had breached the city's threshold.

"The Blind Gate falls under the jurisdiction of the East Quarter," said the Hand. "When Dunthruik holds its majesties the processions start there. The Hands lead the Gauntlet in through the Blind Gate, along the Coll, and into the Royal Plaza. The Right Hand leads a service of thanksgiving to the Master for his dominion and glory; often the Master himself appears on the balcony."

"That must be a wondrous sight, my lord." Eamon had attended majesties in his childhood but had never stood in the Royal Plaza or been privy to a sight of the Master – he and his family had always been in the crowds lining the Coll, the city's main road.

"It is," the Hand continued with a smile, "as you shall no doubt soon see for yourself, Mr Goodman. There's to be a majesty before the new moon."

Eamon resisted the urge to try to catch sight of the moon, lying stone-like, frozen between the clouds, as it faded. He guessed that the new moon – and the majesty – was about a week away.

The East Road was wide and as it wound to the city its flattened earth became a broad, shining mass of different coloured stones paved together into a way of soaring eagles. Eamon walked uncomfortably, trying to avoid stepping on the birds, and looked instead at the gate ahead. The great edifice of stone, bearing crowned eagles of its own, cocooned the city's enormous doors. Eamon knew that the doors were braced and reinforced within by iron bars and that each wall tower had dozens of arrow slits facing both out towards the plain and in towards the open spaces behind the gate.

The gate's postern doors stood wide open and Gauntlet men checked those who passed in and out of them. Not every group was checked; some of those passing into the city with their carts or wagons were familiar faces that brought supplies and wares. Groups of Gauntlet and militiamen also passed, as did the occasional mounted courier – their colours granted them swift passage. Individuals passing the gate on their own business were required to have passage papers if they meant to go beyond the first stretch of the East Road. Men passing on such business waited in a small line at the gate while Gauntlet officers assiduously checked their papers and recorded their departures and re-entries.

The officers were clearly a little behind in their checking that morning as the line of those waiting was long. None would have dared to complain. Most of them appeared to be tradesmen. Some, with carts, would be going just beyond the first stretch of the road to the nearby towns. Among the tradesmen were others, presumably leaving on private errands.

As Eamon and his escort of Hands approached he saw that the officers at the line were poring over a passage paper with unconvinced looks. While the two lieutenants discussed the parchment Eamon looked back to the waiting line. An old man and his wife stood at its head, patiently waiting to pass.

With a decisive nod the lieutenants turned to the couple.

"These aren't legitimate."

The old man looked surprised. "Of course they are," he answered. "They were authorized by the Crown Office yesterday." He pointed to a red seal on the paper. "Mr Rose sealed it himself."

The officer seemed mollified by the seal but his fellow still looked doubtful. He was taking the parchment from his colleague, meaning to study it again, when he caught sight of Eamon's entourage of Hands. At once he, his fellow, and the whole line of waiting men dropped into deep bows.

"Lord Cathair." The lieutenant primly greeted the Hand. "His glory!"

"Lieutenant," the green-eyed Hand, Cathair, answered. The lieutenant rose smartly and the others round him gingerly followed suit. Eamon caught sight of a tremor running through the woman at the old man's arm.

"You have the look of a man perplexed, lieutenant," Cathair spoke with mocking eloquence. "What is it that ails you?"

The lieutenant held out the papers. "My lord, this man gives his business as a journey south to visit his son. The papers are signed and sealed by the East Crown Office, but I query them, my lord."

Cathair looked piercingly at the waiting couple and then gestured sharply. Taking his meaning the lieutenant passed the papers up to the Hand. A small smile spread over his face.

"You are right, lieutenant, that everything seems very much in order," he said. "But a querying never goes amiss. Mr Goodman?"

Eamon stepped to the Hand's side. Cathair held the papers before him. "Your opinion, Mr Goodman?"

Eamon saw the official rigmarole authorizing travel, written in a short hand. The names of the travelling pair, Jovan and Mrs Clarence, headed the note. At the bottom was an elaborate signature, underscored with the emblem of the Crown Office. A red seal, bearing a crown, was next to it. Eamon wet his lips. The seal was smudged, as though it had been done too quickly. It was not the kind of residue he would expect from a Crown Office.

Clarence was watching him carefully.

Eamon looked up at Cathair. "I am but lately arrived, my lord," he said at last. "I am afraid I know little how to judge such matters."

"I will show you how to judge." Cathair raised his gloved hand over the seal. A deep red light formed about the palm. It proceeded to search both paper and seal. The seal gave a ruddy glow, but this neither waned nor increased as the light on the Hand's palm intensified. It was a simple wax mark.

The Hand lowered the parchment and turned to the old man.

"Mr Clarence, are you aware of the process by which passage papers are ratified?" His voice was pleasant enough but Eamon already knew that such a tone from this man could not be trusted.

Jovan Clarence nodded. "Yes, my lord."

"Then you know that ratification by Mr Rose is accompanied by ratification by a Hand serving in his office. Papers ratified in this fashion, Mr Clarence, answer, light to light, to others in the Master's service. It is a simple but effective means of validation."

The old man had fallen silent. Men behind him in the waiting line fiddled nervously with their own documents.

"As has been clearly demonstrated, this paper has not been authorized. Gentlemen, detain Mr and Mrs Clarence for questioning."

"No!"

With a cry Mrs Clarence broke away from her husband's arm and ran as fast as she could out of the gate and onto the East Road. The old man tried to race after her but the Gauntlet caught him and dragged him backwards.

With an indolent smile Lord Cathair raised his arm and a sphere of light, red like the one he had cast at the Hidden Hall, sprang from it towards the fleeing woman. Eamon bit his lip.

"Maddy!" The old man screeched but was powerless to help her. The scarlet orb struck the woman full in the back, sending her to the ground in a torrent of flailing limbs. At a sharp whistle from their master, Cathair's dogs charged the collapsed woman. As the red light faded the howling dogs fell upon their prey; gargled cries came from her. Eamon saw the reddened flash of tooth and claw, and looked away.

Cathair had turned coldly back to the lieutenants. "Mr Clarence will be detained and will reveal what nest of snakes supplied him with these papers."

"Yes, my lord." The lieutenant had to raise his voice to be heard over the insensate sobbing of the man he restrained. Ensigns were called from the gatehouse and the old man was handed over to them. Those waiting in the line lowered their eyes as he was taken away.

With another whistle Cathair called back his hounds. The beasts bounded happily to him, blood and spittle on their muzzles. Cathair urged his horse onwards.

"Get the snake off the road, gentlemen."

"His glory, my lord."

Lord Cathair nodded to them. Eamon passed through the Blind Gate in his wake.

The streets of Dunthruik were crowded with buildings that rose so tall in places that they kept the sun from reaching the streets below. In the early light many men were leaving home and making either for the port or for the North Gate to go on to the vineyards or the distant quarry. In places the Coll was marked with grand buildings, the reserves of the city's noblest families. These had gardens that stretched behind them and open squares that lay before. The Coll ran to the Four Quarters, the heart of the city. From the centre of the crossroads a man could see to each of the other city gates. The theatre stood nearby and, as Cathair continued up the Coll towards the west and the Sea Gate, Eamon saw the palace itself. Its roofs and arches were worked from bold stones, and banners snapped above them.

The Coll led to the palace but they did not go that far. Cathair took them off the road to the left into a well-sized square. A broad plinth, supporting a statue, was at its centre. The Hand advised him that the square was called the Brand.

At the square's far side stood a large building. The flag over it showed an arched crown. Ensigns stood on guard at the steps that led to the doors and, as they approached, Eamon saw the shapes of corridors, offices, dormitories, and courtyards stretching back beyond the doorway and entry hall.

Relief ran through him; the Gauntlet college was achingly familiar. He smiled, remembering the gruel of the early morning runs, the sweat and the confusion, hours upon hours of weapons practice and law and geography, the endless parades and rush to have the uniform spotless before them. His thought wandered back to Edesfield.

"This is the West Quarter Gauntlet College," Cathair told him. "It is where you and Mr Spencing were to be stationed." The mention of Spencing's name chilled him. "As the largest college in Dunthruik, the West is well equipped and impeccably run. You will serve here, under Captain Waite."

"Yes, my lord."

"I will send for you when the Master wishes to see you," the Hand continued, his green eyes gleaming. "Captain Waite will see that you settle in. He has a small room set aside for you."

"That is kind of him, my lord." The privilege of a private room was normally the reserve of first lieutenants and their betters.

Lord Cathair smiled. "I thought that you might appreciate the gesture, Mr Goodman, and arranged it with him."

How could the Hand possibly have arranged it? They had only met the previous day.

"Forgive me, Lord Cathair, I did not mean to offend you by attributing your generosity to –"

"'Redoubled is a small offence made in officious temperament'." Eamon fairly gaped; the Hand was reciting poetry. "You are forgiven, Mr Goodman," Cathair added grandly.

"You are most gracious, my lord."

"I am afraid that I must leave you to present yourself, Mr Goodman. I will send for you."

Cathair gestured for his fellows to carry on to the palace. With shock, Eamon realized the Hands were taking Mathaiah with them.

"My lord –"

"The Master's best physicians keep turn at the palace, Mr Goodman," the Hand answered, offering him a consoling smile.

"He will be entrusted to the best care."

"Again, my lord, you are kind." Eamon hoped desperately that Mathaiah would withstand whatever was held in store for him.

"Tell Captain Waite who you are, and that I sent you. We shall speak soon, Mr Goodman."

Eamon's stomach churned as they went – Mathaiah's form, prostrate still in sleep or by Handcraft, and Cathair's hounds, blood on their jowls.

The walls of the college towering over him, Eamon recalled his task. He yearned for the Dunthruik of his boyhood, the books of his father, the comfort of his mother…

But he was no longer a child. And he had much to do.

He walked up the college steps. The two ensigns on guard did not hinder him.

The doorway led to an open hall where the Gauntlet's golden crown hung on each wall. Through the far archway and across an open courtyard Eamon saw another building on which hung a banner showing a raven. Eamon stopped; it was the same emblem that he had seen on Cathair. He remembered then that the raven was the emblem of the Hand who held that quarter of the city.

Lord Cathair was the Lord of the West Quarter.

Eamon breathed deep to steady his fraying nerves, then turned to fix his thought on the walls again. On the one nearest to him was a wooden panel that bore a list of the names of officers from the college who had gone on to become Hands. For a single college, it was an impressive list.

A small group of cadets came into the hall. They were sweating from training and eyed him discreetly from where they stood. Like Mathaiah the young men were probably in their last year of training. It spoke well of them; during the three years of training as a Gauntlet cadet, it was not uncommon to lose a high number of men to sickness, death, injury, or disqualifying behaviour.

Decisively, Eamon approached them.

"Gentlemen, I'm looking for Captain Waite."

The young men exchanged glances. One of them looked him up and down with a raised eyebrow. It was then that Eamon realized that not only was he not wearing his uniform – that had been left in the Hidden Hall – but these cadets had not seen him escorted to the college by Lord Cathair. Their suspicion, if not their disparaging glances, was entirely justified: Gauntlet rules were severe when it came to civilians on college premises.

"You one of his spies?" one of the cadets asked. "Or one of theirs?" His companions snickered.

Eamon blinked in surprise. Was it common for wayfarers to infiltrate the Gauntlet, or merely a common fear?

He focused hard on the young man who had spoken to him. He was going to have to play the arrogant officer to them. He rolled his eyes and glared.

"Do you know what the penalties are for taking airs with an officer, cadet?" He didn't give the shocked young man time to respond. "Evidently not. Shall I remind you? They involve extra duties, incarceration, lashes, degrading, and a permanent mark on your record which, ultimately, translates into the worst posts and duties when they give you the privilege of a pin." He smiled sweetly as the group exchanged astonished looks. "So, cadet, shall we try that again? If you can answer impeccably then perhaps I will let this little incident drop. Name and rank!" he barked.

The young man leapt to attention and gave a smart salute; he was perhaps a fraction less sharp than he should have been. "Third Banner Cadet Manners, sir!"

"Oh, Cadet Manners, is it?" Eamon asked snidely. "You have shown yourself lacking in any semblance of your namesake. Perhaps you have hopes of becoming an officer?" Manners grimaced but did not answer. "Then you'd better hope that I have a dull memory. You there," he continued, pointing to the other cadets, "form a line; look sharp!"

The cadets leapt into line. Eamon felt sorry for them; he knew how terrifying it was to be berated by an officer, and if they had hopes of getting their names onto the board that shadowed the threshold a single blemish on their records would be a severe disadvantage to them.

"Sign!" he commanded.

The cadets gave their company and full names in turn, following each announcement with a crisply uttered "sir". Smiling, Eamon walked up and down in front of them.

"Better," he told them. "But you won't have a second chance to make such a mistake with me. I am Lieutenant Eamon Goodman, late of Edesfield, and was escorted here by the Lord Cathair to speak with Captain Waite." The young men grew paler. What kind of Hand was Cathair that he inspired such fear? "When a stranger enters this hall you ask him for his name and rank. If he is Gauntlet you ask his business and escort him to an officer. If he is not, you give him one chance to leave and then take him to the brig. Is that clear?"

"Yes, sir!" The cadets gave the answer in chorus. Satisfied, Eamon nodded to them.

"At ease." The anxious line dropped their formal stances. "Now, Mr Manners, where shall I find Captain Waite?"

The cadet looked ashen. "Behind you, sir."

Eamon turned and saw a man who might have been in his early fifties leaning against one wall. His Gauntlet uniform had five bright flames pinned at its collar. The captain began to applaud, slowly and with delight.

"Well done, lieutenant, well done!" He was a tall man and his hair had receded into shades of grey. His sleeves were rolled up and there were long scars along his arms, giving the impression of a captain who had not only seen service but who liked to train his cadets himself.

"Give these young bastards a taste of discipline," the captain growled. "Hop to it, gentlemen! You'll very shortly be late for parade and I'm in a foul mood this morning."

The cadets scarpered.

"Manners, I want to see your boots as black as coal!" the captain bellowed after them, his voice following the fleeing cadets down the corridors. With a small laugh the captain turned back to Eamon. "They're indolent pups, Mr Goodman, but good ones. Come with me to my office and we'll talk."

Not sure whether or not to feel embarrassed, Eamon gave the captain a crisp salute (which made the man smile) and followed him to the officers' quarters.

The captain paused outside one door and opened it, revealing an office with a window that viewed a training yard. Through it Eamon could see a lieutenant drilling young men with bows. A long line of targets had been set up at the far end of the yard and the lieutenant was in the process of assisting a cadet with no strength in his arms to draw the bowstring fully.

The captain watched for a few moments, one hand resting pensively on his chin, then turned back to Eamon. Smiling once more, Waite moved to his desk and ran his hands through a pile of papers.

"That lordly rat Cathair just left you here, I take it?"

"Yes sir," Eamon answered, then, "I mean, no sir."

"I see," Waite answered. "Now, would you mean by your beguiling statement that he didn't leave you here but is a rat, or that he left you here but you would refrain from calling him a rat? One should be more precise in one's responses, lieutenant."

"Perhaps I meant neither, sir. Perhaps the question was indistinctly phrased."

The smile on Waite's face grew into a broad grin. He pulled some papers from his pile and laughed loudly.

"Lord Cathair did say that you would introduce yourself," Waite remarked, "though perhaps that is not what he had in mind." Eamon saluted again and drew breath to announce name and rank, but Waite waved the gesture away. "No need, Mr Goodman. I think you introduced yourself well enough when you gave Manners and his motley collection a good seeing to in the hall. Typical third-year cadets: strutting about as if they own the place one moment, crawling about like the greenest recruit the next. Poor lads. They must have a fearful captain to instil such insecurities in them." He shook his head sadly. Eamon smiled at the self-deprecating humour. "But they'll make Hands, Mr Goodman. All mine do, in the end. Your poor Captain Belaal hates that! He never wanted to be posted to a backwater like Edesfield." He looked up thoughtfully. "Isn't it about as close to Backwater as you can get and still be in the River Realm?"

"Yes, sir," Eamon answered. The town of Backwater, which had garnered a reputation for being more than extraordinarily dull, was about two days' ride from Edesfield.

"Well, it's Belaal's fault, really," Waite mused. "Was terribly insulting to a senior officer just after he made first lieutenant; they sent him to serve in Edesfield where all his superiors – old, balding men – eventually died off, leaving him in charge. Poor Belaal always did have a temper. Always hated me for getting this post. I worked my way up, too – didn't start as a cadet – I was a militiaman-nobody before they put me to the Gauntlet. Let these be a lesson to you," he added, gesturing to the five bright flames at his throat. "I distinguished myself, Mr Goodman; distinguished and made good."

"Yes, sir."

"The question, Mr Goodman," Waite added, "is whether you will be a good man? Or not?" The captain smiled at his pun. "And, if you make good, will you go on Belaal's Hand-scoreboard, or mine?"

The thought of his name ranked on the board drew the breath from Eamon's lungs; he eagerly desired it! But then Hughan's face came before him, and the memory of the sword that had been bestowed on him. Was not First Knight a higher accolade?

Waite laughed. "It appeals to your pride, does it, being a pawn in a competition between old enemies? Well, you were to be assigned to me once your holk came in. So was the other idiot."

Eamon started. The captain shook his head. "Meaning no

offence to Mr Spencing, but I read his files; you were the only good thing on that rotten boat. I am very much looking forward to interviewing the cadet you rescued and hearing his account of what happened."

"Sir, please do not speak ill of Spencing," Eamon began. "He would have grown into a better man than he was."

"Petty, snivelling, conniving, whining, overbearing guttersnipe? Maybe he would have done. One or two of Belaal's did." He fixed Eamon with a firm gaze. "But you were never meant for Captain Belaal. You, Lieutenant Goodman, were meant to walk these halls a little while, and then to walk those." The captain gestured in the direction of the palace. "And I mean to send you there."

Eamon was overwhelmed. Did Waite really mean to make him a Hand? It would be the easiest way to get close to the throned and learn all he could – but there were ceremonies. If what had happened when he swore to the Gauntlet was any indication, then becoming a Hand would be perilous indeed.

"Thank you, sir," he stammered.

"*Tsk!*" The captain pronounced the sound loudly, as though he were shooing away a large bee. "Lord Cathair has put you here to be babysat. But you will be weaned. Belaal made you a lieutenant for some good, if not outstanding, service, and perhaps he was right to do so – though his ornamental promotions have rarely turned out well. I think your actions in the days since your capture and escape qualify the promotion he so quickly gave you. You will join my officers, you will beat my men into shape, and you will learn, lieutenant, many things that Captain Belaal never had the wit to teach you. Then you will serve the Master. You look surprised?"

Eamon felt it.

Waite laughed again. "Do not be so. I have met from time to time with the Lord Ashway. He is the Lord of the East Quarter, and a seer. He has seen much of what you will become." He lowered his voice, "Mr Goodman, Right Hand is not beyond you."

Eamon gasped. Right Hand? The Right Hand was closest to the

Master and lord over all things in the Master's name. The idea filled his veins with fire.

Eben Goodman had been Right Hand.

The fire of ambition turned to ashes and the gasp upon his lips to one of dread.

"Sir –"

"Lord Ashway also said you would make first lieutenant within two days of your arrival," Waite added flippantly, "and get your name submitted for admission to the Hands within a week." Eamon wondered if the captain was joking; perhaps he said the same things to all his new officers. "But let me be clear, lieutenant: there's going to be a lot of sweat, some definite blood, and perhaps a tear or two before then."

"Yes, sir," Eamon answered, smiling despite himself.

Waite laid the pile of papers on his desk. Eamon caught sight of his name. He presumed it to be his file and wondered what it read.

"Your room is the third down this passage on the right," Waite continued. "You can go and array yourself there. Then you'll join the parade. There's a uniform on your bed that I hope will fit you; if it doesn't you can go and see the seamstress. Within the hour you will drill the Third Banner cadets through the course and then we might let you have lunch with the officers. This afternoon you will attend the Handbook, which is a set of drills and classes that I run to prepare my officers for getting on that list. It's a good name, isn't it? This evening you will be posted to gate duty with some of my ensigns at the palace. You'll be there until second watch before coming back here, smartening your uniform and sleeping to be up bright and early in the morning ready for a new day."

Eamon saluted. The security of the routine relieved him – but being posted to the palace disturbed him. He would be more exposed there, but perhaps he would be able to hear some news of Mathaiah.

The captain looked at him. Eamon yearned to please him and rise to Right Hand as had been foreseen… But how could he be sworn to either throned or King when each cancelled the other out so entirely?

Would it not be easier, simpler, to stay and obey this captain?

His eyes passed over the paper that bore his name. Anonymous was the one thing that he would never be.

With an order that Eamon barely heard, Waite dismissed him.

Eamon moved quietly down the corridor, counting the doors. His room was small, and furnished with a bed, a desk and chair, and a window through which spiralled the shadows of a distant arch.

A red uniform lay smartly on the bed, its collar marked with the two flames of his rank. Three flames would be first lieutenant, four draybant, and five a captain. Distinction at two or three flames could set him among the Hands. Beyond captains there were the Master's Gauntlet generals, but to Eamon's mind a captain's five pins were the ultimate mark of authority. He had never seen six.

Half in a dream he touched the flames. They were cool. The whole uniform seemed to call to him. His blood rushed in his veins and strange strength in his flesh; light touched his palm, answering the flames on the jacket.

He had almost forgotten the mark. The sight was like a stab to the heart. He remembered Jovan Clarence and his dead wife, her throat torn by Cathair's dogs.

He had been in Dunthruik all of two hours and he had already seen things that he could never condone. And yet by wearing that uniform… How could he carry flames at his throat and serve the King? Could the King really save any man from the power that sat in the palace, surrounded by Hands and defended by hundreds upon hundreds of young men who knew nothing but the prestige of donning red?

He snatched his hand from the uniform. He could not wear it. He would not. It would devour him; it would force him to betray himself.

It had seemed so simple in the Hidden Hall: go to Dunthruik, pretend to be the lieutenant that the throned wanted him to be, and learn all he could. Stay hidden, like the hall. But how could he?

They would know – of course they would know. Did he really think that he could keep his purpose from the throned?

He felt on the edge of a precipice. He knew the path to escape – the inn on Serpentine Avenue. His limbs tensed, ready to flee.

He closed his eyes and drew a deep breath, forcing it through his body to calm his heart. Then, so quickly that he wondered if he saw it at all, he saw with other eyes.

He saw what seemed to be a man riding on a field of battle before broad city walls. Rain poured down around him, clattering on helm and armour as he raised a shattered standard over his head.

"King's men!" he cried, his voice so strange and loud that it seemed the whole earth should wake and rally to that call. "The West Bank for the King!"

An answering roar rose up; Eamon realized that the calling rider was a woman. More than that: it was Elaina.

The vision was gone. Eamon opened his eyes. His heart still pounded with the clamour of battle but his hand now lay dull before him.

He picked up the uniform. Hating himself, he drew the thing on and gathered his oath to the King about his unsteady heart.

Outside he heard a trumpet call: parade was about to begin. Tucking the papers and the heart of the King safely away, he quickly put on the red jacket, buckled on sword and dagger, and hurried out into the morning light.

CHAPTER XII

Parade was something that Eamon had always enjoyed, for it showed the companies of the Gauntlet at their very best: prim, smart, a moving block of colour and strength. But as he made his way into the courtyard, still tugging at his jacket (which was slightly too big) and straightening his collar, Eamon saw that Edesfield's parades had been a paltry affair where peasants and rogues played the roles of soldiers and gentlemen. In Waite's yard the men, whatever their rank, were as crisp as dew-dotted blades of grass and stood in line just as silently. Swords were slung at their sides and the emblem of the crown blazed on every breast. No muddy boots, no tousled heads, no bleary eyes. It was an awesome sight.

Quickly Eamon identified the column where the officers stood. A first lieutenant was at its head and many lieutenants stood behind him, each the master of a row of men. There was a gap near the front, next to Cadet Manners. Guessing this to be his place Eamon marched neatly over and took it. A worried look passed over the young man's face. Eamon mostly succeeded in not laughing. He had not been in Dunthruik a day and he was already feared!

"Present!" barked a voice. Like an ocean wave the whole body of men drew their swords and held them upright, cross-guards before their faces, in salute. The iron crop glistened.

Captain Waite came down from a platform at the head of the courtyard and began inspecting each man, his years of experience allowing him to move quickly along the lines. He did this mostly in silence; there was little for him to complain about.

Eamon watched the captain, thinking how much more a man he was than Belaal. Waite's face was sincere and his manner, though impeccable, was not uncaring. The men in the yard were testament to the captain's will and skill, and every one of them that went on to become more than a simple ensign would be an extra feather to his cap. There was more than pride and ambition to Waite's careful inspection: it was a labour of love.

The process took only a few minutes. Satisfied, the captain returned to his platform, thanked the men for their impressive turnout, and gave orders for the companies to file out, each to their designated tasks.

As the first lieutenant led his row away it occurred to Eamon that he did not know where the course was. He felt the threat of panic, for the line in front of him was now moving away. With sudden inspiration, he turned to Cadet Manners.

"Lead on, cadet."

The young man gaped, astounded, as though to question this apparent madness: it was a lieutenant's job to lead the line. But an order was an order, and he had received one.

Saluting, the cadet led the line away. Eamon took a step back and looked at each man – the Third Banner Cadets, Captain Waite had called them – as they passed.

Edesfield had been a small college, with only one group of cadets taken in each year, and so the groups had been known by their year: first, second, or third cadets. But in Dunthruik each college would have scores of cadets in each year, and those cadets would have to be grouped together into smaller units for training. The Third Banner cadets would be one of many other college groups, each marked by their year and their own names.

The cadets were all about the same age, fine young men who aspired to the captain's enticing Hand-board. Their faces remained neutral, but he was sure that they all either wondered about their new lieutenant or had already heard wildly inaccurate tales about him. News about new officers spread quickly, especially among cadets.

He joined the end of the line and marched along with it, turning his gaze smartly towards the captain in an honorary salute. A smile crossed Waite's face. He suspected that the captain had been waiting to see how he would deal with the gap in his information. Part of him was amused by Waite's small test; the rest worried what consequence would follow the failing of any of them.

The course was set in a muddy field at the back of the college and made up of a selection of obstacles: deep ditches and tunnels and a wooden frame hung with ropes to climb. There were potholes to avoid, a length of variable terrain to run at speed, and, at the far end of the miserable concoction, another group of cadets to beat in swordplay. The Banner cadets would have to do the course with a heavy pack (weighted, in Eamon's own experience, with bricks). Only the best (or the luckiest) could stay the course and win the challenge that awaited them on the other side of "the river" – the wide, sodden ditch through which they would have to wade to reach their opponents.

Eamon had always hated the course with an undignified and unbelievable passion, mostly because he had only once made it through and then only by the skin of his teeth. While he had been training he and Ladomer had often run it together, and though Ladomer had never failed it Eamon had ended up face down in the mud (usually from the crippling height of the frame) more often than he cared to remember. The frame in the West Quarter College brought to mind the many, many times that Ladomer had come, fairly doubled with mirth, to haul him out of the mud.

The cadets had formed neat ranks at the beginning of the course. At the other side of the long field beyond "the river", another group of cadets was lining up. They seemed a merry company – unsurprising, given that they had the morning's easier task. Eamon wondered which group they were. Being riverside had always been his preferred place. He mused that he wasn't going to have to crawl through the mud on this occasion. No, his task was to make fifteen young men crawl through it.

Eamon strode to the front of the ranks and looked at the young men in his charge. Officer training was given to cadets during their preparation, but such training in Edesfield had been lax and he was not as prepared as he might have liked. Most officer training was done as an ensign. Eamon had admittedly spent his own years as a cadet watching how dozens of officers, Ladomer not least among them, handled their men, through fear or honest enough affection. But to be suddenly faced with a group of young men whose obedience he had to win was daunting. It had been easier on the holk; the cadets there had seemed but boys, and they had known him. These cadets were more like men – well settled in their opinions, competent, capable, close to swearing to the Master – and he was a stranger on their turf.

"Sign!" he barked.

Beginning at one end of the line the cadets gave their surnames. Most of them would be local to the West Quarter. They answered crisply and, when the last man was reached, the cadet added:

"Third Banners all present and correct, sir!"

A bead of sweat trickled down his neck. "I am Lieutenant Goodman. Captain Waite has put you in my charge to make you more than cadets; he wants you to be officers and lauded Hands." He changed his tone. "You had better be swift in demonstrating your capacities, gentlemen, because I can't see why the captain has such faith in you. Packs!"

At his command the cadets picked up the heavy loads that they had to carry round the course. Wooden practice blades, used in training, awaited them at the far end of the course. Some of the cadets disposed of their red jackets, unwilling to get them muddy. Eamon watched the cadets adjusting the straps about their shoulders. He picked one of them at random.

"Mr Ostler."

"Sir?" the young man answered swiftly – and with the slightest trace of insolence.

Eamon chose to ignore it. "Whom are you facing this morning?"

There was a pause. Eamon waited.

Ostler glanced quietly at his fellows, seeking reassurance. Eamon cocked a quizzical eyebrow at him. He was strangely aware of the cadets at the far end of the field and the first lieutenant who strutted among them. But he waited.

"They're the Third Ravens, sir," Ostler answered at last. "The West Quarter's finest."

"Does that worry you, Mr Ostler?"

"We never beat them, sir," Ostler answered grimly.

"On a field of battle, Mr Ostler," Eamon told him, "banners fly courageously in the thickest press. On such a field, a raven is no more than a latecomer and a carrion bird." He matched the cadet's gaze, and smiled. "What you mean to say is that you haven't beaten them *yet*."

The cadets exchanged brief, unsure looks.

"Are you ready, gentlemen?"

"Sir!" At his command they charged the course.

Eamon followed them round it, berating them and encouraging them to remember the beating they had to give the Third Ravens at the other end. His own arms felt the strain as they tackled the frame and slid down the ropes into the mud. As he harried them Ladomer's voice was in his mind, harrying him. He soon found his friend's remembered words on his lips.

"Come on, Ford!" he shouted. The young man had climbed the frame and slowed considerably, almost to a walk. "Run as though the Serpent himself were before you!"

Most of the cadets neared the river at about the same time; they were energetic young men and handling the course well. Eamon followed them, realizing that his status was no protection against mud; it spattered him regardless. He yelled at the stragglers, forcing them to press on to the river.

It wasn't long before the Banners, led by a determined Cadet Manners, were forging a path through the river, up to their thighs in mud. Eamon exhorted them to pull themselves through it and out to the other side.

Manners escaped the river first and grabbed one of the swords on the far side of the ditch. The cadet charged the Ravens, yelling. A few feet behind him the first of his fellows were also emerging. The Ravens, most of them smug, stepped forward one at a time to tackle their filth-ridden foes. Behind them Eamon saw the first lieutenant, a thin man with tawny hair, inciting his cadets.

"Give the third bastards a beating!" he yelled.

Eamon took an immediate dislike to him. He called encouragement to his cadets and to Manners in particular. The young man was making a valiant attempt at his foe but he would be bested, his sword heavy in his weary hands. The cadet he fought answered his thrusts with mischievous parries. Manners tripped, fell, and his opponent declared victory. The next Banner went down seconds later.

"On!" Eamon yelled, but he knew as mud-man after man emerged that the Ravens were simply going to pick the tired cadets off one by one. He sighed inwardly, watching as the defeated hauled themselves off to one side, the victors to another. Both groups cheered their own comrades. The Banners had done the course swiftly and efficiently but only in beating an opponent at the far side could a man be said to have completed it. Ladomer had never failed. "Move your feet, Smith!"

His encouragement made little difference. None of the Banners would finish. But he kept calling them on, rallying them to fight to the last.

"It looks as though I whipped your B-hinds," said a sudden voice by him. The first lieutenant wore the kind of superior smile that Eamon hated.

With effort he forced his tongue to civility. "With respect, sir, I didn't see you fighting any of them," he replied curtly.

"No." The first lieutenant favoured Eamon with a piteous look. "Normally the officer of the winning party duels the losing one, to give him one last chance to redeem his company's honour. But I fear, Mr Goodman, that there's nothing left to save. And," he added, with the singsong intonation of insincere platitudes, "I think you would merely make the predicament worse. Such a pity."

Eamon's blood boiled; it was Spencing all over again. He wanted to challenge the man but such behaviour was not condoned among officers. Every eye was on him. It was his first day in Dunthruik, his first morning as a West Quarter officer. He could not make a spectacle of himself. Responding to the first lieutenant's baiting would only mark him out as an easy victim in the future.

He looked with forced calm at the first lieutenant. "I could hardly duel you, sir. I am, as you see, somewhat muddy, and I fear that you might find your pins tarnished if I answered you."

So saying, he turned his back and strode to his muddy cadets. "Third Banner Cadets, fall in!" It was time for them to get cleaned up.

The cadets lined up in all their muddied glory. They were exhausted, but even in the face of their unilateral defeat they found it in themselves to cheer. Cadets on both sides jeered their opponents while others offered congratulations and praise: their positions would soon be reversed.

But as Eamon led the Banners from the field he felt the first lieutenant's eyes pinned to his back.

A system of water troughs was arranged in one of the college yards and it was to them that Eamon and his company went. Eamon gave the cadets free rein to clean up while he brushed the drying mud from his trousers and jacket. The stuff adhered to the fabric as though to tempest-tossed driftwood. There was mud stuck to his face and hands.

"Good work, gentlemen," he told the cadets. The sun was rising higher; he loosened his tight collar. "You came very close to teaching those pomposities a lesson they deserve."

"Is 'pomposities' a word, sir?" piped up Overbrook. He had a scholarly look and had been among those lagging in the course. The cadet's query elicited snickers and groans, as though only Overbrook would ask such a question.

"It isn't a word!" Overbrook insisted, exasperated. His tenacity was met with more groans and attempts to cover him in water.

"Ignore him, sir!" called Ostler.

"A question often deserves an answer, Cadet Ostler," Eamon replied with a small smile. "Mr Overbrook, you will find that 'pomposities' is indeed a word. Even were it not, I would say to you that the distinguishing mark of our greatest playwrights is their brazen invention of words each time they set their tremulous quills to paper. I would in the latter case, therefore," he continued, "be not only an officer of the Gauntlet, but also a fine playwright in the making."

There was a moment of silence that suddenly filled with noise as the cadets jibed their bested company scholar. Overbrook stared at Eamon for a moment. Then the cadet's face broke into a grin.

"A good answer, sir," he said, and returned to his washing.

They spent what was left of the morning engaged in the weapons drills and practices that were the quotidian affairs of Gauntlet colleges: weapons and swordplay, tactics, River Realm law and geography. Eamon turned his hand to each of them. He was sure that many of the cadets viewed him with suspicion but at least none of them was willing to challenge him openly. They might grumble behind his back (all cadets did), but they would do as they were told, which was as good a place to start as any. Even Manners seemed to be getting over the morning's ungainly introduction.

When lunchtime finally came, Eamon felt exhausted. He dismissed the cadets to their own mess to eat and made his way slowly to the main courtyard. He saw another building, fashioned from dark stones, across the way, and paused. A black banner showing the raven marked the threshold. The building had to be one of Cathair's haunts. It made sense that a Quarter Hand would have offices in his quarter's college. He peered up at the windows but was relieved to see no shapes behind them.

He obtained directions to the officers' mess from a passing servant. His uniform, still patched with dry mud about the ankles, pulled awkwardly at him.

He reached the mess doors and went inside as nonchalantly as he could. Despite his effort every eye from every table turned to him as he went up to the hatch serving food. Lunch appeared to consist of thick soup and some bread. He obtained both from the old woman serving and made his way to one of the tables that was still empty. Sitting down was more pleasurable than it had been for a long time, and as he began to eat – and it became clear that he meant to do nothing more – the curious gazes fell from him.

He didn't stay sitting alone for long. A group of officers approached him, jibing among themselves. One of them was the first lieutenant.

Eamon made an effort to look more involved with his food in the hope that they would leave him alone, but his effort was in vain. The party came to an expectant halt before him; he was obliged to give the odious first lieutenant some mark of respect.

Silently, he rose and saluted.

"Sir," he said, formally. His eyes met the first lieutenant's own. The man looked him up and down, his gaze lingering with withering criticism on the mud stains.

"Might we join you, Lieutenant Goodman?"

Eamon didn't see that he could refuse and so, like a welcoming host, gestured to the table.

"Of course."

The officers sat and Eamon regained his seat. Quietly he looked askance at each of them. Two other lieutenants accompanied the first lieutenant. One of these was tall and lank, pale-skinned and dark-haired, while the other seemed of a slightly more than average build and had an ostensibly friendly face.

"I don't believe we've been introduced?" Eamon began. The friendly looking lieutenant smiled.

"I'm Lieutenant Best," he volunteered. "I command the First Crimsons." He gestured to the lanky man beside him. "This is Lieutenant Fields. He has the Second Arrows. You've already met First Lieutenant Alben."

"Yes, we had an altercation this morning," Alben said with a smile.

Cordially, Eamon shook hands with each of them over the table. "A pleasure, gentlemen," he said, turning his attention firmly back to his food. His new companions failed to take the hint.

Alben took up his mug. "You must tell them, Eamon – may I call you Eamon?" Eamon nodded reluctantly. "How kind – how badly yours did against the Third Ravens today. Well and truly slaughtered." He took a delicate sip of his drink. Eamon supposed that he was probably born of a reasonably well-off family, and liked to show it. "Then again," Alben added, "cadets are young things. They can hardly be held responsible for being set under poor leadership."

"I'm sure Captain Waite wouldn't –" Best began and then, seeing the look on the first lieutenant's face, he reddened and muttered: "Of course, poor leadership, very poor."

Eamon grimaced, trying not to rise to the bait.

Alben ate a while, and then leaned across the table to him again. "Mr Goodman, they say that you were captured by wayfarers and that you surrendered your sword. Is that so?"

Eamon was stunned. How could that be known already?

Taking his silence as confirmation, the first lieutenant tutted his tongue between impeccable teeth. "Surrendered his sword!" Alben raised his voice such that most of the mess could hear. "Would you believe that, gentlemen? To snakes! Foolishness, trite foolishness, and quite unforgivable. A Gauntlet officer should have died rather." He turned to Eamon again. "I hear you came up from Edesfield, one of Captain Belaal's boys?" Alben smiled with empty comfort. "Well, that's nothing to be ashamed of, even if you were given a commission when he was drunk. Or maybe you were given it in return for something else?"

"Backwater folk," Fields added, laughing with force at odds with his slim frame. Best looked momentarily tempted to contradict this searing generalization, but instead chuckled uncomfortably.

Eamon fought still harder to keep back the retorts and impulse to strike Alben. Why was he being so purposefully baited, and how did the first lieutenant already know about the holk? He was sure that Cathair would not have made it public information.

The laughter continued.

"Have you nothing to say, Mr Goodman?" Alben persisted. "Or have we hit so close to the mark that you are robbed of speech?"

Eamon finished a piece of bread and looked the first lieutenant straight in the eye.

"I am sure that the Third Banners will give your company a good lesson tomorrow, Mr Alben," he said. "Should they not, I would be more than happy to answer your curiosity as to my commission at a time and place of your convenience." The words had slipped out before he could stop them.

The laughter stopped abruptly. There was no hiding what Eamon had proposed.

"I hope you're not suggesting a duel, Mr Goodman," Alben said. Officers were not forbidden to duel – indeed, sometimes it was the only way to reconcile differences between conflicting men – but the Gauntlet did not endorse it. Duelling could lead to black marks on personal reports.

Inwardly cursing his lack of restraint, Eamon offered the man a smile of his own. "Quite the contrary," he answered civilly. "I am merely suggesting that you might like me to assist you in making a thorough, practical inspection of your sword; it seemed to me today that it had rusted to your scabbard."

For a moment Alben looked as though he might retaliate. But then he laughed.

"I should be only too glad to, Mr Goodman," he said. "I am sure there will be time for us to settle the matter. Shall we say tomorrow evening?" Eamon nodded silently.

With another laugh, Alben rose and strode away. Fields immediately followed him. Best rose more slowly. He leaned across the table, his large face genuinely perplexed.

"You need to be careful, Mr Goodman," he said. "The Third Banners needed a new lieutenant because Mr Basildon…" The lieutenant fumbled for words and his face grew red. "He was incapacitated in an accident," he finished, as tactfully as he could. "A great loss."

"Thank you, Mr Best," Eamon answered.

With a half smile and a mournful shake of his head, Best left the table.

Eamon breathed deeply, as though the air had cleared at the lieutenants' departure. But as he thought about what had happened he felt his uniform tight and sticky about him.

Already sworn to a duel? He was a fool. If he carried on at this rate the only reputation he would garner would be that of never having lived long enough to learn anything for Hughan.

Sighing, he stood, dry mud falling from his trousers and boots. He left his plate unfinished. None of the other officers watched him as he went. They were, he mused, probably well accustomed to the first lieutenant picking on new arrivals, and had probably all been subjected to it themselves. They had seen what interested them.

He ducked out of the mess hall. The courtyard was now in the full light of the midday sun and it was hot, especially for September. It was a day for swimming, not soldiering. But he had the Handbook to attend and then duty at the palace. Somehow, he needed to find a way to reach Mathaiah. The thought of the cadet remaining in Cathair's charge was not a comforting one.

Eamon reminded himself that Mathaiah Grahaven was a resourceful young man, and that Hughan had faith in him.

Hughan. The name brought him up short.

Rubbing at his palm, Eamon stepped out across the courtyard. He saw Best and Fields moving towards the Long Room where most officer classes were held. Doubtless they were also going to the Handbook; the thought of spending the whole afternoon in their company did not improve Eamon's mood.

His boots crunched the gravel as he walked sullenly after them. Suddenly he heard a woman's laugh.

Alben stood in the shadow of one of the arches of the entrance hall. Beside him was a woman, nobly dressed. The airy laugh was hers.

Eamon looked away. Alben's private affairs were no concern of his, however public they were.

The afternoon passed slowly and Eamon, stuck behind a desk like a schoolboy, followed Waite's Handbook in distraction. The Hand who led the class was one of the West Quarter's own and spoke clearly and convincingly on duties, capacities, and passage papers in particular. But Alben had taken the desk behind and Eamon's skin crawled throughout the afternoon with the sense of being watched and ridiculed. The scent of the woman's perfume – floral, intoxicating – clung to the first lieutenant's clothes and seemed unbearably impudent to him.

When the afternoon drew to a close and the Hand had left, Eamon rose stiffly from his chair. Captain Waite ambled over, shuffling papers under his arm.

"Mr Goodman," he said, jovially. "How have you enjoyed today so far?"

"Well, sir." It was almost true.

"Good man!" the captain smiled. Eamon suspected that his name would be a source of endless amusement for his captain. He resigned himself to it. "I'm going over to the palace to interview this young cadet of yours. Lord Cathair likes to keep me informed as to such matters, which is very helpful of him, don't you find?"

"Indeed, sir."

"As you're to be on duty there, you'll come up with me – your cadets will follow later. I'm told that your Mr Grahaven is a bit... confused; Lord Cathair mentioned shadeweed – nasty, effective stuff. They do say that a familiar face can help to break the after-effects."

"Sir," Eamon saluted.

"Best find yourself another pair of trousers first, lieutenant!" Waite laughed, gesturing to the mud. "I'll meet you in the hall. The seamstress will be able to find you something."

The seamstress did find him another pair of trousers, though they were too tight, and when Eamon reached the hall he felt terribly self-conscious. The captain didn't comment on it. Speaking amicably, Waite led the way from the college out into the Brand.

Central Dunthruik in the early evening showed that night-time was to be a glamorous affair. Carriages, ornately fashioned and exquisitely decorated, were drawn through the streets by pure-bred horses that tossed proud heads. Soldiers were changing posts and Gauntlet red was everywhere, interspersed at intervals with the black of the Hands. Eamon had never seen so many of either. Captain Waite explained that the Hands often attended meetings at the palace. The frequency of such meetings was increasing as the situation with the east worsened.

"Those snakes are starting to be a bit of a nuisance, too," he commented wryly. "Springing up everywhere. Just last week we found one working in the quarter offices. Hands took him in there –" Waite gestured vaguely to a narrow side street; it led along the huge walls of the palace and to a darkly stoned door. "The Hands' Hall. They got some good information from him – had a breacher, like you. Wrecked the man's mind, though. Pity, really, as he deserved to feel every part of his execution. Doubt he felt a thing, he was so shot when they finished."

Eamon swallowed in a dry throat.

The Coll led to the palace gates; these were broad enough for ten men to walk abreast and unbelievably tall. A crowned golden eagle stood at their top, devouring a serpent. As he walked through them Eamon saw Gauntlet stationed everywhere, including above him where an opening in the walls' walkway allowed men to overlook who came and went. Each man stood sharply to attention as Waite passed; Eamon guessed that a good proportion of the palace detail came from the West Quarter College.

The gateway opened out into the Royal Plaza. Eamon stopped and stared.

The plaza was an enormous open space enclosed by the ring of the palace walls. Guards moved atop them and, in the colonnades beneath, Eamon saw doorways and stairways; he imagined that corridors passed through the thick walls and back into the palace itself. The centre of the huge square was divided into four spaces, each marked by a statue of the throned, his arm outstretched to support a bird. From where he stood Eamon could not tell which bird marked each quarter.

The whole square looked forward to the great buildings opposite the gates. These dwarfed every other building in the city. Steps ran up to a grand doorway – this he judged to be the main entrance to the palace. Above this was a balcony that spanned the whole length of the edifice; it was the monumental centrepiece to both the façade and the square, and Eamon knew at once that it was where the throned appeared when the majesties were held. The thought of it stole his breath.

"What do you think, Mr Goodman?"

Eamon tore his eyes from the balcony. "It leaves me speechless, sir," he managed.

The captain laughed. "In that, Mr Goodman, you are not alone. The balcony," he added, "is part of the throne room; the palace spreads back behind it."

"Will we go inside, sir?" Eamon breathed.

"We're going to the Hands' Hall," Waite told him. "It's more usual to take the side entrance for that, but I do enjoy seeing men's faces when they first see the Royal Plaza."

With Eamon close on his heels, Waite followed the inside of the walls before going into one of the small entrances that led into cool and seemingly interminable corridors. They passed dozens of doorways, mostly leading to the right; Eamon imagined that they were skirting the inside of the walls.

"We're passing through the East Wing of the palace," Waite advised him. "On this level are the Grand Dining Hall and the kitchens; below are the servants' passages and above you," he said, gesturing upwards, "are the guest quarters and the eyrie of the Right Hand."

Eamon glanced up and shuddered.

The corridor came at last to another doorway that opened into a broad yard. A gate was in the wall to the left. Waite advised him that it was known as the Hands' Gate and that it was the secondary entrance to the palace. Hands stood at either side of it.

They paused in the small gate yard. Eamon realized that the Hands' Gate was the same side entrance that Waite had pointed out to him from the Coll. A group of stable hands were rubbing down horses in the yard; Eamon thought that he recognized one of the beasts as Cathair's.

"Ah! Captain Waite!" A voice called happily to them and Eamon saw Cathair himself, a moving shadow untouched by daylight, under the colonnade that led to the dark building. "And Lieutenant Goodman, too! Such punctuality, gentlemen! It is most becoming."

"My lord." Waite bowed low and Eamon did the same. Cathair took Waite's hand and clasped it warmly.

"We shall go in together," he said.

Cathair led them into the Hands' Hall. The entry was a wide space furnished of dark grey stones, and evidently a place for receiving guests. A handful of doorways led from it, each one crested with a crowned eagle whose crimson jewels glistened. At first Eamon thought that the gems all shone by reflection, but even those on the darkened side of the hall seemed to smoulder.

Noting his confusion, Cathair smiled.

"Only marked Hands can pass through these doorways, Mr Goodman," he said. "Hands, and those whom they invite."

Eamon nodded silently. It was worth knowing.

Cathair led them to one of the doorways. Eamon tried to see if it had any distinguishing mark but saw none. As Cathair passed over the threshold there was a slight ripple between the dark lintels and suddenly Eamon saw a lit corridor stretching back into the building. It was as though at Cathair's command dark curtains had been drawn aside. The eagle over the posts shone brightly.

Cathair gestured graciously for them to pass within. When he fell into step behind them Eamon again saw the ripple, but from where he stood he could see through the doorway into the hall they had left. The whole effect reminded him strongly of the Hidden Hall. He wondered whether whatever it was that kept both functioning had common roots.

The corridor was long, and many rooms and several staircases, going both up and down, led from it.

They came to a halt before one of the corridor's doors; two men stepped out of it. One was a Hand. The other wore a maroon uniform, denoting him as a Gauntlet surgeon; he carried a stained, empty glass. He bowed.

"My lord," he said. "I have ministered to the cadet: you should find him a little more life-like." Eamon eyed the glass. What exactly had Mathaiah been made to drink?

"Good," Cathair answered. "Life is something which he has seemed to be lacking. Send the notary on your way out, doctor."

"Yes, my lord."

The doctor vanished down the corridor towards the hall, escorted by the other Hand. Whatever was left in the cup he carried stank terribly; Eamon's stomach turned. He hoped that Mathaiah had borne it well.

Cathair, a very picture of nobility, once again held the door open. Eamon passed under the shadow of the Hand's arm into a small room.

It was in many ways not unlike his room at the West Quarter College, furnished sparsely but comfortably with a bed and a couple of chairs. It had a north-facing window looking down into the central courtyard. Through it Eamon saw several Hands going about their business.

Mathaiah lay in the bed, dressed in a night-shift. The covers were drawn down from his breast and the young man breathed shallowly and swiftly, as though he was too hot. His vacant eyes stared, searching the ceiling for something that only he could see. Eamon's heart quickened.

A notary entered, bowed deeply to Cathair and then, at a nod from the Hand, sat to make his notes.

"Mr Grahaven was stationed at Edesfield," the Hand began, looking to Waite. "He seems to have had one or two run-ins with the concept of authority – not hard with Belaal issuing it! Apart from a few careless acts he has a clean – and very promising – record."

"I've read his file," Waite nodded, looking at the cadet wistfully. "Belaal would have wasted this boy. Who knows if his mind is too far gone now to serve at all? Poor scrub." He shook his head and turned apologetically to Eamon. "I don't know if you'll be able to get sense from him."

"He has been senseless since we brought him here," Cathair added. "We do need his account of what happened so as to verify your own record, Mr Goodman, if we can obtain it." The Hand gestured magnanimously to the chair by the bed. "If you would care to sit?"

It was not a suggestion. Eamon reminded himself as he sat that it could all be a trap as easily as a genuine interview, and tried to keep himself alert. But Waite's friendliness and Cathair's unceasing *gentillesse* made it difficult to remember that either of them was his enemy.

He leaned over the bed and peered at Mathaiah's face. If he remembered correctly, shadeweed dulled senses but a known voice was sometimes able to help the afflicted mind to focus, so bringing the victim back to a point of consciousness.

The only problem, of course, was that Mathaiah had been subjected to no such thing. If he was feigning the effects of the poison then he was doing it very well. If he was not…

"Mr Grahaven," Eamon called, softly at first. "Mr Grahaven, can you hear me?" Mathaiah's eyes began to dart here and there, as though seeking him in thick fog. "Mr Grahaven?"

A low groan left the boy's mouth.

Waite shook his head. "He's gone," he muttered. "Damned snakes."

"Perhaps, but perhaps not." A thin smile spread over Cathair's pale face. "Mr Goodman?" he said kindly.

"My lord?"

All kindness vanished. "Breach him."

For a moment Eamon could not understand the brutal command. He had been called a breacher – it was, he remembered, a rare gift among the Gauntlet. Quite what it entailed or how to use it at will, he was not sure.

"I mean no disrespect, my lord," he began, cautiously, "but should not a man with more experience than I be called upon to…"

"Nonsense!" Cathair waved his hand dismissively. "His mind is shattered and so there is nothing to be lost if you prove yourself inadequate. I should perhaps mention that not everyone has been as inclined to accept your story as I have," he added. "You have more incentive than any other man, Mr Goodman, to obtain this boy's report, and the most to lose if you do not."

The glinting, green-eyed gaze held him. Without a word Eamon turned back to Mathaiah and wondered silently – desperately – what to do. To do as Cathair asked he would have to use the throned's mark. Surely that would jeopardize his new allegiance? Wouldn't he be seen? Would he be able to do it at all?

The cadet's face was sickly in the cold light. Eamon laid his hands on it. The skin was hot and troubled. Not knowing what else to do, he closed his eyes.

For a long time nothing happened. The mark in his flesh had always come without a warning; he had never sought it and he did not want to then. With his eyes shut fast he tried to veil his normal sight and open whatever other lids he had. He had to reach that other place. What would they do to Mathaiah if they could take no sensible answer from him? He thought of the city's pyres – and clenched his eyes shut tighter.

The darkness began to lighten. The black became grey and he saw the strange plain where once he had met Aeryn. But there was no red light, no wind, no voice to drive him on. Now the plain was a grey, timeless twilight.

Mathaiah walked there, his eyes turned patiently towards the dim horizon. He seemed to await the rising of a hidden sun.

Unable to fathom what he saw and feeling that he might lose it at any second, Eamon called: "Mr Grahaven!"

The boy turned; his face flew to life and his intelligent eyes twinkled with delight.

"There you are, sir! I've been waiting for you," he said, and laughed.

"What do you mean?" Eamon demanded, more confused than ever. "Are you all right?"

"I'm all right, sir," Mathaiah assured him. "Let go. I'll wake up."

Suddenly the plain was gone. Eamon's eyes snapped open. He had no idea how much time had passed.

Lord Cathair stood behind him watching with chilling interest. As Eamon started back to the world Captain Waite stepped away from the wall where he had been leaning.

"Well?"

Eamon withdrew his hands. His palms were hot where they had clasped the cadet's brow and he noticed with alarm that the fiery eagle could not be seen. Suspecting that its lack might condemn his fragile subterfuge, he tucked his hand away. He was parting his lips to announce that he didn't know whether or not he had been successful when Mathaiah drew a deep breath and blinked hard. His waking eyes regained their sense.

"Sir?" His voice cracked from lack of water.

Eamon could scarcely believe it. "Welcome back, Mr Grahaven!" They shared a smile.

There was a moment of astonished silence. Suddenly Waite laughed aloud and clapped Eamon heartily on the back.

"Good man!" he laughed. "*Good man!*"

"Indeed," Cathair mused, but kept the rest of his thought disingenuously to himself. "Very fine work, Mr Goodman. We will begin the questions," he added.

CHAPTER XII

The interview lasted about an hour. In that time Mathaiah was given food and water and gave account of the taking of the holk and his torture at the hands of the snakes, making particular mention of one called Giles. Eamon admired the cadet's decision to focus on their erstwhile tormentor, for in telling what Giles had committed against them the cadet had barely to lie at all. The cadet's story also proved everything that Eamon had maintained to the captain and the Lord of the West Quarter. Lord Cathair listened with a look of perpetual interest while Captain Waite occupied himself with the fatherly gestures necessary to encourage the shaken cadet to speak.

"I knew it was shadeweed, from the smell," Mathaiah told them. "We'd seen some at college." He shuddered and coughed. "I'm just glad to be awake, sir."

"You did well, Mr Grahaven," Waite told him. Eamon silently agreed.

Cathair gestured to the notary. The man folded his papers, rose with a deep bow and left. A Hand was waiting outside the door to escort him from the hall. Eamon watched both men go with relief. The questioning had concluded.

"We should leave Mr Grahaven to his rest, perhaps," Cathair said.

Eamon rose from his place at Mathaiah's side. He wished that he could know what had really happened. As he stood Cathair drew him aside.

"I have never yet seen a breacher that breaches as you do."

"I hardly knew what I was doing, my lord," Eamon answered truthfully. To one side he could see Waite speaking with Mathaiah. It was a welcome distraction from the uncomfortable attention of the Hand.

"If I told you that this city's greatest breacher had tried, and failed, to do as you have done, would you believe me?"

Eamon gaped. He dared not believe it.

Cathair smiled. "Mr Goodman, I speak truly when I say that there is much potential in you. Do not put it to waste."

Eamon froze. The smiling face revealed nothing.

Did Cathair know?

"Well, Mr Goodman," Waite said as he approached. "I think you need have no fear for your commission; the cadet has given a perfectly acceptable account of the proceedings. I am certainly content with them and it would not be my recommendation to investigate your conduct further."

"I concur with you, captain," Cathair added. "I believe that today's report will be sufficient to quell all murmurings of discontent."

Cathair led the way back to the hall, the threshold falling dark behind them as they passed. After the appropriate valedictories were concluded, Waite led Eamon away. Eamon was conscious of Cathair's eyes on his back as they left. He wondered what kind of attention he had brought to himself.

The Royal Plaza was now filled with carriages, depositing gentry for the palace's evening festivities. The laughter of lords and ladies was already high on the evening air.

The Third Banner cadets were waiting at one of the gatehouses at either side of the broad entrance to the plaza, ready to take the posts of another West Quarter group. Eamon exchanged duties with another lieutenant who seemed grateful to be relieved. Captain Waite gave him a brief but detailed description of his duties before reminding Eamon his duty would last until the second watch.

"There are extra cloaks in the gatehouse, if it gets cold."

"Thank you, sir," Eamon answered, saluting. The captain smiled, and then made his way from the gates onto the Coll. Eamon set the cadets to their posts at once.

Guard duties were all too often a tedious affair and being posted at Dunthruik – even with the imposing grandeur of the Royal Plaza – was no different after the initial novelty. Eamon spoke a little with some of the other lieutenants and ensigns at the gate and learned that duty at the palace was a particular privilege of the West

Quarter. They admitted a large number of guests and saw a good number of couriers and servants passing through the lanterned columns. Eamon listened to a few of the Banner cadets telling tales of their afternoon's lessons and then, when such conversation had dwindled, he watched the stars go by, listened to the music in the palace, and admitted and discharged carriages as the festivities came to a late end. He saw dozens of nobles and their ladies, decked in finery and extravagance, and he saw half a dozen Hands, patches of darkness amid the gaiety. Eamon thought that he saw Cathair among them, speaking to another who also had an emblem marked at his breast. Both men were unusually pale, even in comparison to the other Hands who passed by. Eamon wondered how many of them were breachers and what else these men, so high in the Master's favour, could do. As the Hands left, many of them looked closely at him; he felt that they garnered more about him in that moment of scrutiny than he would like. He saluted them – men on duty did not bow, even to Hands – as they departed.

As the end of the watch neared, the sentries closed one set of the palace gates. Wrought from an interlaced weave of gold, they were clearly more ornamental than practical. The palace's actual gates were enormous wooden affairs, thicker than the length of his arm. It gave him food for thought. He acquainted himself with the stairs that led from the gatehouses to the palace walls; when he glanced back towards the Master's balcony he saw light dancing there behind curtained apertures.

Weariness seeped into every limb and he longed for the work to be done. Exchanging a few further words with the cadets under his command only helped so much to stave off the creeping fatigue.

Not long before the second watch a call from the gate brought him to look out onto the Coll. A lone carriage, drawn by two fine horses, was lumbering towards the gilt gates. A lantern hung from the carriage roof, illuminating a rich coat of arms.

"Open the gates!" called the coachman. "Open the gates for Lady Turnholt."

Eamon turned to the gate's men. "Open them," he said. The soldiers moved to do so and the elaborate gates swung smoothly aside. The carriage came through, casting a strange shadow across the plaza's cobbles. Eamon gestured for the gates to be closed again and for lights to be brought to the coach.

The coachman descended. He was a middle-aged man with a weathered face and the signs of long service on his hands. He went to lower the carriage step.

At that moment there was a crack followed by the sound of wood splitting. Eamon instinctively jerked back from the vehicle and saw at once that one of the axles had broken. A second later the carriage tilted awkwardly on its remaining wheels and then, with a lumbering groan, began to tumble onto its side. The horses neighed wildly, alarmed by the weight throwing them down. The coachman raced to calm them. A valise fell from the roof and crashed into the wet cobbles, spilling fine clothes. From inside the carriage Eamon heard cries.

He yelled a command to his men, who rushed to the carriage side to break its fall. With so many shoulders to bolster it the carriage never hit the ground but remained hanging at an untenable angle. The frightened horses reared and strained and Eamon heard the crack of growing pressure on the remaining frame.

"Hold it, keep it steady!" Eamon stepped from his place supporting the weight to the coach door; its passengers had to be got out.

Kicking the half-lowered step out of the way he pulled open the door. A woman fell through the doorway with a shaken cry. Not stopping to think, Eamon caught her in his arms and pulled her swiftly clear of the carriage before setting her down on her feet at a safe distance from the rocking coach. She trembled and he steadied her. Her breathing was ragged and she still had half a scream on her lips.

"You're safe, madam," he said kindly. He turned to offer her a reassuring smile and then merely stared.

The frightened face looking back at him was one of the most beautiful that he had ever seen. It was round and clear, bearing deep, dark eyes. Her brow was crowned with a cascading coronet of dark ringlets; these were drawn back to reveal a long neck adorned with a shining red pendant.

Eamon's gaze might have gone further but modesty asserted itself in time and he belatedly realized that he still held the lady by the waist. Deeply embarrassed, he snatched back his hands and, shamed by his astonishment, turned away.

"And who might you be?" the lady asked breathlessly.

"Lieutenant Eamon Goodman," he answered, his cheeks boiling. "Your servant, madam."

"A role you performed well, Mr Goodman," she said with a small smile.

Behind her, Eamon saw that his men had managed to right the carriage by forcing mounting blocks beneath the shattered axle. A couple of cadets were helping the coachman to free the horses; boots trampled the lady's fallen dresses.

"I am sorry for your belongings, madam," Eamon told her.

"My maid will see to it." As she spoke a young woman appeared in the doorway of the carriage. The girl also shook, and she accepted the cadets' offers to help her down. Once safely on the ground she went to scoop up the dresses. She was joined by the coachman, who knelt to assist her. He took both clothes and muddy valise from her while the maid came quickly to the lady's side.

"Mr Cartwright will see to your things, madam," she said quietly. Despite being smitten by the strange lady Eamon was able to gain an impression of the girl: no older than eighteen, dark-haired, slimly built, and bearing evident care for her mistress.

"Please come in, my lady, before you catch cold," the girl added.

"I take my leave of you, Mr Goodman," said the mistress, looking to Eamon once more. "Thank you again for your service."

"I should be only too happy to render it again," Eamon heard himself say. Could he really be so bewitched at a single look? The lady turned to go. "Madam, might I be so bold as to ask your name?"

She threw an enchanting smile over her shoulder. "Lady Alessia Turnholt. Perhaps we shall see each other again, lieutenant."

Eamon watched her go, startled. He knew the name. His eyes turned to the maid who walked demurely by her mistress's side. He remembered her name: Lillabeth Hollenwell, his point of contact in the palace. The young maid was a wayfarer.

It was not the only revelation that struck him: the lady left a fragrant floral scent in her wake.

CHAPTER XIII

He woke before the dawn and watched the clouded grey pass by in high swathes. The city's shadows seemed to stretch through the casement, forming the bars of a grotesque cage.

Eamon stretched. There was still a searing ache in his back. He rose and dressed with the speed and enthusiasm of a snail. As he pulled on his jacket he felt the cool weight of the heart of the King fall and rest about his neck. The stone was of comfort to him. Hughan's papers were still safe in his pouch, and as he stood in the half-light he drew them out, drinking in the noble script and remembering the hand that had written them. Both stone and papers were tangible reminders of a world that seemed a distant dream and so he clung to them. Would he be summoned that day to relinquish them to the throned?

In a slightly sullen mood he went to rouse the Third Banner cadets. He was unkinder to them than his guise of rough Gauntlet lieutenant warranted. But, being well accustomed to sleep interrupted by the bawls of irritated officers, the cadets rose swiftly and without complaint. The course awaited them again that morning and there was every possibility, Eamon told them, that they would have the satisfaction of winning. Overbrook told him that it was statistically unlikely. Eamon advised him to keep his opinion to himself.

He led the column of cadets to the field. There had been rain in the night and the grass was cold and slippery. The Third Ravens were already present at the other end of the course, swinging their arms in wide circles and laughing as they prepared for an easy task. Alben strode among them, encouraging them with japes at the expense of their foes. Catching sight of Eamon, the first lieutenant waved cheerily. Eamon scowled and commanded his cadets to sign. One man was absent, apparently gone down with fever and in the care of the college's surgeons. Some officers might have demanded the cadet's presence anyway, but Eamon doubted that being forced to haul himself through mud would do the boy any good. He gruffly acknowledged the absence.

The cadets took their packs and set off. He followed them.

The going seemed as slow and painful as it had the day before. Overbrook lagged but Manners, along with Ford and Ostler, took a definite lead, ripping down the course with impressive speed. Eamon was hard-pressed to keep pace with them, for all three were gifted sprinters. Once again Manners was the first to cross the river, take up a practice blade and charge at his opponents, fire in his eyes and mud up to his waist.

Blades met and crossed. Manners had adapted his strategy and matched his hand evenly to his opponent's. As the meeting endured beyond the customary twenty seconds, Eamon began to wonder if Manners would do it. Every cut and thrust of the cadet's was parried, but twice Manners nearly bettered his opponent.

"Come on, Manners!" Eamon yelled. Other Banners, themselves defeated, took up the cry until the field fairly rang with it. Bolstered, Manners swooped in with a beautiful strike. The swords jarred and the Raven cadet was thrown down to his knees.

The field was torn with cheers and hisses. Manners whooped with delight then turned a radiant, muddy face to his peers, who applauded him wildly.

But in his moment of jubilation his fallen opponent reached out and suddenly hurled Manners down. The cadet was caught off guard; now it was the Raven's turn to press the point of his blade close against his foe.

"Who's won now?" he laughed. He was joined by the other Ravens. Manners grew red. Cries of outrage erupted from the Banners. They swarmed forward.

"It's not fair, sir!" yelled Overbrook. "Manners won!"

Eamon agreed. He stormed forwards and grabbed the Raven cadet by the collar.

"Get off him!" he shouted, yanking the young man bodily away. With a swift move he disarmed the cadet. Manners crawled up out of the mud, his hand curled into a vicious fist and his arm ready to throw a punch; a dark glance from Eamon stayed him. Eamon turned his attention back to the Raven cadet.

"You are ungracious in defeat," Eamon told him. "You will apologize immediately to Mr Manners and cede him the victory." The cadet remained silent. Eamon stared at him hard. "Apologize, cadet!"

"He will do no such thing," said a voice: Alben's. "You go too far, Mr Goodman."

"Cadet Manners won, Mr Alben," Eamon replied through gritted teeth.

"Cadet Manners appeared to conclude the affair on his back; a most compromising position."

Delighted, the Ravens began cat-calling Manners. His face creased with fury.

"Mr Manners," Eamon barked. The situation could too easily go out of control and, much as he would have loved to take Alben down there and then, he knew that he could not. It was not the time.

The Banners were still hurling abuse at the Ravens. Eamon turned on them. "Form rank," he commanded sternly.

The cadets fell silent at once and formed rank, all except Manners, who still glared daggers at his opponent.

"I said form rank, Mr Manners."

Fuming, Manners stalked to his place. Eamon turned roughly to Alben. "Captain Waite shall hear of this, Mr Alben."

The first lieutenant raised an odious eyebrow. "And whose word will he take?" he asked. "That of a man who surrendered his sword?"

An uneasy silence fell. Eamon turned his back on his antagonist. He called for his cadets to tighten their rank and led them away from the field.

He fell in step with Manners. The cadet flexed his hands angrily, as though mocking laughter still burnt in his ears.

"I'll bloody throttle him!" he hissed.

"Tongue, Manners," Eamon advised sharply.

"I won, sir!"

"I know you did," Eamon answered. "You did exceptionally, and mention of it will be put on your record. I will discuss this incident with Captain Waite in person."

The cadet stared at him. "You'd take this to the captain?"

"Yes, cadet. Dishonesty and foul play are never trivial matters." Both were particularly unbecoming of a first lieutenant.

The cadets went on to law and swordplay. Eamon was just dispatching them to the care of more specialist instruction, with his congratulations on an excellent morning's work, when a servant approached him.

"Lieutenant Goodman?"

"Yes."

"Captain Waite's compliments: you're to report to him as soon as you can," the servant told him. "There's also a messenger for you in the hall, sir. You can take your message on the way to the captain."

"I will, thank you."

Bowing, the servant went towards Lord Cathair's buildings.

Eamon dismissed the cadets and went swiftly to the hall, his thoughts tumbling one over another. Surely there was nobody in Dunthruik who could have any cause to send him messages?

He stopped in the hallway and allowed his sight to adjust to the shadowed entrance. Through the gates he could see the busy Dunthruik streets and hear a good deal of bustle. Preparations were underway for the majesty. With the Royal Plaza just along the Coll, a great number of artisans and Gauntlet were beginning to gather, either to go about their own work or survey the work of others.

A small figure sat on a bench under Waite's Hand-board. Assuming this to be his messenger, Eamon stepped forward and then stopped in surprise. The messenger was the maidservant whom he had seen at the palace that night. What business could she possibly have at a Gauntlet college?

The girl rose and curtseyed impeccably.

"Lieutenant Goodman?"

Eamon nodded dumbly.

"I have an invitation for you from Lady Turnholt." She offered him a sealed parchment. He opened it and cast his eyes over the curling script, trying to force them to focus on the words:

Lady Alessia Turnholt kindly requests the presence of Lieutenant Eamon Goodman at supper, a gesture of thanks for his service.

Eamon had to read the letter three or four times before he could look at the maid again. "This is for me?" He suddenly felt very warm.

The maid nodded. "Will you come, sir? I must take back an answer."

"Yes," Eamon said unthinkingly. Then: "If my captain will allow it."

"Lady Turnholt will expect you this evening, at Turnholt House on Candeller's Way," the maid told him. "Please send word if you cannot attend."

"Of course." Eamon felt lightheaded and the parchment burned in his hand.

The maid bowed to him and then began to leave. Suddenly regaining his senses Eamon called after her: "Miss!"

"Sir?"

Eamon paused. "I wish to thank you for your trouble, Miss...?"

"Miss Hollenwell."

"Miss Lillabeth Hollenwell?" How many Lady Alessia Turnholts, and accompanying maids, could there be in Dunthruik?

"Your servant, sir," she answered, curtseying again.

"A friend spoke highly of you and of your service," Eamon told her quietly. After a pause he saw her nod faintly, his meaning understood.

"Thank you, sir." The girl curtseyed and left the college, drawing her cloak about herself as she stepped into the Brand.

Eamon watched her go, his heart beating hard. Beneath her tacit servility Lillabeth Hollenwell was a wayfarer, and his means of reaching the King. Both comforted him.

Lady Alessia Turnholt kindly requests the presence of Lieutenant Eamon Goodman at supper... Eamon read it again just to make sure. It seemed unreal. He breathed in the perfume of the lady – the page seemed suffused with it. What interest could she have in him?

All at once he remembered that Captain Waite was waiting for him. He turned to hurry towards the captain's office and nearly stopped again. There, in the shadow of an arch, was First Lieutenant Alben. The man's watching face was murderous.

Eamon tucked the parchment into his jacket. "Mr Alben," he acknowledged, and went straight past. Alben could storm; they would settle their differences later.

Eamon followed the corridor to Captain Waite's office. The door stood open and at Waite's gesture he stepped inside.

"Mr Goodman," Waite greeted him with a brief smile. Another lieutenant was in the office and Waite dismissed him.

"A good morning?" he asked.

"Thank you, sir," Eamon answered. "Yes. But not, I'm afraid, for Cadet Manners."

Waite raised an eyebrow and Eamon quickly explained what had happened.

"I would like Manners' achievement noted on his record, sir. He gave a very impressive performance. Mr Alben's response was, in my opinion, as unsatisfactory as the behaviour of his own cadet."

"You want to lodge an official complaint?" Waite asked tactfully.

"No, sir," Eamon answered carefully. "I merely felt that you should be informed. Such behaviour hardly seems to befit a man of Mr Alben's standing."

"Hmm," Waite grunted, steepling his fingers together. "I am aware that Mr Alben's methods can be a little unorthodox, Mr Goodman, but he is my college's first lieutenant and there is good reason in that appointment. You do not question that, I hope?"

"No, sir."

Waite laughed. "You have a good sense of self-preservation, Mr Goodman."

Eamon reddened; the remark carried the slur of cowardice. "With respect, sir, if I feel that Mr Alben oversteps the mark I will not hesitate to call him to account for it –"

"You'd duel him, lieutenant?" Waite asked, eyebrows raised.

"– through the appropriate channels, sir," Eamon finished firmly. He met the captain's look. "Notwithstanding such channels, sir, duelling has its place."

"Ah yes!" Waite commented airily. "Where the honour of women is involved!"

"Mr Alben's rank does not license him to do everything that he desires."

The captain fixed him with an interested gaze. "And what of mine, Mr Goodman?"

Eamon swallowed. "With deepest respect, sir – neither does yours."

Waite smiled again, a long, slow smile. He went through some papers on his desk.

"So it would appear that you are a man of principles, Mr Goodman," he said. "Mr Manners has always been an excellent cadet; he narrowly missed appointment to the Ravens himself. He is capable and quick-witted. He does not need so generous a champion as you." When he spoke again his tone was harsher. "When Manners goes to the borders – to Galithia, or to Singsward or Scarmost; when he is in a bloody fight in the Olborough Straits, or caught unawares in the marshes between there and Rothfort, will the bastard he's fighting stay down and politely invite his sword? In your experience, Mr Goodman, does your enemy fawn at your feet because you beat him fairly?"

"No, sir," Eamon answered. His own memories of service on the border provinces flitted through his mind. They had been bloody times. "Ideally, he does not have the chance to fawn. But the Third

Ravens are not Manners' enemy and Manners had no cause to do more than bring his opponent to the ground." Waite watched him, seemingly unmoved. "For the Gauntlet to go from strength to strength, sir," Eamon continued passionately, "it needs to be based on trust. Trust breeds respect and the man with respect has loyalty; the man with loyalty and courage can lead men to places where they would not otherwise go. Mr Alben's methods are divisive."

"Yet men follow him, Mr Goodman," Waite answered. "Cadet Manners will grow thicker skin, and he will survive."

Eamon fell silent. He had kept his promise to Manners but he did not wish to set himself on the wrong side of Waite. It was time to cede the argument to his captain. "Yes, sir."

"I had a request yesterday, Mr Goodman," Waite added after a brief pause. "A request for a warding."

Eamon nodded. Wardings had not been common in Edesfield but he imagined that they were an everyday occurrence in Dunthruik. The sons of those nobles too minor to be made knights who enrolled in Gauntlet colleges were often assigned to experienced officers in the scheme, which was part-shadowing and part-mentoring. The cadet became the officer's ward, a kind of apprentice. After a year or so in such a post the cadet might be transferred to another officer or, if he had excelled himself enough, promoted. Officers in the Gauntlet often competed to become warders as it gave a good gloss to a man's record.

"A warding request is not unusual," Waite continued. "I receive dozens every month. Mark this well, Mr Goodman: the bane of being a Dunthruik captain is this tedious paperwork!" Waite slapped a pile of paper on his desk. "But what was unusual about this request, Mr Goodman, was not that it was made by the young man himself rather than by some doting relative, but that he asked to be warded to you."

Waite leaned over the desk. Eamon swallowed; being a warder would seriously limit his freedom to move in Dunthruik.

"Might I ask who has made this request, sir?"

"Cadet Mathaiah Grahaven," Waite answered, "the younger son of Baron Dolos Grahaven. The baron is a minor noble with some lands near Edesfield."

Eamon nearly burst out laughing. Mathaiah warded – to him? He felt a wash of pride. The cadet had thought well.

"Of course," Waite continued, "from a paperwork point of view there is no issue: it had been decided that Mr Grahaven was to be assigned to this college and that he was to go to the Third Banners, who are a couple of men down at present. He is perfectly entitled to request and obtain a warding and will have it, if you are willing. What I found myself asking myself, Mr Goodman – and I am not a man of little intelligence – was why should he choose *you*? What is it about you that inspires this cadet's evident awe?" Waite smiled. "Would you believe it, but I had no answer?"

The captain pulled out a piece of paper. Eamon saw that it was Manners' file. He watched as Waite began carefully scribing a note on it.

"Before our conversation, Mr Goodman, I was still asking myself that question. But now I think I have answered it." The smile returned to his face. "If you are willing, Mr Grahaven will be warded to you this afternoon after your meeting. He is quite recovered, it seems."

"I'm willing, sir," Eamon answered. Then, catching up with what Waite had said: "Forgive me, sir, if I have been idle of hearing – what meeting?"

"You were to be on patrol duty this afternoon, but Lord Cathair has asked that I send you instead to take what you recovered from the snakes to the Hands' Hall," Waite answered. "Everything will be explained there."

Eamon ate his lunch swiftly, his appetite driven by the energy of his nervous mind.

Waite had given him permission to attend Lady Turnholt's meal that evening, provided that he presented himself in a condition fit for the keeping of the second watch thereafter. The thought of an evening with the bewitching lady would have been enough to put him in turmoil. But what concerned him the most was his summons to the Hands' Hall. Presenting himself before the Hands would be no simple affair, and he knew only too well that it would be an occasion for wit and caution.

He rubbed anxiously at his palm. If the Hands learned of his purpose then he would not even make it to Serpentine Avenue. He reminded himself sternly that he was a King's man and the First Knight. Would he not be protected, should the worst come to pass?

He wolfed the end of his meal and left the mess, aware that Alben had watched him unforgivingly throughout. Eamon ignored it and hurried to the main hall.

He found Cathair already there, speaking with Waite in lowered tones. As Eamon emerged he saw Cathair's pale face break into a grin while he clapped Waite on the back. Both laughed and then Lord Cathair raised a cordial hand towards Eamon in greeting. Eamon bowed.

"Mr Goodman! I shall be your escort." The Hand looked once more to the captain. "A pleasure, captain, as always."

"Thank you, my lord," Waite answered.

Eamon fell into step with the Hand and they left the college, turning down the steps into the Brand and then onto the Coll. Stalls had appeared down the myriad side streets and people threaded through them, bartering wares. The sun rolled low, and a chill breeze from the port sent ripples through blankets and mats that hung from windows and balconies.

The paved road to the palace seemed longer than it had the previous day. Eamon looked at the palace gates where pennons snapped and fanfares played as nobles and knights rode out together. Amid the sounds of the busy city Lord Cathair's continued silence was unsettling. Eamon had grown accustomed to the Hand's banter.

Lord Cathair took him into the palace through the side gate and then to the Hands' Hall. He escorted him through a sequence of stone-guarded doors to the central courtyard where stood another building. Writing was engraved on the door in strange, unfamiliar letters. The rigid and incisive script made Eamon shudder.

A second door, dark as obsidian, lay beyond the first. Wind moved against Eamon's face as it yawned open.

Cathair gestured for him to step inside. "You will be seen very shortly." Nodding, Eamon stepped over the threshold. The door shut fast behind him.

He found himself in an oval room fashioned from the same black stones as the door and threshold. The hall was wide and open. Five chairs stood at its far end, four level and the fifth higher and grander than the others. Each chair had shapes etched on it – he distinguished birds and trees – while the strange writing that he had seen on the doors was everywhere. Narrow windows let in slits of light.

Suddenly five Hands were in the room with him. One was Lord Cathair. Eamon did not recognize the other four. He didn't know how they had entered or how long they had been there. They seated themselves before him, four in the lower. Startled, he understood that they were Dunthruik's Quarter Hands.

The Hands' black garb was rimmed with gold. One bore a red stone about his neck: a black eagle was marked upon it. It was this Hand who took the highest chair. Eamon realized with grinding horror that it could only be the Right Hand.

He bowed low at once. Against the light and the stone he could not see any of their faces; they were carved figures issuing from the surrounding stone.

"Lieutenant Goodman." It was one of the lesser Hands who spoke. His voice was rich and affluent; it wasn't Cathair. "Come forward into the circle."

For a moment Eamon was too terrified to move. Then he forced his limbs to the circle in the central part of the hall. The space before the chairs was lit by the windows, and red stones marked where he should stand. It unnerved him, reminding him of the stones over the doors to the hall. What powers might these hold? Unwillingly, he stepped into their embrace.

Fire rushed in his palm. Closing his fingers he dropped down to one knee.

"My lords," he breathed, wishing to be very far from there.

"Lord Cathair and Captain Waite have spoken much of you," the speaker continued. "The Master wished to meet with you himself but that must wait for the present. Know that we, his Hands, act in his name and with his authority."

"His glory," Eamon answered.

The speaker descended from his chair and strode to where Eamon stood. He had brown, hollow eyes in a face so pale that it stole Eamon's breath. In comparison to this man, Cathair beamed with health.

"I am Ashway, Lord of the East Quarter. Show me the papers."

Not daring to rise, Eamon handed them to Lord Ashway.

He's a seer. Eamon's blood ran cold as Waite's words ran through him. His hand burned. What would happen to him if Ashway discerned that the papers were false? Would it not surely be wiser to confess now, and live?

Words were bubbling to his lips but he somehow held his tongue. Ashway's eyes danced swiftly across the words before he laid his hand over them: the mark on his palm began glowing through the parchment. Eamon held his breath. When their gazes met, the man's face was unreadable.

"The stone, Lieutenant Goodman."

Eamon bowed his head so as to pull the chain up over it. The heart of the King came out from his jacket. It blazed a brilliant blue.

Ashway set his fingers to it and fell still. An expectant silence waited on him. Eamon tried to still his throbbing heart. At last, the Lord of the East Quarter turned to the Right Hand.

"It is the stone, my lord." His voice seemed breathless.

The Right Hand nodded once. Eamon had barely had time to take in the gesture when a spectral face flashed past him and fingers clasped his brow. The Hand's touch was lightning.

Chapter XIII

Searing pain drove into his head. His vision changed.

He saw the plain – but now the sky was blackened. He found that he still knelt and that he was bitterly cold. Pressure and pain beat in every part of his head and he could not fend it off. His hand roared with flames and the eagle rose on his palm, pulsing in his living flesh. All about him seemed fire – all but the heart of the King. It lay against his breast, a beacon.

Eamon clenched his fist in alarm. It stopped neither burning nor pain nor light. He forced himself to look up and saw that visions moved in the rushing wind, fleeting impressions of places and people he knew. They were his impressions, his own memories.

He was being breached.

Striving, Eamon rose to his feet. A figure was in front of him. The face was pale, its eyes aflame, and the figure's black robes guttered in the driving wind. The shape before him was all he could discern.

"My lord," he quivered. "What would you know?"

"Whether you are true." The Hand's voice shuddered in his ears. "Show me the holk."

Suddenly they stood on the holk, or in his memory of it. Eamon saw himself speaking with the captain. He could not stop it. The Hand watched, unmoving, as events unfolded.

Eamon saw at once how this breaching would end: with his secrets revealed and his incarceration, torture, and grisly death. All this was likely to be followed by the chilling testimony of his severed head impaled on a pike over the Blind Gate. Driven by fear he tried to tear away.

A rush of pain as the Hand wrenched his memory in another direction. Recoiling, Eamon gaped.

He had not been prepared for this – what could he do? He could wait as much as he wanted for the King's grace to save him, as it had saved Aeryn, but that would reveal him as effectively as any breaching. The Quarter Hand had to be the city's greatest breacher. How could he hope to hold against such a man? There was no escape. Was he to fail before he had even begun?

Desperate, Eamon stared at the shadowy figure. The Hand's eyes were transfixed by the memories unfolding at increasing speed before them. He saw everything. Eamon's whole mind lay open.

Was it a two-way process?

The thought snapped through his pain. Forcing focus, Eamon stared earnestly at his assailant. A memory appeared – not one of his own. He caught a glimpse of the Quarter Hand, his fingers gripped about Mathaiah's forehead and his powers frustrated by something that he did not understand. This Hand had tried – and failed – to breach Mathaiah.

Scarcely daring to breathe, Eamon glanced at the Hand again. His incursion seemed to have gone unnoticed.

He looked back to his own memory and saw himself rushing onto the deck of the *Lark* to face Giles. In only moments his healing of Mathaiah would be shown and all would be lost. He had to do something. Eamon drew together the tangled thoughts about them, fixed on them with all his heart and willed another vision.

It was that simple. He watched with delight as Aeryn leapt forward and healed Mathaiah in his stead. The Hand looked across at him and a sharp twist of agony ran through him, but Eamon did not falter. He wove his design subtly through his own memories, showing them as they needed to be seen. As Mathaiah had done in his telling of their capture, Eamon was careful to highlight Giles and the man's brutality towards him. It was not hard to do. What damage would twisting and changing do? He did not know and he had no choice. Every thought and word, every single moment was vetted until they reached the present. He trembled with the effort.

The sweeping visions disappeared. There was a final pulse of pain before his own sight was restored. The brain-grinding pressure left his head and he collapsed to his knees, crippled with fatigue. His eyes seemed dark and he could barely think.

The breaching Hand returned to his seat. He seemed to speak to the others but Eamon could not hear them. He was sensate only of the Right Hand's gaze. The Hands' forms flickered around him, brushed by an unseen wind.

"Lord Cathair will see you to your warding." Crawling across his shaking flesh was the voice that belonged to the Right Hand. "Keep the stone for the present, Mr Goodman. Use will be made of it and you very shortly."

"Thank you, my lords," Eamon managed.

He staggered to his feet and bowed, blinking feverishly in an attempt to clear his vision. Leaving the hall, light burned his eyes. He flinched from it with a miserable groan.

His sight slowly returned to him. The first thing he saw was Lord Cathair, surveying him with piercing interest.

"'Any kind of man bear I, save he whose skill is like to mine'."

Cathair laughed at Eamon's obvious shock. "It would seem that a promising breacher does not relish encounters with his own kind?"

Eamon shook his head. He couldn't speak.

"Not every man is breached by Lord Tramist on his second day in Dunthruik, Mr Goodman," Cathair told him. "I trust that you found the experience informative."

Eamon shivered. He realized then that the Hand who had breached him was the same man to whom Belaal had meant to send Aeryn.

Cathair smiled. "Come with me, Mr Goodman."

Lord Cathair led him back to the West Quarter College and to its raven-marked buildings. They passed through the well-lit entrance hall and into a pillared corridor to another set of rooms. Despite being in a Hand's quarters these doors were not marked with the strange red stones. Through one open door he caught a glimpse of an achingly large library.

They came to a corridor lined with marble benches. Mathaiah, resplendent in a new uniform, sat quietly on one of them. The cadet fidgeted with the sleeve of his jacket, and every now and then glanced at the door in front of him. Eamon thought that he could hear Waite's voice inside.

As they approached, Mathaiah leapt at once to his feet and bowed low. "His glory, my lord."

Cathair treated the cadet to a round smile. "I will go and prepare for you, gentlemen."

The Lord of the West Quarter disappeared into the doorway, pulling the door closed behind him. Soon his voice mingled with Waite's. After listening to the indistinct sounds for a few moments, Eamon sat carefully next to Mathaiah.

"Cadet," he acknowledged warmly.

"Sir," Mathaiah smiled.

Eamon looked at him, wondering what he could possibly say. "Are you feeling better?"

"Much restored, thank you."

Cathair reappeared and gestured for them to follow him.

"There's just a small formality, gentlemen," he advised, "and a disproportionate amount of paperwork."

The room held a desk and a few rows of chairs. A notary was behind the desk, shuffling his quill and papers. Several other Gauntlet officers were also in the room, among them Captain Waite and the West Quarter College's draybant, Mr Farleigh – distinguished by his four flames.

Lord Cathair led Eamon and Mathaiah to the desk where the notary was seated.

"We will begin."

The notary began to write.

"Gentlemen, you are here to ratify and witness the assignment of Cadet Mathaiah Grahaven as ward to Lieutenant Eamon Goodman. Captain Waite," Cathair continued, "do you confirm that Lieutenant Goodman is under your command?"

"I do, my lord." Waite's voice was grave enough but had the manner of one who had been through the ceremony a thousand times.

"And do you pledge as to the competence of Mr Goodman?"

"I do, my lord."

"Lastly, will you pledge as to his good faith and service?"

Waite smiled. "I do, my lord," he answered confidently. Eamon's gut twisted guiltily. "To all these I pledge my word."

"Mr Grahaven."

Mathaiah bowed. "My lord."

"Do you confirm that you seek this appointment to give glory to the Master, and do you pledge to be obedient and attentive to Mr Goodman in his instruction?"

"I do, my lord," Mathaiah answered. How could he pronounce the words so steadily? "To these I pledge my word."

"Mr Goodman," the green-eyed Hand turned his glinting gaze to Eamon. "Will you pledge to instruct Mr Grahaven always with a view to glorifying the Master, and do you pledge of your own ability and good faith in this task?"

Eamon felt sick. "To these I pledge my word."

Captain Waite stepped up beside him and took up his right hand; he laid it firmly against Mathaiah's brow. Eamon felt the first tremors of flame in his palm. By the cadet's slightly creased brows he thought that Mathaiah could feel it, too.

"You shall be the ward," Eamon heard himself say, "and I the warder. With my own hand I pledge it." Flames sparked suddenly about his palm, leaping through his fingers to Mathaiah's forehead. Eamon almost jerked his hand back, but before he could the light was gone and Lord Cathair was speaking.

"Thank you, gentlemen, all very swift and proper. I will take the signatures of the witnesses and then you may all go about your business." He smiled. "Congratulations, Mr Goodman, Mr Grahaven: ward well!"

Captain Waite clasped their hands in turn. "Ward well," he said. "Mr Goodman, you're required by Lords Cathair and Ashway this afternoon and have been exempted from regular duties until second watch at the palace this evening. I'm sure I don't need to tell you to do exactly as they ask you."

"Of course not, sir," Eamon replied.

"Mr Grahaven," Waite continued, "you will accompany Mr Goodman, but you need to sign one or two things first."

"Yes, sir." At Waite's gesture Mathaiah made his way to the desk where the notary indicated on what and where he should lay his signature. Waite turned and fixed Eamon with a serious gaze.

"Mr Grahaven has great potential in him," he said in lowered tones. "Keep a good eye on your ward, Mr Goodman. You are to be held responsible for unleashing that potential now."

Eamon remembered his own vision of Mathaiah: a terrifying Hand walking the shadows. He wished no part in that metamorphosis. "I will, sir."

Waite clapped him on the arm in an approving fashion and then excused himself. As the witnesses began to disperse, Mathaiah returned to Eamon's side, his fingers ink-stained.

"I never could keep a quill straight enough," he murmured. "I was the bane of my tutor's existence, sir."

"He might think differently of you today, Mr Grahaven," Cathair interjected, appearing – as he often did – seemingly out of nowhere. "Gentlemen, we have work to do. Mr Goodman, have you the stone you so kindly brought back from your little expedition?"

"Yes, my lord."

"Very good," Cathair smiled. "We shall have need of it."

CHAPTER XIV

Lord Cathair escorted them back to the Royal Plaza where half a dozen other Hands met them. Eamon recognized the terrifying gaze of Lord Ashway. What if these Hands knew what he truly was?

The other Hands chatted as any group of men might, Ashway and Cathair exchanging pleasantries before speaking quietly together. Eamon felt out of place, barred from the strange black world by his red uniform. He was glad to have Mathaiah at his side.

At a command from Cathair the group moved on in silent procession. Eamon grew tenser and tenser but Mathaiah did not seem to feel it. The cadet was too busy eagerly filling his eyes with everything they passed, from the greatest height of the palace to the patterns traced by the cobbles at his feet.

Sweeping across the plaza Eamon was conscious of his every step echoing on the stones, of the expanse of the Master's balcony, and the murmur of voices and music drifting from some distant hall. Flags snapped overhead like the beating of eagles' wings. Yet what he felt most keenly was the stone against his skin. It was cool and still.

They entered the palace below the balcony. The doorway devoured them, the jaws of an enormous beast.

The grand entrance was a huge, open space; all around him staircases led in glittering waves down to the tiled floor. Tapestries bearing crowned eagles boldly worked in red, black, and gold hung from every wall. Eamon cast his gaze up into the face of a great roof: his eyes were met with a roaring splendour of gems that worked dizzying patterns in the sunlight, pouring cascades of coloured light down across the floor below; as they crossed the hall Eamon saw his hand coloured red and gold by the falling shafts of light.

Lord Ashway took them into the lower levels of the West Wing. They went down a set of twisting corridors and a bewildering number of stairs. Eamon began to notice that the stonework grew less ornate and much paler the further they went. Then the hallways became dilapidated and dusty. There was no sound but that of their steady feet.

Were it not for the windows, which looked in towards the palace gardens, Eamon would have found himself completely disoriented. They seemed to be going to the farthest part of the wing.

At last Ashway halted and passed through an open doorway. One after another they followed him across the threshold and into the room beyond. It was well sized and Eamon saw that it would once have been a beautiful place. Great bay windows, now greased and stained, curved from floor to ceiling on the eastern side, looking out towards the Hands' Hall. Crumbling embrasures lined each casement and Eamon knew that they would once have been filled with cushions for the comfort of any who might sit there to read. How his hands ached for the feel of a book!

But that was a lifetime ago.

Marks on the flame-scored walls were all that remained of the tall cases that had once circled them. In places the walls showed traces of pastoral frescoes that had been tarred over. High in one corner Eamon could just see the arching branches of a tree, faintly twining between the swathes of obscuring black. A fireplace was set into one wall, and though its stones must once have been clear and bright it was now charred and blackened. As Eamon imagined how the place must once have looked he felt a pang of regret.

The Hands seemed not to see what had been done to the room, their nonchalance indicating that they had observed it many times before.

"Mr Goodman," Ashway commanded, drawing him across to the fireplace. Eamon felt air moving – but from where?

He looked at the stonework and his eyes fell at once upon an opening in the back of the fireplace, at its very heart: a small hole, marked round with ridges. After a moment he realized that the shape correlated to that of the stone at his neck.

Ashway gestured to the fireplace. "The stone, Mr Goodman. Put it there." His voice quivered. What were the Hands expecting? Eamon glanced at the others and saw that Cathair was also interminably still, as though holding his breath.

Eamon stooped and leaned into the fireplace. He brushed soot and grime away from the hole and felt the smooth stonework beneath. It had been lovingly crafted.

Carefully he drew the stone over his head. It felt dead in his hand. Crouching, he balanced it between his fingers and then slotted it into the hole. He stepped back.

For a moment nothing happened. Then the stone began to glow blue. Eamon heard a click. Lines of light appeared in the joins of the stonework: they flickered and shifted before giving way to a doorway, illuminated from above by the shining heart of the King. Musty air rose out of the opening. The light showed steps leading down into darkness.

Eamon's jaw dropped. But Ashway's face split with a grin that ran from ear to ear. Cathair almost cheered.

"Well done, Mr Goodman!" he cried, his green eyes twinkling. "Torches!"

"Scour the place," Ashway commanded, gesturing downward. Eamon wondered what could possibly be below. "Anything you find is to be brought back here, do you understand? Books, scrolls, folios, volumes, scraps... books, anything." His torch raised high, Ashway looked into the stairwell with an evil grin. "Ellen's Well is breached at last! How she would weep!"

Ashway and Cathair were the first to go down the darkened stair, their torches mere flickers in the engulfing dark. At Cathair's insistence, Eamon was next to follow and Mathaiah was close behind him. The other Hands came after them.

The air smelled vaguely of smoke and the steps were vertiginous and uneven. They led down into a large cellar whose innumerable alcoves were filled with long stone shelves. All were empty. As Eamon's eyes adjusted to the guttering light he saw that corridors stretched off in all directions. Stale air stirred at their approach and the torches disturbed the long-sealed dark.

Ashway split them into pairs and commanded them to search in different directions. Much to Eamon's relief he was paired with Mathaiah. Ashway cheerfully assigned them the task of searching what he called "the tomb tunnel", after which pronouncement he dismissed them to their corridor.

"Why is it called that, sir?" Mathaiah whispered as they walked away from the staircase. He nervously fingered his torch.

"At a guess?" Eamon offered.

There was no need to say more.

They peered down the tunnel before them. "Does the dark worry you, sir?"

"No," Eamon lied. He had never been afraid of the dark. Why did this feel different? "Come on."

As they started down the tunnel, the roof came in lower over their heads, the sounds and lights of the other Hands becoming fainter with each step. They held their torch aloft into each alcove that they passed, but found nothing. Eamon could only reason that that was a good thing. Another good thing was their increasing distance from the Hands – he found Cathair and Ashway tense work.

Mathaiah ducked into another alcove, peered around it, made a disgusted noise at something he had trod in, came back, and shook his head.

"Nothing but a broken bottle in there, sir."

"They used to be wine cellars," Eamon answered. "Hughan told me that Elaina emptied them for her books."

"Sir!" Mathaiah hissed, glancing anxiously back.

Feeling bold, Eamon laughed. "I think we can safely speak if we keep our voices low."

Mathaiah nodded, pacified. "Strange library," he mused.

"I don't suppose it was always this dark."

"That stone, sir: what was it?"

"Bait for the Hands," Eamon told him. "It was Hughan's idea. The throned is obviously looking for something down here. If it is here, whatever it is, we must send word back to Hughan." He felt stronger for saying it.

"How far do the tunnels go?" Mathaiah asked, squinting into the inky dark.

"I don't know." Mathaiah held the torch steady while Eamon searched another alcove. "Hughan told me that the bookkeepers swear the tunnels to be empty. There shouldn't be anything here for us to find. Not," he added, moving on to the next alcove, "that that will have any bearing on how far we have to walk to confirm it." Scaring an errant spider and ascertaining the alcove to be empty, he returned to the main passageway.

"I suppose the bookkeepers emptied it all. It must have been quite a job."

Eamon nodded, imagining the cellar, every alcove filled with knowledge. It would have been an impressive sight. No wonder his father had loved to imagine it in its days of glory.

They went on for a few moments in silence. Hanging cobwebs brushed at their faces and trailed over their heads. The corridor stretched forward until it passed through a cracked archway and pooled into a hall.

Eamon took Mathaiah's torch and held it up, casting light into the room to reveal a dozen long stone boxes. Eamon walked carefully to the nearest and examined it curiously. A stone effigy lay on its top, showing a man with a book and a sword over his breast and a crown upon his brow. A star was shaped on the crown's crest.

"Well, that explains why he called it the 'tomb tunnel'," Mathaiah murmured. He looked at the effigy's face; it was long and noble. "Who is he?"

"I don't know."

"Do you think he... was a King?"

The forbidden word hung in the air. Eamon shook himself. The throned could not hear them there.

"Perhaps he was."

Slowly Eamon stepped to the next tomb. The figure of a woman was carved into the red marble. Intricate words ran round the lid but he could not read them. The stone was scarred, as though someone had taken a chisel to it. Who and why, he wondered? The woman's face was broken. Eamon touched the shattered stone, gently brushing thick dust from its marble brow.

"Sir," Mathaiah called suddenly, "there are papers here."

Eamon hurried to the cadet at once. Mathaiah was crouched on the other side of the red tomb. Tucked into the side of the stonework was a small shelf littered with reams of parchment. Mathaiah was holding one in his hand, turning it to try to make sense of it.

"Poetry, I think," he said, then pulled a face. "And bad poetry, too! Who rhymes death and teeth?"

"It's a particular kind of rhyme," Eamon answered distractedly, stooping to look through the papers himself.

"So particular that it doesn't rhyme?"

"Perhaps it's an intentional break of rhyme, meaning to give emphasis to something else. The broken rhyme might be the critical point of the whole work."

Mathaiah laughed. "I didn't know you were a scholar, sir!"

"A hidden and much maligned talent. I read a lot when I was young: my father was a bookbinder. So was I, before I joined the Gauntlet."

He tried to interpret the papers. They seemed to be a series of sonnets, written in a striking hand. The ink was faded and he could not read a word of the inscription, but to see words withstanding decay in such a place moved him. He looked back at the face on the stone lid. Were the poems hers? Had she written them? Had they been given to her, or written for her? If so, by whom?

"Should we take these back, sir?"

With the exception of Lord Cathair, Eamon did not think that Hands relished poetry. He shook his head and placed the papers back. "They have more value where they are, I think."

"Sir."

Eamon rose.

Breathing deeply, he began to circle the other tombs. Some of them had shelves similar to the one that Mathaiah had found. On some stood chipped pots or ornaments; on one was a tiny iron horse. One of the tombs belonged to a child with a beautiful, round face. With his torch lifted high, Eamon could see traces of paintings on the wall. Some showed knights; some showed gaily painted ladies in springtime, spreading flowers by the River in a time of peace. One, the highest and most faded, seemed to show a man beneath a field of stars. A star shone brightly at his brow, making a crown of light, and his face was turned towards the midnight hue of the River.

Eamon came to the tomb farthest from the hall's entrance. It had an unfinished look and its shelf stood empty bar a large, uncomely insect that scuttled indignantly away. Eamon leaned against the stonework.

The face below him was a man's, stern and wizened. The hands over his breast held a tightly bound scroll marked with a star. In the flicker of the torchlight Eamon saw illegible shapes on the scroll. He traced his fingers across the faded forms. It was as he did so that his eyes were suddenly filled with the hideous strokes of the writing in the Hands' Hall. He went deathly cold.

"Sir?"

But Eamon didn't hear him. His vision blurred and his eyes opened to the chamber. He saw the paintings in the fullness of their colour and vivid hues of stone in the flickering torchlight.

A man was there, dressed in black. A red stone hung about his neck and a strange dagger rested at his side. Eamon stared as the man pushed back the lid of a tomb. Determined sweat plastered his pale face; Eamon watched as he picked up a book from the floor beside him. The book – the same book that Eamon had seen when he lay in torturous dreams at the Hidden Hall – was grimly bound, its dark cover embellished with a grasping eagle and its pages thick with the same writing as Eamon had seen at the Hands' Hall. The sight of it made him tremble.

The man in his vision gripped the book for a moment between his palms. Eamon thought he saw a spark of fire between them. The stricken man cried out and forced his shaking hands to press the book down deep into the tomb. Tears lashed his face, and as the stranger struggled to close the tomb again Eamon saw the heart of the King clutched in his hand.

He staggered against the tomb as the vision released him. All was clear: it was the same tomb, and the man kneeling by it had been Eben Goodman.

Eamon quivered; his ancestor's incomprehensible grief coursed through his veins. He choked back a sob.

"Sir?" Mathaiah whispered, alarmed.

Eamon pulled sharply away from the tomb and drove tremulous hands across his face. He knew what lay hidden there. The throned sought it.

"Sir?"

Eamon could barely speak. "There's a book here."

"What? How do you know that?"

"I saw him putting it inside…" Eamon swallowed hard. He could not take his gaze from the tomb.

Mathaiah followed his look. His face creased with horror. "In there?" he whispered. Eamon nodded. Mathaiah's mouth fell open. "Sir, we can't open a tomb –"

Eamon did not hear the rest. He knew there was a book inside, and he knew that Eben had risked everything to hide it. Every fibre of his being commanded that the thing remain hidden.

But the vision had aroused his curiosity. What was it that Eben had so desperately hidden – something that the throned desired so much that he had once tried to burn his way into the library. Could it really be so very terrible? Hadn't Hughan said that nothing important was left in Ellen's Well? Hadn't the King told him to find out all that he could? He would never know what lay in the tomb if he did not open it.

What price had Eben paid?

"Sir?"

It might help Hughan. He made up his mind. "We'll open it."

Mathaiah watched him silently. Though clearly unconvinced, he gave his assent: "Yes, sir."

Eamon looked around. Finding a hook on the nearby wall he slid the torch into it. The light made the faded figures in the paintings dance.

Eamon pushed his sleeves up and laid his bare hands to the side of the thick, heavy lid. Without a word Mathaiah joined him and at an unspoken signal they both heaved. The scars on his back burnt as he strained against a force so strong that his muscles could scarcely nudge it. Mathaiah's feet scuffed and skidded in the dirt and he struggled to keep his footing.

Suddenly the lid budged and air sighed out of it, bringing with it an unpleasant smell. Mathaiah recoiled but Eamon kept pushing until the lid was halfway open. Coughing, Mathaiah brought the torch back to the open tomb.

Inside was a skeleton, regally composed in fading robes. Its arms were folded over its breast in the manner of the effigy, and its robes trailed gracefully down to its feet. Eamon felt suddenly, and deeply, ashamed. He had opened a tomb, a royal tomb.

"I can't see it," Mathaiah whispered faintly. Beads of sweat lined Eamon's brow. He wiped at it with his bare, shivering arm.

Mathaiah was right: there was nothing to be seen except the skeleton in its resting place of streaming robes. Eamon surveyed the body as objectively as he could, chewing nervously at his lip. The skeleton's back arched upwards a little more than it ought to – as though there was something beneath it.

It was his last chance to leave it.

"Hold the torch high, Mathaiah."

With a calming breath Eamon reached into the deep, cold tomb with both arms. His skin crawled as he pressed his hands underneath the crumbling robes. He searched blindly under the skeleton, feeling cold stone beneath his fingers. Then he suddenly felt something else: leather.

In silence he drew out the book. The leather was dark, roughed, and embittered with age. An eagle still sat boldly on its front, chipped and cracked, though the red-edged pages were crisp.

The mark in his palm stirred. Something began whispering in his mind and Eben's grief filled him: it was overpowering.

He staggered. The book fell from his hands.

"Sir?" Mathaiah gripped his shoulder in alarm. "Are you all right, sir?"

Eamon didn't answer. He had made his choice. Rising, he drew a shuddering breath and slowly pushed the lid of the tomb closed again.

Stepping back he saw Mathaiah turning the book over in his hands. The cadet stared at its strange letters with a furrowed brow.

"What kind of book is this, sir?" he asked uneasily.

"I don't know." He watched as Mathaiah opened the covers and scanned a few pages. The writing was unintelligible and jagged. The cadet's face grew strange.

"This will sound odd, sir, but I feel like I can almost read it."

"Close it," Eamon told him. The pages glared at him and he did not want to think about what they might read.

Mathaiah gauged him uncertainly. "Are you sure we should take this back?"

"It may help Hughan," Eamon answered. He had to believe it. Hadn't the King expressly commanded that they discover what the throned wanted from Ellen's Well? Perhaps they could smuggle the book from the tunnels. Even if they could not, what possible use could it be to the throned?

"Will you carry it, Mathaiah?"

"Yes, sir."

Eamon took one last look at the disturbed tomb; its stony eyes followed him, feeding the maelstrom in his heart.

They retraced their steps to the central chamber. Mathaiah carried the book solemnly while Eamon busied himself with the torch. The voices of the Hands grew louder; Eamon made out Cathair and Ashway among them. Mathaiah suddenly stopped. Eamon had carried on a few paces before he noticed his ward's hesitance.

"Are you all right?"

"Listen," Mathaiah told him quietly.

"It's only Cathair and Ashway –"

"But listen!"

Obligingly, Eamon concentrated on the voices. He then realized that though he knew the voices, he did not know the words. The language was completely foreign to him. He had studied a little of the tongues used in the majority of the merchant states but this sounded nothing like them.

He glanced at Mathaiah. "What is it?"

Mathaiah didn't answer. Instead, he pressed one hand to the cover of the book. Eamon stared at him.

"Did you understand it?"

"Lieutenant Goodman!" called a voice. It was Cathair's.

With one motion Eamon and Mathaiah hurried to the stairwell. The other Hands were coming back in dribs and drabs. Some had already brought back odd scrolls and thin leather books: these Ashway was studying and then discarding single-mindedly. Eamon wondered what fate awaited the papers that displeased him. As they approached, the Lord of the West Quarter treated them to one of his harrowing smiles.

"Come, lieutenant; there is little purpose in trying to sneak about these tunnels, especially when you bear a torch!" Cathair laughed, and might have continued. But as Mathaiah stepped forward the Hand fell silent, his face frozen. Eamon realized then that they could never have hidden the book from the eyes of Dunthruik's raven: his eyes were keen and swift.

Cathair glanced at Eamon. "What have you found, lieutenant?"

"Nothing, my lord —"

The words had barely left his lips before Lord Ashway snatched the book hungrily from Mathaiah's hands.

"Where did you find this?" he hissed.

Eamon's mind whirled. "In a tomb, my lord."

"What a grave matter, lieutenant!" Cathair laughed, glancing sidelong at Ashway. "Mr Goodman, you never fail to impress — or amuse — me! Gentlemen, we will burn those," he added, gesturing to the other papers.

The Hands hurriedly gathered loose papers and parchment as though clearing autumn leaves. Eamon only managed to get hold of a few sheets. The Hands led the way up the staircase, most concentrating on the tricky steps. Cathair and Ashway were bowed over the dark book. Boldly, Eamon slipped a couple of parchments into his jacket. His small act of defiance passed unobserved.

The dying sunlight flashed fitfully through the windows as they emerged. At Cathair's direction Eamon removed the heart of the King from the fireplace. The walls closed over the opening. There was a moment of light and then the King's stone fell dull.

Eamon pulled the stone from its place.

"Keep it, Mr Goodman," Cathair said. "A memento of a successful afternoon's work."

Nodding, Eamon slipped the stone back around his neck.

Back in the plaza, the Hands were dismissed to their burning assignment and Eamon and Mathaiah to the college. Cathair and Ashway vanished swiftly into the palace, the book still firmly clasped beneath Ashway's arm.

"Sir," Mathaiah volunteered after a while, "I think I understood some of what they were saying."

"How?" Eamon asked — though he supposed that the more important question would be "what".

"I don't know, sir. They… they said that it would be ironic."

"What would?"

"If Eben's son brought them back the Nightholt."

Eamon stared at him. For a moment he couldn't think, couldn't speak: he was chilled through to his very core.

"The what?" he whispered at last.

"Nightholt. I think… they meant the book, sir."

A group of Gauntlet passed by. Mathaiah pushed his hands inside his jacket. When they were gone he spoke again: "Who is 'Eben's son'?"

Eamon swallowed. "They meant me. I am Eben's son."

"Your father?"

"No." Eamon found he could not meet his friend's gaze. "Eben was Ede's First Knight. He betrayed him. Then he betrayed the throned. Eben hid the book in the tomb. I saw him."

"I hope we did the right thing," Mathaiah whispered.

Eamon drew a guilty breath. "So do I."

They walked on in silence. Hoping to ease both their minds by changing the subject, he continued: "I wanted to ask you before. What happened to you when we met Lord Cathair?"

"I don't know," Mathaiah admitted. "When we got to the bridge I was just pretending – I know what effect shadeweed is supposed to have and I tried to emulate it. But when he touched me… it was like being immured. I could hear voices, most of the time, but I couldn't see." He shivered. "I don't remember coming to Dunthruik. The first I saw of it was when I woke up, and you were there."

"And the plain…" Eamon hesitated. "The place where I found you. Do you remember that?"

"Now that was strange, sir," Mathaiah smiled, as though the rest hadn't been. "It was frightening at first. But then someone came to me. I don't know where from, or who he was. He… he was like Hughan – and yet unlike him. His face was wrong, yet somehow more right, too, and his voice! I cannot describe it to you. There was a kind of light all around him – blue, or white, or silver all at once…" The cadet paused, as though drawing his thoughts into order. Eamon listened in awe. "He seemed kind, so I asked him to stay with me. He wasn't at all frightening. He knew my name and spoke to me of courage. He told me that I was a King's man and that although I was in darkness it couldn't keep me or hold me. He made me feel better – stronger and less afraid.

"He said that the Hands had brought me to Dunthruik and that they wanted to get into my mind – no, 'breach' was the word he used – but that I shouldn't worry, because they would find it unreachable. He said I was safe and that you would come; he stayed with me until you did and then he left, but I didn't see him go… Then I woke up."

Eamon stared at his young friend in amazement. The tale thrilled a darkened part of his soul.

"I'm glad that he came, sir," Mathaiah added. "Do… do you think that the light round him was like the light that you used to heal me?"

Eamon nodded wordlessly.

After a few moments of silence, Mathaiah looked up. "What will we do about the book, sir?"

"We have to send word to Hughan. Maybe a description of it will mean something to him or the bookkeepers." A plan began forming in his mind. "One of us must speak to Lillabeth tonight."

"Lillabeth?" Mathaiah asked, then added: "Tonight?"

Eamon realized he hadn't told Mathaiah about his evening plans. He reddened. "I'm invited to supper tonight with Lady Turnholt."

Mathaiah raised a pleased eyebrow. "To supper, eh?"

Growing redder, Eamon shushed him. "Lillabeth Hollenwell is her maid and our contact for reaching Hughan. All we need to do is figure out how to get the information to her."

Mathaiah grinned. "I think we can do that, sir."

Candeller's Way was in the North Quarter, and lit that evening by dozens of lanterns that spread along the road like flowers answering the rising moon. They did not find it difficult to locate the house of

Alessia Turnholt. When they reached the gates they were expected.

"Lieutenant Goodman, cadet," greeted the gateman, bowing to each of them in turn. "Please follow me."

The servant led them towards the house. Eamon saw stables to one side and some outhouses to the other, along with a small garden. The lady's carriage was propped by the stables, undergoing repair. The elegant house boasted high balconies with views across the city. Welcoming lights glowed in its windows.

Within, the house was more spectacular than it had seemed from without: panelled walls and hanging drapes of deep velvet surrounded them, while the corridors showed portraits, statues, ornaments... Every part of every room heralded the family's riches and favour.

But, on entering, Eamon's eyes were caught by one thing alone. Standing in the hallway was Lady Alessia, resplendent in a long, red gown, cut low at the neck. Her dress was brocaded in golden threads and she smiled a smile that would melt the heart of any man who did but glance at it. Eamon knew it, and still he looked.

"Lieutenant Goodman!" The lady's voice was high with pleasure and her smile broadened as she came to greet them. "It is so kind of you to join me – and of your captain to let you come!"

"It was kind of you to invite me," Eamon answered, bowing awkwardly.

Alessia received the compliment with a gracious laugh. "Who is your young friend?"

"This is my ward, my lady."

"Cadet Mathaiah Grahaven, at your service, my lady," Mathaiah bowed with a flourish. Eamon was jealous of his ease.

"How lovely!" Alessia enthused, turning to Eamon with an astonished look. "Here but a day, and already entrusted with a ward? You do excel yourself, Mr Goodman." Eamon blushed. "Mr Grahaven is, of course, welcome to join our meal."

"Thank you, my lady."

The lady led them to the dining room; the table had been laid forth so regally that it might host lords as easily as lieutenants. Lady Alessia invited them both to sit and quickly had her servants make up an extra place for Mathaiah. Eamon recognized the coachman among those who followed her commands.

"Gentlemen, welcome to my table!" Alessia smiled, her eyes resting on Eamon last of all. He flushed crimson.

They sat together. Laughing, Alessia plied them with jests and tales of the court and the city while course after course of food was laid before them. Mathaiah ate readily, willingly accommodating the lady's insistence that he should not stint his eating for modesty's sake. Eamon ate far less, engaged as he so thoroughly was in watching the lady speak. He marvelled at the way she could weave her words into a tale full of life, and could not help but appreciate her beauty. He was glad that Mathaiah had volunteered to find an excuse to speak to Lillabeth – he was wondering how he would ever tear himself away from Lady Alessia.

As Mathaiah finished eating he sat back and returned to examining the paintings that lined the wall, something which he had been doing as much as he could during the meal.

"Do you like art, Mr Grahaven?"

It was the perfect opportunity. "Yes, my lady," Mathaiah beamed, "especially the early Dunthruik style. My mother had a couple of works from that period. I was admiring these you have here, my lady." The cadet was looking at a great landscape piece, detailing the port of Dunthruik in the height of summer: the ships were filled with grain. Eamon had scarcely noticed it himself.

"Mr Grahaven, you must know that this is but a poor example compared with some that my father collected!"

Mathaiah's eyes widened. "I would love to see them," he said. "Would that be possible?"

"Of course," the lady answered, half-rising. Mathaiah stopped her with a gesture of his hand.

"Forgive me, my lady – I intend you no disruption. Perhaps a servant of yours would be so good as to show me?"

Eamon marvelled at Mathaiah's smooth handling – he was delighted when their calculated risk paid off.

"That is a wonderful idea, Mr Grahaven." Lady Turnholt rose and pulled a cord. Far away a bell rang. A few moments later Lillabeth entered. She curtseyed impeccably.

"My lady?"

"Lilly, would you be so kind as to show Mr Grahaven the collection in the West Wing? He is a great appreciator of art and I think that he will enjoy them."

"Of course, my lady."

"And do ask Mr Cartwright to have the house retire for the night – they worked finely this evening. You may help yourselves to a small cask of Ravensill Avola, as a congratulation."

"Thank you, my lady," Lillabeth answered with a smile. "Your house will appreciate it. If you would follow me, Mr Grahaven."

Mathaiah rose from the table and thanked Alessia again before leaving. Eamon found himself alone with Alessia.

The lady went to open the balcony doors. A cool breeze blew in from them but Eamon felt hot. Alessia set two small glasses on a side table then turned to smile at him.

"Would you pour me a drink, Mr Goodman?" she asked. "It is always a pleasure to share a closing drink in good company."

Eamon rose and came to her side. She raised her glass and he tilted the bottle so that a deep, red wine came running out of it. It was the same colour as her dress. As he poured, her hand shook a little and Eamon reached out instinctively to steady it. Their hands touched.

"My apologies, my lady," Eamon said, turning as red as the wine.

The lady laughed. "That's quite all right." Slowly, Eamon set the bottle down. She watched him. "Won't you join me in a drink, Mr Goodman?"

"I'm sorry, my lady," he answered, and he was. "My duty precludes it."

"I understand, lieutenant." She set her glass down and cocked her head at him. "Would your duty preclude a stroll on the balcony?"

"No, my lady."

She moved across to the balcony and looked back at him, her dark hair cascading like a cape about her shoulders. "Then perhaps you would accompany me?"

Eamon gazed at her. "With pleasure, my lady."

She stepped onto the balcony, a nymph slipping into moonstruck darkness. Bewitched, Eamon followed her.

The balcony overlooked the garden. What seemed miles away Eamon could hear the sounds of the city. The dome of the Crown, the tall shape of the palace, and the harbour lights all met his eyes. But they did not hold him.

Alessia gestured to one side of the house. "That is the West Wing," she said, "where your young friend will be enjoying a fine collection."

"It was kind of you to let him see them, my lady."

Alessia smiled. "A love of art marks a man of good repute." She laid a playful hand on his arm. "And you, Mr Goodman?" she asked, her eyes twinkling. "Are you a man of good repute?"

Eamon swallowed. His whole being was on fire and in that moment, with the lady's welcoming smile and her fingers dancing delicately on his pulse, with the moonlight shining enticingly on her pale flesh… in that moment he wished very much that he was a man of bad repute.

With great effort he turned his gaze away from the sweet invitation of the dress's low neckline. "I strive to be one, my lady," he murmured. "Only a good man may keep his honour. If I have not honour then I cannot serve or glorify the Master."

Alessia laughed, delighted with his answer. "You speak well, lieutenant!" She strolled across to the balcony rail and leaned against it, facing him. "There are rumours about you at court, Lieutenant Goodman. You so intrigued me with your gallantry last night that I decided to see if they were true. I hope you do not think that rude of me?" she added with a sincere look.

How could he think of her as anything but entrancing? "No, my lady."

"I am glad!" Alessia laughed, seemingly relieved. "Would you object to my seeking answers to some of those matters that most intrigue me?"

Eamon gazed at her, astounded by her interest in him. "I would answer you willingly, my lady."

"They say that you surrendered your sword," she told him, turning so as to look up into his eyes. The turn was enough to set his heart racing, let alone the glimpse of her beautiful neck. "They say," Alessia continued, "that you were taken prisoner by wayfarers and that they tortured you, yet you revealed nothing. They say that you stole precious information, risking your life to bring back the last man of your crew, and that you brought things of great value back to this city and to the Master. Quieter voices, more wary of being heard, say that you breached a man that Lord Tramist, Lord of the South Quarter and finest breacher of this city and the River, could not. They say you are the only man who stands up to First Lieutenant Alben in matters of decency."

He did not care how she had heard such things. Eamon half-heartedly tried to offer her compliments some resistance. "You flatter me, my lady."

"I do not," she told him. Suddenly she shivered. At once, Eamon removed his jacket and eased it over her bare shoulders. She smiled. When she looked at him again he found that she was impossibly close to him. His heart pounded so loudly that he was sure the whole world could hear it.

"They say," she whispered, "that in one meeting you conquered the heart of Alessia Turnholt, and that she seeks to reward you in full for your gallantry." Her eyes filled his sight and heart, forming the circles of his whole world.

Suddenly there was a hoarse, piercing scream – a girl's. It was followed seconds later by a yell. Eamon recognized the second voice: Mathaiah's. The cries came from the side of the house.

There could be no hesitation. Eamon tore himself away from Alessia and hurtled back inside. Flinging open the dining room doors he raced down the stairs, into the hall, through the doors. He heard sounds of a struggle near the stables, where the West Wing opened on the garden. Alessia was running close behind him.

"Stay inside!" he commanded. He did not wait to see if she obeyed. He bolted across the yard.

Lillabeth was pressed against the wall of the house. She sobbed and clutched at torn clothes with bloodied hands. In front of her was a man in a state of half-undress. His breathing was ragged and he was wild with rage, for between him and his weeping prey stood Mathaiah.

"Out of my way, bastard!" the man yelled. "Or I'll have you, too! Go back to your precious warder and leave me to my business!"

The wild man heard Eamon's approach and turned. With a rush of hatred Eamon recognized him: Alben.

With a screech the first lieutenant hurled himself at the cadet. The next moment Mathaiah and Alben were struggling hand to hand in the moonlight, the first lieutenant towering wrathfully over his foe. Alben drew a long dagger and thrust it at Mathaiah's chest. But the cadet was quick and with a feat of strength blocked the man's blow. Mathaiah twisted Alben's arm impossibly at the wrist and Alben was forced to tear away with a scream. He slashed across Mathaiah's arm and the cadet gave a cry of his own.

All this happened in moments. First lieutenant and cadet fell apart and Mathaiah moved back to stand protectively by Lillabeth, drawing his sword with his bleeding arm. His breath was pained.

"Sir!" he warned.

Eamon turned in time to see another man bearing down on him, dagger drawn. He blocked the blow and then drew his blade ferociously across the man's neck. There was no time to think about what he had done.

The corpse fell away from him and he rounded on Alben. The first lieutenant was laughing.

"Beginner's luck, Goodman!" he sneered. "That one was supposed to have garrotted you on your way home. Now I can kill you and your ward myself, a solution that I like much better."

Howling like a devil Alben slashed again at Mathaiah. The cadet blocked the blow but its force was enormous – he staggered down to his knees beneath it, his sword clanging away from his hand.

"Stop!" Eamon yelled, lunging at him.

With a bloodthirsty smile Alben parried the blow. Content that he had drawn the man's ire, Eamon fell back a pace.

"Let me tell you how this evening is going to go, Mr Goodman," Alben said. "First, I'm going to nearly kill you. Then I will kill him, and I will take her, and then I will finish you slowly. You don't object, I hope?"

"They have nothing to do with us, Alben!" Eamon told him.

"They are in my way – much like you." Hurling his dagger into his other hand Alben drew his sword. Terror flashed through Eamon's flesh. He did not know how skilled a swordsman Alben was.

"You want murder?" he cried. "For what, Alben? For Manners?"

Alben erupted. "You expect me to think that you're blind, Goodman? I'm not. Since you came Waite has thought of nobody but you. How do I become a Hand if my captain is dallying with lieutenants? He can dally all he pleases, of course, but not when my promotion is on the line. The incidents at the course are amusements, Goodman, much like you are, and I intended to duel you to teach you your place, like all those other newcomer bastards." Alben's face was hollow and crazed; Eamon fell back before it. "But then, Goodman, you dare to court Lady Turnholt, brazenly, in my face. Sleep with as many whores as you want, Goodman – but not with mine."

Eamon gaped, but had no time to answer and barely the time to think. Alben launched himself, foul blades grinning in the light. Eamon met the oncoming blow and jerked to one side to avoid the slashing dagger strike that followed it.

Their swords jarred and Eamon struggled to hold his own. His stomach cramped as he and Alben tore apart and then exchanged a furious match of thrusts and parries. Fire burnt on Alben's palm: a red light like that in the man's eyes.

Suddenly Alben threw a strike that brought Eamon's sword out of his hand. The pommel-blow that followed struck Eamon hard in the jaw and he was sent, head swimming, to the ground. With a blood-curdling scream Alben threw down his blades and hurled himself on top of him. He clenched his sweating hands about Eamon's throat. Eamon cried out as the palm-fire burnt him.

"I'm going to choke you like a dog, Goodman!" Alben hissed, driving his thumbs down. Choking and gasping, Eamon tried desperately to pull Alben's hands away, but his strength was waning.

Only one defence was left to him. He rammed his hand into Alben's face.

The plain was dark and when Eamon looked with his other eyes Alben stood like a tower before him. The man laughed derisively.

"This will solve nothing, Goodman!"

Eamon staggered. His vision was still blurred; he could do nothing while he was being choked. He could not control it. Alben knew it. The first lieutenant approached him with a grotesque smile.

"So, you're a breacher," he snarled. "Would you like to know what I am? A breaker." Alben thrust his hand into Eamon's face. The hand upon him became a fistful of knives.

He screamed.

In agony Eamon fell fitfully between the plain and the real world. In one he could see Mathaiah trying to tear Alben off of him while in the other were the knives and looming presence. There was nothing he could do. Nothing.

Courage, Eamon!

Suddenly there was strength in him again and he saw the plain. The knives ceased to strike. Alben gaped in horror. Eamon looked at himself and understood that help had come: he was arrayed from head to foot in an armour of bright light.

He opened his eyes to the courtyard. There was strength in his hands and light at his throat where the heart of the King lay. He tore

Alben's hands from his neck. Breath returned to his starved lungs and he hurled Alben from him.

Both men staggered to their feet. Eamon was aware of blue light shimmering by his hands, of Mathaiah and Lillabeth watching in astonishment, and of the cries of approaching soldiers. It was then that he realized what was plain for all to see: that he was a King's man. Alben had seen it. If he didn't act quickly then the approaching soldiers would see it, too.

"You treacherous, wayfaring bastard!" Alben cursed, and drew breath to yell it out loud.

The breath never reached his lips. Eamon snatched up the fallen dagger and hurled himself at the first lieutenant. He had no choice.

The blade went deep. Alben collapsed against the wall of the house. Eamon stepped back, hating himself and hating Alben for forcing him to do what he had done.

Suddenly Alben spoke again. His voice was small, different. As he spluttered blood into the darkness his eyes searched frantically this way and that.

"Eamon!" he pleaded. "Eamon, it wasn't me, he…" The man gave a gasp of pain. "Eamon, please! Save me!"

Eamon felt the ebbing light of the King's grace in him. He knew he could do it. He had done it before. But the soldiers were coming…

The light faded away. Alben's mouth twisted into a sob. Gripping its hilt, Eamon twisted the dagger.

"Lieutenant!"

Eamon saw Waite, Cathair, and a hoard of Gauntlet soldiers. Behind them came Alessia, her running much hampered by her long dress. Eamon understood at once that she had raised the alarm – he did not have time to wonder how she had found Cathair and Waite. With a cry the lady ran to Lillabeth and gathered her into her arms. The maid was weeping.

Waite's face paled as he surveyed the scene. He met Eamon's gaze in a fury.

"You had better have a damn good explanation for this, lieutenant!"

"Sir, I…" Eamon faltered. There was blood on his hands. The first lieutenant was stone still, his wretched face growing cold. He choked back an angry cry.

"What happened here?" Waite demanded, rushing to Alben's side.

"I can explain, sir," Mathaiah said, clutching at his wound. "Alben… he was in a kind of fit… He attacked this serving lady… I tried to help her, and he was upon me… He meant to kill us… Lieutenant Goodman had no choice – he had to kill him."

Waite glanced at his erstwhile first lieutenant. "Alben," he whispered sadly. He pressed his eyes shut.

Lord Cathair stepped forward. "Mr Alben was an exemplary officer, gentlemen, but was known to suffer from bouts of fierce anger. He was receiving treatment for it."

Eamon gazed at the Hand, dumbfounded. The explanation for Alben's madness seemed too quickly offered. Alben himself, dying, had seemed a different man…

"With respect," Mathaiah cried, "the fact that he was receiving treatment would have been of no comfort to this lady had he had his way!"

"Cadet," Eamon warned sharply.

"No, no." Waite's face was grey and he moved with the slowness of an old man. "Mr Grahaven is right." He turned to some of the ensigns who had followed him. "Gentlemen, escort Lady Alessia and her maid back to the house, and entrust them to her household."

At further commands from Waite the bodies of the nameless assassin and dead first lieutenant were removed. Eamon trembled. He had done it – he had killed a man to defend his broken oaths. What else was he capable of doing?

Waite and Cathair were speaking together in low voices. Mathaiah stepped to Eamon's side.

"Are you all right, sir?"

Eamon nodded dumbly. He turned to speak as privately as he could with the cadet.

"Did they see?" he whispered, dashing at tears with bloody, shaking hands.

Mathaiah shook his head.

"I didn't want to kill him." He felt sick. There was nowhere for him to clean his hands.

"Lieutenant Goodman."

Eamon spun about. Cathair summoned him with a gesture. Captain Waite had already turned to follow the soldiers who carried Alben's body away.

Quivering, Eamon bowed. "My lord."

"Captain Waite has magnanimously decided that you will not be required to attend watch duties tonight."

"Thank you, my lord."

"He has also recommended that you return to the college and get some rest. You will have other duties to attend to in the morning. Be sure to be looking your best at parade."

"Yes, my lord," Eamon answered. "But I will escort my ward to the surgeons first: he is wounded."

"Do so," Cathair smiled. "I bid you good rest, First Lieutenant."

The Hand disappeared into the night. Eamon stared after him with burning eyes. "*He said that you would make first lieutenant within two days…*"

Eamon drove his hands across his eyes. The moon in the cold sky told him that it was the end of his second day.

CHAPTER XV

Eamon slept fitfully that night. No amount of washing seemed to cleanse his hands.

Could he not have healed the first lieutenant and then breached him to change his memory? Surely he could have done. But it was too late.

The predawn light seeped slowly through the window. He shuddered, longing for his chill flesh to be warmed. The first lieutenant's dying pleas harrowed him by name.

"Save me, Eamon!"

He thrust his hands back into his water basin and scoured them again. Was this what service to Hughan meant – murder?

He anxiously shook his hands dry. Desperate to distract himself, he paced back to his bed and took from his jacket the papers he had picked up in Ellenswell.

Most were faded with age – odd words or drawings could be distinguished here and there. They angered him. Had he saved worthless papers over a man that day?

Only one leaf caught his eye. On it was a simple sketch: a watchtower on the crest of a hill, overlooking a wooded valley. There was no name, mark, or indication of any kind. Inked soldiers stood at their posts and a flag was raised above them. Beneath the flag, among distant hills, was a man with a bright face. On his breast were the sword and star.

Eamon stared at it, demanding some providential absolution. There was none to be had.

His thoughts oppressed him as he left his room. Even Mathaiah's face, when it appeared at the other end of the corridor, did little to cheer him.

"Good morning, sir." One jacket arm was swollen, betraying a bandage underneath, but apart from this the cadet was merry enough. Eamon tried to smile.

"How are you feeling?"

"College surgeon says I'll be right as the River," Mathaiah answered, patting his injury. "Yourself, sir?"

"Not well," Eamon confessed. "Not looking forward to this morning. I'm glad you're about."

Mathaiah smiled encouragingly. "Wouldn't be anywhere else but here, sir."

Parade was called at the usual time. Eamon took his accustomed place in line. The Third Ravens kept scouring the courtyard for their first lieutenant – everyone seemed to notice the absence. The college's lieutenants spoke together in curiously hushed tones. Eamon could read their conversations from their faces: they all wanted to know where Alben was.

His gut twisted as his double oath consumed him.

Waite came at last. He seemed intolerably tired. The ranks fell silent.

"At ease, gentlemen," the captain called. He did not need to draw their attention: the college was rapt by his gravity. "I'm afraid that I have some unpleasant tidings. We have lost First Lieutenant Alben to wayfaring intrigues."

Stunned outrage rippled through the college. Perhaps he hadn't heard clearly over the beating of his throbbing heart. Was he not to be named? No; his murder was to be covered with the tale of insurgents.

"Snakes are at large, gentlemen," Waite continued, "and this is proof that they have penetrated our city."

Eamon shuddered. Waite could not guess how near to the truth he was.

"Honour Alben's memory with your vigilance, West Quarter.

His death will not then have been in vain." Waite paused, taking the whole college in his gaze. "Lord Cathair and I have consulted on the matter. We appoint a new first lieutenant this morning."

There was another murmur; several of the lieutenants looked secretly pleased, expecting the honour to alight on them. But Eamon already knew the outcome of Waite's consultation. He met Waite's gaze. There was an uneasy formality in it.

"Lieutenant Goodman."

Stunned silence. It was only his third day in Dunthruik, and some lieutenants had reached that rank before Eamon had even joined the Gauntlet. How they would loathe him – and they did not know who he was, and what he had done.

Eamon presented himself before his captain with a salute. Waite's face was expressionless. He held another flame in his hand, a mark ready to join the two already pinned at Eamon's neck.

"Lieutenant Eamon Goodman," he said. "Your blood, blade, and body speak of the Master's glory; will you command men for that glory?"

Eamon could not look the captain in the eye. "For his glory."

"Then for his glory it is given to you to command men, First Lieutenant Goodman. Lift your head, Mr Goodman," he added quietly.

"Sir." Eamon trembled as the captain pinned on the flame – a bitter, undeserved, usurped honour. Waite knew what had happened – how could he make this appointment?

Waite surveyed the ranks. "I present to you First Lieutenant Goodman," he called. "This promotion is ratified by the Master himself, and performed by my own hand." The mark of the throned flared along the contours of his raised palm. "Let any who has bane bring it to me."

Waite lowered his hand. He proceeded to dismiss the ranks. Then he turned to Eamon.

"Congratulations, Mr Goodman." The captain held out his hand. There was little warmth in it.

"Thank you, sir."

"Dismissed."

Eamon hesitated. He owed nothing to Waite. But part of him loved the captain – had loved the captain since that first day when he had heard him laughing in the hall. Their oaths conflicted wildly but still Eamon felt bound to him, and bound to please him. At that moment, he felt the captain's grief and was burdened that he was the cause of it.

Waite considered him piercingly. "Why are you still here, Mr Goodman?"

"Sir, may I speak frankly?"

Waite nodded.

"This appointment, sir… it is against your wishes." Eamon discerned it from the captain's whole bearing.

Waite smiled a sad smile. "Not on professional grounds, Mr Goodman. You are a fine officer and a young man destined for great things. You take responsibility well and defend those who cannot defend themselves. How many of us can say as much? Defending the defenceless is what you were doing last night; I laud your courage."

Waite looked once about the emptying parade ground and then back to Eamon. When he spoke again his voice was quiet. "Of all the officers that I have trained, Mr Goodman, you are probably the one who has been most deserving of this appointment. Alben was a good man, in his own way, and a man of my age dislikes watching young men being buried before him. Writing a letter of condolence to Mrs Alben is made infinitely more difficult when she is of my kin. My sister will forgive me, in time," he added stoically. "She is a good-natured woman."

Eamon's heart ruptured. He had bereaved a mother of her son and the captain of his nephew. What could he say to Waite? That he had killed to defend a wayfarer – the same snake who now bore the murdered Alben's office?

"I'm sorry, sir," he whispered.

"Yours was an unenviable position," the captain answered. "I don't doubt that Alben genuinely sought your life. You could not have done other than you did."

"I wish I could, sir," Eamon managed.

Waite laughed. "I appreciate your sentiment, Mr Goodman. Rest assured that it is not your appointment that displeases me, merely its circumstance. But, as you will no doubt learn yourself, it is often the lot of captains – and draybants, and first lieutenants, and any other man in authority – to see the young gone before their time. Sometimes we have to sacrifice them in war, sometimes for politics (which is far worse), and sometimes for no reason at all." Waite sighed. "Mr Alben was not the first, and he shall not be the last. My personal stake in the matter shall not jade my opinion of you." He drew a deep breath. "I had dismissed you too soon, Mr Goodman," he added, "for I had not yet finished the business side of matters. Will you take the Third Ravens?"

Alben's group? He could not. "If I may, sir," Eamon answered, "I would rather keep the Third Banners. I know it is unconventional," he added, "but the Ravens are already brilliant cadets. I began with the Banners, and I would like to stay with them, sir."

Waite nodded. "Very well. Giving the Ravens to one of the other lieutenants may mollify those over whom you were promoted. You shall keep the Third Banners. To your duties, first lieutenant." He spoke with the gentleness of a father.

Like a son, Eamon obeyed him.

Mathaiah joined the Third Banner cadets that day. Both first lieutenant and cadet found relief in doing what was second nature to both of them – training to serve. But the new pin at his throat was a constant weight on Eamon's mind. How could he train those beneath him to serve the Gauntlet when he himself did not? This led to a darker thought – did his grief at Alben's death mean he did not truly serve Hughan?

As the cadets were piling off to the mess Mathaiah drew him aside.

"I forgot to say, sir – I was able to speak to Lillabeth last night before… well, before what happened. She said she would pass everything on."

Eamon nodded. He hoped that what they had seen would be of interest to Hughan. No, he believed it. He had to believe it.

"What exactly did happen last night?"

"She showed me the paintings, and we talked," Mathaiah explained. "Then she heard noises down by the gates, and said she ought to go down. I offered to go with her but she said that it was probably only one of the stable hands trying to get in. She asked me to wait where I was. A few minutes after she left I heard her scream and went after her. When I got there I found Alben…" the cadet faltered and flushed. "I stopped him, sir. Then you came. The rest you know."

"I'm glad that Lillabeth is safe." The thought of losing their contact was not a pleasant one to him. She and Mathaiah were the only things in the city that reminded him of why he was truly there.

"So am I," Mathaiah added, with feeling. He went on after a pause to ask about Eamon's evening with Alessia. Eamon's reluctance to answer amused Mathaiah greatly.

As a lieutenant in the West Quarter College, Eamon's duties had been straightforward. He had had charge of a group of cadets and been responsible for overseeing their practices and patrols. The West Quarter had eighteen lieutenants and nine first lieutenants, who commanded duties and patrols in the port, the palace, along the River, and through the streets of the quarter itself. Of those first lieutenants, three worked closely with the quarter's three draybants, assigned to the overseeing of the college and quarter logistics, to the upkeep of the quarter's law, and to administrative duties in the college.

First Lieutenant Alben had been the first lieutenant with overall charge of the trainee cadets at the college. As his replacement, Eamon found that his duties grew a little more varied. The signs of respect that he received from others increased and he was called to meetings with Waite and Draybant Farleigh more frequently. It was from the latter that he began to learn the administrative arts behind the running of a Gauntlet college.

Eamon was saluted and congratulated everywhere. Although he was uncomfortable with it at first, he found himself warming to it. He did not descend from a family noted as noble in any way and wondered if first-born sons felt the rush that he did upon being acclaimed. It was a completely new feeling to him. Some watched him with awe, some with scorn, but they all watched. It was the watching that counted.

At the end of the day he went to the officers' mess to sup and found the lieutenants, so silent and cool towards him before, falling over themselves to lavish him with compliments. Even Alben's lackeys had changed their tune; in celebration of his appointment they now brought him a fine bottle of wine and a broad plate.

"Do take a drop, sir. You'll find it an excellent Ravensill vintage," cooed Fields. Eamon reviewed his drawn face, remembering how the man had joined Alben in laughing at the new lieutenant. Now Fields was fawning at Eamon's feet, like a beast quelled by a superior master. "A very excellent vintage."

"Thank you, Mr Fields." The wine was a deep red, the same colour as his uniform. Sipping it, he found it cool and rounded with fruits. It went well with the fine cut of meat which had been presented to him. Fields stood at his elbow ready, like a serving man, to see to his every whim, and the whole mess watched him as though he were the most important thing in the world.

Slowly, enjoying the attention, Eamon ate and drank. When he spoke they listened to his every word, and when he joked they laughed. Even though he knew that more than most of it was artifice, he liked it.

"More wine, Mr Goodman?"

Eamon raised his glass. It was a wine that had first been laid in casks twenty-five years ago and could easily have cost as much as a month's wages for a single bottle. Fields said that such bottles were saved to welcome notable men, and the whole mess agreed with him. It was a token of their respect for him and was but a taster of what he should receive when he became Right Hand, as Ashway had promised. The wines would be finer, the attention sweeter, and all men would fawn at his feet as Fields did then.

The wine filled his mouth and Eamon revelled in it. He would never have drunk its like in Edesfield. At the Star, ale had been enough for him.

The sudden thought of home and the weight of wine in his unusually full stomach brought him up short. He thought of Aeryn, Ladomer, and Telo, and the way they had all sat together under the summer stars. He remembered Aeryn's laughter, a beautiful sound, and Ladomer's fine singing.

He did not finish his drink.

He left the mess feeling lightheaded. Alone again, his thoughts tumbled back to Alben.

He saw Mathaiah coming across the yard towards him, accompanied by a smaller figure – Alessia's maid. The young woman was cloaked against the cool night air.

"Good evening, Miss." All thought of Alben vanished. Eamon's heart leapt to his throat – what message could the girl be bringing this time?

"Good evening, Mr Goodman," she answered, bowing low. "I have a message for you, sir. Mr Grahaven was good enough to escort me from the hall so that I could deliver it myself."

"Thank you for bringing it," Eamon answered. Perhaps it would be news from Hughan?

"There is to be a masque at the palace tomorrow night, sir," Lillabeth said, holding out a piece of parchment. Eamon could already smell the perfume of the lady who fascinated him. He tried to keep his hands from shaking. "Lady Alessia asks if you would be her escort."

"Of course," Eamon answered rather too quickly. "If my captain will allow it." He unfolded the paper and drank in the curling script, relishing every flourish. Alessia invited him to be "creative" in his costuming efforts, teasing that he would have to match her. What would she wear? He found himself imagining a thousand dresses but she looked just as beautiful in each and every one. Her lips were always pulled in that knowing smile that he already believed was kept only for him.

Eamon looked up, his heart beating. "Costuming?" he queried.

"The Right Hand is giving the occasion in honour of the majesty next week," Lillabeth said. "It is a traditional precursor to the September festivities. There is a prize for the most lavish or interesting costume. Lady Alessia advises that you will have to see to your own costume, sir, and that she wishes to be impressed."

Eamon grimaced. He was not a rich man, and though his wages had increased a little with his new position he could never afford something to make him rank alongside Dunthruik's dearest. He had seen their gaudy grandeur and silken sensibilities going to and fro through the palace gates, men and women alike doused in bright dyes from the east and expensive gems from the south and west.

"I'll try not to disappoint," he said, hiding his darker thought. He tucked the letter into his jacket. "Please thank Lady Alessia for her invitation."

"My lady advises that she will send a coach for you tomorrow evening."

"Thank you." That left him his free hours of the following afternoon to scour the streets of Dunthruik for something that wouldn't destroy his purse as well as his reputation.

Lillabeth curtseyed and made to leave.

"Sir, may I have permission to escort Miss Hollenwell back?" Mathaiah asked suddenly. Eamon thought little of it and supposed that the previous night's incident and Lillabeth's importance made the precaution wise. Awkward questions could be allayed easily enough: it was not unusual for Gauntlet to form attachments to young women in the towns and cities where they lived and worked.

"Please do, Mr Grahaven."

The cadet smiled broadly and then bowed to Lillabeth. "Your servant, Miss!" he said. She laughed and Eamon thought he saw her blush. Folding his arms behind his back in a most gentlemanly manner, Mathaiah began walking with Lillabeth back towards the college hall. It reminded Eamon that the cadet was the son of gentry, and for a moment the thought left a bitter taste in his mouth. He thought of the wine that he had drunk that evening. If he had been born the son of a nobleman, even a minor one like Mathaiah…

Astonished at the direction of his thought, for it dwelt on women and on power, he shook his head and tried to concentrate on the cool night air. The wine churned uncomfortably in his stomach. He had had a long day and the next would bring new problems.

"I think you're being too fastidious, sir."

Such was Mathaiah's verdict after several hours of wandering through Dunthruik had produced little to solve Eamon's costume dilemma.

"I know it," Eamon answered. "I'm just not good at choosing, Mathaiah."

"I've noticed!"

Dunthruik had an odd beauty in the afternoon light. The sun ricocheted down the city's tall buildings, casting enchanting shadows across the crowded streets. Many roads were dedicated to a single trade where every man was in competition with his neighbour. Eamon had thought that beginning in the drapers' area might have helped, and had sincerely hoped to find just the right thing in his first search. But the small shops, often lit by a single hanging light that filled the room with smoke, were disarrayed, and vendors pushed and bartered, sensing a stranger, though of course they always maintained a level of respect once they saw the glistening flames of a first lieutenant at his throat.

The search had been difficult. Going through the darker, narrower alleyways – routes less often trod by the Gauntlet – they had come across foul lanes and broken buildings. Rats ran in many of these streets, trailing cess and filth behind them, and lame, blistered dogs wandered the blackened road ends. Beaten beggars lay on some corners, and in marked places bodies were piled high, waiting for transportation to the city's pyres. They passed dour buildings where grotesquely painted women plied their own trade to any who would pay. It was a side to the city that Eamon had never seen before, and wished he had not seen at all.

Eventually they had found a small street in the South Quarter filled with dressmakers, some of whom served the most lavish levels of the city's gentry. They had tried looking through the tangled web of garments in the back of the shops – for those robes on display near the window cost more than Eamon could ever have afforded in a year – but nothing was right. Things were too big, too tight, or too expensive.

"Fastidious." Mathaiah repeated his diagnosis with a doleful shake of his head. "You can wear something that's too tight for one evening, sir."

"I don't want to," was Eamon's petulant reply.

"People do it all the time," Mathaiah told him. "Especially in courtly circles."

"I suppose you know all about that," Eamon muttered, more viciously than he meant. He had spent the night in unpleasant dreams that reminded him of his less than illustrious roots. While his father had been a bookbinder from Edesfield province, his mother had been the second daughter of a quiet city merchant. Mathaiah, on the other hand, had been born to rank and privilege. Like many minor noblemen's sons, Mathaiah had been assigned to the principal Gauntlet college in his region. Mathaiah said that his father had done this so that his son, who was not quite of a rank enough to be made a knight, would be kept out of trouble, and laughed. Eamon marvelled at his seeming lightheartedness. He had not yet asked how it was that the young man, spying in the deepest heart of enemy territory and living every day under the threat of discovery, could be so content.

But Mathaiah had not yet had to kill for his colours.

"They used to make me wear breeches that were very much smaller than I was," Mathaiah continued. "They called it 'fashion', sir. Mother disapproved but my father said that it was proper, especially when we had to attend meals. Berehem and I just put up with it, he better than I." Mathaiah smiled at the recollection of his older brother and Eamon was glad of it. Since Giles's revelation that he had killed the older Grahaven Mathaiah had been reticent to mention him, but in the last few days this wound seemed to have healed a little. There was no ostensible motive for this melting of attitude. "You can't tell me that you never had to endure the wiles of fashion, sir!"

"Only occasionally." Eamon's own memories of smart meals involved dinner at his grandfather's, when his mother had tucked him into smart shirts and stuffy jackets, and his grandfather had proudly placed him on his knee and announced, to the gathered company, that his grandson was "a great man born of a Goodman". He remembered the smell of sweet wine caught in his grandfather's beard.

"Still," Mathaiah told him, "there are times when it has to be done."

"Such as?"

"Now, for a start. And you'll have to wear something uncomfortable when you marry, sir."

"When I marry?"

"It just occurred to me, that's all!" Mathaiah protested, reddening.

Eamon shook his head. "The oddest things occur to you! I shall console myself with the knowledge that the same dismal law will apply to you, Mr Grahaven!"

"I think no less of you for it, sir," Mathaiah grinned.

A couple of passing women stopped to stare at them and then hurried by. Eamon noticed it, just as he had noticed the way that people now watched him: with fear. He was a man of standing. Though he didn't want to admit it any more than he wanted to tell Mathaiah of his feelings in the officers' mess, he liked it.

They stopped at the end of a street. A well stood in the dilapidated square, overgrown with ivy that had begun tearing the stonework apart. Small children huddled by it, watching Gauntlet and gentlemen go marching or riding by on the main road just beyond the street mouth.

Eamon saw another draper's shop. An old man sat outside. Their eyes met and Eamon saw a mocking glint in them, as though the man saw straight through his smart uniform to his fraudulent core. It shamed him.

"Let's try over there." Mathaiah gestured to the shop and its stolid guardian.

"I don't think we'll find anything there."

"Do you, or do you not, have to make an appearance at a Dunthruik masque in a couple of hours? I'll warrant that you don't even know what you're looking for."

Eamon remained silent. Mathaiah was right; he hadn't the faintest clue.

Mathaiah led the way and the old man watched them with an unfaltering gaze. A tough wooden sign hung over the doorway and a cart of disused fabrics stood by the old man's chair. Some women were rifling through it but when they saw Eamon approaching they gathered up their things and hurried away.

The old man said nothing as they reached the door.

"Good afternoon, sir," Mathaiah greeted politely. Eamon risked an uncomfortable glance. The man's gaze pierced him. He shied away.

"How can I help you, gentlemen?" His tone was frigid.

"Mr Goodman is in need of a costume, sir," Mathaiah answered, gesturing once to Eamon. "Might we trouble you to look here?"

"Be my guests, gentlemen." His voice was gruff but Eamon thought he had seen raised eyebrows at the mention of his name.

They stepped inside. A smoky lantern burned unattended in one corner. Racks were loosely bound to the wall and from them hung dozens of cloths and clothes. Several baskets sat nearby, each one brimming with vestments of every size and colour, except blue. There was no blue anywhere in the city.

Eamon turned his hand nervously to one of the baskets and began looking through the clothes hidden there. Most of them were gaudily coloured, bright bodies with outrageous limbs, dresses emblazoned with bold patterns. He did not imagine that he could possibly find what he needed there – unless he wanted to go dressed as a court jester.

"There's nothing here," he whispered. He did not want the proprietor to overhear them.

"What are you so worried about?"

"Nothing," Eamon lied.

"Persevere a little longer, sir."

Eamon sighed, keeping his thoughts to himself. Mathaiah continued his merry churning through another one of the baskets and at length moved to a third one. Eamon tried to look as busy.

"Perhaps you should try the rack, Mr Goodman," called the old man.

Something about his tone caused Eamon to follow the suggestion. Slightly more elegant things were hung there, most of them dresses. He found his thought turning to what Alessia might – or might not – be wearing, and reddened.

Suddenly his hand touched something cool and smooth. He pulled it out from its hiding place between flowing, crimson gowns, and held it in his hand for a moment.

On a splintered hanger was a dark pair of trousers with a thin silvered stripe running down the seam. With it hung a pale blue shirt, thinning in the sleeves. It had a dark blue cloak with a high collar. But it was the shirt that caught Eamon's eye, for on it were the faded remains of a stitched sword and star.

He stood stock still, struck dumb. How could that emblem be

staring back at him from the wall of a draper's shop, in the crumbling heart of Dunthruik? It could not be real! And yet even if it was a false, mocking costume, something about it called to him. The flames at his throat grew uncomfortable as he stared, enthralled, at the sword and star.

He became aware of Mathaiah beside him. The garments' significance was not lost on his ward. Eamon's hand loitered on the embroidery, tracing the faded colours in amazement.

Did he dare?

A smile grew on his face. "You were right, Mathaiah; there is something here."

"Sir, do you think it wise to –?"

"Why don't you try it on, Mr Goodman?" The old man stood in the doorway now. His eyes were keen, his words more so. "Try it on. See if it fits you."

There was a small room rather like a cupboard at the back of the shop. Eamon slipped between the shadows, taking the uniform with him. While Mathaiah and the old man exchanged obligatory pleasantries Eamon stripped off the hot weight of his uniform and exchanged it for the old garments. Though a little thinned in places the trousers were well made; their silver seam shimmered in the lamplight. The shirt sat easily on his shoulders and the cloak, as it fell about him, enfolded him comfortingly. He felt the embroidery over his heart and was encouraged by it.

Grinning, he emerged into the shop-light. Silver facings ran dimly about the cloak hem, sparking like stars.

The old man and the cadet stared at him.

"I think it fits."

The shopkeeper nodded. "There's just one more thing." He hobbled forward and tugged with a veined hand at the chain showing at Eamon's neck. The heart of the King spilled forward to shimmer in the light. "Now it fits," he whispered, his old eyes rimming with tears.

"Sir," Mathaiah breathed worriedly, "you can't –"

But Eamon did.

That night Eamon left his quarters and strode boldly through the corridors. He met Waite in the hall, where he was receiving the captain of another quarter.

"Yes," Waite was saying, "he has a great future in him; Lord Cathair was telling me…" One look at the first lieutenant he was trumpeting silenced him.

Eamon saluted primly.

"What are you doing, Mr Goodman?" Waite's voice quivered between mirth and outrage.

"Attending the masque at the palace, sir."

"You brazen hussy," Waite clipped.

"Thank you, sir."

Waite could only laugh. "Carry on, Mr Goodman."

Saluting again, Eamon left. Wherever he passed, soldiers stopped and stared. They knew that the uniform he wore was embellished with the Serpent's symbols; he knew that gaping faces followed him. He didn't care. The emblems shone brilliantly in the light.

Deep down, Eamon didn't know if he was being brave or reckless: he purposed to go to a ball given by the Right Hand, as escort to a noblewoman high in the throned's favour, proudly boasting the colours of the enemy. It was dangerous and stupid, inviting all the wrong kinds of attention, and he knew it. But the uniform of a King's man was a glorious contradiction in a city of gold and red – and it was the uniform he ought to wear. Something about it was balm to his troubled soul. What harm could befall him when he served the King?

Such thoughts had led him to decline Alessia's offer of a coach and Mathaiah's of an escort. Being in bold mood, he walked openly to the palace. It would certainly get him talked about but he intended to pass the uniform off as an arrogant joke.

He marched merrily. Hanging street lanterns swung in the wind. The road was alive with carriages, and men and women had lined it to watch the procession of the masque's attendees. The air was filled with perfumes and music.

Eamon skipped among the milling crowds. He knew that they stared at him, aghast and open mouthed; he left shocked gasps everywhere he went. It exhilarated him. If only they knew how truly he showed himself that night!

A gust of wind brought the whisper of distant thunder. Eamon did not care – it would not rain that night.

He reached the palace gates. The ensigns on guard might well have arrested him on the spot were it not for a nearby voice crying with delight: "Mr Goodman! Is that you?"

Eamon turned. Alessia was waiting for him near the gate; she clapped her hands to see him. As the guest of such a highly born lady, the guards were obliged to let him pass.

Dozens of carriages had begun to arrive, each bearing jewelled cargoes. Alessia drew him to a secluded part of the plaza.

"Let me look at you." Taking his hands in hers, she lifted them so that he stood like a mannequin while she examined every detail of his costume. A mischievous glint appeared in her eye.

"I see you don't like to fail a challenge."

"You said that I needed to match you, my lady," Eamon answered. Though whatever he had worn it would have been impossible to do so. Alessia had bound her curled tresses about her head so that they cascaded down her back. A tiara of glistening gold nestled in her hair and a stream of gold lay all about her throat. She wore a dress of dark, dark red and about her shoulders hung a golden cloak with red designs woven into it. Every fold of the garment was designed to suggest the curved body underneath. Eamon felt a rush of pride.

"My turn, Mr Goodman." She pirouetted slowly before him. Her perfumed hair passed by his face. He drank in the smell. "Does it please you, Mr Goodman?"

"You look wonderful," he enthused before adding a demure "my lady."

Her beautiful smile played over her lips. "I trust that I shall not look amiss on your arm this evening?"

Eamon shook his head speechlessly: surely she knew he would be the envy of every man at the masque?

Alessia seemed to read his thought and laughed gently.

"You are the talk of the whole palace, sir. And tonight, First Lieutenant Goodman," she said, slipping her arm into his, "I am wholly yours."

Remembering nothing of what he wore, where he was, or even who he was, he led Lady Alessia across the Royal Plaza, under the Master's balcony, and into the palace.

CHAPTER XVI

The steps into the palace hall were lined with lights and banners, displayed like hunting trophies, bearing the emblems of the attending nobles. Eamon tried to concentrate while Alessia showed him her family's crest, an eagle in full flight grappling a shield in its talons; the shield bore a crown like the Gauntlet's emblem. He thought that he heard her telling him that the family had earned the crest for killing a prominent enemy of the Master's many generations ago, but the notion washed meaninglessly over him. All he was conscious of was the way in which the whole world was in her eyes.

They went from the hallway into corridors leading through the East Wing. Each passage revealed a greater one and glistened with unimaginable grandeur; dozens of tapestries covered the walls. They alternated between great crimson folds, embellished with an upright crowned eagle in golden thread – the emblem of the city of Dunthruik – and black lengths embellished with the birds of the city's quarters: raven, owl, falcon, and harrier.

The corridors turned at last and met their end in grand, open doors. As they approached, Eamon's ears were filled with delightful refrains of music. He could also hear the distant murmur of voices, sometimes punctuated with laughter. Alessia told him that the doors led into the throne room itself, which was used on such occasions to host the Master's dearest.

A sudden chill pierced Eamon's heart. "Will he be there?"

Alessia laughed. "Your enthusiasm does you great credit, Mr Goodman, but I am afraid that you are to be disappointed. The

Master won't be here tonight; only the Right Hand. That is honour enough for us."

Eamon smiled. "Your company is all the honour I need," he told her, delighting in the gentle laugh and demurely lowered eyes that answered him.

As they came to the doors he saw that the panels bore the angled script he had seen in the Nightholt. Intoxicated by the lady at his arm, his eyes passed blithely, blindly, over the writing. He gave it no further thought.

A raised platform stood just beyond the doors, leading down to an enormous hall filled with lords and ladies in all their finery. Some had come as famous heroes, some as musicians and playwrights; a quill here, a lute there. Some had come as animals: there were ladies with great nests of hair arrayed to impress height beyond their stature, and one knight had an ebony tail attached to the back of his coat. Apart from the flippant knight, all those robed in black were Hands. The ladies wore dresses that billowed outwards when they danced. Small trains of serving girls, trying vainly to keep their mistresses in order, followed the ladies. There were masks, masks – everywhere masks. Large and small, ornately worked in precious metals or in wood. Among all the artistry barely a face could be seen.

So Eamon saw the lords and ladies laughing and dancing in the great hall of Dunthruik. He wondered briefly if below them, in the kitchens, cooks and slaves sweated and toiled, and farther down still whether prisoners cried and travailed. But in the throne room music formed the most regular noise, and the lords and ladies ignored the beautiful melody. Nothing mattered but the glittering dresses and the swirling masks.

Just inside the door were a small band of servants, two trumpeters, and Lord Cathair. The trumpeters played fanfares to announce those who arrived, while another servant marked names on a list and Cathair absently surveyed their work. As he and Alessia entered, the Hand's sharp green eyes flashed with surprise.

"Mr Goodman," Cathair began. Eamon braced himself for a barrage of criticism. For a moment he held his breath: what if Cathair failed to take it as a prank?

Cathair suddenly laughed and laid an amiable hand on Eamon's shoulder. "My dear Mr Goodman!" Cathair chuckled. "This is a masque, yet you have come unmasked!"

Mind racing, Eamon froze. Cathair knew! Catching movement in the corner of his eye, Eamon prepared to defend himself. They would not take him easily.

He whirled towards what he had seen – only to find that the gesture that had arrested him was Alessia raising a small mask to her own face. Suddenly he understood. Terrified then that his reaction marked him as a guilty man, he bowed low to the Hand, placing his own hand over the emblems at his breast.

"I have no answer to that, my lord."

Cathair smiled. "No harm done, Mr Goodman; no harm done."

He was saved by the startling blast of a trumpet.

"Lady Alessia Turnholt and escort," the announcer cried, "First Lieutenant Eamon Goodman of the West Quarter."

When Alessia's name was called nobody really acknowledged it; Lady Turnholt was well known in Dunthruik and would be, Eamon supposed, long after his own name had passed into the dim shades of obscurity. But at the announcement of the long-expected Goodman, hundreds of eyes turned to look at him. This was the man whose name was the talk of the whole court, the man who had escaped snakes to reach Dunthruik and become a first lieutenant in mere days, the man who had become the companion of Alessia in less time than it had taken him to become a first lieutenant. It was the man rumoured to be the greatest breacher the city had ever seen and the man who, if the darkest whispers were to be believed, would one day become Right Hand himself. Such a man was worth looking at, and so they looked.

Eamon felt what seemed a thousand eyes fall upon him. A startled silence covered the whole hall like a pall. Hundreds of masks dropped, and hundreds of aghast faces were revealed. The lords and ladies of Dunthruik had seen him, and seen what he wore. Eamon's heart – so sturdy in the streets of Dunthruik and so untroubled while he had walked with Alessia – faltered.

Only the music continued undisturbed.

Eamon felt a tug on his arm. Alessia was leading him to the top of the stairs that led down into the long hall. The eyes held him prisoner, following his every move; they would not let him go.

Those standing near the bottom of the steps backed away as he alighted on the first stair. His heart beat fast and he, who had loved being watched all that day, now longed for the eyes to cease. What could they see? He did not know. There was no mask in the world great enough to cover him. He would have to cover himself.

At the top of the stairs was a page bearing a tray of goblets – welcoming beverages for the guests. He did not seem to note Eamon's outrageous costume as he offered him a drink. The wine was a deep gold, cool and bubbling.

With a slick movement, Eamon caught a drink. As he raised the goblet high, the chandelier light struck it, lighting his palm with gold.

"My lords and ladies," he called, "a toast! To the Master's glory, and to exquisite company!"

Holding the wine high a second longer he downed the glass and then, with an unforeseen flourish, he took Alessia's hand and raised it to his lips. Alessia coloured and smiled; Eamon's heart flared hot.

To his relief, the company echoed his toast back to him and then, seeing the kiss, laughed and returned to their doings. The dancing recommenced.

Alessia leaned towards him and spoke softly into his ear. "It would seem, Mr Goodman, that you are a fearless man."

"What is there to fear when I serve the Master?" Eamon asked her, aware of Cathair watching him with a strange glint in his eye. It was an unsettling look – like that of a creature who watched its prey, lauding its efforts to escape. What if Cathair…?

Alessia's voice drove his fear away. "Come with me, Mr Goodman," she said, descending into the hall. Eamon followed her.

The hall was magnificent – a great stone mosaic forged of red, gold, and white gems. Descending towards it was like stepping down into a lake of frozen fire and the lords and ladies were as spirits, summoned forth and dancing on the flames. Fifteen sumptuous paintings ran around the balcony openings, each depicting an impressive scene figured in bold, uncompromising detail.

Eamon did not see them all, but would later remember some of them. One showed a city emerging out of flames that drove away a great serpent. Another showed a figure, robed in brilliant red, stemming the flow of the sea with his outstretched hand, allowing ships to pass, while his fiery hair trailed behind him in the wind. Another showed this same figure with his arms raised in a gesture of benediction over five men robed in black. These pictures led in a grand procession to the head of the hall where another raised dais stood. Eamon stopped and stared.

On the dais was a throne. It was grotesquely large, with cushions and armrests that might support a giant. Its stone frame was encrusted with gems and the wall behind the throne had been painted so that the seat was framed with a great crown. But it was above this crown that Eamon's eyes were drawn, to the largest painting of them all. It showed the same fiery man, crimson cloak and hair billowing in the wind. His grey eyes were piercing and he held aloft a book in his left hand; both book and palm roared with flame while a crown of fire burned on his high forehead. Behind the man was a great battlefield where men could be seen killing other men. From the bodies of these fled bleeding snakes. In his right hand was a sword that shimmered with flame; beneath his foot was the writhing body of a unicorn. The beast's horn had been smashed, and bloodied flecks raced in the creature's wild eyes. The sword had gorged open the beast's pitiful throat, and from the gouged mass of flesh and blood beneath the blade came a serpent, its eyes and throat spitting curses as it too fell and died. And a familiar image lay, faintly marked, on the breast of the snake: a sword and star.

Understanding flooded Eamon's mind and gall burned his throat. His raging heart was ready to leap from his mouth. The heart of the King lay heavy on his breast as though it too cried out; Eamon clenched his hands tightly. The house of kings had been figured as a serpent crushed beneath the Master's foot.

Eamon shivered; he alone knew them to be lies to steal the throne.

His vision changed. Beyond the arches of the hall's balconies hung the darkened night. The walls bore no paintings and the ceiling was blue, littered with silver stars. The great doors were barred.

A solitary man sat on the steps by the throne – not the great, stony monstrosity which Eamon knew lay before him but a tall, elegant seat with a star set at its head. A blue banner covered the wall behind him, showing a sword and a star. The old man cradled a sword across his lap.

A great noise rang through the hall. The doors buckled before a tremendous strike of red light. A figure strode through the splintered wreck of wood. He was dressed in crimson; he carried a bloodied banner showing a unicorn and three stars. He cast it derisively onto the floor, calling a mocking challenge to the old man whose whole house had fallen.

The old man slowly rose to his feet, lifting his small sword. The grey-eyed man laughed. Black-robed men followed him as he struck the last guardian of the King's house.

The vision was gone. Eamon saw jewelled throne and golden crown.

"Mr Goodman?" He stirred and looked up to see an older woman, dressed darkly. Blinking back his thoughts, Eamon bowed to her.

"Your servant, madam."

"Mr Goodman," she said, "I hope you'll not think it wrong of me, but I must ask something of you."

Eamon nodded. A man stood at the woman's side. There was no joy in either of their faces; there were tears in the woman's exhausted eyes.

It moved him. "Please make your request, madam," he said, "and if I can rightly serve you in what you ask, then I shall do so."

"Please, Mr Goodman, tell me about my son." She reached out for her husband's hand. She held it and trembled.

A sick feeling wormed through him. "Your son, madam?"

"First Lieutenant Alben," the man interposed. His voice was harsh. "He was our son, Mr Goodman, and we would know more of his death."

Pain pressed on him anew. "Mr Alben," he answered carefully, "I believe that you will find yourself in receipt of an official letter regarding the matter from Captain Waite. It is hardly my place to speak in his stead."

"Waite be damned!" the man retorted. His wife let out a quiet sob. Those nearby turned to look at them but the man did not notice or care. He stepped towards Eamon and jabbed at him with a condemning finger. "His letter said nothing! We want the truth, do you hear?" As he spoke his eyes fell on the sword and star. He grimaced.

"What kind of man are you, Mr Goodman," he growled, "that you can wear that Serpent's mark only hours after your colleague was slaughtered? What kind of man are you!"

Eamon faced the man with as much calm as he could muster. He was glad of the rumble of voices and music, and for Alessia's presence. He drew a burdened breath.

"I am the kind of man that will grant you your request, understanding why it is made." Alessia stiffened. Did she fear for him? The thought emboldened him. "Mr and Mrs Alben, your son was a worthy officer, and he died well. I was with him at the end and can vouch for his courage. He had a great hand in battle and the Master had blessed him with many gifts in reward for his dauntless service." He shuddered, remembering the pain of breaking. "It was in great sorrow that I parted from him," he continued, "for he was a powerful captain of men, and I have no doubt that he would have gone on to become greater still."

Alessia pressed his hand. But Alben's father glared at him as though he were utterly reprehensible. "You have nothing for me but honeyed words, drawn from Waite's own sickening comb." The man turned on Alessia. "Are you not ashamed of yourself, lady?" he glowered. "My son is not a day in his tomb and already you have another man to warm your bed!"

He spat at her.

Outraged, Eamon surged forwards. "Spit at a lady?" he called hotly. "Have you no shame?"

"No shame? I have no son! Do you hear me?" Alben bellowed. "I have no son!"

"Mr Goodman, please," Alessia whispered, pressing his arm.

Only she could have restrained him. Eamon forced himself to be civil. "I am grieved for your loss, Mr Alben, and have given all that you asked of me. First Lieutenant Alben was a man who showed his breeding in his every gesture, and I pray you that you would respect his memory by allowing some of that same grace to touch you."

Alben fell back, shaken. He bowed formally.

"Good evening to you, Mr Goodman." He took his wife on his arm and the crowd parted to let the black figures pass. They left the hall.

Eamon watched them go, shaking. Alessia trembled beside him. "Are you well, my lady?"

She smiled weakly. "I think I need some air."

Eamon looked around. Farther down the hall there were steps that led up to the Master's balcony. Cool air drew in from the arches and he could see that nobody walked there.

He took Alessia's pale hand gently in his own and led her through the watching crowd and up onto the balcony. Both of them breathed with relief as the cool air balmed their faces. Lights had been set in the plaza which, moving, showed like stars in a troubled sky.

They stood in silence for a while, only the music reaching their ears. The musicians began to play a melodic dance that lifted Eamon's spirit. He looked across at Alessia. She watched the plaza below, deep in thought.

"My lady?" She fingered her golden mask, and did not answer. "I'm sorry that he treated you in such a way," Eamon said gently, thinking that he discerned her burden. As he watched her in the moonlight he felt something stirring within him. Was it something deeper than his passion for the lady's beauty?

"His son was little better," Alessia confessed, offering him a pale smile. "But he is gone. And you are here." She reached out and touched his cheek. Her eyes searched his. "I am so glad that you are here." There was no trace of the seductive, teasing smile which he had come to associate with her. In that moment she seemed more real to him, and more alive, than he had ever seen her.

Eamon stood still, relishing her touch. She still held the mask in her other hand but, after a few long moments, she laid it carefully aside on the balcony rail. Its golden eyes stared out over the empty square.

"Mr Goodman, I am wondering whether you might ask me to dance with you?" Smiling shyly, she took his hand and set it against her waist. "Or shall I have to ask you?"

"That would be most improper," Eamon answered, scarcely able to breathe. Her touch elated him. Yet the crimson dress reminded him of the figure painted in the throne room, of the murder and treachery that had unfolded there. He told himself that she was nothing to do with that history, nor that fire.

He took her hand and raised it in his own. "Lady Turnholt, would you do me the great honour of dancing with me this evening?"

Alessia raised her eyebrows, delighted. "For the whole evening, Mr Goodman?" she asked, but she had already pressed herself close to him in answer; her eyes danced beneath his.

Eamon laughed. "Dance with me, lady!" he cried, his voice filled with passion and delight. "Dance with me until the very stars are razed from the sky!"

He swept her out across the balcony; she laughed and he joyed to hear her. As they danced and danced together in the moonlight, neither of them wore a mask.

Eamon didn't know how many hours had passed when they at last came in. The throne room was warmer and the guests, who had been picking all evening at lavish food, now sipped closing drinks. Some Hands, Lord Cathair among them, were speaking together on the entry dais. Eamon and Alessia went to find something to drink – neither of them felt any desire for food.

Suddenly a fanfare was played. Through the grand entry doors processed a figure robed and cloaked in black, a large, obsidian mask hiding his face. Despite it, Eamon recognized the Right Hand. A shudder ran through him. The man had undeniable presence. As the trumpet call died, its place was taken by uproarious applause.

The Right Hand raised his arms for quiet. "Lords, ladies, and gentlemen, I thank you for honouring both myself and the Master by your presence here this evening. I hope that you have had ample chance to avail yourselves of the glorious bounty of the Master's benevolence towards those who serve him and whom he loves."

The assembled company cheered and goblets were raised in every quarter. Eamon applauded along with the rest.

"Honoured guests," the Right Hand continued, "I take this opportunity to thank you again for your great service to the Master."

"His glory!" cried a voice; a whole chorus rallied to it. Eamon joined it. Alessia put her hand silently in his.

"It is my great pleasure to announce that this evening's costumes were magnificent. You are all worthy of prizes and of praise! But alas – only one prize can be awarded. It was a difficult choice!"

The Right Hand paused as some laughed and applauded. Eamon was amazed – he was so different from the cold, harsh man in the Hands' Hall.

"The Master was especially amused by the audacity of this evening's winner." Eamon suddenly felt pierced by the man's gaze.

"Please congratulate First Lieutenant Eamon Goodman of the West Quarter, and his rather unmistakable garb."

Eamon froze. He hoped against hope that he had heard wrong or strayed into a nightmare. He could not stand before the Right Hand dressed as he was! And yet, being summoned, he could not refuse.

Applause had begun and Eamon forced shaking legs to carry him to the Hands. Each step seemed to take a lifetime to climb. The Right Hand's darkened eyes were always upon him.

Eamon bowed low. The Right Hand clasped Eamon's hand in his, with crushing strength.

"A fine and bold display you have made this evening, First Lieutenant Goodman." Eamon's knees threatened to give way. "The Master is looking forward to meeting with you himself."

"Thank you, my lord," Eamon answered, quailing with terror. Mathaiah had been right: he had been a fool to dress as he had done. Why hadn't he listened?

A burst of movement caught his eye. A young man, dressed in a servant's livery, came to the dais from the corridor. His grim face was set on Cathair. Eamon caught the glimmer of a knife in his hand. The crowd, gathered below, could not see him, and the Hands had their backs to the open doorway. The guards in the doorway faced into the hall. He was the only one who could see the dagger – and the only one who could stop it.

Sweat beaded his brow. Would not the Hand's death be a blow to the throned and a victory for the King? All he needed to do was stand by… But he could not.

At the last possible moment he tore his hand from the Right Hand's congratulating grasp and hurled himself with a cry at the would-be assassin. He and the young man crashed to the floor, taking a small table and dozens of glasses with them. Eamon clenched his left hand about the knife-holding fingers and twisted the wrist back hard.

The sound of smashing glass and astonished cries filled the room. Eamon ignored it. Strengthened by fury, the young man struggled to get his hands free and cast Eamon away. It was clear from his wild cries and even wilder mismarked blows that he had never tried to kill someone before.

With a brutal crack Eamon crunched the man's wrist against the ruddy paving, sending the knife spinning. The young man yelled in furious pain. Gauntlet soldiers ran to Eamon's aid and hauled the boy up to his feet. The panting face seemed vaguely familiar.

The young man began cursing. "How dare you?" he yelled. "How dare you!" With a final burst of strength he wrested one arm free and tore the sword and star from Eamon's breast. "You are no King's man!" the man screamed. "How dare you!"

"Send him to the Pit," said a voice at Eamon's side: the Right Hand's. He spoke quietly now and the soldiers obeyed him without question.

As the screaming young man was dragged from the hall, pouring maledictions on Eamon's spinning head, the Right Hand turned back to the alarmed crowd.

"Silence!"

As willingly and immediately as soldiers, they obeyed. A stunned hush descended upon them, like a wave rolling to the shore. Out of the corner of his eye Eamon became aware of Lord Cathair. The Hand looked shaken and was watching Eamon with new wariness.

"Lords, ladies, and gentlemen: Mr Goodman is, as you have seen, a man worthy of praise," the Right Hand said. "Let us thank him for his timely intervention."

The Right Hand began to applaud, and what the Right Hand did the people followed. Soon the whole hall was alive with clapping. Eamon was awed by the power of the man beside him. Would he one day stand in that place, reaping multitudinous and compliant adoration? He smiled.

How could he want to become Right Hand?

The Right Hand clasped his hand again. "A most timely intervention, Mr Goodman," he repeated, before adding meaningfully: "It will not go unnoticed. You have my thanks, and Lord Cathair's, I do not doubt."

"Thank you, my lord." Eamon could not hear himself think over the raging applause. Alessia's face beamed at him.

How could he not love this? How could he not seek it for his own? What could Hughan offer him that could outshine what the Master lavished on him daily?

He breathed deeply, trying to clear his head. The Right Hand's warm, strong grip clasped his arm, urging him to cast all notion of the King from him; with his left hand he clutched the tattered remains of the sword and star.

CHAPTER XVII

"You still seem incapable of telling me whether or not you enjoyed yourself at the masque, sir," Mathaiah said.

"Perhaps I still am."

They were sitting together in one of the inns near the college, taking comfort in a drink of mulled spices. Over the last few days the weather had grown much colder and news of snow had come from the northern reaches. The passages to the north and east would soon begin to block, rendering trade more difficult, and the port would drop to minimal functioning as the ships took to wintering instead of trading. It was a time when the city became more insular and, with it, more superstitious. Over the winter months the dead were rounded up from street corners and burnt in the pyres. Such burnings had already begun, and Eamon had seen great billows of smoke on the city's plain. The price of bread had increased as grain became more tightly rationed with the closing of many trade routes. Yet while the poor starved and dreaded the coming icy blasts, the lords and ladies of Dunthruik feasted on venison and gorged on honeyed cakes until their stomachs could hold no more. Eamon had seen first hand what gifts were lavished on those who glorified the Master.

"It's been three days since the masque, sir," Mathaiah persisted. He had listened with great interest to Eamon's account of the hall and the throne – details that Eamon, in his embarrassment over Alessia, was all too eager to relate. She served the throned – what could he possibly say to defend her to as staunch a King's man as his ward? He could not justify what he felt for her, not to Mathaiah.

"I know," Eamon answered at length. But his memories of the masque still troubled him. He would not have exchanged the time he had shared with Alessia for any price, but that joy was overshadowed by the snakes, by the Right Hand's dark mask, by Cathair's eyes and the howling assassin. The gruelling nature of the work he had done at the college since had driven none of it from his mind. Besides all of this was the memory of his return to the West Quarter College on the night of the masque. He had found Captain Waite waiting for him. What the captain had meant to say he did not know; when the man had seen Eamon's torn uniform and heard his account of what happened, he had fallen silent. Thoughtfully pursing his lips, the captain had patted him amicably on the shoulder and bid him goodnight.

Eamon took a long sip of his drink. He was accustomed to ale but his stomach, having been given nothing but wine to drink since he had become an officer, was weary of alcohol. Even in the mulled drink he was privileged: upon hearing his name the bartender had insisted on brewing for him the most expensive leaves in the house, brought long ago from Istanaria, the pinnacled city east of the mountains, in the land of the Seven Sons. Eamon hardly believed that he deserved to drink it.

"Hughan should know about what I saw," he said quietly. It had taken him some time to tell Mathaiah about the old man in his vision. But his ward had not batted an eyelid at the revelation: he had nodded sagely, as though the whole affair was the most logical thing in the world. Eamon admired the cadet's calm and reassuring manner.

"You'll tell Lillabeth?"

"Yes, sir."

Eamon thanked him. Mathaiah was a dear friend – he could never have foreseen how dear. The young man was faithful and trustworthy, and Eamon was glad to have him by his side. The cadet also seemed to have grown his own attachment to Alessia's maid: he often spent his free hours visiting her and some of that time, Eamon knew, was used to pass on messages for the King. There had not yet been any news from Hughan. The silence played on his troubled mind, but he had to trust himself to the King's judgment.

He rubbed tired eyes, then looked at Mathaiah over his drink. It was the day of the majesty, and the whole city had sprung into life. As first lieutenant of the West Quarter College, his own task that evening was to lead the quarter's ensigns, cadets, and officers in the procession from the Blind Gate to the Royal Plaza. Eamon had spent the morning going through the ceremony's protocol with his own cadets until they knew every moment wherein it was permitted for them to breathe. Though he was confident that his men would cut a very impressive figure in the Royal Plaza, he knew that he would be watched from every quarter; his name had spread like wildfire since he had saved Cathair's life at the masque. He still kept the heart of the King beneath his shirt, but the three pins of his first lieutenancy weighed against his throat. He fiddled anxiously with one as he thought.

What kind of First Knight was he, who so willingly served – and saved – the King's enemies?

Mathaiah seemed to read his mind. He chinked his mug against Eamon's, rousing him from his reverie.

"It'll be all right, sir," he encouraged. "You're doing all right."

Eamon laughed gently. "What would I do without you, Mathaiah?"

"Goes both ways, sir."

They took a little while to finish their drinks, watching people going about their business. Upon seeing a three-flamed uniform most men gave them a wide berth, but some came and stared at them. Mathaiah found this amusing, but Eamon hated feeling that each man was impressing the details of First Lieutenant Eamon Goodman's face into their minds. Those moments when none watched him were moments that he indeed relished. The irony of this did not escape him.

As they drank, Eamon became aware of a young woman watching him particularly intensely. Huddled in a far corner of the inn, away from the light of the window, she had a tiny child cradled in one arm, which she rocked from time to time. Her dirty hair was tied back and her eyes were sunken with fatigue. The longer she watched him the more disconcerted he became.

"Do you see her, Mathaiah? The one staring at me."

Mathaiah glanced up, then took another drink. "I don't think there's any harm in her, sir."

"It's as though… as though she expects me to do something." He felt irritated by the attention of the stark eyes. A quick glance over his shoulder confirmed that the woman's gaze was still resolutely on him. "What could she possibly want?"

"Perhaps you could ask her, sir."

It seemed a mad suggestion. Eamon stared at the herbs in the bottom of his mug, listening to the murmur of nearby voices. The others in the inn were cadets, ensigns, merchants, and all of them had looked at him from time to time, but none had stared as this woman did. Eamon tried to shut out the sense of the piercing gaze upon him. The baby began to cry. The girl tried to quieten it, her voice trembling.

Suddenly he rose. His chair scraped back across the floorboards; everybody looked at him before swiftly pretending to look away.

Eamon turned angrily to the young woman. She watched him warily as he approached, but made no move to leave. The baby whimpered. The young mother rocked it and watched him.

The cry grated. "Is there something the matter, Miss?" Eamon asked roughly.

The young woman started. "N-no sir."

Eamon looked at the child. Its face was deathly pale and the tiny fingers were blistered and yellow with cold. The sight filled him with pity.

"Is something the matter with your child?" he asked, more gently this time.

"Please, sir," the woman whispered, "are you First Lieutenant Goodman?"

Eamon did not see how her question answered his own, but he nodded.

Her face lit like sun over a winter sea. "Sir, my boy is sick. Snakes cursed him, so my husband says – they have terrible power! I want my boy to live. They say that you are favoured by the Master, and that you have power in you; that the snakes can neither harm nor stand against you." She brushed a tear from her lowered eyes. "They say that you can undo what the snakes do."

Eamon stared. How had he gained so fearsome a reputation – he, work against Hughan? His heart sickened at the thought.

The woman's voice was desperate: "Sir, I beg of you – take the curse off my boy."

Eamon gaped at her. Remove a curse? He could not – there was no curse. The baby was unwell and likely to die swiftly in the coming cold. Many lost children to the combination of the winter's cold and the fevers that frequently accompanied it. It was not an unusual occurrence – yet the mother had not resigned herself to it. She held Eamon in a plaintive gaze, moving the babe in her arms as it cried. Eamon felt a desire growing in his heart: he wanted to see the baby well.

Slowly he reached out and laid his finger by the baby's hand. After a few moments the tiny fist latched on to him and the child grew quiet. Eamon looked down kindly at the boy and felt warmth welling inside him. He remembered how, on the deck of the cold holk, he had pressed his hands hard against Mathaiah's wound and called for help he had known could never come. He tucked the tiny palm that he held between his own. Now he knew differently.

Eamon felt the King's grace at work. He thought that maybe, just maybe, he caught a momentary glimpse of blue light passing from his fingers into the tiny hand that he held. He knew then that the boy would live.

The child smiled at him. With a yawn and a stretch, he fell asleep.

Eamon loosed his finger from the child's grasp and looked back to its mother. She gazed at her child, and him, in amazement.

"He's sleeping," she whispered. Tears came to her eyes. "He's… *sleeping*…"

"He is not cursed," Eamon told her, wondering at his own confidence, "nor has he been cursed. There are snakes and wayfarers about, Miss; that much is certain. But keep your sight clear and you will distinguish snake from man and true man from false." He paused, the heart of the King burning at his breast. "As for your boy, he will be safe all winter long."

Tears ran down the woman's cheeks. "Thank you, sir," she said. "His glory!"

Curtseying awkwardly she ran from the inn. As she hurtled past the window and disappeared into the labyrinthine streets Eamon heard her joyously squealing her husband's name.

Then he became aware of the others in the inn. The barman stared at him openly.

"Well," he exclaimed, "who would have thought it! And in my inn, too." He raised the glass he had been cleaning. "His glory!"

The other men in the inn took up the bartender's call. How Eamon wished that he could tell them how the child had truly been saved! Swallowing the desire, he strolled to the bar and laid a handful of coins on the table.

"Some drinks for these fine gentlemen, innkeeper," he said, hoping it would help witnesses forget what they had seen.

The bar resounded with a cheer.

Eamon returned to Mathaiah. While all in the inn were otherwise occupied, they left in silence.

They walked quietly through the street, the sun barely warming their faces. Eamon's mind raced. He was plagued by Alben's death and distraught at saving Cathair's life. Now he had used the King's grace to heal a child. What kind of man was he? He could not be indistinct in his loyalty. He had to choose – why did he delay?

"Are you all right, sir?"

Explaining his turmoil to Mathaiah would help. Eamon drew breath, but the thoughts never left his mouth.

"Well I never!" cried a sudden voice behind them. "Well I never! Can it be? Is that Eamon Goodman, the fearsome Ratbag of Edesfield?"

Eamon halted mid-pace. He knew the voice – knew that its owner was miles away. But there was only one person in the whole of River Realm who would call him "Ratbag".

With bated breath, he turned. On the street corner stood his old lieutenant and dear friend.

"Ladomer!" Eamon cried. Filled with laughter, he raced forward and heartily embraced his friend. "You're a sight for sore eyes!"

"You didn't expect to see me here, did you?" Ladomer grinned.

"No indeed! You must tell me everything!" Stepping back, Eamon remembered Mathaiah. The cadet hung a few paces behind them. "Oh, this is Cadet Mathaiah Grahaven, my ward."

"From Edesfield College?" Ladomer said, eyes narrowed in recollection.

Mathaiah nodded. "Yes, sir."

"Ah, that's right! The banner-renderer." Mathaiah pursed his lips uncomfortably but Ladomer only laughed. "Fear not, Mr Grahaven! It had been mended when last I checked."

"That's good to know, sir."

Ladomer turned back to Eamon. "And you – you're a warder already?"

Eamon beamed. "Have you counted the shirt burns?"

Ladomer gazed at him, making a show of looking to Eamon's throat. His dark eyes widened in astonishment.

"Three shirt burns?" he said. "In less than a *week*?"

"You expected less of me, Mr Kentigern?"

Ladomer threw back his handsome face and laughed out loud. "They snapped you up quickly, Ratbag!" He thrust out his hand to clasp Eamon's. "Mr Goodman," he said, raising his hand as though he held a sword for his formal gesture, "I salute you!"

"Don't be an ass!" Eamon retorted, shaking his hand free with a laugh. "I'm just the same as I always was."

"Conceited, ill-dressed, doubly left-footed, physically challenged, and scared of women?"

Eamon's jaw dropped. "You're a harsh, cruel man!"

"They are such undervalued skills in the modern age," Ladomer answered, bowing, "and I thank you."

Eamon dealt him a playful buff on the shoulder. "What are you doing in Dunthruik?"

"Belaal sent me up to liaise with one Captain Waite over some paperwork or other," Ladomer replied flippantly.

"Waite?" Eamon was delighted. "He's my captain!"

"Really?" Ladomer grinned. "Then perhaps I shall see you for a few days while they sort the papers."

"What kind of papers?"

"As I promised you I would, I came looking for a city appointment," Ladomer told him. "Belaal said there were a few positions available, and my record is good for the city, so he and Lord Penrith agreed to send me up." He lowered his voice. "There are several lieutenantcies vacant across the quarters, including one in the West where you are, but it seems that I am being considered for a role in the palace."

"The palace?" Eamon knew of no lieutenants serving there.

"They want to assign a new lieutenant to the Right Hand."

Eamon gaped, remembering the darkened face and mesmerizing words of the throned's closest. "The Right Hand?" The idea of Ladomer binding himself to the man chilled him. He could not bear it – how could he warn his friend to keep away?

Ladomer laughed. "You needn't look so concerned. In all likelihood they will take one look at me and send me straight back home. But moving paper for such things always takes a certain amount of time so, even if they do, I expect to be in the city at least a week."

Eamon smiled. "Well, then, I shall enjoy your company while I have it."

Chapter XVII

"I have to go – they're expecting me at the palace." Ladomer drew him slightly aside. "Listen, I heard about the holk and your capture. I was so relieved, Eamon, when I learned that you were safe. Do you know if Aeryn made it?"

Eamon paused for a fraction of a second. He couldn't take any risks. "She was alive, last I saw."

Ladomer relaxed. "Thank the Master for small mercies! Belaal seemed to think that she was connected to the snakes. Can you believe that? Shows the kind of man he is! Aeryn was far too sophisticated to be allied with such simpletons. Now, if he'd told me that *you* knew something," Ladomer added, a mocking twinkle to his eye, "I might have believed him…"

Eamon forced a loud laugh. "What nonsense!" he cried, terribly conscious of the stone at his neck.

"My very thought," Ladomer agreed. He took Eamon's hand and clasped it firmly. "I'll see you soon."

"I hope so," Eamon replied. He meant it. "Take care of yourself."

"You too, Ratbag!" Ladomer winked and then hurried off along the road, his uniform pristine in the afternoon light.

Eamon watched him go. He felt the weight of his treachery falling anew on his shoulders. Becoming a King's man meant leaving Ladomer behind him – and he did not know that he could.

"You were going to say something, sir?" Mathaiah watched him earnestly.

Eamon shook his head. "It was nothing," he said.

Later that afternoon Eamon was summoned to Captain Waite. He went obediently, and wasn't surprised to find that Lord Cathair also awaited him.

"My lord; sir."

"At ease, first lieutenant."

"Thank you, sir." Eamon looked at the Hand. The darkly swathed man looked paler than ever that afternoon. Green eyes flashed brightly in the dwindling light.

"Mr Goodman, I came to offer to you my personal thanks for the service you rendered me several evenings ago," the Hand said, laying one hand against his breast in a delicate gesture.

"It was my duty, both to you and to the Master. You need not thank me for performing my duty, my lord."

"Still I am, as you may imagine, pleased with your intervention." Cathair smiled. "How does it feel to be back in your right uniform, Mr Goodman?"

Eamon shuffled uncomfortably. "Perfection itself, my lord."

"You should have seen him, captain!"

"I did," Waite answered quietly.

"Ah, your first lieutenant cut a very gallant figure at the masque, captain. He has created an indelible impression on us all. Unfortunately, due to the little ruckus that followed Mr Goodman's election as winner of the evening – a most prestigious award! – his prize was overlooked." The Hand looked back to Eamon. "With the notable exception of that occasion when Lord Rendolet came as a woman – a matter to which, I must add, he owes any and all notoriety he may possess – the masque prize usually goes to a lady and so tends to take a floral form. However, the Right Hand felt that such a gesture, regardless of its good intent, might not be so well received by you, Mr Goodman. He has taken the liberty of arranging for a few extra coins to find their way to your wages for this month."

"Thank you, my lord."

"Don't spend them all at once, Mr Goodman!" Cathair told him with his accustomed smile. "Now, to return to the matter of the assassin." A sudden chill ran through him, as Eamon remembered the furious wrench that had torn sword and star from his breast.

"Following your various administrative and patrol duties for Captain Waite, you are to accompany me to the Pit this afternoon." Eamon paled: the Pit was Dunthruik's most notorious prison, and Eamon had no desire to see it. "Are you fond of poetry, Mr Goodman?"

Struck dumb, Eamon could only stare. Poetry? "Yes, my lord," he managed.

"I am myself very fond of the lyrics from the first days of Dunthruik," Cathair told him. "'Round, around my lady went, round around my lady fair; about her brow a crown of stars, an eagle's flower in her hair.'" He recited the words softly but watched with an intensity that seemed to go beyond the verse. Eamon swallowed. "Do you know it, Mr Goodman?"

"No, my lord."

"You are a man of little learning, Mr Goodman!" Cathair tutted. "Perhaps you should ask Cadet Overbrook; he has the look of a scholar to him."

"Yes, my lord."

"I ask you whether you like poetry because, as you halted this man's attempt at my life, I felt that it would be *poetic* for you to inquire of him what he intended."

The chill went deeper – the delicate word "inquire" could only mean one thing...

To the Hand he could only show a smile. "Nothing would please me more, my lord."

The wind buffeted him as he walked to the palace, his steps swallowed by Cathair's shadow. Mathaiah followed them. Cathair chatted to them and sometimes broke spontaneously into song. He had a fine, deep voice, and seemed distressingly cheerful.

He led them to the Hands' Hall and through a string of stone-guarded passages. Eamon was too anxious about what was to follow to really note where they were going, but Mathaiah looked everywhere. Seeing the strange writing on post and doors, the cadet's eyes widened, and Eamon wondered what new revelation had reached him.

The corridors halted in a small hall at a single staircase. The stairs led down into interminable darkness, only broken at irregular intervals by torches. The steps came at last into a subterranean hall filled with doorways. Cathair led them through one of these.

They emerged into a cavern lit by a dying brazier. A strange, slight breeze disturbed Eamon's face.

There was a hole in the middle of the cavern floor. It was about the width of three men standing together and a terrible stench – sweat, fear, blood, and excrement – issued from it. A long ladder and a trellis stood by the hole. More ominous doorways circled the whole chamber. Only Hands stood guard there.

Cathair stepped up to the brazier and kindled it to life. Gasps and groans leapt pitifully from below. Eamon exchanged anxious glances with his pale ward. It was a place of terror. It was where they would both end up if their treachery was discovered.

"Welcome, gentlemen, to the Pit," Cathair proclaimed cheerfully. "It affords most affable accommodation to dozens of wayfaring whores and bastards." Unadulterated horror flooded him. "Oh, it's much bigger down there than it looks up here," Cathair added. "We drop them in for a little while, to reflect most seriously upon what they are. Sometimes we leave them there. More than one unhelpful person has died in there, I am sorry to report. And it is so very difficult to efficiently remove cadavers." He shrugged lightly. "But we get by."

Eamon gagged. At a command from Cathair, the Pit's Hands moved to the edge of the chamber's ghastly crevice. They stretched out their arms. A red glow formed about them; it spread down into the hole. A scream answered it. Eamon watched, aghast, as a body rose up, hoisted as though on strings. He understood then that this red light came with the throned's mark. The fiery levitation was more painful than rope or chains would ever have been.

The body was disgorged and Eamon recognized the young man whom he had stopped at the masque. The boy's face was swollen and purple, his naked torso pocked with ugly welts.

The Hands dropped their prisoner by the mouth of the Pit. His cut arms barely had the strength to support him and he collapsed at once, gasping.

Striding forward, Cathair reached down and took disparaging hold of the boy's chin. Yanking the head backwards almost farther than its neck could bear, the Hand turned to Eamon with a smile.

"Do you see, Mr Goodman, what happens to those who betray the Master? But this is just the beginning of payment for that coin."

Was this message not also for him?

Further Hands were summoned from some dark recess of the chamber. They ruthlessly dragged the young man through one of the doorways.

The room beyond was small and silent, with a single torch fixed to the wall, which Cathair lit. The trembling prisoner was bound to the chair in the centre of the room. Along the walls were various instruments of torture, and Cathair stood silent while he allowed the young man's terrified eyes to pass over them, taking in the shape, size, and power of each. Eamon knew the names and functions of the tools, and dreaded that the boy would be made to suffer them.

"There is something missing, if I could but think of it," Cathair mused. "Ah yes."

The Hands returned with another man. He was dumped on the floor where he lay and writhed. In disgust, Cathair kicked him hard. Eamon winced. He could do nothing.

"Up, snake," Cathair hissed.

The old man hauled himself upright and leaned heavily against the damp chamber wall. The point of some evil instrument glistened by his forehead. Eamon saw that the man's face had been cut almost beyond recognition: one eye had been gouged, leaving a dark, scabbed mass of crimson.

Mathaiah retched. Eamon held himself in check by a thread, for he recognized the remains of the man before him. Cathair had stopped him at the Blind Gate on his first day in Dunthruik.

Cathair stepped lightly between his two prisoners, his pallor and robes giving him a deathly aspect.

"Mr Clarence?" he said to the older man. "Please allow me to introduce you to Master Clarence. But soft! I believe that you have met."

The young man heard the words upon Cathair's lips and managed to bring his eyes into focus on the bedraggled other. He stared uncomprehendingly, then stretched his bound hands out.

"*Pa!*"

Eamon blenched. A glance at Lord Cathair showed crippling delight in the Hand's eyes. It stifled all Eamon's will. Cathair was boundless in his strength and vile in his means. He could not be stopped.

"Do you see, Mr Goodman, the kindness that the Master offers, even to the snakes?" Cathair asked. "See! A father and son sweetly reunited." A groan died on Clarence's lips.

"You bastard!" the son screamed. "Murdering bastard!"

"Young man," Cathair said with mocking gentility, "your father has been my most honoured guest in recent days. I even took care of your dear mother's funeral expenses on your behalf. Let me assure you that my dogs enjoyed the event especially."

The boy let out an incoherent cry of rage and grief. "I'll kill you!" he screeched: "I'll kill you!"

Cathair leaned close to his prisoner. "I very much doubt it," he sneered. "Mr Goodman."

Quaking, Eamon tore his eyes away from the sobbing, screaming, swearing boy.

"My lord?"

"Breach him."

Eamon gaped. What could that possibly achieve? "My lord –"

"I want to know who forged the papers."

Eamon glanced guiltily at the young man. The prisoner spat. "Damn you! Damn you and your usurper!"

"I said breach him, Mr Goodman."

There was no other way. Eamon pressed his hand against the young man's head, the flesh sweaty and grimy. The boy struggled furiously in his bonds. In his ire he hurled curses at Eamon, and as each curse landed anger rose.

This boyish simpleton had no idea what position he had been

forced into. Fire flecked unbidden on Eamon's palm. And then the world changed.

The plain was dark and he was strong. The boy was nothing before him, and in Eamon's ears was a voice he had not heard for many days:

See how he defies you? Crush him, Eben's son. Crush him with all my strength!

Yes. Eamon knew he could do it. The boy's mind was breached and lay open before him, a fruit split apart by the incision of a knife. He saw the boy's whole life, every secret thought and word, every anguish, every joy, every love and hatred. It was wretched and pitiable. With one gesture, he could stop it all.

Breaching was more than tearing open the pages of a mind to read all written there: it was the power to cast them into torment and flame or to destroy them utterly. It was his power.

The young man stared at him in horror. Eamon towered over him. The prisoner backed away on broken flesh.

Crush him, crush him!

"Stay away from me!" the young man cried.

Rise to your place, Eben's son!

The young man screamed in pain. "You cannot harm me!" he yelled. "I am a King's man!"

A ruddy flare was forming in Eamon's palm. Such power! He would send it against the insolent wretch… He drew back his hand to crush his foe.

Suddenly the King's grace dropped down, engulfing the young man in a wash of blue.

Eamon started in terror. He could not strive against that! He could not – it had saved him, and he had sworn to serve another.

With a cry he thrust the red light away – it cracked harmlessly over the plain. Driven by the sight of blue he tried desperately to withdraw, but the grim voice demanded that he hold.

Do as I command, son of Eben!

No! He did not want to! His heart cried out to the King's grace, begging it to aid him in his struggle.

Breach him.

The light grew. Eamon pinned his flaming arm against his breast. Why did the grace not help him? He called again for strength to stand against the command that his hand so ardently meant to follow. Was he not also a King's man?

Suddenly the blue light was on him – the heart of the King answered it with sapphire brilliance. The red was quenched at once. He was released.

The boy stared at him. "Who are you?"

His will his own once more, Eamon met his gaze. "I serve the King," he panted. The boy's look became incredulous. "Please, forgive me my part in bringing you here. I will do everything I can to help you."

He opened his eyes; the torture room was before him. Echoes of agony died on the boy's lips. Eamon heard the old man crying for mercy.

"Stop, stop! He's just a boy. I beg of you, my lord! Stay your hand!"

"Mr Goodman?"

Blinking hard, Eamon lowered his reddened palms. "He doesn't know who forged the papers, my lord," he said firmly.

"No," Cathair agreed. "But *he* does." Cathair turned burning eyes to the dolorous man. "Have you not heard your only remaining son screaming, Mr Clarence? Have you not heard him begging for mercy?"

"Yes, my lord, yes!"

"Have you not seen that my servant can break his mind at my whim?"

"My lord, I beg of you –"

"Does it seem a reasonable exchange to you, Mr Clarence?" Cathair spoke the words as though they were the most logical in the world. "A name, a single name, for your son's very life?"

"You will let him go?"

Cathair nodded. "I will release him," he promised solemnly. Eamon gasped – no, he could not –

"Pa, no!" But it was too late: the name was uttered.

"Benadict Lorentide. It was Benadict Lorentide."

An awful silence. Cathair stood back, satisfied. "Thank you, Mr Clarence," he said, touching the man's shoulder with consoling lightness. "You have been most cooperative. Mr Goodman."

"My lord?"

"Kill the boy."

Eamon froze. Kill the boy? He couldn't! There had to be another way...

Mathaiah stood, pale and shaking, in the corner; there were Hands at the door, and Hands beyond it. Cathair was a Quarter Hand. Eamon had no help. He could not disobey; and Cathair, whatever else he knew, knew that. The Lord of the West Quarter relished it.

"You promised me that he would live!" Clarence howled.

"I promised you that I would release him," Cathair answered smoothly. "What better service could I render him than to release him from his muddy bondage to this earthly world? Mr Goodman."

He could show no fear, no reluctance. Eamon drew his dagger and pressed it against the young man's heart. In that moment, when the dagger was all the bond between them, the young man met Eamon's gaze.

Eamon wished he could say he was sorry, wished he could beg the boy's forgiveness, wished that he could promise that good would come of his sacrifice. He could not. He put his weight to the blade, closed his eyes. The dagger crunched as it sank through flesh and bone and stopped abruptly against the chair.

The old man screamed.

Blood ran down the dagger to drip about his fingers. He gripped the pommel tight. Enraged tears stung behind his eyes. He could not show them.

Cathair watched approvingly, and smiled a horrible smile. "Thank you, Mr Goodman," he said. "A most effective blow." He looked disparagingly at the weeping man, who grovelled with grief.

"Miserable fool," he pronounced archly. "Mr Goodman, go back to the college and fetch your cadets. Arrest Mr Lorentide, all of his kin with him, and as many of his neighbours as you can find. No doubt all snakes. Bring them to me at the college. An example will be made of them."

Eamon lowered in a bloody, quivering bow. "Yes, my lord."

CHAPTER XVIII

Eamon reeled as they ascended the disorienting stair. Blood – everywhere was blood. His very heart was matted with it. It stained his hands, burnt his face.

One of the Hands from the Pit escorted them through the reddened doorways to the palace gates. Eamon gulped down the cool air, as though it might somehow purge him.

He bowed towards the Hand. "My lord," he said, "I will go directly to carry out Lord Cathair's will."

"Good man," the Hand smiled. "These snakes are to be found in the East Quarter, where Coronet Rise meets Acacia Way. This man, Lorentide, holds a minor post in the local Crown Office and his wife owns a small grocer's shop. A relatively well-off family. Get them all, first lieutenant."

Eamon didn't know how the Hand knew this, but he did not dare to ask. He bowed again and then watched the Hand return to the Hands' Hall.

He watched long enough to be sure that he had truly gone then turned to Mathaiah. The cadet clutched at his throat where bile had burned it.

"Are you all right?" Eamon whispered.

Mathaiah nodded weakly; Eamon steadied him. Clarence's son had not been much older than his ward. He swallowed down the bitter swill in his mouth. He had murdered. Murdered – and for what? A man with a crown? An eagle's oath? He wanted to howl, swear, curse, but duty forbade it.

Had killing Alben been so very different?

"I'm sorry that you had to see…"

"I'm sorry that you had to do it."

Eamon glanced furtively about. There were soldiers everywhere and any of them could take an unwelcome interest in them at any time. He might not have been able to save Clarence's son – but he would not stand by while the Lorentides were slaughtered.

"Come on, quickly."

"Sir?"

Eamon needed to think fast. Cathair certainly expected to receive prisoners for his grisly tortures – as many as could be obtained. It was also clear that the official to be arrested was a wayfarer and that he had somehow managed to forge Lord Ashway's permission for Clarence's pass. The Hands would want to know how the man had managed to come so close to accurately forging the paper. It was a crime that would merit a prolonged and painful death. With luck, the family would have heard of Clarence's arrest and found some way to hide themselves – but there could be no guarantee of that. If Eamon did exactly as Cathair had ordered, then the whole family might be captured.

The smell of the Pit was still in his nostrils. It was no way to die – cramped in the dark at the mercy of a Hand. Yet that was the fate to which Eamon would condemn the wayfarers if he arrested them – and if he brought back none at all then Cathair might guess at where his own allegiance lay. The choice was between himself and the Lorentides – just as it had been between himself and Alben.

No. Eamon shook his head. He would not make that choice again. One man had to be brought to endure Cathair's rabid fury – but perhaps the others could be saved.

They were by now on the Coll and hurrying towards the Brand. Eamon could make out the flag over the West Quarter College, hanging limp and still.

"Mathaiah," he said suddenly, "go to the Lorentides'."

"Sir?"

"Go now; warn them. One of them is going to have to give

themself to Cathair, or he will keep hunting them until he finds them all. But tell the rest of them to go. Get them out of here, clear out their neighbours."

Mathaiah glanced at him, astounded. "I'm in uniform!" he hissed. "What do I tell them?"

"Not your name." As his plan grew so did his urgency. "And not mine. Don't even tell them who wants them or why. Just tell them…" he paused. He had to think of something – they were getting close to the college gates. There was one obvious name to give – did he dare?

"Tell them that the First Knight sent you and that, as they value their lives, they have to go."

As he gave the command, peace filled him: it was a choice made for his true colour and for his King. "I will delay the Banners for as long as I can, but you will need to move swiftly and discreetly." He looked steadily at his ward. Mathaiah watched him with wide eyes.

"Yes, sir."

Eamon was trembling. It was dangerous for both of them, but he would not turn back. "Be careful, Mathaiah."

Mathaiah disappeared into a side street among the thronging merchants, ensigns, and aristocrats. Eamon breathed deep. He drew himself upright and marched into the college.

Knowing that his cadets spent that time of the day in geography he went straight to the study chambers. Without knock or preamble he swept inside.

His fifteen cadets – most of them thoroughly bored – sat in the room. Of them only Cadet Overbrook was hunched over his bench furiously scribbling notes. Lieutenant Best was taking the class and was at that moment pointing at a large map of the north-east border where the Shimmer, one of the tributaries of the River, tumbled down from the mountains near Greypass. As Eamon entered unannounced the lieutenant looked up in surprise; the cadets leapt to their feet to salute.

"Good afternoon, first lieutenant," Best began.

"I'm sorry to interrupt you, Mr Best," Eamon answered. "I must rob you of your students; orders from Lord Cathair." The cadets exchanged glances.

"Of course," Best continued, carefully not noticing the blood on his first lieutenant's uniform. "You may take them immediately, sir."

"Leave your things," Eamon barked. "Be in the hall in three minutes."

"Yes, sir!" The cadets hurried out of the room.

As Eamon watched them go he heard Best's voice at his arm: "Is everything all right, sir?"

"Just an arrest to see to, Mr Best," Eamon replied, trying to make it sound as nonchalant as possible. His heart was beating fast.

"And that…?" Best began, looking at the blood.

"Not mine, Mr Best."

He took his leave and hurried to the hall. He had to make everything look as though he wished deadly efficiency, but knew he needed to give Mathaiah the time to get to the Lorentides before him. The Coll and Coronet Rise were the two roads that divided the city into quarters, the former running from east to west and the latter north to south. Acacia Way was in the East Quarter near the Crown Office and was a reasonably prosperous area. Thanks to the attention he had himself paid to Best's geographical knowledge and to Giles's map, Eamon was quickly able to calculate that he could probably prolong the time it took them to reach the wayfarers if he insisted on taking the Coll rather than weaving through the smaller streets. The Coll would be teeming with preparations for the majesty, and the Four Quarters, the city's heart and crossroads of Coll and Coronet Rise, would be filled with people. Adding a group of fifteen marching cadets would augment the confusion considerably. It was the perfect way to slow everything down.

"What are we doing, sir?" Manners asked. He was first to arrive in the hall.

"Lord Cathair has identified some snakes in the East Quarter," Eamon answered. "He is sending us to arrest them."

The cadets looked excited at the prospect of some real Gauntleting. Eamon regarded them sternly.

"Gentlemen, be at your most proficient. If possible the suspects are to be taken alive and unharmed, though you may use force if they resist you. Lord Cathair will doubtless have questions for as many of them as we can bring back." And, he thought, if those who gave themselves up were unharmed, there was the slightest chance that they might be freed later, to make a good escape in their health.

"Sir, shouldn't someone from the East Quarter be performing an arrest in the East Quarter?" asked Ostler.

Eamon hadn't thought of that. He gave the best answer that he could. "Lord Cathair unmasked these snakes and he has sent us, Mr Ostler."

"Yes, sir."

"Your ward, sir?" Manners asked. His absence was conspicuous.

"Mr Grahaven was otherwise engaged but I have sent word for him to join us," Eamon answered. It wasn't a total lie.

Eamon led his men onto the Coll and towards the Four Quarters. As he had hoped, the road was choked with people.

The Four Quarters came into sight up ahead. The façades of tall buildings formed their angles. The quarters' faces were high and sombre in the light, at least one perpetually caught in shadow as the sun circled the city. At the highest part of each building was an upright eagle, its bold wings outstretched and a crown upon its brow.

Every street around the Four Quarters was filled. In all the confusion caused by the preparation for the majesty, diverted carriages and carts had blocked the central passage. Irate traders and merchants hurled colourful abuse at each other from their stationary wagons, and raised their voices at the Gauntlet ensigns trying to get the traffic moving again.

It was better – or rather, worse – than Eamon could have hoped. It took time for the carts to be cleared to the side so as to grant them passage. He took his men left at the crossroads and north up

Coronet Rise onto Acacia Way. The trees that lined the tidy road seemed ghostly reminders of an older time.

They soon reached the small square that held the Crown Office. It was the place where much of Dunthruik's administrative work for the East Quarter was done, and where Benadict Lorentide worked. The small area hosted a number of affluent shops, but only the office flew the throned's eagled banner.

Eamon surveyed the square. On his right, by a water pump, were carts of fruit and, above it, the Lorentides' decent home. He caught fleeting sight of Mathaiah coming into the square from the north. The cadet fell in step next to Manners and was welcomed heartily.

"We're in for some real action today, Grahaven!" Manners told him cheerfully.

"I'm looking forward to it!"

"Mr Manners and Mr Grahaven, keep yourselves in order," Eamon commanded sternly. Both fell quiet at once. Eamon stole a glance at Mathaiah's face: he read neither success nor failure from his ward's eyes.

He called a halt and split his cadets into several groups. Some he assigned to go through the Crown Office itself, others to block off potential escape routes, some to hold suspects in the square, and others to go through the nearby buildings and the Lorentides' home.

"Anyone deemed to be suspicious or of interest, and anyone who resists your enquiries, will be brought to holding in the square," Eamon told them. "I will vet them before we perform any arrests. To your tasks, gentlemen."

"Sir!"

The cadets dispersed. In the square and nearby streets men and women stopped. As the cadets hauled suspects out into the square the onlookers began to look alarmed.

Eamon went boldly to the Lorentides' home. As he had hoped he found nobody in the main hallway. He instructed the cadets with him to search every room before hurrying upstairs himself.

He was trembling with hope. The house seemed empty. But as he reached the top of the stairs he heard a voice.

Eamon froze. Mathaiah, who had followed him, looked at him in horror.

"I'm sorry, sir," he whispered. "There was nobody here when I left; they said that the nurse wasn't due back until this evening, that they would find her before –"

Eamon glanced behind them. The other cadets were still searching through the lower rooms.

"Stay at the stairs here. Don't let anyone pass."

"Sir."

Eamon tracked the voice down the corridor. It sang with the contented oblivion of a child. Reaching it, his heart sank.

A little boy sat in the centre of the end room, a wooden soldier in his hand. The soldier wore a red jacket and his smooth back was embossed with a painted crown. They boy looked up expectantly.

"Daddy?" He frowned with disappointment. "You're not daddy," he stated crossly, before he glanced between the toy in his hand and the man before him. "You're a Gauntlet?" His voice was terribly loud.

Eamon stepped over to him, every muscle in his body tense.

"Yes, I'm Gauntlet," he said, crouching down.

"Are you one of daddy's friends?" the boy struggled a little over his words. He could be little more than four years old.

"Yes, I am."

Grinning, the boy reached out and clasped Eamon's hand. "I'm Dorien Lorentide," he announced.

"Good to meet you, Dorien," Eamon answered, pressing the tiny hand in his own. He was horribly conscious of sounds downstairs and of people gathering – or being gathered – in the square. The only way out for this child was not to be found.

"Dorien, I need you to do something for me," he said. "Will you? It's very important that you do exactly as I say."

The little boy nodded. "You're daddy's friend. All right." The unquestioning obedience was unsettling.

Eamon looked around for inspiration. "I want you to hide in this chest here," he said, gesturing to the large chest in one corner. "You must be very quiet, Dorien! Nobody must know that you are there. You must not come out until we have all gone away. No matter what you hear, you must not come out. Do you understand?" His cheerful tone belied the fear he felt as the footsteps drew nearer.

"Is it a game?" the boy asked, his eyes lighting.

"Yes, a very important one." Eamon rose and opened the chest; the smell of treated furs rose at him. "In you get, Dorien," he added, shepherding him into the hiding place.

The little boy clambered to his feet, clutching the soldier. The painted crown glistened as the boy climbed into the chest, complaining about the smell. Settled among the furs he seemed terribly small.

"Are you comfortable?" Eamon asked.

"No."

"I'm sorry. Don't come out," he repeated earnestly. "You must stay there." He hesitated before adding, "And Dorien, if you stay quiet and still, then you will get a prize. Do you want a prize?"

The boy beamed. "Yes!"

"Good. Stay there."

Eamon smiled, laid a finger to his lips, and carefully lowered the lid. Manners' voice called up the stairwell: "Clear downstairs, sir. We only found a nurse."

Eamon nearly swore. "There's nobody up here," he managed. He hurried down the corridor and stairs. Mathaiah followed him. Manners stood expectantly below. Was he suspicious of Eamon's speed? He would have to hope not. "Let's go and sift through whatever rabble we've collected."

Most of his cadets had returned to the square, herding an anxious group between them. Some of them were women holding food in their arms, a couple with a servant or maid to assist them – they had evidently been shopping. These Eamon dismissed immediately. It would not do to arrest such folk. No neighbours had been found;

their only quarry was Lorentide's nurse, who was hustled brusquely into the square. She was a young woman with dark hair. The majority of the remaining people were officials from the Crown Office. As they cowered he felt the strange – though not now unaccustomed – tug of power at his breast. What a thing it was to be feared!

"Which of you is Benadict Lorentide?" he demanded.

One man stepped forward. He looked pale but resolute. "I am."

Eamon fixed him with an unfeeling gaze. "Mr Lorentide, for the Master's glory, I declare you under arrest for consorting with and conspiring to assist wayfarers in their operations against him." He growled for the benefit of the onlookers, and spoke as though sincere. It alarmed him. "Where are your family?"

Lorentide drew himself up proudly. "They left the city three days ago. Your cruel Master will not find them!"

"We shall see what your tongue shall say to that once it has been loosened," Eamon retorted. He glanced at the man beside Lorentide. He was large and had a puffed face. Eamon took him to be in charge of the office.

"Please, sir!" the official whimpered. "We have nothing to do with this man! We merely serve the Lord Ashway, and we have served him well for many years. We have much work to do!" he added plaintively.

"I will let you go," Eamon answered darkly, "but know that if you have had illicit dealings with this man, then Lord Ashway will discover it and will exercise a less lenient judgment than I." He nodded to the cadets who then permitted the office officials and servants to leave the square. Several of them cast fearful looks over their shoulders at their colleague as they went.

Lorentide and the nurse remained in the Gauntlet circle. The woman began to sob. Lorentide laid one hand on her shoulder, a gesture from which she took little comfort – it tore Eamon's heart to shreds. They had to be sacrificed – for the sake of the boy.

But part of him watched the stalwart man and weeping woman and relished how their lives rested in his hands.

Eamon turned to the cadets. "Third Banners, these two are under arrest. Take them to the West Quarter College and commit them to Lord Cathair. Meet any attempt at escape with force."

"Sir!"

It was a ridiculous sight: fifteen Gauntlet cadets shepherding two prisoners. Eamon almost dared to breathe. Two prisoners should be enough to satisfy Lord Cathair, and the rest of the man's family was safe. Safe, that was, if Benedict Lorentide was a man who could hold his own before a Hand. But over that, Eamon had no power.

As he led the cadets away he heard something that filled him with horror:

"Daddy!"

He turned. Dorien Lorentide was running out of his house as swiftly as his small, stumbling legs could carry him, his arms outstretched towards his father. "Daddy!"

Time slowed. Eamon reeled. Lorentide turned grey. The boy pushed through the cadets until his tiny hands could grip his father's knees. The child laughed out loud.

"You've finished early today!" he said with delight. Then he looked up at Eamon. "Do I get my prize?" he asked.

Eamon beat down the grief rising in his throat. Why could the child not have done as he had asked? *Why?*

"Is this your child, Lorentide?" he demanded. He met the man's gaze and willed him to disown the child. It would be a cruel heirloom – but all Lorentide need do was state it with enough conviction, and Eamon could command that the boy be left behind. How he wished the man would say it!

They held each other's gazes. Then, with the grace of a loving father, Benedict Lorentide stooped to gather his boy into his arms.

"Hello, Dori," he said. "I'm here – we'll go together." Tears quivered about his eyes; Dorien pressed them away with kisses.

Eamon gaped at him. Would the man sacrifice his son? Now what could he do – surely not deliver them to Cathair?

The cadets, now uncomfortable, watched him, and officials gazed at him from the Crown Office. He swallowed back his sorrow.

"Take them to the West Quarter."

There was no question, no discussion; only the child's laughing face as his father carried him away.

For the second time that day, Eamon committed a father and his son to Cathair.

The majesty began not long after the sun had set. Lights burned all over the city. Thousands of people lined the roads, trying to get close to the Royal Plaza, while Gauntlet patrols walked every street and dotted the long lines to keep the crowds in check. Crown-shaped lanterns ran from the Blind Gate all the way along the Coll to the palace, and in the harbour every ship flew a crimson banner in the Master's honour; they snapped in the wind like drums. Every tower, every building, and every home had red cloth bound to its posts, declaring the ownership of the Master, and every man, woman, or child who lined the Coll bore red.

The procession began outside the Blind Gate. It was there that Gauntlet companies, each led by their Quarter Hand, captain, and officers, were gathered. Drummers followed each detachment, filling the air with a heart-stirring beat.

Eamon took his place among the West Quarter's officer lines, waiting for the order to begin marching. He caught glimpses of men from the other quarters lining up behind them. Of course the West marched first – it was the Master's own quarter.

A shadow passed over him. He jumped.

"Mr Goodman!" Lord Cathair was about to take his place in the first of the West's lines, but changed his course to turn his smiling face towards Eamon.

Cathair was the last person that Eamon had the stomach to see. "My lord," he answered, bowing low.

"I really must thank you for your excellent work today," Cathair told him. "No, really! Excellent work. I'll confess, I am disappointed that we did not take the whole Lorentide brood, but there is time enough for that. Bringing the boy was a stroke of veritable genius: rendered his father much more cooperative." He laughed. "You have a very great – and wonderfully sinister – potential in you!"

His mind was crowded with images of the tiny child in the Pit and the picture became confused with Clarence's son and the smell of blood. He tried to force everything from his mind. "Thank you, my lord."

"Mr Goodman, you will march in the first line," Cathair added, "beside your draybant."

A shiver of fear ran through him. What new madness did this portend? "Yes, Lord Cathair."

Cathair nodded with satisfaction as Eamon shuffled through the line to Draybant Farleigh's side.

"Enjoy the majesty, Mr Goodman!" he called. Eamon doubted very much that he would.

Trumpeters over the city gates began to play, calling the Gauntlet to march. The West was followed by the South, the East, and then the North. Lord Cathair walked centrally before the West Quarter's men. By him walked another Hand, who carried a tall banner showing raven and vine. The other quarters' columns were led by their own Hands, and similar banners: an owl and ash for the East, falcon and oak for the North, and a harrier and yew for the South.

Drums answered the trumpets. The crowd cheered as the Gauntlet passed through the Blind Gate, then walked the length of the Coll towards the palace. The throned's eyrie stood against the sky. Music and shouting filled the air, and streamers fell in the road all about them.

The procession reached the Royal Plaza. Its beauty struck Eamon forcefully: the colonnades were lit with torches, and red fabric, bearing the Master's eagle, had been wound about their pillars. The plaza stair beneath the balcony was littered at every step with candles – an enormous shining crown forged there in wax.

The Gauntlet procession came to an ordered standstill, each group gathering in the quarter of the plaza which bore its token. As the jubilant music died away a figure appeared on the balcony. Eamon recognized at once the long steps of the Right Hand. He was vested in exquisite sable robes and his voice, powerful and obediently followed, rang out clearly across the crowded plaza. His words seemed uttered directly into Eamon's own ear.

"The Serpent is defeated," he announced, "and the land is crowned." The speech was heavy with the rhythm of ritual.

"The land is crowned in glory," came the cry. Eamon was astounded to find that his lips moved to the words of Dunthruik's liturgy.

"The glory is the Master's, for he has cast down the Serpent's brood. Serve him. Behold the majesty of him who delivers you from the broken house whose star has set. Behold him, and rejoice."

"His glory!"

A great light erupted on the balcony, blinding all below. Eamon's eyes were caught upward as the chant continued:

"His glory! His glory!"

Fire moved in the air, a burning crown on every palm exultantly raised, hungrily stretched towards the balcony.

"His glory!"

There, bathed in the light of the burning crowd, stood a figure in crimson with red hair, his brow a crown of living fire. As he raised his hand in benediction the chanting reached an untenable volume, yet still it grew:

"*His glory! His glory!*"

The fiery figure lifted his head and spoke in a voice like the roaring wind: "I call forth these strong hands to serve me."

A shiver cracked with crippling force down Eamon's spine. He gasped: how often had that voice – that selfsame voice! – spoken in his mind?

"Of the North Quarter Oldin, Tulloch's son; of the East Quarter Richart, Dromel's son; of the South Quarter Vintan, Grinward's son."

Eamon's heart quickened to an unbearable pace; he knew the eyes of the distant, flaming man were on him. Loving and mocking in their intensity, they pierced him through. Could it be? He desired – and dreaded – to hear what would be spoken.

"Of the West Quarter Eamon, Eben's son."

Eben's son! And so he was. His whole soul burned and the jubilant crowd roared about him, their one voice universally acclaiming his worthy proclamation, and his alone. The Master had called him by name and he had answered.

He had been nominated to become a Hand.

The grey eyes saw and welcomed his skill, offering power in return for service. What else could he desire?

The Master laid a benediction over the people and disappeared from the balcony, followed closely by the Right Hand.

Eamon's cadets whooped in delight and poured praise on him. Among the tiers of seated nobles in the plaza his eyes suddenly picked out Alessia. She smiled. The fire in his heart grew greater.

"Congratulations, Mr Goodman," said a voice at his side. It was Cathair's; it no longer seemed hateful to him. "Did I not say that you would be rewarded?"

Elation nourished strange thoughts. Congratulation was all around him and he barely had a moment to think. Yet in the web of his victory he was conscious of Mathaiah's troubled face. Eamon scowled. What did Mathaiah understand of such reward?

The procession soon devolved into a general party; many departed in search of wine and women. The candles burned bright on the steps and the music played into the night.

Eamon found himself by Mathaiah.

"Congratulations, sir." The boy's face was worn with worry. Eamon rolled his eyes.

"Whatever's the matter with you?" he asked, noting with only a touch of alarm that he did not really care for the answer. What did it matter, the voice asked him?

"Nothing, sir."

Mathaiah did not approve. It was obvious. But he didn't understand. "Don't you see what an opportunity this will be? If I can become a Hand I will be able to learn much." And what power he would have! He might even become Right Hand himself…

"Yes, sir," Mathaiah consented. His look remained. "Sir, doesn't it worry you that –?"

"Mr Goodman!"

Eamon's heart soared: Alessia! The wondrous lady was walking across to him, her crimson dress fluttering in the evening breeze. Reaching him, she kissed his cheek.

"Congratulations, Mr Goodman!" she whispered, her voice close by his ear.

"If you'll excuse me, sir," Mathaiah said quietly, "I think I will retire for the night."

Eamon glanced at him with guilty eagerness. "Already?" With Mathaiah gone, he would be free to go with Alessia. All he could think of was her touch on his skin.

"I've seen enough for one day," Mathaiah told him. Was that an agitated tone to his voice? "Goodnight, *first* lieutenant."

Eamon frowned. What should the word "first" mean to him?

Alessia tugged gently on his arm. "Mr Goodman," she said, "would you accompany me home?"

Eamon smiled, delighted by her radiance and thrilled by the kiss that lay still upon his cheek. "It would be my pleasure, lady!" he replied gallantly.

Together they walked the red-lit streets towards the North Quarter and turned from there into the gates of the Turnholt estate. Alessia flooded him with compliments; her eyes and hands upon his inflamed him utterly.

They reached her doors. She turned and smiled at him.

"Won't you come in, Mr Goodman?" she asked. "I have something for you; a gift of congratulation, if you will."

Part of his heart cautioned him to stay his step, to consider the import of crossing the threshold on that night in answer to those words. But it was only a very small part of his heart. His veins sang with the Master's acclaim, drowning out the warnings.

He stepped over the threshold and followed her.

She led him up the staircase and along the upper passageway. Dozens of rich paintings gazed down at him and every wall bore an eagle that clasped a crown-bearing shield. The eyes of that noble predator, great bird and mark of a great family that served the Master, watched him as he followed her who was heir to that same crest.

They met no servant and all about was quiet. They came at last to a doorway at the far side of the house. Even the sounds of the majesty's revels seemed far away. Smiling still, Alessia opened the door and stepped inside. Past her slim figure Eamon could see a bedchamber.

His heart stopped.

Seeing him pause, she came back to him. She took his hand. "Come, Mr Goodman."

He followed her. The room held a great bed over which hung the eagle and the shield. Tall windows that overlooked the garden lined one side, curtains draped about them. From those windows the reflected light of the majesty, of a thousand candles burning in the night, filled the room with a low glow.

Eamon trembled. Fear and passion clashed in his heart like mighty armies.

Alessia gently closed the door. She stepped back to him, caressing his fingers in hers. He knew what gift it was that she intended. He longed to receive it, and yet...

He pressed her hands. "My lady," he whispered, "you honour me – how you honour me! – but I cannot –"

Alessia laughed. With a fairy grace she pulled his face down to hers. She kissed him and Eamon felt his whole being driven to answer it. How could he not? He pressed himself against her, drinking in her loveliness, feeling her face and hair with his hands.

She stepped back from him, lingering her lips on his, and as she smiled at him she seemed surprised. He burnt – how he burnt! – with greater ardour than the mark on his palm had ever burned.

In the ruddy half-light he saw that one sleeve of her crimson dress had slipped from one white shoulder. Abashed, he reached to set it back; she stopped him. There was sudden seriousness in her face. Eamon saw something deep in her – far deeper than the seductive smile that had drawn him to her chamber.

"Three nights ago, you asked me to dance with you," she breathed. "How we danced!" She looked at him anew, her eyes now soft and shy. Her fingers trembled as she guided his hand to her bare shoulder.

"Eamon," she whispered. How sweet his name sounded, pronounced by her sweet lips! "Eamon, will you dance with me?"

And he did.

CHAPTER XIX

He woke in the grey light, when the world waited for dawn to rise in bridal splendour. He, too, joined the waiting, thinking nothing but that the dawn had to come and that, when it did, it would be beautiful.

Slowly, he gathered his senses. The long, red drape over the casement stirred in the breeze. A mirror gazed at him from the far wall. In it was the reflection of the bed in which he lay. He saw himself, roused from a dream to find that it had not been a dream.

He heard breathing beside him, the slow, deep breathing of sleep untroubled by any shade or shadow. A hand with warm, slender fingers was curled in his. Dark hair lay all about him, showing streaks of forgotten gold. The gentle scent of perfume was by him, and it was this that made him turn his head at last to see what he, in his bliss, had almost forgotten: Alessia. Her resting face, still and wondrous, lay near his.

Long he looked at her, tracing every contour of her dear face with his eyes and memorizing its every shape. He reached out and passed an awed touch across her forehead. She was so very beautiful. How was it, he wondered, that such a beauty had seen fit to bestow herself on him? That she had chosen to do so made him love her all the more.

The thought startled his waking mind – was what he felt for her love? And yet, having given all of himself to her, what else could he call it?

The first streaks of the dawn appeared at the window, casting ruddy light over his discarded uniform. Eamon looked to it and remembered his duties.

He eased his hand from Alessia's and slipped out from between the bedcovers. The floor was cold beneath his feet and he moved to stand on the crimson rug. As he dressed, his eyes strayed often to the lady as she lay in her bed.

At last he set his jacket over his shoulders and buckled his sword to his belt. Alessia had not stirred. Her hand was curved still in a phantom of his as she lay sleeping. He leaned over and kissed her forehead, feeling its warmth beneath his lips. He wished that he might stay with her.

He went at last to the door. He slipped through it and pulled it closed behind him.

A cool air lay in the house. Far away he heard the sounds of servants in the kitchens, stoking the fires. It was late September. The smell of baking bread rose to his nostrils and he heard a voice singing. As he went silently down the stairs, fastening his jacket, the voice came closer. He looked up.

Lillabeth stood on the steps, a jug of steaming water in her hands. Hearing movement she had looked up and now she saw him.

The jug nearly slipped from her hands. Officer and maid froze upon the stairs, each transfixed by the astonished gaze of the other. Eamon gave no explanation for his presence: his bearing told his story intimately, without the utterance of a single word.

He fixed the last fastening on his jacket and offered Lillabeth a nervous smile.

"Good morning, Miss Hollenwell."

She neither smiled nor answered him.

Eamon hurried down the stairs and disappeared into the grey morning.

He worked his way swiftly from the house onto the Coll. He was to be at parade in the college for the second hour and his absence would be unacceptable. If he was to become a Hand, he would have to earn it. He remembered Alessia's voice in his ear, praising him and exhorting him to fulfil himself in his service to the Master.

Like so many others, she had seen that Eamon Goodman would be great. As a man and as a Hand, he could have no equal before the throne.

Eamon struggled to focus his thoughts on something, anything – the early calls of the Gauntlet as the watches changed, the frosty cobbles crunching beneath him. But all he could see was Alessia's face tilted towards his own, and all he could feel was his heart, burning, as he held her.

"Good morning, first lieutenant."

Startled, Eamon looked up. Lord Cathair came down the Coll, a piece of night that the sun could not drive away. The Lord of the West Quarter wore his accustomed smile as deftly as his black robes.

"My lord."

"Up a little late this morning, aren't we, Mr Goodman?" Cathair inquired pleasantly. Eamon flushed.

"Yes, my lord."

"I do adore the morning, Mr Goodman," Cathair continued. "It speaks to a deep and most poetical part of my soul." The Hand spread his arms, as though to encompass the whole morning in his dark embrace.

The sun was just appearing on the horizon and the Hand smiled at it. "Ah, Mr Goodman!" he called. "'Dawn steals from secret bowers and rises, inflamed by her passions, to light the day. Does she know what colours her fellow wears until he comes to her again? She does not. But she rises and is content.'"

Lord Cathair's poetic mood alarmed him. Cathair seemed not to notice. "Perhaps this work is also unknown to you?"

"I regret that it is, my lord."

"Again, you disappoint me. Perhaps you should ask Cadet Overbrook."

"Thank you, my lord; I will."

The Hand gestured once to dismiss him. Bowing low, Eamon turned and began to hurry on down the road. As he was leaving, Cathair called after him:

"You will find the fruits of your labours of yesterday in the Brand, Mr Goodman. Be sure to inspect them."

A chill coursed through his veins. His pace quickened. Smoke… charred flesh.

He ran. The Brand was before him. Eamon stopped.

Three stakes stood at the centre of the square, exhausted kindling stacked all about them. Blackened, disfigured remains were caught in writhing about the poles. One was smaller than the others. Dark smoke still emanated from them.

People milled around the square, darting in and out of shuttered buildings. All avoided the gruesome centrepiece bar a lame, welted dog and carrion birds that had not yet dared alight upon the faggots.

Eamon's eyes stung. He went slowly towards the poles like the crows. Wretchedly, he halted at the edge of the kindling by a wooden board. A notice had been fixed to it, telling of the crimes committed against the Master by the grisly remains. The notice bore Lord Cathair's seal. It stoked the hatred in his heart.

Those who break the law deserve death, spoke the voice within him. *Be proud of what was done here, Eben's son, and for your part in it; you glorified me.*

Eamon steadied himself against the board.

The burning had been done that night. While three wayfarers had writhed and screamed and met their brutal deaths in the Brand, he himself had been… How could he? But she had been beautiful and he had been her joy!

A deserved joy, son of Eben. Just as they earned suffering through their treachery so you earned pleasure by your service. All that you reaped, you merited.

The memory of the night returned to him with force. With the voice driving him, Eamon glutted upon it, his heart lusting after the time when night would come again and he might return to her. A tremor of passion seized his limbs and he turned his back upon the gutted, blackened ligaments. What were they to him?

A loud crack reached his ears.

Lifting his heel, Eamon saw a small wooden soldier, its red coat marked with a golden crown. It was snapped at the heart.

For a long time Eamon stared, held captive by the broken form. The thought of himself and Alessia caught up together was cast aside by that of a little boy, running from his house, calling for his father with joy.

"There you are!"

Eamon dashed back his tears. Soot and smoke, bile and passion clung to him.

Mathaiah approached. His ward had drawn in a lung-full of smoke when he called and was coughing.

"Mr Grahaven," Eamon tremored.

The cadet came to a halt before him. He was pale. "I have been looking for you half the night. It's about the book, sir."

"The book?" Eamon repeated the word dumbly.

"The... Nightholt." The word came haltingly from Mathaiah's lips. He swallowed hard. "I was dreaming, sir... I saw it. I can..."

"What?"

"I can understand it, or most of it. I can read it. They were terrible dreams, sir," he whispered. "That's why I was... why I needed... where were you?"

"I..."

Alessia, flushed and radiant. He shuddered, unable to drive her from his thought. How could the First Knight recount that he had spent the night in the arms of Alessia Turnholt while King's men burnt to death?

"I'll not tell you," he said suddenly.

The answer jarred Mathaiah. As their eyes met, Eamon saw concern replaced by injury; he squirmed as the young man's face coloured in the following silence. His ward had guessed, and guessed rightly, where he had been that night.

He judges you, son of Eben! He judges and reviles you. See how it is written on his face!

Eamon glared. "My business is my own, Mr Grahaven," he spat.

Stunned, Mathaiah stared. "Sir –"

"I'll not have you judge my doings, cadet," Eamon growled. "They are my affairs, and mine alone."

"With respect, sir," Mathaiah answered quietly, "that isn't true. You are not your own."

Will you have him disdain you, son of Eben, and call you liar?

"You would have me answer to you, whimpering child of a Backwater lordling? A boy who weeps because he has bad dreams?"

Mathaiah seemed taken aback. Eamon didn't care. "I would have you answer to another," Mathaiah replied.

You answer to me alone, son of Eben.

"I have no answer to give you," Eamon retorted.

Mathaiah stared at him. "Did *she* teach you to speak like this?"

He envies you your joy, Eben's son.

"She taught me things you do not know, cadet," Eamon answered snidely.

"Then she has served her purpose well."

"Purpose! What do you know about her purpose?"

"Are you so blind, sir?" he cried. "Look at yourself! *Listen* to yourself! See what she has done to you! She has waylaid you, just as they meant her to, and is trapping you so that you will betray your promise. That is her purpose. She is a honeyed jar."

"Then why not speak before, cadet? I will tell you why: you have a jealous tongue."

"You… you cannot think that of me," Mathaiah breathed.

It was his own fault; the boy was bringing it on himself. "You have taught me what to think of you, Mr Grahaven."

See how things stand, son of Eben? You cannot trust him. What can he understand of so rich a man as you? My glory and her touch are all that can enfold you. They are all that you need. Cast this child aside: scorn him utterly.

Eamon's rage was hot and there were traces of fire on his palm.

"I was a fool to entrust friendship to a mere boy. Be sure that I will not do so again."

Mathaiah recoiled; a look of unutterable hurt passed over his face. In the silence that followed, the young man gaped, appalled.

Eamon looked down at him. He felt no remorse. The boy deserved it. He was nothing but jealousy and judgment. What did he know? "It's time for parade, cadet."

That night Eamon returned to Alessia. He had spent the whole day thinking of her until his heart could bear it no more. With her and in her embrace, he told himself, his thoughts would be his own.

She was in the hallway when he arrived and stood as though she had been expecting him. Perhaps she had. Eamon cared nothing for the servants, who saw him as he came in, or for Lillabeth, who watched him as she served them an evening meal. His lady spoke sweetly to him and fuelled Eamon's passion.

When they had eaten she led him upstairs once more, as he had hoped she would, to her chamber. No sooner had she closed the door but he fell on her, lavishing her face and neck with kisses. She laughed, and caressed his cheeks.

"Eamon, Eamon," she said softly, "has it been so long since we last met?"

"It has been an eternity to me."

But he did not tell her that the power behind his passion was born in Mathaiah's words against her, nor, as she returned it, that his exultation came from his certainty that her kisses disproved all that his ward had said.

With October a harsh winter settled on the city. The icy wind drove in from the north and the harbour was besieged by waves so tall that they struck through into the harbour mouth, damaging wintering ships. The breakwaters had to be reinforced, a task in which many men lost their lives to the dun waters.

Eamon went to Alessia on many of those long, autumn evenings. With every night that they passed together he became more and more convinced of her love for him and of his for her, and so he grew in his belief that he had to rely on her alone. During those cold nights a fire always burnt at the grate in her chamber and Eamon loved to watch her undressing in its glow, and to allow her delicate hands to undress him also.

One dark evening she laid her hands on the heart of the King at his breast and asked him what it was.

"An old trinket," he answered carelessly. "A relic of days long past."

So she took the heart of the King from his breast, as she had done so many times before. But when he came to dress the following morning he did not place it back around his neck.

As the months turned on, through November and December into January, supplies of food began to dwindle, though in the palace fires roared and those dearest to the Master feasted upon meat and wines from Ravensill.

The pyres outside the city burned constantly. Fever was rife, especially in the South Quarter, and tales spread of physicians murdered for refusing service to those who could not pay. As the winter drove on, the tally of the fever's victims increased. At the end of December traffic moving in and out of the city ceased entirely. On clear days the mountains to the north-east could be seen under a perpetual cap of snow. The roads beyond Dunthruik's sphere turned treacherously muddy, and ice fretted parts of the River. Driven by hunger and a desire for warmth, dozens of young men applied to join the Gauntlet, where a daily ration of food was provided. These men replaced those who were lost to the fever or in the increasing number of skirmishes with wayfarers. Some of the men who survived such encounters returned with rumours of an amassing Serpent army to the north and east, and of grim battles in the frozen fortress towns in the provinces of Singsward, Orlestone, and Haselune.

Eamon grew greatly in reputation during those months: his cadets were among the best in the college and, together with Draybant Farleigh, Eamon helped to run the college efficiently. He interviewed young men wishing to enlist and saw in their eager faces the enthusiasm that he had once thought lost, but now found renewed with every morning. He helped Captain Waite with his paperwork and oversaw several wardings. Each time he witnessed them Mathaiah came to his mind, and each time he resolutely drove the thoughts away.

Eamon accorded well with Dunthruik. His reputation, his position, and his lover all went before him; each was a source of joy to him. When he encountered Lillabeth on the stairs of Alessia's home he did not falter, but walked past her proudly. What concern was it of hers what he did? And what did he care if she spoke of him to Mathaiah, as he was sure she did?

During December, Cadet Overbrook was among those to fall ill with the fever and be confined to quarters. The word among the cadets was that the young man, never renowned for stamina, would not last the winter.

Despite being advised not to approach those struck down with the fever, Eamon went to see the cadet. He found the young man in a room with darkened windows that already bore an air of death. Remembering Overbrook's loves, Eamon later returned there, taking with him a number of books. He set the young man the task of locating some quotes, the majority of which he had dredged out of memories of his own reading.

"I'd be particularly interested if you can find this one," he added at the last, repeating the roundel that Cathair had first spoken to him in September. Overbrook smiled weakly.

"I'll try, sir."

"Good man."

To this work Overbrook set himself with relish and, when he was not quote-hunting, he drew detailed maps based on some geographical volumes. These he showed to Eamon, and Eamon brought them to the attention of Captain Waite. The cadet's work was impressive and, as a result, new field maps for several regions were commissioned. As Overbrook began returning to strength, the college cadets, who had seen how Eamon had worked to keep the young man focused on something other than impending death, grew more fond of their first lieutenant. Yet even as the college rang to Eamon's praise Mathaiah Grahaven kept a cautious distance from him. Eamon found that it was no fatigue to scorn and ignore the cadet. He had long since ceased giving news for Hughan.

Indeed the King very nearly slipped from his mind, except for those few nights when, unable to be in Alessia's bed, he rested in his own. There the heart of the King, closeted away many weeks before, shimmered, casting an eerie glow over his room and pervading his dreams. On those nights he covered the light with blankets, and huddled alone in the cold.

It was also during this time that Eamon came to know the Hands who held each quarter: Lord Cathair, the West; Lord Ashway, the East; Lord Dehelt, the North; and Lord Tramist, the South. With their characteristic pale faces and piercing eyes, it was a chilling business to see all four discussing city policies. Eamon met on several occasions with the Right Hand, who commended his progress, and continued to promise that the Master would meet him soon.

In the new year Lord Cathair took to showing Eamon about the Hands' Hall and palace, demonstrating their hidden nooks and crannies. The Hand had ceased chanting oddments of poetry at him. Eamon came to know the city very well, and was able to chart swift and complex routes across it. He was charged with capturing any suspected snakes – a task to which he initially responded with reluctance. Yet Lord Cathair's praise and the Right Hand's compliments made it increasingly easy to commit men and women to the care of the Hands. He was present when his prisoners were tortured and soon began setting his hands to the instruments to effect it, putting into practice the theoretical training he had so despised in Edesfield. It was not difficult, and their blood was easily washed from him. But of Lillabeth he did not breathe a word; Alessia was fond of her.

From time to time Lord Cathair entrusted him into the care of Lord Tramist. A powerful breacher, the Lord of the South Quarter was capable of extracting much from those he interviewed. Eamon was coached in how to pressure and bend a mind into revealing what its keeper would rather hide. He began to learn the workings of the far-off plain, and just how much pain to inflict on men so that they would open, but not break. Lord Tramist conservatively lauded his impressive skills.

But sometimes, when he tried to breach a wayfarer, the searing brilliance of the blue light intervened. Against it neither he nor Lord Tramist could press, and those too protected by it were killed or cast into the Pit. Eamon found satisfaction in seeing such men hurled into the choking blackness. It was all they deserved for rejecting the Master. How could he ever have considered doing as they did?

But sometimes the blue light haunted his dreams. On such nights Alessia's kisses barely served to free him from his thought and, seeing his burden, she would take his face between her hands and hush him. Then he would bury himself in her, forgetting his troubles; yet when at last they would lie still and sleep, the light would return to him, and call on him by a name he was trying to forget.

So the winter went on. As the months passed, the time that he spent at the college decreased substantially. If he wasn't with Lord Cathair or Alessia, he was often on duty at the palace, aiding in inventories or inspecting the West Quarter Gauntlet on duty there.

In those months Ladomer, who had been officially instated in his role as lieutenant to the Right Hand, also came frequently to visit him. They spent much time together in a nearby inn, talking about the Master's policies and their own hopes for the future. Eamon found that his heart turned more and more towards that accolade which had always been before him: that of the Right Hand.

This was the thought that occupied his mind one grey day when he met Ladomer for their usual drink.

"Are you listening to a word I'm saying?" Ladomer asked, waving a playful hand in front of his face.

"Sorry?" Eamon asked, recalled from his distant dreams of power.

"I suppose I wasn't talking about Alessia, was I? So there was nothing worth listening to!"

Eamon smiled a little. Apart from Alessia herself, he confided most things to Ladomer or to Waite, depending on their nature.

Ladomer pushed a mug to him over the table. "My point exactly. Drink – it will do you good."

Eamon took a deep draught.

"There's something on your mind," Ladomer told him. "Don't try to deny it! I can read you like a book."

"You don't read books," Eamon replied idly.

"Neither do you these days," Ladomer countered.

"No," Eamon mused, trying to maintain his focus against the obsessive bent of his thought. "I'm a little distracted, Ladomer," he confessed.

"By Alessia?" Ladomer scoffed. "Come, come, Ratbag! You've been bedding her for months. Surely the distraction stage has worn off by now?"

"Not by Alessia," Eamon answered, offended.

"Oh?" Ladomer eyed him curiously. "I thought she was your whole world! Well, if it isn't Alessia, then you must tell me what it is!"

Eamon met his gaze and held it for a long time. Ladomer was his closest friend. Surely it wouldn't hurt...

"Come on, Ratbag!" Ladomer insisted. "It's no good keeping secrets from me; you know I always find them out, one way or another, in the end."

"You must promise not to speak of it," Eamon told him sternly.

"Not to speak of it? My, we are being dramatic this morning." He solemnly raised one hand. "I give you my word."

So it was that Eamon at last confessed to Ladomer the way in which the promised power of the Right Hand held him in thrall every moment he lived.

For a long moment, Ladomer stared at him. "Well I never!" He whistled quietly. "I have heard some impressive things about you, especially from Lord Ashway – he loves wandering around the palace corridors playing the prophet – and Lord Tramist speaks highly of your breaching skills. But you, become Right Hand!" He lifted his mug high. "Now that would be worth seeing."

The words encouraged him and his friend's confidence spurred him to his duties with renewed vigour. For with every day that he served, with every cadet he trained or snake he breached, he was coming closer to earning his place as a Hand. And the closer he came to becoming a Hand the nearer he came to the greatest prize.

"Just a little more," Cathair advised him one frosty morning in late January. "The Master is most impressed with you, Mr Goodman!"

One day late in January he went to see Alessia. She was expecting him, and all the servants – by now well accustomed to his presence – greeted him. To those who were kind he gave a few coins, and they praised him for it. He walked proudly, fully expectant that promotion to the Hands would come any day. In his pride he demanded Alessia's touch. Gone was his surprise and delight each time she favoured him with her love; now it was a right, his right. Now he favoured her.

As he kissed her that night she pulled back from him and took his face in her hands. Then she studied him hard, strange care on her beautiful face.

"What is it?" Eamon asked, leaning forward to kiss her bare throat.

"You've changed, Eamon," she said, a touch of sorrow to her voice. "He's changed you."

"Who has?"

But she did not answer him.

The following day, Eamon was strolling down the Coll towards the college. He had some papers to see to, and needed to go over the list of suggested lieutenantcies with Draybant Farleigh and Captain Waite. He had plenty to occupy him – yet his mind was filled with

Alessia and weighted with her strange sorrow. What had she meant? How had he changed?

He saw someone climbing the Coll. Recognizing Mathaiah, he stiffened. His ward was dressed smartly and bore his jacket lightly over his shoulders despite the cold. Mathaiah had excelled himself in service over the last few months and was one of those shortlisted to progress directly to lieutenant on his swearing. In this sense, Eamon's tutelage had served him well. Yet Eamon felt that Mathaiah Grahaven was doing all he could to undo that distinction by letting other cadets outdo and defeat him, or by making easy mistakes in his lessons. It seemed nonsensical to him.

Snow drifted in the air that day. Eamon made to pass by his ward without a word, as had become their custom. But this time Mathaiah called him.

"Sir?"

Part of him wanted to ignore the voice and simply keep walking. But an older part of him, a part that he had thought lost forever in his world of Hands and bedclothes, stopped. He turned.

"Mr Grahaven?" He watched his ward against the grey sky. The cadet seemed somehow older; there was strength and nobility in his bearing that Eamon had not seen before. He noticed that the cadet held a small pouch. The young man fixed his hand more firmly about it.

"What is that, Mr Grahaven?"

Mathaiah smiled. "Something I've saved for." Frozen figures passed them by on either side. "Sir," he continued quietly, "there is something that I need to tell you."

"Speak freely, Cadet."

Mathaiah laughed sadly. "We were friends once. Then I spoke freely. Now I must just speak."

A cold stab of anger drove through him. "Mind your tone, Grahaven."

"For months," Mathaiah told him, his voice a sharp whisper, "you have been steadily driven and drawn away from what you came to Dunthruik to do. Your sword and name are tarnished with blood, but you still have your name. It is not too late to turn, first lieutenant." Mathaiah paused. "I can see, we all can, that the throned is netting you, baiting you, goading you. And he has a powerful piece, sir. But he does not own you. Not yet."

How dare the boy judge him! "Do not harp upon this theme, Mr Grahaven," Eamon hissed, "or you will find yourself in a pit of trouble."

Undeterred, Mathaiah leaned in closer. "You have not turned me in, sir. I believe that's because a part of you knows what you should be doing. And part of you knows the truth. She's his, sir. She always has been, and from the day that you saw her first with Alben, she has been played to capture you."

The biting wind drove into his eyes. "I love her," he snarled.

"Maybe you did once. Maybe one day you will again. But now she is simply yours, just as you are becoming his."

Eamon's blood raged. How dare Mathaiah say such things! And yet... the rage pointed to something that he had been long fighting to deny. For the first time in many months he reached for the heart of the King and the comfort that it had once offered him. Both were gone.

"I have important matters to attend to, sir. Once, I dreamed of your attending to them with me. Now, I cannot even think to ask it." Mathaiah clutched the pouch, and steeled his eye. Did he detect a tear? "Good day, sir."

He turned and disappeared into the snow. Eamon could only watch him go.

It was the seventh of February. Bitter winter winds from the north still blew, but the ice over the plains was thinning, the roads slowly becoming passable again. For nights, Eamon's dreams had been filled with the Pit, with the memories of breached minds, with Hands and banners and eagles, and with a blue light that had never quite left him. It did not call him first lieutenant.

He stood on Alessia's balcony watching grey clouds roll over the sea. He knew that she was dressing behind him but he did not watch her as he often did. Instead his eyes turned towards the palace. More than a week had passed since he had spoken with Mathaiah, but his ward's words still haunted him. He felt a weight at his heart and knew it to be the weight of guilt – guilt so softly spoken that a kind word could yet steer its keen bite away.

Alessia came to him and touched his arm. Instinctively, he took her hand. On some days, he felt as though that hand in his was all he had.

"You're very thoughtful today," she said softly, turning him to look at her. She was wearing a dark green dress that he had not seen before.

"You're very beautiful today." He gathered her to his side, trying to strengthen himself by her warmth and presence.

What if...? He could not believe it. What if Mathaiah had spoken the truth?

He looked urgently at her. "Alessia, why do you love me?"

"What kind of question is that, Mr Goodman?" she countered playfully.

"A serious one. Please," he insisted, laying a finger to her lips to still them. "Please. I need to know."

"Isn't it enough that I love you?"

Though he longed to answer yes, all he tasted was doubt as she quickly pressed her soft lips to his.

That afternoon he met some of his cadets in the West Quarter College hall. He saw Manners and Mathaiah speaking quietly together in one corner. As the two spoke Manners' eyes widened, as if he had heard something amazing. Eamon suddenly yearned to join them. What friendship he had been without these past few months! Surely Mathaiah would speak to him?

"Mr Goodman, sir!" Cadet Overbrook hurried over, papers in his hand and a wild, exhilarated look on his face. "Sir!"

Eamon smiled. He was fond of Overbrook, despite his being

neither strong nor athletic. The young man would probably be far happier in a schoolhouse in some quiet town far away from Dunthruik than he would ever be as a Gauntlet ensign; he had the patience and wit to be an excellent teacher. Since his bout of fever, Overbrook had been industriously engaged in redrawing many of the maps that the Gauntlet used, a duty that had mostly liberated him from the aspects of Gauntlet life that he hated. Unfortunately, the cadet was down to his last maps; full duty beckoned him again in a couple of weeks.

"Mr Overbrook."

The cadet came to a halt, dropped some papers, stooped to pick them up, saluted, dropped some more, picked them up, and beamed. "I've found it, sir!"

"Found what?" Eamon asked, wondering how the young man ever found anything.

"The last of those references that you asked me for," the cadet beamed.

Eamon stared blankly before understanding: Cathair's poetry.

"I'm sorry that it took me so long, sir," Overbrook continued. "It was so difficult to find that I was starting to think that you might have invented it, but I found it. I had no idea you were so well read, sir!" He pulled a ream of notes from his mapping papers. "It was a poem quoted in *The Edelred Cycle*."

Eamon frowned. Although he had heard of it he had never read it. He did not think that his father had owned a copy. "What's that about?" he asked, genuinely intrigued.

"It's a poem, written after the Master liberated the River from the Serpent," Overbrook answered. For the first time in many months, the terminology crept into Eamon's spine to make him shudder. "It tells how the Master came from the east and infiltrated the court to find a way in which the Serpent might be deposed. While there he becomes involved with a noblewoman who is close to the Serpent, and a large part of the work deals with their hidden love and his hidden task." Overbrook was grinning with excitement as he told the story. "Edelred eventually turns one of the King's closest advisors and friends – who also happens to be the brother of the noblewoman. The roundel is about her, sir," he added, "and some attribute its roots directly to the Master. In some versions of the text, though, the 'flower' spoken of in the short verse isn't an 'eagle's' flower, but a 'traitor's'."

Eamon stared at him. "A traitor's flower?"

"There's some discussion as to whether the flower was given to her by her lover, or her brother," Overbrook explained. "It all matches with a growing tragic subtext, because when the noblewoman discovers Edelred's purposes she tries to change her brother's mind and dissuade him from following the Master. Finding that he cannot be moved, she tries to warn the Serpent, but the Master catches her first and, whilst assuring her that he loves her, kills her. It is a pity, for she is a fine character," Overbrook pronounced sadly, "but she was going to betray him."

Eamon listened with growing alarm. How much of the tale was true? "What happened?"

Overbrook grinned. "The Serpent was killed, his house vanquished, and the Master took the River Realm," he said. "There's a phenomenal description of a battle at some watchtower somewhere," he added, flicking through his notes. "Sometimes there are problems with the narrator's stance there – he seems to be more on the Serpent's side than on the Master's – but some manuscripts gloss the most suspect passages…"

Overbrook went on but Eamon didn't hear him. Suddenly he was on a cold floor in an inn far away, listening to Aeryn speak the words of a long forgotten song: "Dark, dark the foes of the throne, sly in the mere."

He shut the voice from his mind. "Thank you, Mr Overbrook."

Overbrook fell silent, seemingly disappointed. "That's all right, sir," he said, reluctantly tucking the papers away. But his eyes soon fell on something else, a slightly incorrect detail in one of his map plans; he bumbled away, marking corrections.

Eamon was left in the hallway, his head reeling. If the story was true… why did it trouble him?

Pressing his forehead, he looked up to see Mathaiah's steady gaze fixed on him.

"Mr Goodman."

Waite appeared in the hallway. Eamon saluted formally at once. "Sir."

"A quick word, first lieutenant."

Trying not to think, Eamon followed the captain into his office.

"Mr Goodman, have a seat," Waite said. He too had changed in the last few months; his hair and face were streaked with grey. In recent weeks he had left many important aspects of running the college to its draybant and first lieutenant, for he had been away increasingly, attending to business at the palace with the other quarters' captains.

Eamon came in and sat down. Waite closed the door before going heavily back to his desk. "Lord Cathair requires your services this evening, Mr Goodman."

Eamon's heart leapt. If he could distinguish himself before Lord Cathair he might at last clinch his Handing.

Waite steepled his fingers and sighed. After a reflective pause he lifted his eyes. Eamon realized that the captain was treating him to his confidence.

"There's serious business afoot, Mr Goodman," he said. Eamon imagined so; only very serious business would call the captains and Hands away to the palace as regularly as they had been of late. "Some deadly rumours have been circling all winter. Perhaps you have heard some of them. Harryings on the north bank; incursions into the east; rumours of an army, gathering in Southdael province."

Eamon froze. Of course he had heard of increased wayfaring activity – he had often helped to extract the information regarding their hiding places. But he had heard nothing about an army – least of all in Southdael! The province was on the West Bank, just on the other side of the River mouth from the city.

"The last few wayfarers that we've pressed about the matter have only verified these persistent voices. It is disturbing news. Most disturbing…" Waite trailed off, and seemed suddenly to come to his senses. "Take Overbrook with you when you go," he added. "There's map-drawing to be done."

Later that evening Eamon tore Overbrook away from his painstaking study; only the promise of further map-drawing really convinced the cadet to join him. Eamon didn't mind; he was fond of all his cadets. When the others caught wind that Overbrook was to go on a special mission with their first lieutenant, they appeared in the hall to jealously watch Eamon and Overbrook's departure. Overbrook, his arms laden with paper and bearing a satchel of equipment at his side, beamed at them.

"Where are we going, sir?" he asked as they followed the Coll together.

"I'm not entirely sure," Eamon confessed. "Some work for Lord Cathair." Overbrook looked disconcerted. "Does that bother you, Mr Overbrook?"

"No," Overbrook replied quickly. "That is to say, the work doesn't bother me. But Lord Cathair…"

"Looks like death warmed up?"

Overbrook grinned, relieved. "That's one way of putting it, sir!"

They continued to the Hands' Hall. Overbrook chatted the whole way, waxing lyrical about the map of Dunthruik that he had been drawing. It was the work into which he had put the most effort, and of which he was most proud.

"It's nearly finished." he said. "I just can't get the scale of the distance between the Blind Gate and the River quite right…"

Eamon laughed. He was sure that the map was a work of art.

Cathair was waiting for them at the hall. He stretched out his hands in welcome.

"Ah, Mr Goodman, perfect timing!" Four other Hands were with him, each carrying a bow. "I'm glad to see that you have Mr

Overbrook with you." The cadet clutched nervously at his papers. Eamon offered him an encouraging smile. Cathair also bestowed a broad smile on the cadet. "We shall have need of your expertise, Mr Overbrook."

"Thank you, my lord."

Cathair led them into the Hands' Hall. By now Eamon was familiar with almost every door – down to the peculiar patterns in each stone block – but as they went he noticed Cathair's pallor with renewed eyes. It filled him with long-forgotten misgiving. Passing the angular writing in the hall, Eamon remembered Mathaiah's assertion that he could read it.

The first stars peeped through the cloud cover. At the heart of the central courtyard, Cathair called them to a halt. The Hands pressed round. Eamon was glad of Overbrook at his side.

One of the Hands raised his arms. Eamon felt a strange drowsiness grip him as ruddy flames rose up. He did not know if they were real or imagined. There was a lurch; his senses reeled. The ground seemed stolen from beneath his feet.

Suddenly the wind was blowing into his face and he could no longer smell the sea. When he opened his eyes he was not in the city. He stood on a plateau. To his left was a wooded decline. Beyond that was a ridge and, away beyond the trees, light.

When he looked he saw that Overbrook appeared as astonished as he felt. Only the Hands seemed unperturbed. As the mover lowered his arms, Cathair spoke:

"I would say that we are in the right place." His face was luminous in the moonlight. "Come, gentlemen."

Cathair led them to the edge of the ridge. Feeling less confident than the striding Hand, Eamon crept after him. Overbrook followed uncertainly and they looked down together. What they saw astonished them.

The valley below was filled from crest to dell with an encampment. In the distance, from which Eamon imagined that he was looking north, the bright moon lit coils of the River. The camp was filled with lights, horses, and weapons: spears, bills, lances, swords. Armoured figures moved between the tents. Dozens of fires burned and shapes were huddled about them, cooking or laughing. Voices carried on the chilly air, some of them singing.

It was an army. Not enormous – perhaps a couple of thousand, with more filing through the southern gorge as they watched – but well equipped. Eamon knew there would be pickets, scouts, and guards on the nearby ridges.

But what struck him most was a single pennon flying high, glimmering in the steady moonlight. There, worked in blue and silver, was the sword and star. His heart rose into his throat.

Was Hughan there?

"Rumour's voice runs true," Cathair murmured. "Mr Overbrook."

"My lord?" He sounded stunned.

"Take your papers along the rim. Lord Oldgrove will go with you. Make your sketch accurate. Mind the Serpent's pickets."

"Yes, my lord." Overbrook and Oldgrove slipped off in silence.

Eamon gaped at the army. How had Hughan managed to amass such numbers during the winter? He was shocked to realize that he had been so absorbed with his own lusts that he barely remembered the King's face. But now it came back to him, as clear as he had so often seen his own in Alessia's glass.

Hughan had entrusted him with a task. Eamon recoiled. All winter long he had spared neither thought, help, nor duty to the King. His shame and grief came suddenly to life, howling to be heard. No longer could he ignore its powerful voice.

He swayed, nauseated and faint.

"It was Lorentide who first led us to this," Cathair murmured, breaking Eamon's thought. "He had been forging papers for months to get snakes out of the city. Of course if we had caught him sooner we might have been better served, but we must shed no tears for that; most of the vermin were heading for this wretched army, so we shall kill them in the end. They've been gathering strength all winter. Since they came over the mountains just before the press of winter the Easters have started joining them, too," he added, gesturing along the flank of the camp to a deep emerald and orange banner, bearing a sun. "Doubtless the Serpent has convinced them to aid him. Who knows how? Bartering promises he can never repay and telling them that they have some part in all of this, I imagine." Lord Cathair shook his head and sighed.

Eamon stared at the foreign banner. For months there had been rumours of trouble in the east, and Eamon had himself seen Easters at the Hidden Hall. If Hughan had been gathering support from beyond the mountains, then it was little wonder that things in the east-bordering provinces had grown grim.

"We'll crush these snakes," Cathair growled. "Dust to dust."

Eamon settled back in silence, his head spinning. He had never heard of Hughan's army until that day, yet he was sure that his hands had been instrumental in revealing it. The throned had to crush it before it reached its potential.

Could he let that happen to Hughan?

What will it serve to help him now, son of Eben? You are mine.

Surely the voice was right. He tried to placate himself: there was nothing he could do.

But the voice lied. Hughan had told him so. And, whatever else, Hughan was his friend – they had grown up together. Would he let Ladomer die, if he could prevent it?

But Ladomer wasn't the Serpent.

He wiped cold sweat from his brow. He was more a servant of the Master than he had ever been, but he had to send a warning: the King's encampment had to move before the Hands destroyed it.

A sudden cry rent the air – agonized and swiftly silenced. Cathair stiffened and the other Hands, dotted along the course of the ridge, fell still.

Eamon knew the voice. Not stopping to think, he leapt to his feet and tore across the hilltop, not doubting that his figure was perfectly obvious to any picket or sentry who watched, but he didn't care: let them see. He hurtled towards the ridge.

Seconds later he stopped, appalled. A wrathful cry erupted from his throat.

Oldgrove was dead on the ground. Cadet Overbrook lay beside him, a pool of blood widening from his punctured gut. His papers were strewn around him – he clawed at them.

"Sir!" he gasped – and gasped no more.

Over the cadet's bleeding body stood a familiar man. His hands held a dripping sword.

"You bastard!" Eamon yelled.

It was Giles.

CHAPTER XX

Blood soaked the ground and the grisly moon glared back at him in the gore. Eamon stared balefully at Giles, his mind reeling madly between the carnage that lay at his feet and his grief. The cries of the holk's cadets and the smell of blood on weathered wood poured back into his mind; his stomach lurched as the first bodies hit the water. Now Overbrook was among them, another pale and bloated face. And Giles laughed.

His hands shook with anger. "*Bastard!*"

Giles shook the term away. Eamon's hand flew to his sword in fury. This time he would not meekly surrender it. Giles would pay for what he had done!

"I wouldn't advise that, Goodman." Giles's voice broke dangerously through the dark.

"I'm not in the habit of taking advice from bastards!" Eamon spat.

"I have half a dozen archers in these trees. At my command they will shoot you."

"And I have Hands," Eamon retorted, too angry to think. Overbrook had been a young man with a future. Now mud swallowed his corpse.

Giles fixed him with a condemning stare. "For what good that will do you," he hissed, gesturing to Oldgrove. He surged forward. "And we're high on that Hand list now, aren't we, Mr Goodman? Yes, very high on that list, because we've been very cosy and very busy, nestled in Dunthruik, haven't we?"

Eamon didn't answer. The pins at his collar clenched his throat.

Giles was almost within cutting distance now but Eamon still had not drawn his sword. He couldn't: words, more perilous than arrows, pinioned him.

"You've always been one of theirs, ready to grovel and fawn as they desire," Giles sneered. "I should have killed you when I first had the chance, Mr Goodman. Yes, I would have been the object of Hughan's scorn for a while, but what have I achieved in letting you live? I've allowed you to hunt wayfarers, to breach them, to hand them over to my enemies, to betray and murder my allies." He gave a clipped laugh. "I suppose it just goes to show that even a would-be king makes mistakes. How many wayfarers do you think I would have saved, Mr Goodman, if I had struck you dead like the pathetic traitor that you are? How many will I save if I do it now?"

Eamon's pulse quickened. A thousand faces were suddenly in his mind's eye: the people of Dunthruik, cowed by his shadow. He remembered cries, pleas for mercy, as he pressed still harder upon the heads of countless wayfarers, wresting words from anguished lips. He had offered up each bloodied utterance to the Hand as though on an exquisite, golden platter, receiving in turn a nod, a smile, and the longed-for promise of black. He saw the Pit, smelled its vile stench, felt a numbness where once he felt revulsion at what was exhumed from the cavernous welt. Eamon's eyes no longer stung when he went to the Pit and he no longer flinched from the sight of the red light drawing bleeding prisoners out of the depths with as little effort as he had drawn a hundred confessions.

With a cry he tore his mind away from his guilty recollections. He rounded violently on Giles.

"You will not lay a hand on me," he cried. In the eaves around him he could hear sounds of a struggle; the Hands had engaged King's men in the woods. It would not take them long to dispatch them and come to him; all he had to do was endure this madman a little longer…

"Why not?" Giles roared. "Why should I pity you? What pity have you shown? Every child you've breached, every step you've taken in that accursed city, you've taken for the throned, and he has taken to you quite warmly." Giles pressed furiously towards him until their faces nearly touched. His voice dropped to a growl. The words that he then uttered were between them and the night alone.

"Do you think that I don't know what you have done, First Lieutenant Goodman?" he hissed. "That nobody knows what you do? Do you think that Hughan doesn't know each excruciating detail of every treachery you've committed? Let me disabuse you of that notion, Mr Goodman: the King knows. The whole bloody wayfaring world knows, and I'm sure they weep themselves to sleep with it at night! Because they trusted you, and you are false."

Eamon's heart stopped. It lay stone cold in his breast. "No!"

"No?" Giles mimicked his voice ruthlessly. "It's too late for your pitiable 'no', Goodman! There was never any hope in you. Tell me how you have ever served Hughan? You're the throned's whore as much as that Turnholt bitch is yours."

It was a step too far. Eamon's hands clenched hard and the prick of the mark burned on them. What right had Giles to speak to him of Alessia! He knew nothing! He was a worthless lackey and Eamon had always hated him.

Strike him! Strike him now.

His hand tensed upon the hilt; still he held back.

"You want to kill me?" Giles laughed derisively, snatching the map from Overbrook's stiff hand. He cast his eyes indolently over it as he spoke. "Try, if you dare! You've never been a King's man, and you never will be. You have never even deemed the scorn of being called a wayfarer, much less a snake. But I'll tell you something that Hughan will never know, Mr Goodman." Suddenly Giles was close to him again. Fire spread from Eamon's palm to his heart. "He won't know that we had this conversation. All he will know tomorrow morning is that scouts found your body riddled with arrows. And he will smile – yes! *smile* – and say that you received exactly what you deserved."

"No!"

With a howl of utter hatred Eamon hurled himself forward, blood rushing in his burning veins. It was not fear of death that moved him but the cutting words, the gait, the laughter, the dead body on the ground, and the terrible, unbearable thought of Hughan's face delighting in his death.

He pinned burning hands about Giles's throat. The man was caught off guard and Eamon bore him to the ground. Arrows hissed past his shoulder; one seared past his arm, drawing blood. He heard Cathair's voice behind, and from the corner of his eye he saw a red light arching outwards. A moment later one of Giles's archers screamed, consumed in a bloody glow.

But Eamon had no interest in the Hands or the archers; all his thought was bent on the winded man beneath him. Giles lashed back. Eamon swerved to avoid a crushing blow. He knew that Giles was stronger than him and that he was a fool to think he could take the villain down. But dizzying rage coursed through him, leaving room only for vengeance. He gleefully pressed flaming hands down on his enemy's throat.

His attempt was swiftly foiled. Giles wrenched himself over, and in a moment Eamon found himself pinned under the man's powerful body. He felt knees pressing down on his stomach, exerting excruciating pressure. Suddenly his right arm was bent backwards into the ground. While he grappled to free himself, Giles pounded his face. His vision jarred, turning black; he was about to lose consciousness, but he clung fiercely to it. Giles would not get the better of him – not this time. His fiery resolve steeled to the oath and stared up through throbbing eyes. Giles had drawn a dagger from his boot; it was curved violently in his fist.

"I'm going to kill you, treacherous bastard! Take this to the grave: you betrayed Hughan!" Howling, he slashed at Eamon's throat.

For a split second Eamon found his hand unpinned. A villainous smile crossed his lips. With cool precision he thrust his hand into Giles's face; the flame on his palm was like a burning sun. The dagger never touched him.

The plain was a familiar place to him. He laughed. Giles was frozen before him. Certainly the man still had his strength, but

Eamon had the advantage. He relished the look that passed over his enemy's face.

"You wouldn't bloody dare!" Giles roared.

Eamon favoured him with a placid smile. "I bloody would."

He tore open Giles's mind; the man would pay for what he had done and Eamon would enjoy every single moment of it. He wanted to make it hurt; he wanted it to hurt badly. He wanted to watch the man in agony and hold the memory so that he might savour it at his leisure.

Giles's face contorted in agony; it squirmed and writhed beneath his hand, but the struggling man refused to cry out.

"*Bastard!*" Eamon yelled, and pushed harder.

Giles's whole mind lay before him. He saw in intricate detail what the wayfarers had been doing in recent months. He saw Hughan travelling beyond the mountains to the eastern halls, braving hidden, treacherous passes, and receiving a pledge of loyalty from a leader, a dark-haired man with a thin face and keen green eyes, who spoke of their common cause and a disgrace to be undone. He saw the locations of Hidden Halls up and down the River where the wayfarers had been stockpiling weapons for months. He saw the beginnings of cavalry, hundreds of horses stabled by Stonemead. He saw that, even in the next few days, wagons of weapons, the very wheels of war, would be travelling towards the ridge camp. He saw hundreds of people in towns and villages all along the River being won over by Hughan and his messengers. The wayfarer cause was growing, preparing for an assault on Dunthruik. Hughan planned to move in the spring.

He cared little for all this. Most of all, Eamon felt Giles's violent, burning hatred of him. Everywhere he looked it lashed at him like lightning, and it lashed in vain, for he was more powerful. It incited his rage. No blue light came, and there was no defence for Giles against the growing pain that he inflicted with each piece of information that he extracted.

"Stop it!" Giles yelled at last, wild agony in his eyes.

Eamon leaned close to him. "Why should I pity you?" he laughed, and plunged on.

Still he waited for the blue light, still it did not come, and still he tore through the strata of Giles's mind. He saw the man fighting in the border wars where the merchant state of Galithia had clashed with the River Realm, fighting to avenge his murdered parents and stolen patrimony; scores of Gauntlet soldiers fell before the man's sword. And at last he understood why the light had not come.

Giles was no King's man. His support for Hughan was a tool for vengeance, a marriage of convenience. Giles did not care if Hughan was a king, and did not care if there had ever been a house of kings over the River.

You know all that you need, Eben's son. Break him.

With renewed vigour, Eamon did as he was commanded.

At last Giles erupted in a blood-curdling scream. But Eamon did not pull away his hand. Instead, he tore away layer after layer of the thoughts that he saw, and as he read and rent them he cast them aside; the fire from his hand destroyed them utterly. The more Giles screamed the harder he ripped, and with each cry Eamon felt gruesome satisfaction lodging in his blackened heart.

"How many more shall I destroy, Giles?" he roared furiously. "Tell me to stop, if you can! Surrender your sword to me, if you can. I won't spare you!"

Giles screamed.

Eamon.

The voice cut through his thought, stripping away the flames. He shuddered. It was not the fiery voice that he knew. It was gentle and grieved.

Eamon.

On, son of Eben!

Eamon.

With a shuddering cry he opened his eyes. He tasted blood in his mouth. Giles's dagger was on the grass, festering in steaming blood. Red light was dying among the trees and the Hands were hurrying towards him. Were the King's archers dead? His swirling sight struggled to grasp the trees.

"Mr Goodman!"

He scarcely heard Lord Cathair. Suddenly Eamon looked down, choked on a cry of horror, and staggered violently to his feet.

Giles lay there. His arms and legs were braced in twisted, gut-wrenching positions, and his pale face was plastered in sweat and blood. His fingers were dug into the earth. As Eamon watched, the man clawed, gibbering blood and spittle from a torn, incomprehensible mouth. His eyes were palled with a white sheen that seemed unnaturally bright in the darkness. The now silent air was punctuated by his shrill, quivering gasps.

Eamon stood motionless, a scream begging to be released from his cavernous lungs.

"What have I done?" the words tumbled out of his mouth. His burning hands trembled. They were muddy.

"You've done well, Mr Goodman," Cathair advised. He held his side as he spoke; Eamon was aware of blood on the Hand's uniform. Was Cathair injured?

"It seems that you are a very fine breacher indeed," Cathair added, seemingly unperturbed by either his wound or the dead. "I heard talk of supplies?"

Eamon started. Had he spoken out what he had seen? He had done it, sometimes, standing before Cathair in the rooms by the Pit, but he had always controlled it. This time he had not even made a choice.

He shook.

"This is not the place to discuss it," Cathair told him suddenly. Torchlight was running up the treeline. "We must go."

The Hands hastily grouped themselves together and the mover raised his hands. Giles still twitched on the ground; his back was arched and his arms withered. The sight transfixed Eamon hideously.

"Mr Goodman."

Eamon looked away. He saw Overbrook's body on the ground. He could not leave the cadet.

"My lord –"

"Very well, but hurry up."

They hauled the bodies of cadet and Hand into their circle. Eamon grabbed Overbrook's map with trembling hands. As he passed, Giles screamed, shied away, and shook convulsively.

Eamon staggered away. The lights were near on the hillside. The Hands were about him and Overbrook's face gawked palely at him in the light.

What had he done?

He buried his face in his hands and the ground under his feet was swept away.

They watched him, early in the morning of the eighth of February. They watched him in the streets, from windows and doors of the West Quarter; they watched him as he turned his shaking steps along the Coll to the college. Some shrank back, some gaped. Others looked once and shrugged, for such things were to be expected in the Gauntlet.

They watched him as he went leadenly into the college. They watched him in the hall. Salutes crumbled and good mornings went unsaid, for when they watched him the cadets, the lieutenants, the servants, and the clerks also looked at what he led: Overbrook's body, stretcher-borne. They knew that it could so easily have been, and might yet prove to be, their own.

Captain Waite met him in the corridor. He held papers in his hand – drafts of orders, requests to be ratified. He saw what followed Eamon, and lowered his eyes.

"Good morning, sir."

"I see we have a condolence to write."

"Yes, sir." His lip trembled. Had he worked all winter to save Overbrook from the fever for a bloodied map and a punctured gut on a cold hillside?

Giles's twisted face danced before him – he tried to force it away, but he could not. Tears gripped his eyes, and the whole world watched him as he led Cadet Overbrook's body to the infirmary.

The companies at the college paraded quietly that morning, the air that rested over them like the pall that covered Overbrook. Though an official statement had yet to be made, the news of wayfarers and a stab in the dark had spread.

Eamon felt that the whole college watched him at parade. Manners stood next to him and, by him, Mathaiah. Both had pale faces though both, like all the Third Banners, seemed careful not to watch him too closely. Of that, at least, Eamon was glad. He was shaken to his very core and the mark on his hand – the flames – seemed unbearably clear. He felt his exultation over Giles's pain and could still smell the stench of blood, the wreck of a mind destroyed – the memory was so strong that it almost had a smell of its own. They had carried Overbrook away, but what would become of Giles?

What would Hughan think?

How could Hughan ever know that he had done it? And yet even as he offered the cold comfort to himself he knew that the King would know. He felt anyone that looked at him could tell it at a glance – his very being betrayed it. Could they not smell it on him? He had become a monster that night. He was terrified that what Giles had said was true and that there was no way back for him. He had betrayed the King, and yet… What power he had had in return for that treachery! And what strange joy he had felt in the use of it.

He shook his head and glanced across at Mathaiah, yearning to confess what he had done. But he could not tell Mathaiah; if he did that Hughan would certainly learn of his evil. He and Mathaiah had stopped speaking long ago.

Eamon watched as Waite climbed the small platform at the head of the parade ground. He fixed his eyes on the captain as though it could somehow save him from floundering in Giles's blood. Waite was solid, real… he surveyed his men without a trace of his usual humour. It had been months, Eamon thought, since Waite had joked. That, surely, was Hughan's doing – and he felt a surge of anger towards the King.

"At ease." Waite spoke solemnly. His look was weighted and the ranks, unaccustomed to being asked to stand at ease at parade, stood nervously.

"I'm afraid we have unpleasant tidings this morning," Waite continued. "Third Banner Cadet Overbrook, a friend and fellow to many of you, was killed in action during the night. He was a dependable man and will be sorely missed. There will be a remembrance for him this afternoon."

Eamon didn't follow much that Waite said after that, for the thought of a remembrance brought back to him uncomfortable memories – of Alben in his hearse, his sallow face falsely composed. Waite had presided over that office. Overbrook had been one of Eamon's own men. He would have to lead the service, just as Waite had for Alben.

About mid-morning he found himself near Waite's office. The captain was labouring under a perpetual pile of papers. "Mr Goodman?"

"Sir?"

"Might I have a moment?"

Obligingly, Eamon entered. He snapped a salute as best he could. His hands had not yet stopped shaking. "Sir."

Waite did not speak immediately; he was writing the letter of condolence that would go to Overbrook's family.

Eamon tried to wait patiently as the captain continued to write. He was nervous and Giles's face still twisted before him. Beyond that was his fear of the voice that had held him back. What might he have done, had it not?

Waite put a flourish to the end of the letter and laid his quill aside. With great care he folded the parchment and sealed the malleable wax with the mark of the West Quarter College.

"I'd like you to deliver this to Mr Overbrook and invite him to the remembrance. It will be this afternoon, at the tenth hour."

Chilled, Eamon nodded. "Yes, sir."

"I have written that Cadet Overbrook glorified the Master in his stalwart service and, in his final hour, brought us news with which we may strike against the wayfarers. Lord Cathair told me about what happened. He said that he will come to interview you after the office."

"Will you be there, sir?"

"Yes," Waite answered slowly. He paused for a moment. "Is everything all right, Mr Goodman? You seem agitated."

Eamon's head was swimming. He hated himself for what he had done to Giles, hated himself for taking Overbrook to his death, and was terrified about what Hughan must think of his First Knight now. And Aeryn! What would she think of him when Giles's body was brought back to the camp?

He suddenly longed to spill out his guilt to Waite, to purge himself of its weight. But for that release he would have to give himself up, reveal his long treachery, and lose the captain's trust just as he had lost Hughan's…

Why shouldn't he? If he confessed himself to Waite now, fully and utterly, his impeccable record with the Gauntlet might save him. He could be forgiven and welcomed with open arms by the Master, before being drawn into the fold that had always longed to hold him. He could prove himself against the wayfarers; they could never trust him now. Let them laugh at him! They would not laugh when he was the Right Hand and he exacted a cruel vengeance from them for their mockery.

His thoughts shook him. When he looked up he saw that Waite watched him still.

"Mr Goodman?"

Eamon struggled. "Overbrook was a good man, sir. I feel… responsible."

Waite smiled sympathetically. "I know. Unfortunately it is the burden of command that we bear. The loss of any man is deeply felt, especially when he is your own. But you must remember that he is one man, and there are many that you lead. You must be strong for them. To your business, Mr Goodman."

Eamon took the letter, saluted, and left the room.

He listened to his footsteps echo in the corridors. Soldiers and officers were moving towards their messes for lunch. Eamon caught sight of Mathaiah and Manners speaking together. As he passed by they glanced at him. Manners offered him a smile, but Eamon could not match Mathaiah's gaze. It bored into the dark parts of his soul.

He hurried from the hall.

The clerks told him that Overbrook's father lived alone near the South Quarter, attended by a few servants. He was an old man. Eamon did not know if he had any other children or whether his son's death would at a single blow rob him of the prop of his age and house.

Eamon felt the letter in his hand but his thoughts could not hold there long. Giles – always to Giles they turned. How could he live out his life bearing it? And what choice would he have but to tell all that he had learned to Lord Cathair? What redemption could there be for him now? He called down curses on himself as he walked the Coll.

Your redemption, son of Eben, lies in my service. The voice was strong in his mind, a firm counsellor. *In that service you will redeem your blood from its ancient treachery.*

Eben had betrayed the throned. Eamon shook angrily. Had Eben not done so, Hughan would never have lived and Eamon would never have found himself in this situation. That treachery trapped him. He reviled Eben Goodman.

What kind of man had Eben been? Incapable of staying either course, he had been traitor once to Ede and then to the Master. Had Eben known the oppression, the weight and conflict that beat relentlessly in him? Had Eben known it and chosen it as the inheritance of his house? If Eben Goodman had had but the resolve to keep one vow – just *one* – none of what Eamon now faced would lie before him. How long, he wondered, did he truly expect to live as he was living?

Give yourself to me, son of Eben, and you will atone for your house and live.

He had walked to the Four Quarters. From the heart of the city he could see straight to the Blind Gate.

"First Lieutenant Goodman!"

Some passing Gauntlet and militia – led by a striking draybant – saluted him. Eamon met gazes with the man. The stranger nodded courteously to him.

"Draybant Anderas, to his glory."

"His glory," Eamon answered, saluting. "A pleasure to meet you, sir."

The draybant smiled broadly. "The pleasure is and shall remain mine, Mr Goodman. I hope you'll not think me jealous for saying so!"

They clasped hands in greeting. The stranger seemed only five or six years older than him – young for so high a Gauntlet post. Draybant Anderas was clear-skinned and smiling. His eyes were blue and his hair a dusty gold.

Eamon tried to place him. "South Quarter?"

"I suppose we aren't all as famous as you, Mr Goodman," the man replied good-naturedly. "East Quarter College; I report directly to Lord Ashway. We recently lost our captain to the fever – the Hands are yet to ratify his replacement."

"My condolences," Eamon said, grateful for the distraction that the meeting provided him from his own sorrows.

"On serving the Lord Ashway, or the loss of a captain?" Anderas asked, and laughed. "I jest, Mr Goodman, I jest! Captain Etchell was a fine man, and your wishes are well received." He smiled, his eyes falling as he did so to the letter that Eamon carried. He turned his head to one side. "Condolences?"

Eamon nodded wordlessly.

"I'm sorry," Anderas replied. "I'm sure he was a good man."

"He was, sir."

"I had better let you to your business: condolences are best not left long." He seemed about to move his small squadron along, but then paused. "Might I ask a question, Mr Goodman?"

"Yes, sir." How different this man was from Alben, from Fields, from the lieutenants and draybants he had known since he had joined the Gauntlet! Was this not how all Gauntlet should be?

"We've heard all about you in the East Quarter, of course, and envied the tales of derring-do." The man smiled, and where others might have lowered their voices in asking what he then did, Draybant Anderas did not. Eamon admired him for it. "Is it true, Mr Goodman, that you surrendered your sword?"

"Yes, sir."

"It is a matter of curiosity – I hope you will forgive my prying. Might I be so bold as to ask why you did so?"

Eamon saw the men in the patrol gazing at him. "I wanted to save my crew," he answered with a sad smile. "They were also good men."

The draybant nodded as though he had suspected the answer, and flicked a pleased gaze towards his men.

"A noble endeavour, Mr Goodman. Inspiring leadership." Anderas was silent for a moment, as though enjoying the righteousness of the intent. Then he reached out and clasped Eamon's hand again, warmly. "I have had the pleasure today of making acquaintance with a legend in the making, Mr Goodman, and I thank you. I hope we shall meet again."

"Thank you, sir. I shall look forward to it."

The draybant gathered his men and they marched towards the East Quarter. Eamon remembered leading his own cadets along that road, the day that he had been to capture the Lorentides.

A draper by trade, Mr Overbrook lived very near the Four Quarters. The family house was well kept, speaking of modest wealth. Eamon knocked on the door with a heavy hand.

Some moments later Mr Overbrook appeared. His eyes, blue as

his son's had been, took Eamon in at a moment and counted the flames at his collar before speaking.

"Good afternoon, first lieutenant. His voice carried the intonation that Eamon had known in the young cadet. "How may I be of service to you?"

Eamon's throat was dry. The man's eyes fell on the letter. Mr Overbrook became quite still.

"Might I come in, Mr Overbrook?"

The cadet's father nodded dumbly. "Y-y-yes," he stammered, "I suppose you had better."

The afternoon brought a cold, shrill wind and the threat of rain. Cadet Overbrook's remembrance was short and his corpse was escorted to the college pyre by a procession of cadets. They held their blades high while the palled body was set upon the bier, and Eamon spoke a few words, recognizing Overbrook's service and heroic death. As the pyre was kindled and the cloth took to flame, a fanfare played.

"This life was given to his glory, and crowned in that glory he shall be." It was an infinitesimally small comfort, Eamon thought, to the boy's father, who wept as the flames snapped at the pall.

The Third Banners were silent when they returned to their duties; there was an empty place in the room where they studied that afternoon, and unused books upon it.

Later, Eamon went to the Third Banners' dormitory to go through Overbrook's belongings. His map of Dunthruik, exquisite in every detail, lay untouched on the communal table. It was littered with inks and compasses.

Slowly, Eamon shuffled the instruments aside. It was a paper worthy of honour. He decided to suggest to Waite that it be framed and hung in the hall. Overbrook would have appreciated the gesture.

Waite was in the hall. Eamon entrusted the cadet's remaining things to Lieutenant Best, who proceeded to escort Mr Overbrook home. The old man's shoulders were hunched with grief as they went down the college steps into the rain.

Eamon joined the captain.

"We buried two men today, Mr Goodman."

"Sir?"

"He lost his wife when he fled the Breusklian border," Waite observed morosely. "He has no other sons, and his daughters live far away."

Eamon turned to gaze after the man. There seemed to be nothing to say.

As they faced the Brand a dark figure stepped up. Although he walked a little stiffly, Lord Cathair seemed to carry no other trace of his new wound. The West Quarter Hand was accompanied by a series of other men – some Hands and some Gauntlet officers, captains, and draybants from other quarters. Eamon hoped to see Anderas among them and was not disappointed: the draybant walked by Lord Ashway, and was among the last to mount the steps. The very last to come tumbling in from the rain was Ladomer. His old friend grinned at him.

"I'm taking notes," he said, answering Eamon's unspoken question as he passed.

"Welcome, my lords; gentlemen," Waite said, clasping hands with each of them in turn. "I hope you will find the college here suitable to the task."

"My quarters will be ample," Cathair answered. "I apologize that no other venue was available. The Right Hand had some important business to attend to that could not wait, and I am afraid he cannot join us. Lieutenant Kentigern will be keeping notes for him during the meeting." To hear Ladomer referred to by his surname brought back memories of Edesfield. How in the River Realm had Ladomer managed to land such an important role? And how could his friend stand being an administrative officer rather than an active lieutenant?

"Follow me, gentlemen," Cathair said.

"You too, Mr Goodman," Waite added.

Cathair led them to his quarters, then down long corridors lined with bookshelves. At last they came to a large, ornate room. A grand table stood at its centre, laden already with maps and circled with chairs enough for the number attending.

The room filled with Hands, captains, and officers from all over the city. The groups representing each quarter sat together along one side of the table. Eamon found himself sitting next to Ladomer.

"You all right, Ratbag?" his friend whispered while the others were taking their places.

"No."

"Your cadet?"

"No." For a moment he felt that everything would come flooding out of him. The accursed fire was in his hand; he clenched his fingers over it and trembled. He could not tell Ladomer – not now...

Cathair saved him: the Hand rapped his fingers on the table for silence. Ladomer fell studiously to his note making. Eamon watched the curling script out of the corner of his eye.

"His glory," Cathair began. The room echoed the words back to him. "Gentlemen, let me begin by assuring you all that the Master's full authority is behind me in this meeting, and that it is at his request that it has been called. Mr Kentigern, please keep your notes for the Right Hand accurate; they will be archived for reference at a later date."

"Yes, Lord Cathair."

"As you know, gentlemen," Cathair continued, "last night Mr Goodman, some others, and I went to investigate the rumours that we have been receiving as to this Serpent army. Word reached us weeks ago that this self-styled heir to the so-called house of Brenuin had himself been to Istanaria during December, and that the Easters had pledged some kind of alliance to him. Our agents did try to assassinate the Serpent while he was in the city, but the attempt miscarried. Our agent was lost, but the last word we received from her indicated that Easters would be coming to join the Brenuin forces in some numbers. This has since been confirmed thanks to the efforts of some excellent breachers here in Dunthruik – my thanks especially to Mr Goodman in this regard; he has been indispensable to me in the last few months while we have been trying to track this encampment down."

Eamon accepted the praise with a bowed head. It felt surreal to him: he was sitting in a room filled with Hands, hearing about spies he had never known existed and hearing Hughan referred to by the name of the royal house fallen with Ede. That name filled the room with stillness and Cathair seemed wary to speak it.

Hughan Brenuin. As he sat there Eamon suddenly remembered the day he had thought Hughan lost. He had searched the fields outside Edesfield, the day the snakes had come, searching the bodies left behind for the boy who had been his closest friend. He had searched until the earth was cold and clammy, crying out the name he loved and knowing that no answer would come to him. He remembered Hughan and Aeryn, standing together in the Hidden Hall watching him leave; they had pinned their hopes on his shoulders. Past and present seemed to coalesce into an indistinguishable mass, broken only by Giles's face.

He had failed.

"The Serpent keeps at least one camp on the West Bank, between Hoefield and Lower Ashford," Cathair continued. "It has tributary access to the River and is well protected by Ashford Ridge to the north. Some details have been noted of its layout, but we were unfortunately unable to make as thorough an account of it as we should have liked, due to a small skirmish."

Eamon stiffened. Would no mention be made of Overbrook's sacrifice?

"Mr Goodman, however, was successful in breaching the leader of the skirmishers and has some interesting information to offer us. It is on this information that I wish to have your opinions, gentlemen. Mr Goodman," he added, "if you would be so kind?"

Eamon reddened as all eyes, some of them awed, some of them envious that the upstart officer should have distinguished himself yet again, turned to him. Lord Tramist in particular glowered.

"Lords and sirs," he began at last – what choice did he have but to tell them? "There are convoys going to the encampment, supplies and weapons coming up the East Road." He paused, heart stinging. Cathair raised an eyebrow at him. Eamon guessed that he had spoken much more aloud when he had breached Giles; he could not now refuse to say it. Cathair had already heard it once.

"Go on, Mr Goodman."

Ever more mired in the filth of his broken oaths, Eamon went on to detail what he knew of halls, supplies, and alliances. "The Serpent himself hopes to take Dunthruik in the spring," he finished at last. "His support is great in every quarter of the River Realm. He is confident."

A general murmur rounded the table. With every word spoken it was as though a vice tightened around him, wrenching his gut. He had betrayed Hughan's plans, and worse, those plans had been taken by force, torn from Giles without pity. What hope was there for him now?

"And we are unprepared," murmured Ashway, drumming his fingers. "Lords, I propose that the power of the local Gauntlets in the provinces be extended; they must take in anyone suspected of wayfaring tendencies. The Serpent's brood is great enough and we can ill afford for it to take further hold."

"If you would excuse the interruption, Lord Ashway, such a proposal has already been sanctioned by the Master," Ladomer put in. Eamon looked at him; his friend's eyes were shining. "There will be a culling."

"Thank you for your timely mention, Mr Kentigern," Cathair nodded. "The jurisdiction for such measures in Dunthruik will fall to the Quarter Hands, and full orders should be ready for implementation in the next week. Captains, you will prepare your colleges accordingly."

Eamon saw a grave look pass over Waite's face.

"The Master wishes to break up the Serpent's encampment before it grows out of proportion, hopefully scattering or eliminating any allies that have already gathered. A group has already been sent out to deal with the camp at Ashford Ridge."

Horror seized him. Hughan would have no warning! The King's men would be slaughtered.

"Convoys will also be interrupted," Cathair continued. "Should these measures not prove effective enough, however, the quarters will turn to the walls."

"Are we expecting a siege, my lord?" Anderas asked.

Cathair smiled, his green eyes twinkling. "Keeping a house, Mr Anderas, necessitates a little spring cleaning from time to time. Should this Serpent by some chance reach the spring alive, he will find our house quite clean. A precaution, if you will."

"Yes, Lord Cathair."

Eamon listened as they discussed cull strategies for the city and provinces. Tempers grew heated, were abated, and fired again. All the while he heard Ladomer writing beside him. At times his friend shook his head with a sigh or a quiet laugh. In his place, Eamon would not have dared.

It was dark when the meeting concluded. The officers dispersed to await or implement orders. Waite was held back by Cathair; when he emerged he granted Eamon an avuncular smile. Eamon bowed solemnly to the leaving Hand. His whole world whirled about Giles's scream; nothing else could hold beside it in the vortex. Everything reminded him of it, and of what he had become.

He wanted to lose himself, to absolve his grief and clear his churning mind from Overbrook and Mathaiah and Alben and Giles and Cathair and Hughan, who took turns to glare and cast him into consuming shadows. There was only one place he could go.

The servants admitted him without question, greeting him with a cordial good evening. They offered to take his jacket. He declined.

"Is Lady Turnholt here?"

The old woman, one of the kitchen servants, shook her head.

She wiped her hands carefully down her apron. "No, sir. She was invited to dinner at the palace."

"Will she be back tonight?"

"Yes, sir, but late."

"May I wait for her?"

"Of course, sir. Would you like some supper, sir?"

Eamon nodded dumbly.

Supper was laid for him in the dining room. He ate swiftly, wolfing the fine food and washing it down with wine – more wine than he would normally have drunk. He drained his cup as though the thick red liquid could somehow quench his burning conscience. It did not. He drank until his head throbbed.

When he had finished eating he was escorted to the drawing room and invited to await the lady's return. The servants were kind to him. Eamon rested heavily in a cushioned chair and watched as Lillabeth lit the fire. He felt awkward in her presence. He waited in silence, twisting his fingers together.

"May I offer you any other service, Mr Goodman?"

"No," he told her curtly, waving her away. Curtseying, she did as she was bidden. He was left alone.

The drawing room was a grand affair, with great paintings on the walls and marble busts on pedestals in the corners. There was a balcony but its doors were closed. Even so the curtains moved slightly in a breeze that crept through the casement.

Eamon sat close to the fire, trying to let it warm him; he was tired and every part of him ached. The light cast over his skin mocked him, and he could not silence the sounds in his mind.

He heard screams and felt convulsions as though they moved through his own bones. Power crawled in his skin – the voice was there. He saw the long throne room, its stones filled with nightmarish shadows, but still he knelt before the flaming figure from whom the voice came.

You have done well, Eben's son, and you will be rewarded. He deserved the death that you delivered him.

"He's not dead! I didn't kill him!"

Shadows leapt. Could Hughan's camp already be under attack? And a cull was being prepared for the city – all because he had delivered news to Hughan's enemies. He had done it as blithely as he had delivered the Nightholt to the Hands. The tears on his face burnt as though formed from molten metal.

"*He's not dead!*"

You do no wrong in killing the Serpent's brood, the voice soothed. *Your blood is cleansed in shedding theirs, Eben's son. I know your blood: I know its taste, its smell. I know you, better than you know yourself; and I know you serve me. It is right that you kneel before me, that you glorify me. You can do no other!*

The shadows clawed at him and in the fire was the Master's face. The mark on his hand answered; he could not shy away.

Everything you are, Eben's son, you are because I made you thus. Did you truly think to exchange your fealty to me for that to a Serpent? Eben destroyed that House and you will complete his work for me. You will strike and breach and break as many men as I command you to, Eben's son, and you will glorify me.

"No!" The mark on his hand burned and burned. However much he struggled it would not let him be free. "*You lie!*"

You are mine.

Eamon started in his chair. The house was quiet. Alessia had not returned. It was late.

He tore off his jacket and hurled it across the room. Through misted, stinging eyes he looked down at his palm: it burned with a glow ruddier than flame. He loathed it.

The crown mocked him. He could not bear this mark – he would not bear it. He had to free himself of it. How he rued the day that he had sworn!

Suddenly he was on his knees by the fire, dagger in hand. If he could just force the eagle from his flesh he would be free. He could renounce all oaths to every man. He could renounce his blood, take another name, and flee to the south or to distant merchant states across the sea. He would destroy the heart of the King and carve this mark from his flesh. Then he would be free!

He felt and did not feel the pain of the dagger's point driving into him, just as he believed and did not believe that he could remove the mark. He did not know how deep it ran or how deep he cut, but he felt sure that he could destroy it. He pressed the blade under his skin; it ran red in the light.

Eamon.

The voice reached out to him, staying his hand. He fell back on his haunches and wept thick, hot tears. Hand and blade were marked with blood.

There was a step, then a gasp at the door.

"Eamon!"

The door slammed shut and feet ran to him. Cool, light fingers wrapped about his and Alessia knelt beside him. But he did not look at her; he could barely see. All he could feel was the blade where it lay in his bleeding hand.

Alessia laid her hand on the dagger. "Eamon," she said gently. "Don't."

"Stay away!" he sobbed. Rage welled up inside him but he could not drive her away – he could not take the dagger out of his hand and he could not push it farther into his bloody palm. The grim voice he knew so well mocked his incompetence. He fairly howled as it laughed at him.

"Make it stop!" he cried, hanging his head against her shoulder. "Make it stop, please!"

"Eamon, Eamon."

Alessia's fingers touched his face, brushing at his tears. He did not stop her as she drew the blade out of his hands. He sobbed and trembled as she bound a handkerchief about his wound. Laying the dagger carefully to one side, she clasped her beautiful hands over his.

"My love, what have you done?" she whispered.

He turned to look at her. Everything churned in his mind, toying with him and goading him, and there were was no one he could turn to. He could tell no one. But to live with what he had done... he could not. Sobs wracked through him. He could not lead a double life alone.

"I've lied to you, Alessia." His voice was contorted with terror in the knowledge of what he had to do.

She was smiling at him. Her grip on his hands tightened. "I can't imagine you doing that," she said lightly. "Let's worry no more about it. You've just had a difficult day."

She leaned forward and kissed him so hard that he could barely breathe. For a moment he lost himself there. What did he need to say to her? Nothing, nothing... he could stay forever in that kiss.

No, he would no longer lie to her – or himself. He pulled himself away and took her face between his hands, as he had done what seemed so long ago – that first night he had loved her.

"No, Alessia, you have to listen to me," he said urgently. Were there tears in her eyes? It grieved him that he was the cause of them. He had to seem a madman, and perhaps he was.

"It's all right," she told him. "You need say no more than that you love me."

Eamon quaked. "I do love you, Alessia. You are all I have. I can tell no one else but you, and I must speak before it destroys me."

She fell silent and raised her hand to his against her cheek. Blood showed on the handkerchief, dotting the crest embroidered there. She looked at him with deep, suffering compassion on her face. She was everything to him, and he treasured the profound nature of those eyes that truly, deeply loved him.

"I love you," she breathed, a tear trailing down her cheek. "Speak freely, Eamon. Freely."

There was courage, and the promise of release from his torment, in her loving eyes. He loved her; he wanted her to know the truth. That was all that mattered.

He laid his life in her hands and told her everything.

CHAPTER XXI

He started at the beginning.

He told her how he had had two dreams when he was a young man: to go to the university or to join the Gauntlet, and that his father had asked him to wait before doing either. He told her about his father's books and trade, and the night his father had died. He explained how he had become a bookbinder, setting aside what he had dreamed of, and the fire that had destroyed everything he had called his own. With nothing left but a desire to do something notable and worthwhile, his dream of joining the Gauntlet had returned to him and been fostered by those close to him. He had had skill and, above all, a true desire to serve. He had been at home in the Gauntlet college and comforted by the training, the uniforms, the parades, and the chance to serve something greater than himself. Of all the cadets at Edesfield he had been the most passionate about his forthcoming swearing. He spoke of his terror the night that wayfarers in the woods near Edesfield had bested him, and his joy at being granted the opportunity to swear nonetheless. Nothing had ever been so important to him.

He told her what the sworn had not: about the hideous weight that had met his hand when he touched the pommel, and the eagle that had been driven into his flesh. He spoke about the power that had gone into him and the voice that had appeared in his mind. Of all the cadets who had sworn that day he alone seemed to have noticed the new poison in his blood.

He told her about Telo, the great-hearted keeper of the Star, of the burning and his own part in it. He spoke about Aeryn and her capture, and about the holk that had borne him away from Edesfield as a hastily promoted lieutenant alongside another who despised him.

"That's where I met Giles. He was the wayfarer who led the attack on my ship. He…" He began to quiver violently. "He is the man whom I broke last night."

Alessia looked at him gently. "I don't understand."

Eamon met her gaze. Although, safe in the midnight quiet of the bed they often shared, he had spoken to her about his work for Lord Cathair, he had never described the plain, the voice, the terrible power. He had never told her about what breaching truly was, or what it did, or by whom his power to do it was granted.

Now he spoke of it all. He saw her growing pale as he recounted how a breaching was conducted and what he saw when he did it. He trembled as he told her how it felt to be breached, for he knew that also.

"It burns, Alessia," he shuddered. "It tears and grips and rends and sunders and punctures and penetrates and *burns*. You can do nothing to stop it: a breacher will see what you know, he will take it from you, and if you resist him he will call down fire upon you until you can only beg him to take all he wants and let you die. Breaching is a rare skill among the Gauntlet. The Master's mark gave it to me. I have used it upon dozens of men – women and children too." His bleeding palm throbbed. "I have done it, Alessia, and, of late, I did not care that I did. I did it to Giles. I wanted to. He was not protected."

Alessia pressed his hand tenderly between her fingers. "He was your enemy."

"That does not justify it," Eamon whispered. There, kneeling by the fireplace with her hands on his, he understood it clearly at last. "He… he said things about me. Things I didn't want to hear. Because they were true."

"What did he say?"

"He said that I had…" Eamon fell silent. Did he dare to tell her the rest? Alessia watched him, eyes round with compassion. His desire to be true engulfed him.

"He called me a traitor," he said at last.

Alessia stared. "A traitor?" She laughed. "Eamon, you are no traitor – "

"He spoke the truth, Alessia."

"How could he?" she breathed, reaching forward to lay her hand by his face. "I don't believe it."

Eamon felt his resolve quail. Drawing a deep breath, he took her hand again.

"I was telling you about the holk," he said. Alessia nodded. "Giles was the man who captured it and killed my crew. He meant to kill me too, and he would have done, except…" It hurt to remember.

"What happened?"

"It… it was Mathaiah." The name came heavily, painfully from his lips.

"Your ward?" Alessia asked softly. She knew that Eamon was estranged from the young man. He had never told her why.

"We were friends then," Eamon replied, marvelling at the bitterness in his voice. "He… Mr Grahaven saved my life."

He looked at her in surprise. How could he have forgotten? Yet he had – just as he had forgotten the thousand gestures of kindness and encouragement the cadet had always freely offered him.

He pressed the handkerchief closer to his slowing wound. "He took a blow that should have killed me. He should have died. He was bleeding in my lap. I have seen blood before, and much of it, but I had never seen such rage. I was terrified, Alessia." He had never confessed it before. "I was terrified that Mathaiah would die; that I had met death and would be swept up with Spencing and the others – another corpse to silt the River." He wept with remembered fear. Alessia touched his face, caressing the tears to one side.

"Your fear did not seize you," she said. "That is courage. It does not make you a traitor."

Did she not understand? "Mathaiah was dying. Yet he lives. Do you not ask yourself how?"

"Does it matter?" Alessia whispered. "It is a grace that he does so."

How near the truth she struck! "It was. It was the King's grace."

She stared. "The… the King's grace?"

"Do you remember I told you that sometimes, when I tried to breach men, there was something that stopped me? A kind of blue light?"

"You told me," she whispered.

"It is called the King's grace; it aids those who serve him in times of trial. I have seen it hold men safe from breaching, and that night I saw it used to save a man from death. Mathaiah was healed."

Alessia held his gaze for a moment. "Aeryn healed him?"

Eamon looked up at her. How easy it would be to say yes! But it was not the truth.

Now they had come to the crux of everything, to the fatal contradiction. This was what he had to tell her and what she needed to know to understand him and his grief. It was what he needed to utter to her so as to be free.

But what would she think of him? What could she think? She had heard his tale as that of a Gauntlet officer who had perhaps gone too far, and she had been sympathetic to him… What could she say – and be obliged to do – if he told her the truth?

He shook his head. He had to tell her. He tried. The words cloyed in his throat. He swallowed hard. So much rested on it, so much could be lost…

He had to be true.

Determined, he looked up at last. Alessia watched him with confusion. He straightened a single tress of her dark hair, letting it settle over her shoulder. Then, with his heart hanging upon a precipice, he met her gaze.

"Aeryn didn't heal Mathaiah," he said quietly. "I did."

The truth was spoken.

Alessia's eyes widened in disbelief.

Would she say nothing? "I healed Mathaiah," he said again. He wrung his hands.

"But that would make you…" She stopped short and met his gaze. He tried to hold hers. "That would make you a wayfarer."

He looked back at her. He wanted to answer yes, but he did not deserve the name that she gave to him. Not after what he had done; not given who he had become.

"I don't understand." Alessia was frowning at him and her eyes passed over his injured hand. "You were already sworn to the throned. It's…" She shook her head. "It's impossible. Surely you cannot bear his mark and be one of them?"

"But I do, and I am. I am not the first who has done so."

"What do you mean?"

"After I was captured I was taken back to one of the wayfarers' Hidden Halls," he told her. "I learned that swearing one thing and doing another is a common curse of the Goodmans. The throned only sits where he does because a Goodman put him there. It… it was my ancestor who betrayed King Ede." The fierceness and fear in his voice startled him. Who could betray such a man as Ede or Hughan?

Why had he done it?

"They cannot hold you responsible for that," Alessia told him firmly.

"The wonder is that they don't!" Eamon told her. "Or at least," he added quietly, "Hughan doesn't."

Alessia blinked hard. "Hughan?"

Eamon nodded silently. "He is Ede's heir."

"You've met him?" Alessia's voice was filled with awe. As Eamon nodded again her expression became that of a child watching a fairy tale come alive: the throned gave out that the wayfarers had no true heir among them. "Is he really Ede's descendant?"

"He is the true King," Eamon answered. The simplicity of the truth stunned him. Even Lord Cathair had acknowledged it: Hughan Brenuin was Ede's heir. Eamon remembered every detail of Hughan's face, the justice and kindness with which the man commanded the wayfarers. How just and gentle Hughan had been with him, swift to encourage him and to call him by his true name. Hughan was kingly indeed.

"Why did you come to Dunthruik, Eamon?" Alessia asked suddenly.

"To serve him."

Had he ever known whom he served? It was Hughan who had called him First Knight; under that name and with Hughan's blessing, Eamon had come to Dunthruik to aid the King. Or had he come to rise to Right Hand, to be vested in black and serve the glory of the flame-faced Master?

He had done neither.

"Eamon." Her grip tightened on his hand. "You cannot serve them both."

"I know."

"You have to choose."

It was the truth he had long sought to evade. Now he faced it. "I thought I had chosen," he whispered. "But I never did. I suppose I thought that I could pick and choose my fealty. But I can't. It has to be all, or nothing.

"The throned wants to begin culling wayfarers. He knows where the King's camp is. It's probably under attack now – Lord Cathair said that men had already been dispatched to see to it. The throned knows where the supply convoys are and where they're going, because I broke Giles's mind and uttered his secrets aloud as I breached him. He's going to try to destroy them, and kill the King." Eamon trembled as the enormity of the situation struck him. "The throned has only one way to quell the wayfarers and secure his dominion: he has to kill Hughan, for he is the very last of the house of Brenuin." It was a task in which the throned wanted him to play a critical role: *"you will complete his work…"*

Urgency drove him to his feet. "This is my fault. I have to warn Hughan."

Alessia rose with him. "There will be others who can go –"

"You don't understand," Eamon answered. "The throned has a book – something called the Nightholt –"

"A book?" Alessia sounded incredulous.

"Mathaiah and I brought it back from Ellenswell. I don't know why it's so important, only that it is. If only I knew what it said…" He laughed bitterly. "Mathaiah said that he could read it. It was written in that writing that's on the doors to the throne room, and plastered all over the Hands' Hall. I didn't want to believe him; I chose not to. Can you believe that, Alessia? He never failed me, *never* lied to me once. And I *chose* not to believe him!" He did not add why; the wound was still fresh. "I don't suppose I can ask him now. But I have to speak to him. I must get word to Hughan."

She gripped his hand. "Eamon, don't just go and –"

"I have to."

"Why must you do it?" Alessia's voice caught in a sob. Eamon suddenly saw the fear in her reddened eyes. "Why must you do it?" she whispered.

"I must because I am not simply a King's man." The logic of it was painfully obvious at last. "That's why I was sent. Even though I had the throned's mark, even though it was likely that I would be discovered, even though it was more than likely that everything would fall if I were taken, the King sent me." It astounded him. "I'm his First Knight, Alessia."

She stared at him, seemingly struck dumb. "First Knight?"

"Yes. It is why, even though I have done wrong, I must choose rightly now." He looked at her again and saw that she had grown pale. "What is it?" he asked, setting his hands upon hers.

"N-nothing."

Suddenly he felt ashamed. Her hand trembled beneath his and there were tears in her eyes. What had he put her through? "Alessia," he breathed, "I'm sorry. I didn't mean to hurt –"

"You're an informant, aren't you?" she interjected.

"I was meant to be one. It didn't really turn out that way. I only marvel that I haven't been caught yet." Sometimes he had felt certain that Lord Cathair knew the truth – sometimes he felt that the whole world could see through him. But nobody had ever tried to stop him. Why, he did not know. Perhaps they had seen how he could not choose. Perhaps he had never been worrying enough to warrant stopping.

He drew himself out of his thoughts and looked at her again. There seemed to be a growing weight across her shoulders, but she held his hand tightly.

"Have you… have you ever done things against people that you love?" she asked.

It cut him terribly. He had. Everything he had done for Cathair had been against Hughan. He could not even begin to think of what he had done to Mathaiah.

"Yes," he answered weakly. "It is nearly unbearable. But perhaps I can still redeem some of what I have done, even if I cannot undo it." It seemed a forlorn hope.

The dwindling fire crackled quietly in the grate, its flames lighting the eagle over the mantelpiece.

Suddenly he stared at her, remembering that she was Lady Alessia Turnholt, ally to the throned.

He started back.

He was a fool! If she did not reject him for what he was she would now be caught in the same net as he – and perhaps she would take every word he had said back to the throned. He panicked. "Alessia, I shouldn't have… I have to go… I…"

"Is that why you loved me?" Her voice was quiet. It caught and stilled him completely. "Was I a stepping stone to him?" Her hands shook in his.

With all the force with which he had been ready to flee he reached out to take hold of her face.

"That was never why I loved you," he told her. "It isn't why I love you now. I love you because… because you chose to love me." He searched her deep, dark eyes with his own. "The only thing that I have clung to in these days is you, Alessia. Neither king nor throne has been in my heart as you have been. Despite all of my falsehood you have been true, and now you have helped me to see my duty clearly again. I love you. I have doubted much the last few months – but I have never doubted that."

He had expected to calm her with his words but her voice came back to him with sudden, unbearable passion.

"You have to leave Dunthruik!" she told him, seizing both his hands until it hurt. She startled him.

"Why?"

"You cannot stay!" She was nearly sobbing in her urgency. "They will hurt you. Don't stay!"

Eamon forgot his own troubles. He gathered her into his arms and held her tightly, running his hands across her beautiful hair.

"Please don't stay," she whispered. Her heart beat fearfully against his.

"Alessia," he answered. "Dear Alessia. By what grace I do not know, but I have been kept safe so far. If I can still do what I was sent to do, then I must."

"He will find out!"

"We don't know that."

"And if he does? What will he do to you?" She clung to him. "Please, Eamon –"

"Alessia, don't you see?" he laughed, and suddenly his fears were far away. "I can't leave Dunthruik now, any more than I could if the throned had already bound me and cast me to torment in the Pit. I have my duty to the King."

She held him silently for a long time. "You won't go?"

"How could I? Even had I no oath, no promise, to keep me here, I would not."

Alessia glanced at him in confusion. With a loving laugh Eamon pressed her close.

"Alessia!" he breathed. "You are here."

Light was beginning to touch the walls as the sun sleepily climbed the sky. Alessia was quite still now, as though she could see that he would not be moved. He smiled at her and raised her chin. Shivering once, she smiled back.

Gently, he drew her to him again and spread out his cloak so that they were wrapped in its folds. Together, they watched the sun colour the sky.

The roads were quiet that morning and he made his way back to the West Quarter unnoticed. The only movement on the Coll was of servants, who were stolidly beginning their long days, and the Gauntlet patrols that exchanged watches. Eamon heard his boots on the cobbles, as he had on hundreds of other mornings, and in his cloak he smelled Alessia's perfume.

His heart was clearer. Giles's screams continued to haunt his mind, but though they were still terrible, they held less power over him. He knew now Giles had been right – he had betrayed Hughan. He accepted it.

Alessia had seen him to her gates and kissed him, laying her hands about his neck and saying that she loved him. The words rang in his heart, undulled. He knew her and now she knew him, more deeply than she ever had before. It had been beyond his hope to share it with her, but he had done it, and she loved him still. How, then, could he be sullen?

"What ho, Ratbag!"

Startled, he turned to see Ladomer strolling up the Coll. His friend bore his customary papers and, though a little pale, was his usual, cheerful self.

"Good morning!" Eamon called. He almost sang it.

"Good morning, good morning!" Ladomer sang back. "Where do you go, with such delight, so early in the sun-kissed morn?"

"Is that poetry?" Eamon scoffed. It sounded utterly absurd coming from Ladomer.

"I'm very creative, you know."

"You've been spending too much time with Lord Cathair," Eamon countered playfully.

"Too true, too true," Ladomer laughed, ceding victory. "Going to the college?"

"Yes indeed." Eamon yawned and arched his shoulders back in his jacket. They were stiff and sore, but he did not mind.

"Want to carry my papers for me?"

"No."

"It was worth a try."

"Yes, it was." Eamon laughed, then yawned again.

"Tired?" Ladomer fell into step beside him.

"Yes and no."

"Perhaps you have been spending too much time with your lovely lady, Mr Goodman?"

"Perhaps!"

"Then 'tis little wonder that you're tired!" Ladomer winked.

Eamon thumped him. "None of that, Mr Kentigern!"

"Come now, you deserved it. It would certainly be why I was tired, if she were mine!"

"If you want to know, we were actually only talking," Eamon told him, mock-petulantly.

"I can't believe that for a moment!" Ladomer chortled. "What about?"

"Mind your own business!"

"I am." Ladomer adopted a pretentious tone. "The personal conduct of officers, down to the goriest detail, is of great interest to the Master." He smiled. "The Master's business is the Right Hand's business, and the Right Hand's business is mine. I am, as you see, his personal papershuffler – a duty I execute with utmost efficiency and pride."

"My talk was of a personal nature, and of little interest to the Right Hand."

"Sweet nothings or no, I fear I shall have to take you both in for questioning. How do you fancy the Pit, Mr Goodman?" he added brightly. "I hear it's very pleasant at this time of year!" The latter had been spoken with every inflection of sincerity, but unable to keep it up Ladomer burst into great-lunged laughter. Magnanimously, he offered to drop the subject.

If Eamon had taken much longer to reach the college he would have been late for parade. As it was he arrived as the cadets were drawing up and swiftly took his place among them. Each offered him cheery good-mornings; he smiled in return. He even smiled at Mathaiah. His ward stared at him, surprised.

As he watched Waite inspecting the ranks and giving the morning's news, he reflected that as he meant to get news to Hughan his ward was still the best way to do it. He wanted to laugh out loud: he was going to speak to Mathaiah! In that moment it held no dread for him. He could still prove himself. He could become what Hughan had seen in him.

"There's one last piece of news, gentlemen." He tried to concentrate on the sound of Waite's voice. "You are all aware that Mr Goodman was engaged in action against the wayfarers two days ago. He comported himself with extreme dedication in that effort, and once again rendered invaluable service to the Master in the endeavour."

Eamon flushed with embarrassment. One or two Third Banners cheered. Waite hushed them with his hand.

"In view of this effort," he continued, "it is my proud duty to announce to you all that Mr Goodman will, as of today, sadly no longer be with us."

Eamon froze. What did Waite mean?

Waite was smiling at him. "Gentlemen, I have here a note from the Master himself, approving a recommendation from Lord Cathair. Let me read it to you:

"'It is our august will that Eamon Goodman, first lieutenant under Waite, captain of our own West Quarter, should this day be summoned from that station and elevated to the rank he deserves. Let him be made a Hand.'"

Waite turned the paper so that all could see the eagle that sealed the bottom of the parchment. It glinted. "Congratulations, Mr Goodman!"

There was a split second of silence. Then, as though with one accord, the whole yard erupted into a cacophony of cheering and applause, and cadets and ensigns were calling his name. For a Hand to be chosen from their ranks brought honour on every man there. Waite fairly beamed as he applauded. Any semblance of an orderly parade vanished as man after man came to clasp Eamon's hand; the other officers, no doubt secretly pleased that the appointment would raise one of them to his place, clapped him round the shoulder.

Then Waite himself was among them; he took Eamon's hand and clasped it with vigour and warmth. "Well done, Mr Goodman!"

Eamon couldn't think, could barely hear, and almost couldn't see. So many faces around him, so many calls and cries – it was overwhelming.

But one sight remained with him: his ward's face, grey amid the cries of joy.

He stood in the hall, dressed in the finest jacket that the college had. His shirt had been pressed, each pin at his collar polished until the flames fairly burned. As he stood he watched while a carpenter diligently carved into the wooden board: *First Lieutenant Eamon Goodman, made Hand on the 9th of February in the 533rd year of the Master's throne.*

Above the board hung Overbrook's map. Waite had had it framed and set there with a memorial plaque.

Eamon's heart beat so quickly he almost couldn't distinguish it from the strokes of the carpenter's chisel. He was to be made a Hand that very afternoon. The initiative for the Handing, inspired by Eamon's selfless and unfaltering service over the last few months – one that had reached its peak when he had breached Giles – had been Lord Cathair's. The Master had been similarly impressed and was rumoured to have ratified the suggestion in moments. The voice within counselled him that he richly deserved the reward being offered to him. So tenderly did it speak that he scarcely noticed it, and he did not stop to wonder what the Master's lightning ratification might imply.

He saw sudden movement in the corridor as a cadet scurried past, his head lowered.

"Mr Grahaven!"

Eamon had called out before he had even thought about it. Perhaps, had the dictates of rank not forbidden it, Mathaiah might have kept walking.

"Sir."

"Would you lend me your company a moment, Mr Grahaven?"

Reluctantly, Mathaiah walked across to him. The young man had a wary look and seemed terribly conscious of the name being marked onto the board. His glance flicked to it as he saluted formally.

"How may I be of service, sir?" His tone was cool.

Eamon suddenly found that he didn't know what to say. What could he say? That he had told Alessia everything, that he felt restored, that he was going to be a better man henceforth – perhaps one deserving of the name Hughan had given him?

He could say that Mathaiah had been wrong. He could confess his sudden fear about being made a Hand; the pronouncement had laid a strange hold of joy and terror on him. He could ask Mathaiah to take news to Hughan. He should do that at least, and do it at once, while he had the chance.

Most of all he wanted Mathaiah to know that he had been wrong about Alessia.

"Sir?" Mathaiah asked. "Was there something? I have duties to attend to."

"Yes, Mr Grahaven, there was something," Eamon began lamely. Where was his courage now? "I wanted to tell you –"

"Mr Goodman! Good afternoon!" The voice that called his name was loud and familiar. Eamon turned and smiled.

"Lord Cathair," he answered and bowed low. He was aware of a dark look passing over Mathaiah's face as he did the same.

"Well, I have to hand it to you, Mr Goodman," Cathair smiled. "You've made a fine spectacle of yourself this time. One might almost say a *hand*some spectacle!"

"One might," Eamon returned, reminding himself that he was not Cathair's equal.

At least, not yet.

"Ah, and Mr Grahaven too, looking fit to race the length of the Serpentine and back before I can count to ten!" Mathaiah bowed again. "A fine young man, very fine. What a pleasure to see you, Mr Grahaven."

"Thank you, my lord," Mathaiah answered. "I was congratulating Mr Goodman on his appointment. He will be sorely missed by those of us who looked to him in this college."

Eamon glanced at him; there were traces of bitterness in the last.

"You may look to him still, Mr Grahaven; he will be a Hand of the quarter under me, and all the more worthy of looking to!" Cathair laughed again. "I shall go and gather Captain Waite, Mr Goodman – he often needs gathering these days, but I have luckily had much practice in it – and we shall go to complete the formalities. You may await us here."

"Thank you, my lord."

Cathair disappeared down the corridor. The chiselling stopped and the carpenter descended his ladder for some tool or other. Eamon smiled.

"You were wrong about her, Mathaiah," he said. He turned to speak to his ward, then stopped.

Mathaiah was gone.

Glancing round the empty hallway he felt sudden despair. If he could not reach out to Mathaiah, to whom he had once been so close, how could he expect to reach out to Hughan?

He stood numbly until Cathair and Waite joined him. Then he followed them to the shadows of the palace.

He remembered the long corridor that led to the throne room. He remembered the portraits, the coats of arms, the awful banners and emblems that lined the walls in cascading rivers of red silk. He remembered the peculiar ring of the paving stones underfoot, the glitter of gold in every arch and high window, now lit with drifting sunlight instead of burning torches. He remembered the doors, great, oaken lumbers, and the strange writing that adorned them.

Waite and Cathair walked either side of him, each one solemn as they approached their goal, the throne room itself.

Cathair turned to him. "Many are overwhelmed when they first stand in the presence of the Master," he said. "I expect you to be among their number." Eamon swallowed. "I also expect you to behave in a way that befits you, honours me, and glorifies the Master," Cathair added. "Is that clear, Mr Goodman?"

"Yes, my lord," he whispered.

"Good."

Eamon looked back to the great doors. He thought of Alessia, and wished for her hand in his.

A man dressed in red – perhaps from the throned's own servants – admitted them. The throne room's mosaics filled Eamon's eyes with light, blinding him as he came onto the molten lake of stone. Before him was the throne's dais. It rose to a great height, and as Eamon walked the length of the hall he knew that all around him the man with red hair looked down; only now, the eyes did not mock but rather welcomed. Eamon found his eye drawn again to the unicorn, and to the grisly snake that fled its breast.

Hands stood on the steps that led to the throne in two sombre black lines. They were the Quarter Hands: Ashway stood to the right, Tramist and Dehelt to the left. Above them, nearest to the throne, stood the Right Hand.

It was then that Eamon saw his face clearly for the first time. Like Cathair's it was pale, but more youthful. There was something strange about it – Eamon felt almost as though he knew it. And yet he also knew that he had never seen that broad forehead or the deep, fierce eyes. He knew only the clasp of his hand and the stirring voice: perhaps those were enough.

Cathair and Waite stopped at the foot of the steps and Eamon halted a few paces behind them. Sweat had broken out on his brow and he fought the urge to wipe it away with his sleeve.

"Who is it that approaches?" called a voice: the Right Hand's. Eamon remembered that voice and how the crowd had answered it at the majesty. It demanded him.

"Lord Cathair of the West Quarter and his servant, Captain Waite," Cathair answered solemnly. Eamon realized with a start that the ceremony had begun. "We have come to lay a new servant before the Master."

"Then the Master will test him," the Right Hand replied, turning to face the throne. He bowed low; all the Hands and Waite dropped down at once to one knee. Eamon followed them.

The long curtains behind the throne stirred. Eamon risked a single glance and then dropped his head.

He was there.

The Master. His fiery head bore a crown and his steel-grey eyes shone more keenly than the thick jewels upon his brow. He was like a pillar of fire, red and roaring in the light, and a great cloak, rimmed with black, hung from his powerful shoulders. A sword hung at his side, its scabbard encased in glinting jewels, and dark writing – the same writing as in Nightholt and Hands' Hall – adorned the top of the blade's length.

"Rise."

They rose. Only the Right Hand met the Master's dreadful gaze. "Master," he said, "a new servant is brought before you."

"I will test him."

Every nerve in Eamon's body went stone cold. The voice coursed through him, robbing him of strength and filling him with fear. He knew that voice – how he knew it! – and it knew him.

He began to tremble. He could not go through with this! They would kill him, and strike at Hughan, and the house of Brenuin would be razed from the earth. It would be his fault for letting himself be made a Hand. There was no courage in his limbs and no cry in his throat. He was lost!

"Test him, Master," Cathair said. There was something close to adoration in the Hand's voice. "Test him and make him true."

All except the Right Hand sank to one knee again. Eamon tried to kneel. His knees were so weak he feared he would fall. He could not bring himself to do it. He was struck immovable by the terrible grandeur of the one by the throne.

The Master came to stand before him, his hair like wreaths of living flames and his face, though pale, terrifying, showing not weakness but indelible strength. Eamon quailed. How could Hughan, of mere flesh and blood, hope to stand against this being? The grey eyes were on him, driving into his very heart.

"Will you bow to me, Eben's son?" The voice was glorious and hideous.

"Yes, Master," Eamon stammered. He staggered to his knees until the hem of the throned's robes were before him, and still he felt as though he stood too tall.

He heard the unsheathing of the great sword. He shut his eyes, pressed his face against the ground, and quivered.

"Will you renew your pledge to me, Eben's son?"

"Yes, Master," he whispered. He reached out and touched the pommel of the sword that he knew was stretched towards him. He laid his injured right hand over its eagle, feeling pain as sore flesh and metal touched.

"I renew my pledge." He felt the throbbing red light growing around the mark in his hand but he dared not look up. His hand shook. "My blood, my blade, and my body are all given in your service."

"Will you swear a new oath to me, Eben's son?" The Master's voice seemed both within and without his mind. It permeated him, reverberating through every pore and fibre.

Eamon nodded speechlessly.

"Will you swear to be mine and mine alone, a hand swift to avenge me, obedient to and glorifying none but me alone, forsaking all other oaths and service, even to the end of your days?

CHAPTER XXI

Will you be as my Hand in this city, and in these lands?"

"My hand is witness to my pledge; I ratify it," Eamon answered, holding his hand aloft.

"You cannot serve them both," Alessia's voice warned. But a new vow was weaving its tendrils round him. He could not shake himself free. It was too late.

Suddenly the throned's hand was on his forehead; it was a cool hand, bearing power.

"I will test your service, Eben's son." Eamon knew with dread certainty what would follow: he would be breached.

The ground fell from under him. His whole world became the hand pressed hard against his head. He opened his eyes and gasped.

He did not see the plain.

He saw a broad expanse of tangled woodland in the arms of a valley. Men lay dead there; some wore blue, others red. Their arms and shields were unfamiliar to him, but on some he saw the sword and star and on others the Master's eagle. Men fell around him. A watchtower was in the distance, its roof and pennons caught in a torrent of flame. The charred stonework spewed a guttering coil of smoke. The nearby woods burned, filling the night with ash as well as blood and death.

He saw a man ride through the press of the dead. His sword lifted high, the heavens seemed to light the blade. His bright helm was ringed with a shining crown. The rider called and men rallied to him.

The King, for so he was, rode down the narrow field. There was a man before him, seemingly wrapped in flames. The man laughed, red hair shaking about him like a mane. His face was violent with delight.

The King rode on towards his foe. There seemed to be no force that could stop him and no power that could stand against the piercing brightness of his sword. But the riding King did not see the man who suddenly rose from among the fallen dead, and he did not see the stroke of a reddened blade arching towards him.

With an unearthly scream the King's steed plummeted to earth in a froth of fear and blood. The King was thrown down hard. As he fell his helm was cast aside and he saw the man who had struck him.

It was the First Knight.

Even as the King fought to regain his feet the flaming man came upon him, sword long and terrible in the light.

The blade plunged down, piercing the throat of one that called still upon the name of his First Knight.

"Even thus are you mine, Eben's son."

As the vision began to fade the throned was before him. There were sobs of anguish in his throat. Burning tears rushed down his cheeks and he shivered with cold fear. The Master was over him, an unbreakable tower of fire and steel.

"You will never undo that stroke. The house of Brenuin is fallen and the service of your house is given to me. You are bound to me. You will be true to me."

Eamon lowered his head. His hope lay, shattered and bleeding, like the broken corpse in the valley of Edesfield.

"I am true to you, Master," he whispered. Inwardly, he wept.

He felt a searing pain on his forehead and resisted the urge to cry out. The throned was withdrawing his hand. The fingers left a new, heavy mark upon him, one that he could never remove. Broken and bound, he knelt before the throned.

The Master stepped back.

"I have tested my servant, Eben's son, and found him true." The voice was victorious. "Let him be my Hand, in this city and over the River."

Eamon trembled as Cathair and Waite drew him to his feet. His arms were drawn back and his red jacket was taken from him. Cold air passed over him; he felt vulnerable, naked. The Right Hand came to him, bearing a black garment. Thick, black clothes were set upon him and a cloak was darkly clasped about his shoulders. The Master smiled at him.

He was a Hand.

He was to be stationed as a Hand of the West Quarter and awarded lodgings in the Hands' Hall. He was assigned to the especial care of Lord Cathair, who would in effect ward him until he grew accustomed to his role. His duties had not essentially changed: he was to continue assisting Captain Waite at the college, but he would also have duties at the palace – and work from the Master himself – via Lord Cathair and the Right Hand, when it was allotted to him. He would learn about the deepest workings of the city, be privy to its politics, economics, and trade disputes, and be an integral part, so Cathair told him, of setting policy on the upcoming culling.

The black cloak was heavy and cumbersome as he walked slowly up the Coll, overtaken by dozens of Gauntlet and servants. He had accompanied Captain Waite back to the college and collected his things. He was to take them back to the Hands' Hall, after which Cathair had insisted that he should join the West Quarter's other Hands for a celebratory drink. His forehead still burned – perhaps that was what people shied away from as he passed.

A cool wind came in across the sea with the eventide. He turned to face it. All the hope that the morning had brought was shrouded in black. He had reaffirmed fealty to the wrong man; strengthened the wrong oath. He had been a fool to think that he might do otherwise.

Hearing footsteps approaching, Eamon looked up. Mathaiah Grahaven was watching him.

"Good evening, Lord Goodman," he said, bowing.

Eamon's heart curdled. Lord Goodman. Had he not always dreamed of coming as far as he had done that day? Why, then, was the title so grievous to him?

You will go farther even than this, son of Eben.

As Eamon shook the voice away the young man turned to continue along the Coll. Suddenly his voice leapt to his throat.

"Mathaiah!"

The young man turned warily. "My lord."

That joy again! And none could gainsay him this due. The title was his. He had earned it.

"Mathaiah," he said, shaking himself as though by it he might cast off his oath. "You must take a message to Hughan."

Mathaiah gaped at him. His face set into a disbelieving line. "A message?" he repeated. His tone grew hard. "Your garb is message enough!"

The words cut to his heart. "Don't you understand?" he cried. "Hughan is in danger!"

"He is now, my lord," Mathaiah retorted curtly. As he stalked away his face was streaked with tears.

"Mathaiah –!"

He will not listen to you, the voice told him. *He never did.*

The door was answered slowly when he knocked, and he stood, shivering, in the cold. He felt more vulnerable in black than he had ever felt in red.

He had been to drink with the Hands. Lord Cathair had toasted his health and long service, and Eamon had stayed as long as he could deem polite before leaving, ostensibly to retire. He had even done so. But his room had been cold and dark, engulfed by the wings of the palace and the hall's red stones. The stones now answered to his hand – he could go where he wished. But he did not want to be in the Hands' Hall. He did not want to be alone.

Shadows moved in the dark around him, and as he waited by the door he heard the last whispers of the city. Most lights were doused, though those at the palace still burned; its great windows were like eyes weeping flames. He watched the moon creep from behind a cloud.

At last he heard fingers unbolting the door. A servant welcomed him with tired eyes.

"Mr Cartwright, is Lady Turnholt here?" Eamon asked.

"Yes, Mr… my lord," the servant corrected himself, starting at the black. "She's in her chamber."

"May I go up to her?"

"Of course, my lord," the servant replied, lowering his eyes.

Eamon thanked him and made his way upstairs. Light flecked the corridor and he knew that it emanated from the fire in Alessia's room. He followed it, the way so familiar to him that he barely thought about it. His shadow grew behind him as he approached the door. It stood a little ajar.

He knocked.

There was no answer. Carefully, he peered inside.

Alessia was sitting at her dressing table, her hair undone all along her back. A brush lay still in her hand and her eyes gazed far away.

He walked to her and gently touched her hair. Seeing black in the mirror she turned, terror on her face.

"My lord," she began, shaking.

"Alessia!"

Her eyes widened in relief. "Eamon!" she whispered, hurling her arms about his neck. "It's you!"

"Of course," he answered. "Who else should it be?"

"Nobody, nobody!" Alessia cried, and pressed her lips against his until his whole world was her wild hair and wilder kisses. He laughed and caressed her, until at last she stepped back to look at him.

"What happened to you today?" she asked. She seemed unsure whether she should smile or weep. Her hands lightly touched his forehead where the throned had marked him. He did not know if she could see it, but her fingers were a balm to his troubled brow.

"I got some new clothes," Eamon answered, trying to make light of it. "Do you like them?"

"They do suit you… but perhaps I liked the old ones better." Alessia smiled. "Black seems to swallow you a little."

"How should I dress to please you, my lady?" Eamon asked.

She laughed and laid her hands upon his shoulders. The black cloak felt stifling on him and seemed, as he held her, to dwarf them both.

"The colour and dress matter little to me," she told him, "while it is you who wears them."

Overwhelmed, he kissed her gentle lips, losing himself in her warmth – a warmth that penetrated the cold recesses of his soul. It was all that mattered then.

He stayed with her that night. The grey dawn stole upon them all too swiftly. In that half-light he held her close and wished that he could lie there with her forever; that her lithe limbs, soft laugh, and deep heart might be his whole world.

But he knew it could not be. His discarded black haunted his sight.

"Do Hands have to go to parade?" Alessia murmured.

He shook his head and buried his face in her neck. "No," he answered, "not now, not today, not ever."

"You're lying!"

"You're worth it."

She fell silent and then looked at him seriously. Her hands touched his back; her fingers explored his scars. He did not mind.

"I have never asked you…" she said at last. "When were you flogged?"

"On the ship."

"What did you do?"

"Nothing."

She was silent. He watched her thought in her eyes until she met his gaze again. "If you didn't do anything…"

"There was a miscarriage of duty; the three cadets were under my command. So I claimed the fault as mine, and took their punishment." He remembered the bite of the lash, the rip when the knots caught his flesh, the cadets' terrified faces. "They were just boys."

"Mathaiah," Alessia guessed with her usual, deadly accuracy. "He's important to you, isn't he?"

Sorrow filled him. "I tried to tell him," he told her. "About the danger to the supplies, and the cull that's to happen here. He could have got a message out but he… he wouldn't listen to me." He fell silent as the enormity of the statement hit him. They had each saved the other's life. Now there was no measure of trust between them.

Alessia kissed his cheek. "I'm sorry."

"So am I."

They rose together and Eamon delighted in helping her to dress. He tenderly brushed her fine hair and offered her his hand. He did not don his cloak, but rather gathered it over his arm. They went downstairs together. As Alessia held his arm, he felt the happiest man in the world.

They had scarcely reached the last step when a familiar, but unexpected, voice reached them.

"Ah! The love birds. Good morning, Lord Goodman; Lady Turnholt."

Alessia went quite still at his side. Ladomer appeared at the foot of the stair. Lillabeth followed him; she had obviously let him in.

"I'm sorry, my lady," she began.

"It's all right, Lilly," Alessia answered. Was her voice shaking? Why?

"What are you doing here, Ladomer?" Eamon asked.

"My apologies, Lord Goodman," Ladomer answered, bowing. "Lord Cathair sent me to find you. There's work to be done."

It sounded ominous. "What kind of work?"

"There's a supply convoy to upset. You've been chosen to lead the endeavour."

Eamon's heart sank. It would be one of Hughan's; one he had learned about from Giles. Why was he being sent to destroy it?

They were testing him. They had to be.

"Cathair is dispatching a team tonight. You'd best make your farewells," Ladomer added, seeing Alessia's face. Eamon looked to her, standing stiff beside him as though struck dumb.

"Eamon," she whispered, fearfully and urgently.

He laid a finger to her lips and hushed her. "I'll be all right. I'll come back," promised, and kissed her. She clung to his hand, and as he pulled away he felt her fingers trembling. "Alessia?"

What she would have answered he never knew, for Ladomer laughed. "Don't worry, Lord Goodman!" he put in cheerfully. "I'll keep an eye on her for you!"

"Not too close of an eye, if you please," Eamon replied firmly. He looked back to her. "What is it?" he whispered.

She held his gaze and almost imperceptibly shook her head. Her fingers pressed his hard.

"I love you," she breathed.

Eamon touched her face one last time, seeing emotion written there that he did not understand. "I'll come back to you," he told her.

"Come on, Lord Goodman!" Ladomer called, chivvying him towards the door. "Lord Cathair is waiting. I'd put on your cloak," he added. "It's cold out there!"

"Thank you, Mr Kentigern," Eamon answered. He threw the cloak over his shoulders and fastened it. Before he knew it he was beyond the door and in the chilly grip of the February morning. He glanced back over his shoulder.

Alessia stood, pale and beautiful, in the doorway. Lillabeth was at her side and, as he stepped from the Turnholt gates, he saw Alessia reaching out to take Lillabeth's hand.

Ladomer guided him to the Hands' Hall, chatting incessantly about the amount of work there was to be done. He did not ask about Eamon's ceremony – in fact, he made no comment on the promotion at all. This Eamon found somewhat odd but he did not comment. Perhaps Ladomer was jealous.

The hall had a large meeting room, protected by red stones and marked with the same writing which Eamon noticed more and more wherever he went. There was a table inside and dozens of chairs, all empty. Cathair and Ashway stood by the table, speaking quietly together; a couple of maps were unfurled before them. There were several others in the room, Waite among them, as well as a couple of other Hands who served in the West Quarter. Although he had seen them a few times and drunk with them the previous night, Eamon did not know their names. They looked young men and were most likely recently promoted, as he was.

The other man present in the room was a welcome sight. As he saw Eamon he grinned broadly.

"Lord Goodman," he said, coming across and bowing. "Congratulations on your appointment!"

"And you on yours," Eamon replied, noting an extra flame at the man's collar, "Captain Anderas!"

"Yes, the weather and the wayfarers served me well in that," Anderas told him. It was Gauntlet practice to cross-post captaincies, promoting men from other areas so as to avoid favouritism; but the East Quarter had been in need of a captain and Eamon imagined that Draybant Anderas had been the best of the men that the quarter had to offer.

"Good fortune indeed," Eamon told him warmly as they clasped hands.

"Gentlemen, your attention." Cathair seemed in no mood for his accustomed pleasantries. He summoned them sharply to the map. "Business is of an urgent nature today. This shows the area near Stonemead, by the eastern mountains. Stonemead is here and this is the length of the East Road, picking up from the pass here and running to the River here." He traced the directions. The road had been the main route over the Algorras to the Easter cities long years before. It was broad, in places still well maintained. Old women told stories of the days when the Easters came along the road from Istanaria, the great eastern capital, bearing fine goods.

"The Serpent has a convoy of supplies coming down the road from the Easters. How they made it across the mountains so early in the year we don't know – we shall have to ask anyone who survives. The convoy is travelling the road with a view to joining the main forces when it can." Cathair shook his head, muttering something to the effect of wishing a gory death on each one of them down to the hundredth generation, should it be reached. He was in a foul mood. "Bloody snakes took the fortress at Greypass just before the winter set in, and with Easters pouring over the border there we weren't able to take it back. Logistical nightmare," he offered with a faint smile. "Otherwise we would have nipped this little expedition in the bud.

"But, gentlemen, that's where you come in. Local Gauntlet units have been pinned down and reduced by skirmishes and a harsh winter. They are thus incapable of taking on this task alone. Dunthruik blood is needed to complete this mission, encourage those units and show that we have not ceded the area to the Serpent." The Hand's voice was bitter.

"You want us to take the convoy, my lord?" Eamon guessed. It seemed logical. He looked at the map. Differing levels of terrain were indicated in sweeping contours. It was hilly and wooded to one side and flat on the other. He realized that the map was Overbrook's.

"The convoy is of a reasonable size, likely escorted by Easter archers." Cathair pulled a face as he mentioned them, uttered horrific expletives directed towards the archers' mothers, then regained himself. "We're sending a reasonable force to deal with it. The men will be East Quarter ensigns and officers, a group of the city's knights, and a joint group of East and West Quarter Hands. It is a force over which you, Lord Goodman, will have charge."

Eamon stared. Shouldn't an East Quarter Hand have charge? Ashway scowled as the pronouncement was made. It unnerved him. Eamon imagined that as Cathair was the Hand over the West Quarter – the most important and demonstrably most prestigious of the four parts of the city – he likely outranked Lord Ashway. Whatever Ashway's own view on how the mission ought to be ordered, Cathair was in command. It renewed Eamon's fear of the Hand that bore the raven.

"Thank you, Lord Cathair," he managed.

"Road block to force the convoy to stop," Anderas murmured, thinking aloud. He ran a hand through his hair as he pondered the best place. "About here. Pinewood village. Probably deserted these days. The convoy will have no choice but to clear it, and, unable to go round it, they'll be encumbered with what they're carrying and by the ditches."

"Then we ambush them," Eamon continued. He had always enjoyed tactics in his Gauntlet training, and there was something soothing about pointing at a map and making plans. "We put part of the force behind these hills, and the rest in this hollow here – just behind your village, captain. We draw and hold off the escort," he added, gesturing in an arch over the curved lines, "then come at them taking the front, rear, and flank of the column."

"We kill the guards and any who give us trouble, but keep the drivers to bring home whatever portion of the bounty needs to come to the city; the rest we leave with the regional units," Anderas finished, and smiled broadly. "A fine plan, Lord Goodman!"

"Thank you, Captain Anderas."

Cathair had watched them both with interest. He smiled. "I seem to have chosen capable hands for the matter, gentlemen," he said. "You'll be a large group of men, one hundred or so, including logistical support. I will send a few surgeons with you, too. The movers will take you on to your meeting point with the local units, whence you shall proceed to Pinewood. Clearly bring back some of the wagons. Dependent upon your losses and situation, leave some ensigns and a couple of officers there to bolster the local units. The rest of you must return to the city to maintain quarter capacity. There won't be any movers on the way back."

The room echoed in assent to Cathair's commands.

"Very good, gentlemen," Cathair concluded. "Logistics for you will soon be in place. You leave at midday."

They were near one hundred and fifty men that marched through the streets of Dunthruik that afternoon, each accoutred with the tools of their trade. Hands and Gauntlet ensigns, militia and knights, all gathered with a common cause. Morale was high.

Eamon rode at their head. He neither was nor ever hoped to be a skilled rider, but trotting the beast down the Coll and being marvelled at by all was not beyond his ability. Indeed he enjoyed it.

Captain Anderas rode near him, his steed a rich gift from Lord Ashway on his promotion. The captain was content to speak either to the animal or to Eamon, as the moment took him. He laughed much, which cheered Eamon immensely.

Lord Dehelt, the Lord of the North Quarter, rode with them. He was chief of the Master's movers. A small group of Hands was with him. He spoke very little.

Though he scoured the streets for her as he rode out, Eamon did not see Alessia.

When the procession passed the Brand and the West Quarter College, he was touched to see many of the cadets crowded on the steps. The Third Banners cheered him.

But he did not see Mathaiah, and that he rued. He had somehow hoped that one more exchanged glance would soothe all the ill will which ran between them. The Blind Gate loomed before him, its stony height ornately fashioned with the eagles of Dunthruik.

Suddenly he was through the gates. Open fields, farms, groves, and the River lay before him. The land was beautiful but his thoughts were not on it; he turned in his saddle to look back at the city gates.

"It will be nice to get out for a while, won't it, Lord Goodman?" Anderas commented.

"Yes," Eamon answered uncertainly.

Anderas laughed. "I don't think I've been out on proper active service since I became a first lieutenant."

"When was that?"

The captain pulled a face. "Too long ago, my lord, to be mentioned in civilized company!"

Eamon laughed with him, but he felt faint. He had come to Dunthruik, months ago, with a heavy heart. Now, he was loath to leave it.

CHAPTER XXII

They were a large group and the movers strained to perform their task. They could not move men more than a certain distance. Even the Hands, too, had their limits.

They were moved in groups of thirty and deposited about twenty miles from Pinewood. Eamon commanded that pickets be set around the area. He then watched in fascination as the second, third, and fourth group of men came. One moment there was nothing but the empty field, and the next it was filled with knights and infantry from Dunthruik. The other Hands from the East and West Quarters came on horseback in the last group, riding with enviable elegance.

Not long after they arrived, the pickets reported the approach of the local units who were to join them. Eamon watched as groups of ensigns and officers came from the north, uniforms ragged and breath clearly visible in the cold air.

"There aren't many," Lord Dehelt murmured. He and the movers had orders to wait with them until the local units arrived. Watching the slither of red coming towards them, the Lord of the North Quarter shook his head. "Not many at all."

Eamon tried to tally the arriving men; there seemed to be about seventy of them. "Every man who can be added to our number will be of help to us, my lord."

"That is true," Dehelt nodded. He seemed much younger than the other Quarter Hands. "Though your task may be easy, Lord Goodman," he added, "the force that you command might not be."

Eamon glanced at the Hands, knights, and Gauntlet, each from different quarters and regions. "They will recognize my command," he said, more confidently than he felt.

"You are young, Lord Goodman," Dehelt answered. "You must hold your authority. Lord Cathair has, in public and in private, put much stock in you. Do not disappoint him."

A chill ran through him. "I will not, my lord."

"I wish you good work, Lord Goodman. His glory."

"His glory," Eamon replied, bowing.

Dehelt and the movers withdrew, leaving Eamon feeling shaken.

"Lord Goodman." Anderas bowed. Another man was with him – one of the local arrivals.

Eamon took hold of himself. He would not be spooked like a horse. "Captain."

"This is Lieutenant Walden, the ranking officer from the Greypass groups."

"Good to have you with us, Mr Walden," Eamon said, turning to the first lieutenant. "I understand that you and your men know this area well."

"Yes, my lord," Walden answered. His scarred face was grim. "The snakes have been exercising against the Gauntlet here since the end of August, and kept it up even in the depths of the winter. They cut our garrison off from the other units in this area and took the town from us. First Lieutenant Bailiff gave the surrender," he added bitterly. "My men and I were outside at the time, my lord – we made it to Stonemead. The snakes had taken that, too, and the stragglers who had escaped joined our company. We've been in the wild since then. We lost men to the cold, and in skirmishes. It has been a long, hard winter." He looked up with a grizzled glint to his eye. "We will glorify the Master with our vengeance."

The man's fury unnerved him. "I am sure you will," Eamon told him. "I wish to congratulate you on the number of men which you bring to me today. To do so – in spite of the perils of snow and snakes – speaks highly of you. We have food, drink, and cloaks for your men," he added. "Make sure that they all receive them."

The lieutenant bowed. "Thank you, my lord."

"Welcome to the company, Mr Walden," Anderas added, and dismissed him.

The man saluted sharply and, with a limping step, returned to the lines. Eamon wondered if each man was as determined – and grim – as Mr Walden, and how a convoy of Easters would fare against them.

The East Road was broad enough for many to walk abreast and be flanked by the knights. The knights cantered along with their heads held high and their armoured breasts resplendent in the crisp afternoon. To be counted among such men was an ancestral honour, and well they knew it. Only sometimes did they descend to relieve their beasts and walk beside them, carrying their saddles in their hands. Most of the militia, and not a few of the Gauntlet, reviled the knights for their wealth, privilege, and arrogance. But even the knights were subject to the Hands. The Master's darkly clad servants interspersed the lines, flecks of black among lines of red and steel.

More than once Eamon found himself gazing back over the column that followed him, marvelling that he should be among those in black. To have such a tide roll in his wake brought a swell of pride into his heart. That pride urged him to forget how untried he was in his new office.

The road led towards mountains that formed the eastern borders of the River Realm; a great ditch sank at either side of its potted breadth. In the distance, Eamon saw the peaks of the Algorras capped with snow that would soon melt and join the tributaries that ran to the River. He found himself imagining the pinnacled cities of the Easters and the Land of the Seven Sons. The mountains had certainly kept the Easters out of the Master's grip, just as the desert in the south had made passage to those regions impossible. Only the merchant states had given pledges to the Master. Most had sworn allegiance, albeit begrudging, many years ago, and all such states vied to be first among the Master's allies. Few of the merchants had ever dared to openly resist Dunthruik, and those who had were well monitored by the Master's servants. Were it not for the wayfarers' impending action, the Master would likely have sent the Gauntlet north and west in force that spring, to fully quell trouble among his allies.

Being a Hand did not assure Eamon a place in Dunthruik. What would happen if he were sent to the borders to fight the merchants? What would happen if he were sent against the King's men?

And if Hughan did succeed in bringing an army against Dunthruik, and the Master fell in torrents of ash and smoke… what would become of him, the man who had betrayed the King? Perhaps, if he had truly been the First Knight, something might have been left to him. He might have been able to stand with honour at Hughan's side. But he could not hope in that. Had he not renounced that office when he had permitted them to cinch black robes about him? The Master had spoken rightly: his blood had been claimed long ago, and was bound in ways that he could not escape.

"Lord Goodman, are you well?"

Anderas's voice broke his thought. The captain rode beside him and looked at him with concern. For the briefest of moments, Eamon thought of Mathaiah.

He gripped his horse's reins more tightly and offered the captain a smile. "A little pensive," he answered.

"Something that befalls the best of us," Anderas agreed sagely, then laughed. "Forgive me if I speak too informally, Lord Goodman."

"It is no trouble, captain."

"I'm afraid that I still think of you as a Gauntlet man," Anderas explained. "The black has yet to blot out the red. I shall henceforth better my tone." He tried to force a sombre look, failed, and laughed again.

"I am still growing accustomed to the black myself," Eamon replied, touched. It seemed unfair to him that he should outrank Captain Anderas. Surely it was clear who was the worthier?

"How are you faring with it?" Anderas asked. "The black, I mean?"

"The cloak's a bit scratchy round the neck," Eamon answered confidentially, "but they have so far let me wear a comfortable shirt underneath."

"So I have been saved from a terrible fate!" Gauntlet officers that were promoted to draybant or beyond were never then made Hands, whatever their skills or triumphs; they were kept for the Gauntlet. "Besides," Anderas added, "I'm told that red suits me."

"It does," Eamon replied, and he meant it. Anderas was everything that red should have been.

"That must be why they sent me along on this expedition," Anderas mused.

"Oh?" He understood the logic in first lieutenants or draybants being sent on such a mission, but not a Dunthruik quarter captain.

Anderas looked up with a wry smile. "Lord Ashway wanted a high-ranking East Quarter officer to go with his men. We haven't appointed a new draybant yet," Anderas added, "so it was decided that rather than send First Lieutenant Greenwood, I should go."

"Lord Ashway did not approve of Lord Cathair entrusting this mission to me."

"They have their disagreements on such matters, I understand," Anderas told him. "On this occasion, their disagreement has had an agreeable outcome for me. I am sure that Lord Cathair's trust in you is well placed – but I haven't been out of the city for a while, so when Lord Ashway told me that I was to accompany this mission I did not question his command. Though I did not say as much to him," he added with a grin, "I am very pleased to be riding in such illustrious company."

"I hope that you will not find yourself disappointed, captain."

"By you, my lord?" Anderas shook his head. "You do not seem the kind of man who disappoints – except, perhaps, Lord Ashway."

Eamon smiled.

They followed the road all day. The terrain varied between hills and woods and, especially north of the road, relatively flat expanses. It was much the same story to the south, though as they drew farther east the woods filled with thick pines that led back to the embrace of the distant mountains. Clouds gathered over them like dense eyries.

They passed by several small villages and some farmland. Often people stopped to watch them and crowded onto the road to catch a glimpse of the Hands, who rose like spectres from the stony road.

But the road also bore unpleasant tidings. More often than Eamon would have expected, corpses lay abandoned at its edge. Sometimes they passed the remains of overturned carts with broken axles, their bodies shattered, their cargoes emptied and their drivers left for carrion fowl. More than once they passed gatherings of hastily dug shallow graves, bearing the remains of red uniforms fastened down with heavy stones. Sometimes there were no graves; instead a copse of trees was adorned with hanging bodies that twisted and turned on their nooses in the wind. These Eamon ordered to be cut down. The whole road groaned with the detritus of battles between the Gauntlet and the wayfarers. It was clear that the Gauntlet, cut off by the winter and hemmed in by their enemies, had often fared the worse.

They reached Pinewood as night drew in. The clouds over the mountains cleared, leaving a dark sky and a cold wind. The wind swept down from the bitterest reaches of the north, the sky alight with stars as bright as the fiery palms had been at the majesty.

Eamon called for camp to be made. The day had been long, and strength would be needed the next day to begin work on the roadblock. The village was deserted, as Anderas had guessed, and the men settled themselves into the hollow behind it, risking small fires. Eamon allowed it, knowing that they were sheltered by both hollow and ruined buildings. He posted a far-reaching net of sentries. Most of the men were in good spirits – their wayfarer foes would be little more than peasants with oxen and would be easily crushed. They joked while partaking lightly of the provisions that they had with them.

As night grew deeper Eamon climbed the hollow to the village and went to walk among the ruined buildings. Stones and timbers lay everywhere, driven down by the winter's crushing malice. Halting near the road, he turned his gaze down its moonlit glint. The ditches on either side of it were muddy, filled with rainwater and melted snow. Both would present problems the following day, especially if ice formed during the night. From what he had glimpsed in the gathering dark it seemed that the plan he and Anderas had proposed to Lord Cathair was viable. They would have the whole of the next day to block the road and, if Giles had been correct, the convoy should pass the day after. It seemed both interminably far and terribly close. He wondered where the convoy was that night, and whether wayfarers' eyes gazed back at him across the distant dark.

Anderas approached. He carried a tin mug in each gloved hand. They steamed in the cold air.

He offered one to Eamon. "Something to warm you up a little, my lord."

"Did Lord Ashway send me with the East Quarter captain or a butler?" Eamon answered, gratefully accepting. He pressed his hands hard about the mug, waiting for the warmth to reach through his gloves and spread into his hands.

"Do not be fooled, my lord, by my fine jacket," the captain told him, starlight shadowing his breath. "From my earliest ensign days, I knew that I was destined for that rare form of butlery which composes a Gauntlet captaincy. It is a privilege, my lord," he added.

Perhaps it should not be; Eamon doubted that he was worthy of the man's service. "You seem to forget," he told him gently, "that you are a captain, captain. You need not address me as though you were a draybant, or as though I were a Quarter Hand – you are far more than the one, and I am far less than the other."

Anderas laughed. "How right you are! My apologies, Lord Goodman."

"You also do yourself wrong to equate your captaincy with butlery... Is butlery even a word?"

Anderas grinned. "What do you say, Lord Goodman?"

Eamon was suddenly, painfully, reminded of Overbrook. "I think that you invented it."

Anderas inclined his head a little. "Then, Lord Goodman, invented it is; but I wish to claim full responsibility for its invention when they next compile one of those lexical nonsenses."

Eamon looked at him in surprise. "You would call it invented, simply because I said it was?"

"You may not be a Quarter Hand, Lord Goodman, but you are a Hand," Anderas answered more seriously. "As such you will find that there are few who will gainsay you, even in jest."

Eamon stared speechlessly. The captain took a sip of his drink, and gave a short gasp as he found it too hot.

"I know that I have just seen it being taken from the fire," he mused, "but somehow I am, as always, surprised by how hot it is."

Eamon laughed. "Be comforted by this, captain: I shall learn from your misfortune." He blew at his before trying it.

They fell silent and looked, by one accord, back to the road. Eamon sighed.

"We did this, didn't we?"

"'This', Lord Goodman?"

"The war; the skirmishes; the Gauntlet, and so us." Eamon looked at the village's broken walls, wondering what had happened to its people. Of those who had escaped he did not know. Those who had stayed, or had allied themselves either to the Gauntlet or the wayfarers, would have become more bodies, hanging on ropes or rotting on the brittle earth. "We did this."

"It may not appear so in Dunthruik," Anderas told him, "but we have an enemy with whom, openly or not, we are at war."

There was little more to say. They stood silently, sipping their drinks, in the starlight. After a long time, Eamon returned his mug to Anderas with thanks, and went to join the other Hands.

The morning dawned clear. Chill shadows lay across the men.

Eamon was among the first to rise, frozen and unrested.

It took them the best part of the day to erect the blockade. Using the tools they had brought and some others they found in the ruined village, they felled trees across the road and poured rubble from the desecrated village into the gaps. The men worked hard and the Hands oversaw them, occasionally helping to lift trunks of wood or masses of stone. The knights did little but ride their horses about the plain.

"Their lordlinesses can't bear to dirty their delicate white hands," one of the other Hands, Febian, commented as they worked. He said it just loudly enough that the nearest of the knights heard it. The knight returned with a look that could have curdled milk. Eamon almost laughed, but thought it better to advise Febian – also a West Quarter Hand – to mind his tongue instead.

The day ended. They returned to the hollow and Eamon again posted sentries, concentrating many of them eastward along the road to watch for the convoy. He imagined that they would hear it long before it appeared; nonetheless, he ordered the fires to be reduced that night. Bar a couple of minor injuries – cuts, scrapes, or falls – obtained during the day's work, there had been no real problems. It filled him with deep satisfaction as he watched the camp settling down to wait.

As the stars turned in the sky he strolled to the road. Anderas went with him.

"How are the men?" Eamon asked.

The captain stood burning himself on another warm drink. "They're making the usual jokes, the usual threats of vengeance and usual promises to kill the Serpent with their own hands. The men from Greypass and Stonemead are taking things a little more seriously, but that is hardly surprising."

He paused, drinking. Eamon wondered how many battles the captain had seen. The next day's operation was to be simple. Its ease was one of the reasons the mission had been granted him: it was a chance to show that he merited his promotion, and Cathair's faith in him, without expending too much effort.

What if he should fail the test?

Anderas glanced at him, interrupting his worried thought. "So much for the men. How is the commander?"

"Nervous," Eamon confided. He liked Anderas; something about the man's manner inspired his trust. That, he realized, was because Anderas reminded him strongly of someone else.

He tried to stop himself thinking of the resemblance, but the thought took root. Captain Anderas reminded him of Hughan.

"I would be nervous if you weren't," Anderas told him. "Only the knights aren't nervous. They have no real idea what they're doing. As far as they're concerned they ride their horses, prance about a bit, hack at something here and there, and then it's back in time for drinks and campfire heroics. I suppose we're not so different," he mused. "It's just that we know that we don't know what we're doing. And we're better at telling the campfire stories."

"Was that supposed to make me feel better?" Eamon chortled.

"My stressing of our common humanity, feelings and failings in the face of uncertainty, you mean?"

"Yes."

"No. But, in fairness, you didn't let me get to the really important part."

"No?"

"No. The point I really wanted to stress was the necessity of courage in the face of uncertainty, and the giving of steadfast and glorious service to the Master." Anderas smiled. "Does that help?"

"You incorrigible man!" Eamon laughed. "Good night!"

"Good night, Lord Goodman."

Eamon spent an uncomfortable half an hour checking on the watchmen, examining horses' tethers and pacing the hollow, his thought blacker than his cloak. How could he possibly think to strike against Hughan the next day? He had never meant to do it – and yet the blockade was built.

What will you do, Eben's son? Dismantle it during the night? You cannot. You will not. You are mine.

At last he lay down to sleep, but rest was a long time in coming to him. He huddled in his cloak, wishing that it were blue and wishing that he would find Alessia by him when he woke.

But it was not, and she was far away.

Just before the dawn, a sentry returned hurriedly to the camp. His breath steamed in the early light. He came to a breathless halt before Eamon, who was discussing the last details of the attack with the other Hands, and dropped into a bow.

"My lords!" His face was flushed with running and excitement. "The convoy has been sighted – a few miles away."

"Shall we begin deployment, Lord Goodman?"

Eamon swallowed. Why should such men take orders from him? Some of them had probably been made Hands before he had joined the Gauntlet! But he could not falter.

"Begin deployment."

The Hands inclined their heads very slightly to him and went to their horses. Their task that day was simple: to draw off whatever escort the convoy might have. The knights would aid them by keeping any of the escort from returning. Taking the wagons fell to the Gauntlet and militia.

The hollow became a nest of activity as the men began checking their weapons and moving into position. Eamon gave the Hands and knights their final orders, and watched Anderas doing the same for the Gauntlet. Then, accompanied by the young officer who would be his aide during what followed, he took his place on the other side of the road. From there he would oversee the operation and be hidden in the eaves of the woods.

As he settled into position Eamon saw the full blockade. It was heavy with dew in the dun light, a looming mass that spanned the whole road. He reasoned that once the convoy arrived it would not take long. Each man was well versed in the part he would play in the attack; they had been through such details at length the night before. But fear pummelled the pit of his stomach. If this was how he felt, how were the men faring?

The men weren't double-sworn.

Suddenly he saw shadows against the grey dawn, grinding slowly forward, appearing and disappearing behind the bends of the road. What seemed hours later the shadows became more distinct and he saw the first riders cast darkly against the early morning light. The convoy's escort. They seemed tall in the sun's low rays; the horses bore the sleek, powerful look of the best eastern breeds.

Eamon had seen Easters closely only once before, at the Hidden Hall. Staring at the figures on the road, he was suddenly thrown back to the stories of his childhood, to tales of eastern travellers, bold men who had ventured to the southern wastes and deserts, encountering strange foes and stranger friends.

In the stories they had been men of adventure, tall and dark-haired. The men riding towards him did nothing to dispel his long-held impressions. They wore fine clothes woven in greens, browns, and oranges, and Eamon chanced that he could see a blazing sun marked out on their breasts. It was like the emblem he had seen both at the Hidden Hall and at Ashford Ridge.

Behind the riders came the first wagons. They moved two abreast at a steady speed, drawn by horses and oxen. The farther the first wagons advanced the more he could see coming up behind them, until the whole road became a snake of beasts, vehicles, riders, and men. The column was enormous. It was much longer than he had imagined it to be. He pushed down the first spark of worry.

The first Easter riders caught sight of the blockade. Eamon heard them calling to each other, saw them gesturing to it. They might think it to be a natural block at first but they would soon discover their error. He could see the front of the convoy clearly now; the men were probably fathers and sons. At the riders' commands, some of them began detaching animals from their wagons so as to draw their vehicles closer together.

Suddenly the sound of drumming hooves marred the morning. The Easter riders started; the Hands were coming out of the south.

They were swift as eagles, cloaks beating behind them like stormy wings as they arched at the convoy with a breathtaking speed.

There was frantic movement among the wagons. One of the Easters fell; a driver near him tumbled to the ground amid frightened cries. The throned's cavalry rode undeterred. Drawing close they suddenly struck away. A group of mounted Easters wheeled to pursue. Black and green danced on the plain; the Easters called in their strange tongue as they harassed their harriers. They could not know that they would soon be attacked by the hidden knights.

Eamon watched the Hands knotting among the Easters before drawing them still farther from the alarmed convoy with playful mockery. Shouts rose in the convoy and drivers tried to calm nervous, bucking animals. The wagons drew even nearer together. Eamon knew that a second charge would follow, to draw away the remaining riders. Even as he thought it the second group appeared. The remaining Easter riders made to follow them.

As the cavalry pulled away Eamon glanced back to the road, watching for the movement that would betray the Gauntlet rising from the hollow. The convoy ground to a noisy halt in front of the blockade. Eamon winced. The men standing farthest forward would be the first to die when the trap was sprung.

Shouldn't he call it all off? Letting the column pass would aid Hughan... But it was too late for that.

There was a flash of red in the hollow and the Gauntlet appeared like bloody spectres, brandishing their weapons with exultant ferocity; a great cry accompanied them. Eamon waited for the convoy to collapse into a mass of panicked screaming; for men to begin falling as the Gauntlet surged onto the road like an angry tide.

The convoy did not panic.

The Gauntlet pressed on. Eamon gaped at the steadiness of the column. He knew that two-thirds of his company were now moving to the flanks and encircling the rear of the convoy. Killing the drivers would be easy. The battle was a foregone conclusion, the convoy clearly outnumbered and surprised. Why was nobody panicking?

Something was wrong.

There was a flash of movement near the front of the convoy. Suddenly the air became thick and the Gauntlet fell beneath a hail of arrows. The projectiles cut through the ranks, shredding them as though with a single, insoluble blow.

Eamon gasped. Where his men had reached the convoy spears appeared, no less deadly than the arrows. Bodies, living and dead, tumbled down into the muddy ditch, taking some of the advancing men with them.

Bolts, arrows, spears… It couldn't be! The horsemen were the only armed men and the Hands had drawn them far away…

Suddenly the answer hit him.

Not all the wagons had carried logistical support. His stomach churned with the sickening certainty of it. Some of them were carriages of war, bearing armed men. They had to be. It was these men – unknown to and unprepared for by him – who now swatted the Gauntlet like flies.

Eamon blanched and quivered. He hadn't known. Giles hadn't known. Scores of men were falling lifeless on the roadside.

It was his fault.

He could only watch. Soldiers scurried for cover and squeezed into the narrow gaps between the wagons, hoping to evade flying and thrusting death, but there was no shelter for them there. Some of the militia tried to exchange arrows with their foes, but to no avail. Eamon stared. How many war wagons were there? How many archers, how many polemen? He had no way of knowing. His men were being shredded – and there was nothing he could do.

What about Anderas?

He looked wildly towards the rear of the column – but he could not see it any more than he could see the Hands or knights. Like the front, the rear would have been littered with unexpected defenders and his men, expecting peasants and two dozen archers, did not carry enough armour or padding beneath their red jackets to protect them from the convoy's ire.

The Gauntlet went on. Oxen lowed, horses screamed and started, drivers fell; Eamon imagined the Gaunlet's fight among the narrowed wagons, gored to death by scrabbling beasts. The dead that day would be his.

Suddenly there was colour on the plain. The Easter riders were returning. Eamon gagged. Where were the Hands, the knights? The Gauntlet could not fight the archers, the wagons, *and* the Easters!

The Easters rode unharried at the beleaguered Gauntlet.

Eamon assessed the fray. With enemies hunting them within the convoy and riders encircling them without, his men were bound to run. He had to legitimize it.

"Sound the retreat," he commanded.

The shrill notes of the trumpet burst across the field and there seemed a moment in which everything stopped to hear it. Then everything resumed its grisly pace. The Gauntlet began threading and then pouring out from among the wagons, some dragging injured comrades. A maelstrom of arrows followed them. The Easters spurred their steeds into a gallop after them, yelling with victory.

It was a rout. The men dashing for the cover of the woodland were shot; the horsemen rode down some, crushing them beneath iron-shod hooves. Some reached the treeline and pelted down the densely wooded slopes to the emergency rallying point.

Eamon watched the men breaking, watched their bodies mangled by gore-spattered steeds. Gall sat heavily in his stomach and throat.

"My lord?" questioned his aide.

Eamon could not answer. Dozens of men from one of the flank detachments spewed across the plain in a desperate, tumbling run for the woods. He watched as a group of them fell, littered with arrows – only a couple of men struggled on towards the treeline. One of them was Anderas, bravely dragging a wounded man.

Another volley of arrows was loosed. One struck through the throat of the wounded man, turning him into a dead weight. There was a rain of blood and then Anderas went down.

That was when Eamon found himself racing towards the battle. The alarmed cries of his aide grew faint behind him and the noises of screaming men, ground in the muddy, bloodied earth, were all about his ears. He burst out of the tangled trees.

He expected a volley to take him before he reached the captain; with every pace he ran he anticipated the thudding jolt. Had he had any sense he would have cast aside his cloak – on such a field, death followed the colour of the throned's closest. So be it! He welcomed death – it would release him from all his oaths. The desperate thought drove him as he ran.

He skidded in the mud by Anderas's side. The captain was trapped under the body of his comrade; his face was wracked with pain as he tried to struggle free. An arrow was deep in his leg. He suddenly froze with shock.

"Lord Goodman! Are you mad!"

Eamon didn't stop to think or answer. With a cry of rage, he dug his hands under the body and hurled it aside. This bloody field was of his making – he would not see Anderas pay its price.

He hauled Anderas to his feet. He blindly looped his arm under the man's shoulders and they began to beat a retreat towards the trees, just two among dozens of soldiers still trying to escape the convoy's furious rebuttal. Eamon's world shrank to the jerking treeline. Anderas gasped for breath as blood seeped from his thigh. It might be a fatal wound and running would not help it – but they had to run.

Suddenly the earth shook and the beat of hooves drummed in his skull. The Easters bore down on them, their strange voices high in the air. His time had come. He would not be ridden down!

It was an odd moment for pride. His lungs ached. He stopped. The captain understood. Together, they turned to face their pursuers.

Two riders careered towards them, bows in hand and arrows at the string. There was nothing to say. Eamon's cloak lay grim over his shoulders. He wished that he could tear it off. Around them dozens of men escaped into the treeline. All the available riders made for his black cloak. His death would at least save some men.

Hand and captain stood and shook and gasped together, but the blow did not come. There were at least four riders approaching them at an incredible speed, but no hiss of arrows struck the air.

Suddenly one of the Easters was before them. He rode a grey horse and a dark green sun burned on his breast. His face was narrow, his skin tanned, his hair dark. His bow was in hand but, looking down, his expression changed. He lowered his weapon.

Eamon met his enemy's gaze squarely. There was no doubting that he stood in the Easter's power, but he was not afraid. The tall man tugged his reins into his hands.

"Harry us no further, Hand." The words were harsh, strangely mixed with the eastern accent. Eamon did not answer.

The Easter turned his horse and galloped back to the injured convoy. The other riders followed him. None of them looked back. The last of the Gauntlet reached the treeline.

Eamon felt terrible relief and shame. He did not know what had moved the Easter to spare them, but it did not matter; his heart beat wretchedly. He laid one hand over it to ease the pain.

"By the throne!" Anderas rasped, half-laughing, gasping with pain and fear unworked. "You have a certain style, Lord Goodman – a very particular style – and not a little luck."

Eamon helped Anderas hobble back to the treeline. The calls of the dying and jeers of the victorious washed over him. They staggered under the cover of the eaves. The battle of Pinewood was over.

The fallback location was a large glade, thickly wooded on all sides but with a narrow approach from the south by which the horses could be walked to it.

Bloodied men filled the once tranquil space. Eamon looked at them in dismay. A brief count had shown that half were dead.

Another two dozen were missing or unaccounted for. They had lost three of the Hands, one knight, and over seventy ordinary soldiers and Gauntlet officers. Only a score of the sixty men from Greypass had survived; they stared vacantly at the surrounding carnage.

Eamon held a quick meeting with his officers and the remaining Hands. As they gathered tales from the various parts of the deployment they grew grave. The whole convoy had been littered with hidden war wagons. Many men had been lost in the initial volleys and dozens more had been killed while seeking shelter between the vehicles that should have been so easy to capture. The few vehicles that they had managed to take had been lost in the retreat. They did not know how many losses the enemy had taken, but it was reckoned to be a smaller portion of a much larger force.

Only one thing was certain: the Master's men had been defeated.

Eamon ordered their return to Dunthruik; there was nothing to be gained in sending anyone to the local divisions. His order was received with stony silence.

"Look on the bright side," Anderas told him that evening. Eamon had sought the captain out among the wounded treated throughout the afternoon by the surgeons. The arrow had been removed and the wound cleaned, but when Eamon had asked what the man's chances were the surgeons had answered him with pale looks.

"There's a bright side?" Eamon didn't see it. Nine more had died during the day from their injuries and the air was punctuated by moans of the wounded. He shuddered. Benighted with defeat, he would have to lead the survivors back to Dunthruik. The thought of Cathair terrified him.

And the Master? What would be said of him to the Master? It was beyond utterance.

"We were vastly outnumbered, and surprised," Anderas grimaced. "It was not our fault. We'll do well to take back so many survivors."

"Will Lord Ashway see it in that light?"

Anderas laughed grimly. "No! Will Lord Cathair?"

"No."

Anderas laid a trembling hand on Eamon's arm. "They weren't here, Lord Goodman."

"But I was. It should have been easy, Anderas!"

"It isn't always easy, Lord Goodman."

But it should have been. When Eamon lay down to sleep that night, hissing bolts, beating hooves, and dying men haunted him.

The following days' return journey to Dunthruik by the survivors of Pinewood was made in silence. They followed the same road that the convoy had taken. Eamon sent groups of sentries ahead to watch for an Easter rearguard that might yet do them harm. The precaution only added to their slow pace, but revealed that at least part of the convoy had gone south only a short distance from Pinewood; the rest had gone on.

Stops to tend to the wounded were frequent. More men died as they went and Eamon had them laid by the roadside. It was too cold to dig.

The overwhelming sense of shame grew daily. Eamon knew of no way to assuage it – perhaps there was none. At least it unified them. They consoled themselves with the knowledge – or hope – that what had happened had not been their fault. Still they feared their return to the city. Despite the danger posed by the Easters and wayfarers, some of the militia slipped from the ranks, deserting the company during the dark hours.

When the column made camp during those nights Eamon often sought Anderas. His wound was turning ugly, but the surgeons said that amputation would certainly kill him. Anderas bravely denied that anything was wrong. Eamon wondered if there was any hope for the captain at all.

Every moment they were goaded by wheel tracks frozen in the muddy road – their quarry had passed that way before them. It made the road an agent of their shame.

It was the third morning following the battle. The road had run steadily west and a little south, towards the River. Eamon knew that a couple more days would see them to Dunthruik. Anderas's worsening plight was a distraction from the awful welcome that awaited him at the Blind Gate.

Eamon was riding a little way back from the front of the marching lines that morning, trying to encourage the remaining wounded, gathered in carts and buried under all the cloaks that could be spared. They had been moving for perhaps two hours when the lines came to a halt. At first Eamon assumed it signified an unsteady part of the road that would need to be negotiated with care, but the delay persisted. He spurred his horse on to the front of the lines.

They had come to a small hamlet. A couple of Hands and a Gauntlet officer were examining the road.

"What is it, gentlemen?"

"It was here," snarled one of the Hands – Lord Febian. His fingers pointed in a wild, clawing gesture at the ground. There were traces of grain and wagon marks. "The rest of the bloody convoy was here. It off-loaded supplies and went north off the road."

"If it no longer goes before us then we may reduce our vanguard sentries," Eamon answered, trying to keep his voice measured. He was deeply surprised to see that the tracks went north – he had thought that the wayfarers' strength was in the south – but didn't have time to consider the matter. The Hand's tone was feral and men were breaking rank to find out what was happening.

"It stopped here," Febian continued, then shrieked, "and these people helped them!" Angry assent rumbled through the ranks like thunder.

Things threatened to rupture. Eamon glanced anxiously at the village – there were people there. Some had come to look at the soldiers and many now froze in the streets, afraid – rightly so – that any movement on their part might trigger violence. Eamon's men wanted vengeance for what had been done to them. They wanted to take it there. Eamon could not allow it.

He dismounted and stepped close to the Hand. "Don't incite a massacre, Lord Febian," he hissed. "There has been enough blood. There will be no more, do you understand?"

"Yes, Lord Goodman," Febian growled.

"Whose blood has it been?" roared another Hand, jabbing at Eamon with an accusing finger. "Ours! And they shed it. They helped the bastards who killed our men and destroyed our pride. They will go on to strike at the Master. Shall it be said that we saw the Master's enemies and did not strike them? It is our duty!"

Eamon could have killed him where he stood.

"I said no more blood!"

But the Hand's words had grown to a howl; they were joined by the bitter squall of the company's fury. It was too late.

Some of the villagers ran; it triggered an enormous cry as scores of vengeful men broke ranks and poured into the dirty streets. Aghast, Eamon tried desperately to stop them as swords, knives, and daggers flew to their hands. Fingers became talons that carved flesh with the speed of steel.

The incensed mass streamed into the village. The screaming started.

Eamon hurled himself back into the saddle. The square was a mass of moving flesh, some of it already dead, and the soldiers a crimson wave. Men and women tried to flee and were stopped, some beaten to the ground and others dragged away from the square to be tortured.

Eamon yelled and shouted, cried and commanded, but in their rabid frenzy none would hear him. He shook and balked and raged and stared in horror; the violence that he saw was not perpetrated against the King, but against absent soldiers. He wept. It was a glut of madness that he could not stop.

The camp was quiet that night. Eamon sat once more at Anderas's bedside, his bed little more than a stiff bundle of cloaks on the hard ground. He had brought the captain something to drink. Anderas struggled to take a sip, growing weaker by the day. It was too much for Eamon to bear.

There had been rape and murder, hangings, men impaled, and children disembowelled before their parents. Houses had been burned, their contents hurled onto the streets and hacked with manic blows. Blood had been poured into the well along with dozens of small bodies. He did not know how many had escaped, or been left, wounded and alive, to suffer.

"You couldn't have stopped it," Anderas murmured. Eamon shuddered. "Forgive me for saying so, Lord Goodman, but you were a fool to try. They could have turned on you, too."

Eamon could not answer him.

"Perhaps on your tour of duty in the north you never saw similar," Anderas added weakly, "but it is not uncommon – especially when our enemy is as hidden as this Serpent is. Defeat – shame, and the death of brothers in arms – puts a kind of madness into men's blood. But right senses return. Many of these men will not sleep soundly for a long time."

What good was broken sleep? "It will not atone for what they did," Eamon snapped.

"It won't," Anderas agreed. "You should rest, Lord Goodman." His breathing sounded sickly and shallow.

"Yes," Eamon murmured, but he did not move.

They remained silent for a long time. Anderas fell asleep. Eamon saw him shuddering beneath the cloaks as the chill moon rose. The camp was quiet.

Anderas was going to die. The surgeons had informed him that the wound was past their skill. It was rumoured that the Easters used arrows with poisoned tips but the surgeons believed that the wound had turned with infection. Anderas fought it bravely, but was doomed to meet with as much success as the battle in which he had garnered the hurt.

Eamon watched the captain's pale, sweating face, sorrow and

anger grinding hard in his heart. He would not have lost the battle if he had been a wayfarer. He could have saved the village if he had been a King's man. If he had ever been the First Knight he could save Anderas, even now. But the throned's mark was on him. He had never been – and could never become – the man whom Hughan had believed him to be. He saw that now. The battle was lost, the village was slaughtered, and Anderas would die.

He laid his hand on the captain's brow. It was clammy beneath his touch. Would Anderas last the night? Choking back a sob, he brushed his hair aside. Why should Anderas die for what he had not had the courage to be?

He closed his eyes. He pleaded with the blue light, the King's grace, begging it to overlook his oaths and transgressions, imploring it to come and save a man whose life surely deserved saving. Was it not but little to ask?

You are not a Serpent's man. Cease your unseemly pleading. No grace will come to you, son of Eben. You serve me.

The voice worked cruelly in his mind and his hope fell, crushed. No grace would come. Anderas would die.

He tore his hand away and rose. He could not stay there.

They had camped by the roadside again that night, among a small cluster of hills that offered shelter from the wind. The hillside was dotted with campfires; he heard their distinctive crackling. He did not know – and barely cared – where his feet took him. None noted him, a shadow among shadows at the edge of the firelight. He swept on into the hills until the noise of the camp was far behind him. He walked until his feet began to climb and he was scaling the hillside, his lungs burning with effort. He gasped in the cold air.

Suddenly he stopped. The rocky hillside lay all before him. But there was something different about the half-lit shadows. Part of him remembered the feeling of so long ago, when Ma Mendel had first led him to the Hidden Hall. As he gazed hard at the windswept grass he felt a similar sensation.

Scarcely daring to breathe, he walked forward until he stood between two of the stones. He was staring directly into the hillside. He smelled the cool earth. He reached out with one hand, and stepped forward.

He opened his eyes to the inside of a hall. It was rounded and worked with grey stone. Dull paintings, faded with age, marked the walls. Dust lay thick on the floor and burnt-out torches were bracketed to cracked wall-stones. Behind him he saw out onto the moonlit hillside and down to the field of campfires.

The hall was deserted. It gazed out over the stony hillside, an unseeing guardian that watched the road to Dunthruik.

Why had he come in? Perhaps he had hoped that the place would be filled with wayfarers who, seeing his black cloak, would have fallen upon him and killed him before they realized who he was – or wasn't. He remembered the face of the Easter who had spared him and the eyes of those from the desecrated village who, with their screams, had begged him to spare them. He thought of Anderas, pale and shivering under borrowed cloaks while death choked him…

The moon cast a long arc of light over the hall wall. He looked up. His eyes stung – was he weeping?

There was a shape cut into the stone. Blinking hard, he made out the blade of a sword. It was matched by a star whose light, made real by the moon, hallowed both the carved blade and the house whose emblem it was.

With sudden fury Eamon slammed clenched fists against the wall. Clods of dirt fell from it. He let go of his voice. An anguished, enraged howl, which he had held inside himself since the battle, erupted from his lungs, reverberating in his throat. He roared. Sobbing hard, he sank down to his knees in front of the stone. Watched only by the moonlight he called on the name of the King in despair – and no answer came to him.

CHAPTER XXIII

It was still dark when he came to his senses. Tangled dream fragments faded around him: voices, and a light so faint that it had died before he had really seen it.

He struggled to open his swollen eyes, wondering what hour it was. The stars had moved. The trees were shifting in the breeze, their distant branches strangely silent.

He shivered and stretched, glad for the first time of his robe of shadow. His memory returned. There could be no peace for him. There was nothing left to him. He feared both the King and the flame-haired thief of the crown.

He stood slowly. He had to go back; he had to lead his men to the city. He tried telling himself that until he had dispensed of that duty nothing would befall him.

Why was his choice so impossible?

He did not want to leave the hall, but he did not want to stay. How could he face revealing his loss and shame to the whole city? Already he saw the heaving mass of Dunthruik rushing at him in scorn.

But it was nothing compared with how Hughan would receive him.

Grief-stricken, he left.

He retraced his steps to the camp. Spirals of smoke showed faintly against the grey sky. The sounds of men and horses grew louder and he soon found himself passing the grazing beasts. They were curiously calm, oblivious to wars and oaths. One of them – a tall, muddy-coated creature – paced towards him. Eamon rested his hands on the horse's muzzle. It was warm, and some small comfort.

He continued to the part of the camp where the surgeons guarded and treated the wounded. Soldiers were stirring, pale faced and grim. Eamon could hardly bring himself to greet them.

The surgeons were already awake; he wondered if they ever slept. By the surgeons' fires he saw a figure laid out beneath a pall. The sight filled him with leaden dread.

"Lord Goodman," greeted the leading surgeon.

"Lieutenant," Eamon answered. The half a dozen Gauntlet surgeons were the only men who had not partaken in the massacre the day before. "What news?"

"We lost another during the night."

"I'm sorry to hear it," he managed.

"We could cure the majority of these wounds in the city," the man told him. His frustration was evident. "Even Captain Anderas's hurt would have been relatively straightforward."

Eamon's heart plummeted. So he was dead.

"We could have saved so many more, my lord," the lieutenant continued, "had we anticipated the kind, and number, of injuries to be sustained in the attack." The officer blanched. "I'm sorry, my lord. I spoke out of turn. I didn't mean –"

"Peace, lieutenant." Eamon swallowed, struggling to contain his grief. "Your task these past days has been hard, and your work honourable. It does you no ill to speak the truth."

The man looked astonished. "Thank you, my lord," he stammered.

They stood in silence. Eamon summoned his courage. "May I see Captain Anderas?" He owed the captain at least a farewell.

"Over there, my lord." The surgeon gestured to the dwindling fires.

Heavy-hearted, Eamon walked to where he had left the captain the previous night. If he had only had the strength to choose and keep an oath! Then none of this would have happened – none of them would be dead.

"You look terribly lugubrious this morning, Lord Goodman."

Eamon started. Anderas sat propped against a tree trunk, making the most of a dying fire while he waited for his turn to be helped to the wagon.

Eamon stared. Anderas was alive! He looked frail and his cheeks bore a ghastly pallor but he was alive. Eamon felt the impulse to rush and embrace the man, but the weight of black made him awkwardly hold his ground.

"Something the matter, Lord Goodman?" Anderas croaked.

"They told me you were dead," Eamon stammered.

"They told me I was fortunate. What a terribly embarrassing conflict of information!" His laughter was broken by coughing.

Eamon struggled to grasp the enormity of the truth. It was beyond the comprehension of his hope. "But... they said you would die."

"Should it salve your mind, my lord, I am still in grave danger," Anderas answered. "But I might make it back to the city. If I do, they say that they can probably clear the infection."

"Let it be so!" Eamon rejoiced.

"I shall second that. Truthfully, I did not expect to see the light of day again," Anderas confided. "But there seems to be new strength in me since the night began."

Eamon laughed with relief. Neither knowing nor caring where the captain's strength had come from, he beamed from ear to ear. "Would you like some breakfast?"

"Yes," Anderas answered, surprised. He had not willingly eaten for several days. "Yes, I think I would."

They ate a meagre breakfast together as the camp prepared for the final leg of the journey to Dunthruik. They were likely to reach the city before nightfall. Part of him hoped it would be dark when they arrived, so that they could disguise their shame in the shadows. But that morning, sitting with Anderas and marvelling at his second wind of life, Eamon felt a small measure of peace. Their dried bread and mostly stale cheese seemed to be a feast tailored for great lords.

Anderas ate ravenously. Eamon offered him the remains of his own dwindling portion.

"You look pale this morning, Lord Goodman," Anderas commented between mouthfuls.

"I didn't sleep well." His mind suddenly conjured Cathair's grim face. "Pale?" he repeated.

"There's more colour to you than to the Lord Ashway, Lord Goodman," Anderas continued. "You'd have to not sleep for hundreds of years to match him, I fear."

Eamon managed a laugh. "I am just tired," he assured him.

A startled look passed suddenly over the captain's face. Eamon noticed it at once.

"Is everything all right?"

"Yes… yes, Lord Goodman," Anderas stammered, shaking.

"No," Eamon rose sharply to his feet. "I shall call a surgeon."

"No, no, my lord – Lord Goodman," Anderas managed. He caught Eamon's arm. "Really, there is no need." His cheeks coloured with embarrassment.

"If you need a surgeon –"

"I don't. Thank you, Lord Goodman."

Unconvinced, Eamon sat again. "What's the matter?" The man looked as though he had seen a ghost. Perhaps he had.

"I…"

Eamon watched as Anderas wrestled with some unknown thought. Their eyes met. Was Anderas afraid?

"It's nothing, Lord Goodman. I just… remembered a dream. That was all."

Eamon could not pursue the matter further; the lieutenant surgeon approached to advise that the wagon was ready to receive the captain.

It was mid-February when they began the last miles to Dunthruik. The River glistened to the south. Ahead of them, Eamon saw hills sloping to the mouth where Dunthruik nestled, feeding on the River's torrents.

Though heavy hearted, Eamon was proud of those who marched with him that day – they had escaped death, refused to desert, and were determined to reap the crushing reward for their defeat. How could a tarnished man – how could any of them – reclaim their honour? Wherever they went, to whichever colleges, units, or companies they were assigned, they would be known as the men who had failed at Pinewood. They would all pay the price for Eamon's folly.

What would he say to the throned? How could he possibly hope to become Right Hand with Pinewood over him? And Hughan… he could never justify what he had done to the King. He had abandoned his choice. Had the King's grace deserted him, leaving him only the torment of the throned's voice?

He had never felt such uncertainty. He knew only that he was a man without honour. It was that which drove deepest. Whatever he had done, and against whomever he had done it, he had betrayed himself.

He longed for Alessia, for her hand in his, for her understanding gaze and her words of comfort. What if she renounced him, too? How could she associate with him after what he had failed to do? His shame would touch her, too, in every circle of the court. He could not ask that of her – and he was terrified that she would not freely offer to bear it for him.

The shadow of Dunthruik touched the landscape before them. All at once he saw the city towers and their snapping pennons. He had not even passed the gates, and yet already he felt the piercing gaze of the throned upon him.

What a sight they made to the city watchmen: the bedraggled survivors of an unexpected massacre. They had gone out in glory; they would re-enter less than half their number, with a dozen wounded men and missing half a dozen deserted ones. They would return with a tale of defeat to break their names and match their broken bodies. It hovered, vulture-like, over his men. He wished that he could bolster them against the terrible welcome awaiting them, but his voice stuck in his throat.

Slowly they wound their way on to the city. Those who lived near the Blind Gate had seen them approaching, for there was yet light enough to bear witness to their return; those on the road stopped in shock to watch them pass. Eamon rode at the head of the column, his head as high as he dared to raise it. He did not meet the looks of the onlookers, and tried to ignore upturned faces.

The gate grew large before him, a thick edifice of stone graven with the emblems of the Master's city and glory. The gate guards watched from every orifice of the walls, while people gathered along the streets within. All gaped.

Eamon felt every eye upon him as he led the column through the gates, past guards standing uncertain and still. They went in silence; people whispered. He could not allow himself to imagine what they said.

He led his men to the Brand. People stared at every turn – rich and poor, old and young, Gauntlet, merchant, peasant, noble; it made no difference. They all knew who he was and saw that he had failed.

They halted in the Brand and Eamon, wearied by scrutiny, dismounted. He was grateful for the shadow of the college.

"Lord Goodman?"

Ladomer stood on the college steps, papers in hand. He rushed forward. Formality was swept aside.

"Eamon, what happened to you?"

Eamon fought the tremor in his voice. "I must see Lord Cathair."

"He's just received Lord Ashway for a meeting –"

"I must see him at once. Please, see what you can do, Ladomer."

Ladomer stared a moment longer, then hurried away. Eamon watched the end of the column filtering into the courtyard behind him. The cart with invalids clattered over the stones. The lieutenant surgeon leaped down, calling for men for infirmary duty. Eamon hurried to help as they unlatched the sides of the cart and began unloading the surviving injured men. Anderas was the first to descend, his face deathly but tenacious. Eamon gripped his hand as they laid him on a stretcher.

"You're here, captain," he said, willing him to live. "Just a little longer. They're taking you back to the East Quarter. You will be healed."

Panting, Anderas nodded.

The injured officers were gathered and taken to their relevant quarters. A couple of other Hands, Febian among them, came to stand by him. They looked nervous, and shifted the weight of their robes uncomfortably on their shoulders. They looked to Eamon, awaiting his leadership. He said nothing. Words had failed him long before.

Ladomer re-emerged. He bowed, face coloured with worry. "Lord Cathair advises that the Right Hand will see you in the Hands' Hall at once."

Eamon trembled. The wrath of the Right Hand... would be more than he could bear.

"Thank you, Mr Kentigern," he whispered.

As the evening light dwindled westward, the brands at the Hands' Hall were lit. The doors stood open, the strange script upon them as unreadable as it had ever been. The letters seemed to snag and cut at him.

No explanation he could give would satisfy the Right Hand.

He drew breath, trying to steady fraying nerves and shaking hands. The Hands who had gone with him to Pinewood followed him over the darkened threshold.

They waited in the antechamber. Eamon stood silently. The other Hands did not speak or meet his gaze. They were kept a long time.

The central hall was exactly as he remembered it. The Right Hand sat at its head, the westering light showcasing his face. To either side of him sat Cathair and Ashway, one more grim-faced than the other. Cathair's look was unspeakably dark; Ashway's was one of anger and sinuous pleasure.

The Right Hand was unreadable.

Quivering, Eamon knelt. "My lords," he breathed. He waited for the command to rise.

It never came.

"I understand that there has been a misadventure, Lord Goodman?" The Right Hand's voice cut palpably across the room.

Eamon flinched. "Yes, lord." What else could he say?

"You will recount it, Lord Goodman, omitting nothing."

Eamon looked up; the Hands behind him remained upon their knees, their heads bowed. He understood: the duty of bearing the wrath of the Right Hand was his alone.

Trembling, he gave account – the careful plan, the convoy's arrival, the initial attack; the press of arrows, thick in the air like a fly-swarm. The dead, littered among the wagons. The beaten retreat.

"You gave that order, Lord Goodman?"

"Yes, my lord."

"You turned tail before the enemy!" Ashway cried in disgust.

"My men were being slaughtered!" he answered hotly.

"Better dead than shamed by flight!" Ashway retorted.

"If there is any shame in the affair, then it belongs to me alone!" Eamon rejoined. He would not allow Ashway to tarnish the names of the men who had lived to see their homes and families – men who had lived to serve the throned and fight again – with cowardice. "If there must be blame, let it fall on me."

"Such theatrics!"

"Hold your tongue, Lord Ashway," the Right Hand spoke sharply. Ashway fell silent, instantly cowed. "All shame in this matter is rightly apportioned to Lord Goodman. It was on the basis of information obtained by him that we planned this attack, under his hand that we set these forces, and at his command that those forces acted." He looked down at Eamon. Eamon paled. "How many men did you lose, Lord Goodman?"

"More than half, my lord. Some in the battle, some to their wounds. A very few deserted."

"He cannot even keep his own men in defeat!" Ashway hissed. "Your precious pupil has proved what trust he merits!" he added, glaring at Cathair.

"I discharged my duties to the best of my ability!" Eamon cried, emboldened by passion. "I cannot be held accountable for the actions of armed men about whom I knew nothing!"

"Did you not just pronounce that you were accountable for everything disreputable in this venture?" Ashway countered.

Eamon looked to the Right Hand. "I performed my duty," he said, obstinacy setting in his voice. "My lord, if you would just let me speak with the Master –"

"The Master is not interested in your defeat," the Right Hand answered. Though his voice was steady, almost placid, it tore at Eamon's heart. "It was a simple task that he, and Lord Cathair, gave to you. You failed them in it."

Eamon was crushed. "Yes, my lord."

"Did you not also try to hinder your men from obtaining their rightful vengeance on the Master's enemies as you returned?"

Eamon didn't answer. He supposed that the news could easily have reached the city; they had been less than two days' march away. If he confessed it they would strike him hard...

"Yes, my lord," he said at last.

"Why did you do that, Lord Goodman?" the Right Hand asked coolly.

"There was no reason to strike down the villagers, my lord." It sounded like a vain explanation, even to him.

"No reason, you mean, apart from evidenced Serpent sympathies?"

Eamon could not answer.

The Right Hand's eyes showed no trace of feeling. "The destruction of the village might have alleviated your disgrace, Lord Goodman, had you played an active role in it. Instead, you meant to halt it. Not once, but twice you have failed the Master by not exercising yourself in the responsibilities entrusted to you. You barely merit those colours."

Eamon lowered his head. The weight of the rebuke was enough to lay him in a tomb.

"How may I redeem myself, my lord?" he whispered.

"That is not for me to decide. But I should henceforth discharge my duties with extreme attention, were I to find myself in your position."

"My lord." He had been flogged until he lay, broken and bloodied, crawling in the dust.

The Right Hand watched him carefully. "You will assist Lord Cathair with the preparations for the city cull," he said. "Be sure to merit this grace of mine, and to apply yourself to the task. You may rise when we have left, Goodman."

Eamon bowed his head with murmured acquiescence. One by one the seated Hands left, and those who had knelt behind him followed at some unseen command.

Eamon waited until their footsteps were echoes in the distance then raised his head. The black stone glared at him.

Silently he rose and bore himself from the hall.

He emerged alone, shivering in the dark. High above him he could see torches in the palace and thought that he heard music playing in its many chambers. The lords and ladies of Dunthruik were oblivious to his defeat and humiliation. He did not know what he would have said to the Master had he been permitted. Perhaps it was better to be chastised by the Right Hand alone. He was, after all, still alive.

Whether he would be once Cathair had finished with him, he did not know.

Cathair had lodgings in the West Quarter College, but he also had expansive chambers in the Hands' Hall. It was from there that he directed much of his business. He would find out what was required of him.

Eamon wove his way through the dark stone passages to the doors that marked Cathair's abode. The angular script lay on them and two ravens were graven into the wood. Some Gauntlet stood nearby and though they let him pass, they did not bow.

He came into the room that formed the more public part of Cathair's quarters. It was rounded, with windows looking in across the courtyard; through them Eamon could see the edifice of the Hands' Hall, its doors grim in the moonlight. The room had several doors leading from it into other chambers. Before Eamon was a table and an arrangement of long, cushioned chairs that would easily seat several people. The upholstery bore strange patterns. He wondered whether the swirls of brown were typical of the lands to the south, and when Cathair might have travelled the deserts. It was an unusual feat if he had done so and an even more unusual gift if he had not.

Something clattered. Suddenly all four of Cathair's dogs were around him. The beasts easily reached his waist and Eamon knew, from months in Cathair's company, that should they choose to jump they would be taller than he was. He was assaulted by the memory of his first arrival in Dunthruik. These dogs could maul a man to death.

The dogs growled, baring teeth between snarling lips. Holding his hands well away from them, Eamon stood in an invisible contest of wills with the hounds – who sniffed at him, growled, and occasionally feinted for his arms with their long teeth, daring him to run and give them excuse for a chase and rending. But he held his ground.

At long last he heard a voice. "I see that you take the Right Hand very literally indeed, Lord Goodman."

Cathair emerged from one of the other doorways, a dimly lit room visible behind him, his papers spread over a desk and books aligned in deep shelves. The Hand's eyes had a menacing glisten to them, which rekindled Eamon's fear of his pale-faced enemy. Cathair had not spoken once during his interview with the Right Hand, but his anger had been clear.

"He bade me to assist you, my lord," Eamon replied timidly.

"A foible of his own, little according with my desires. You are an abominable humiliation, Goodman!" he spat. "You have disgraced me and the whole West Quarter through your pitiable, unforgivable remonstrance."

Eamon didn't answer. He tried to match the green eyes, but could not. Cathair was right.

The dogs snarled; one snatched at his hand. He began shaking. Cathair came striding to his dogs. His eyes grew cool. "Do you like hounds, Goodman?"

Eamon swallowed. Was that a faint smile about the Hand's lips?

"I myself am very fond of hounds," Cathair snapped at him, a fifth dog. "I like hounds, Mr Goodman, because they are unswervingly faithful to me." Cathair touched the head of one of his beasts. "They awake when I command it, eat when it pleases me, bite and rend when I ask it of them. They recognize the justice of my punishment when they do wrong and then return, fawning and whining, to lick my hand in their penitence."

"Yes, my lord," Eamon managed. The dogs growled at him, but patiently awaited their master's commands.

"Another thing I like about my hounds, Goodman," he said, "is that they are good at discerning men who are enemies to me and to the Master."

Eamon's heart went cold. Cathair's green eyes were those of a preying, circling beast, preparing to make the kill.

Every muscle in Eamon's body was tense. Should he feign ignorance, reject the insinuation in outrage, or collapse to his knees in confession and beg forgiveness? Sweat broke on his brow. If he did not do the last then surely the culling in Dunthruik would begin with him, with his blood spilled on the Hand's floor? He quaked with horror. If that happened he could never seek Hughan's forgiveness or redeem his name.

So he resolved to answer.

"A hound is but a hound, my lord, a nose a nose, a scent a scent, a man a man. All can be fooled, however faithful."

"You also are a hound of mine, Goodman, and I am the hand that has fed you," Cathair replied, with severity that might sear flesh from bone. "I am a Hand that metes out vengeance, death, and judgment. Remember that." He paused. "Men were sent to Ashford Ridge to destroy the Serpent's camp. They fared no better than you did at Pinewood."

Eamon stared at him. The Ashford expedition had also gone out under Cathair's auspices but the force had been much bigger, well prepared, filled with experienced men. How could it have failed? He dared not ask; Cathair's gaze was grim.

"Understand from this that today is not a day to test me, Goodman," Cathair growled. "Did you know about the Easters hidden in the convoy?"

The question surprised him. Was it to become an interrogation? "No, my lord."

"Did you seek at any time to hinder the efforts of your men in the engagement, giving orders contrary to the glory of the Master?"

He blanched. He wished that he had. "No, my lord."

"Did you contrive to assist the enemy?"

Eamon stared at him. "Why are you asking me these questions, my lord? My only desire was to serve the Master." That, at least, was true.

"Because I know too well, Goodman, that yours is a house of biting dogs," Cathair spat.

Suddenly he whistled. It was a shrill sound, freezing every part of Eamon's being. He prepared for the worst, feeling with soul-destroying certainty that he had betrayed himself without ever – which was worse – intending service to Hughan.

Claws rattled away across the floor. He blinked hard. The hounds had flocked to the far end of the room and crunched happily at thick slabs of meat in a bowl by one of the doors. Sweat chilled on his forehead.

Cathair offered him a beguiling smile. "Come, Goodman," he said. "We must not disappoint the Right Hand."

It was late that night – so late that it was nearly morning – when Eamon emerged from Cathair's quarters, shivering. He tried to garner an impression of the time from the position of the stars, but his head swam with fatigue and a stomach-churning nausea he had been obliged to hide.

Not long after he had joined Cathair a number of other West Quarter Hands had arrived. Few had acknowledged him, no doubt fearing contamination from his sullied name. He had listened with growing unease to what was discussed.

He had seen the preliminary plans for the culling of wayfarers in the city, plans concerned with the logistical arrangements for the arrest, torture, and execution of any suspected snakes. Orders for it had to be drafted, dispatched, and filed, and holding areas prepared for the processing of those arrested. That "processing" was to involve breaching, torture, and confession, and find its end at the pyres.

A clear hierarchy for jurisdiction had been compiled where the Hands, second only to the Right Hand and the Master, had the highest power to decide the fate of those imprisoned. In each quarter of the city specialized units of Gauntlet had been formed to hunt the wayfarers, each answering to their captain and two specially assigned lieutenants. Cathair had not been idle while Eamon was at Pinewood.

The cull, which had been delayed while lists of probable victims were drawn up, would begin in the following days. It was to be brutal, based in part on a reward scheme. Any who informed on another and were then proven to have told the truth would be given money to thank them for their interest in the Master's authority. If proven wrong they would face no punishment. The criteria for "proving" wayfarer sympathies were slim and Eamon wondered what proportion of the River's population would escape unscathed. Messengers would go that night, and more the next morning, taking authority for the cull to every regional Gauntlet unit. Eamon shuddered to think of the red uniforms prowling through Edesfield, bringing charges of treason where there was perhaps not even the basis for suspicion. How many men would burn, like Telo or Lorentide? How many would be forced to implicate others, like Clarence? How many would lose their lives, wayfarers or not?

Grey touched the sky behind the palace. Drawing his cloak around him, he returned to his own quarters. It was a small room, far from the central hall, but could only be reached by passing the guarded doors. Apart from such details it was much the same as the room he had had at the West Quarter College. The bed was larger and more ornate, decorated with stylized hands and rimmed with the haunting script. It was draped with dark covers and on the wall hung a long banner, bearing the Master's eagle. It glowered at him as he sank wearily down.

He lay back. He did not bother to undress or even to remove his muddy boots. His mind was full of the culling, of the Hidden Hall and its faded emblems, of Hughan and the throned. It had all seemed so clear to him once, and yet... Why was he only capable of betraying – first one lord and then the other?

"*You must choose.*" Alessia's words came to him again. He wished that she were there with him. No, not there; he wished that they were both far away. He wished that either the King or the usurper had claimed victory, and that he had been exiled to a distant land to live out the rest of his years. He was desperately tired. How could he face another day in Dunthruik, another day of treachery and torment? He wanted to be free – of the city and his oaths.

It was the one choice from which he was barred.

"Some of the men you brought back are very badly hurt," Ladomer observed.

Eamon had slept fitfully through what remained of that night and had risen with the dawn. He had spent a large part of the day signing and sealing dispatches on Cathair's behalf – he had quill-ache. Having given the last papers to the last messenger he had been dismissed, and decided to see how Anderas was faring. Emerging from the Hands' Hall he had met Ladomer. It was late afternoon.

"Very badly hurt indeed," Ladomer added.

"Of course they are; it was a massacre," Eamon answered, irked. Couldn't his friend imagine what it had been like?

"So was Ashford Ridge. Have you heard?" Ladomer shook his head. "I can't understand how it can all have gone so wrong."

Eamon sighed. Any operation commanded by Ladomer Kentigern would, he supposed bitterly, have been completed without a single problem and brought glory down to the tenth generation of any man so much as loosely related to those who had followed him. He grit his teeth and said nothing.

"Some of the Ashford Ridge survivors say that they were outnumbered, and ambushed and harried as they retreated," Ladomer continued. "They lost more than a hundred and sixty men, and none of the Hands returned. It's a disaster for the quarters' Gauntlet groups. It's a good job that the commander didn't make it back alive – Cathair would have had his head, and might well visit his wrath on any survivor who comes back. And then, after all that, you," he added incredulously. "What in the Master's name happened to you?" Ladomer hefted his customary papers from one arm to another and looked Eamon squarely in the eye. "I'm surprised Cathair didn't kill you on the spot! The Hands were convinced they sent the best man for the job."

"Told you that, did they? Don't be an ass. You know as well as I do that they gave it to me because it was supposed to be an easy way to prove my credentials and Cathair's praise. That's why this is so awful." He pressed at his head. It ached.

"You've still got the cloak, haven't you?"

"Yes." For what good that did him.

"Well, then, don't make a catastrophe out of it," Ladomer answered. "They can demote you, you know."

The thought sent a shiver down his spine.

"Actually, I think Lord Tramist demanded that you be demoted," Ladomer told him, "but he was overruled. Consider that, Eamon! Someone overruled Tramist in your favour. It implies that you have already proven something."

Eamon shuddered. It was not an encouraging thought; he didn't want Tramist as an enemy.

"Word has it that there was a snake in the ranks that gave your block away," Ladomer persisted, lowering his voice conspiratorially.

Eamon glowered. "Word has it wrong," he spat. He wondered if he felt so wrathful because it should have been true. "Our information was wrong," he thundered as Ladomer raised a placating hand, "and we didn't expect bloody war wagons!"

"That's all that happened?" Ladomer seemed disappointed.

"No, Ladomer, that's not all that happened. Men died."

Ladomer didn't answer. A few minutes later, he airily changed the subject.

They reached the East Quarter College. Ladomer left him at the steps. Eamon quickly found out where Anderas was and went to see him.

Despite his injuries, it had been deemed that Anderas was to continue acting as the East Quarter's captain. He was being kept in his room. When Eamon entered he saw that the captain was on his bed, propped up and holding reports in his hand. His first lieutenant, Greenwood, stood next to his bed, studiously pointing out details on the papers.

Greenwood immediately bowed when Eamon entered; Eamon had to actively forbid Anderas from clambering to his feet.

"I hardly think that necessary, captain!"

"It would be most improper of me not to, Lord Goodman," Anderas insisted.

"Let me rephrase my statement: do not trouble yourself!"

Anderas relented. Eamon saw a strange look in his eyes. He wondered what it meant.

"How are you feeling?" Though still pale, the fact that Anderas had considered standing boded well.

"Much better," the captain confessed. "They're forcing me to imbibe some horrible substance that would probably be more at home in the city sewers, but cheerfully claim that it will clear the infection."

Eamon grinned for the first time in days. "I'm very pleased to hear it."

Anderas raised an eyebrow. "That the substance is horrible, or that it will clear the infection?"

"Both," Eamon answered with a smile. "Captains tend to arrogance unless kept in good check, I hear."

"Being on the mend, they have found me something to do," Anderas told him, glancing at his papers. "We still haven't selected a new college draybant but First Lieutenant Greenwood is good enough to keep me informed. He wanted a signature, for some of this culling nonsense…" Anderas paused, putting his name with a flourish. "There. Well, he has it now. Thank you, Mr Greenwood."

"Sir." Greenwood saluted, bowed, and left the room. Eamon moved to the bedside.

"Have you come to discuss the cull with me as well, Lord Goodman?" Anderas asked, leaning back with a weary sigh.

"No," Eamon answered with a laugh. "I've come to tell you about the weather."

"With all due reverence, I can keep a fair eye on those developments from here," Anderas replied. "You'll see that I have a window for just such a purpose."

"Ah, but you can't trust your own eyes in this city," Eamon remarked.

"Do you mean to say that it handicaps us?" Anderas asked with a faint smile.

Eamon groaned. "That, captain," he said, "was a pun worthy of Lord Cathair."

"Then I've been in this city too long!" Anderas answered, and they laughed together. Soon Anderas sat back and looked at Eamon with tired but hopeful eyes.

"I would be most obliged if you would tell me about the weather, Lord Goodman," he said.

The sky was beginning to darken when Eamon eventually left the East Quarter College. He felt better for having passed an hour in Anderas's company.

He heard thunder rolling over the sea and quickened his pace. The storm was far away, but it made him feel nervous. He hoped to close himself in his room and sleep.

He followed the Coll towards the palace. The torchbearers were at work and the building took on an overwhelming shadow shape in the half-light.

There were many men and women on the road that night. He noted none of them until one spoke to him.

"Eamon!" it said, sounding surprised, overjoyed, and afraid all at once. He knew the voice.

"Alessia," he breathed. A moment later the hooded figure was caught about his neck, holding him tightly. He drew her to one side of the busy street. "What are you doing here?" he asked, hardly daring to let her go lest she should disappear into the night.

"I came to look for you," she answered, her voice hidden in his shoulder and the hood. It had imprisoned her dark hair, which seemed to him an intolerable crime.

"For me?" He could barely believe it. "After what I did, you can bear to look for me?"

"I always will," she replied. "I'm so glad that you're safe," she added, holding him closer. "I heard that terrible things happened at the battle."

His heart pounding, Eamon clenched her to him as he had longed to do every night since he had left the city. "They did," he whispered. "I am so glad, Alessia, that you are here."

It seemed an eternity that they stood there together. He did not care who saw him. He drew strength and comfort from her.

"I have something for you," she said at last.

He gazed at her curiously. "You do?"

"Yes. Seats for the theatre."

"A gift better suited to victory than to defeat, surely!" Eamon asked – but he could not feel sorry about what had happened while she held him.

"A gift to toast some greater, and as yet unknown, victory," she countered. There was something strange about her voice.

He lifted her face towards his. "Are you all right?" he asked, searching her eyes.

She pressed his hand. "Will you come with me?"

"Tonight?" Eamon asked, astonished. "Now?"

"Yes."

Eamon laughed quietly and kissed her. How could he say no?

She had clearly foreseen his answer, for beneath her brown mantle she was already finely dressed in a long, purple dress that suited her as perfectly as everything did. They walked and talked quietly together. Eamon thought that her pace seemed swifter than he knew it – and her voice less free. Perhaps she feared to be seen with him after all. But she held his hand unbearably tight and stayed close by him. He felt unpolished and under-dressed beside her.

Dunthruik's Crown Theatre lay on the Coll in one of the most affluent parts of the West Quarter. It was a tall building with a rounded, gilded roof supported by columns capped with crowns. At the entrance to the theatre stood two enormous eagles, crowns on their heads and breasts, and crushed between their stony talons crawled the frail, twisted bodies of snakes. Enormous braziers hung down from the rooftop; they burned like the fallen stars of an apocalypse.

Everyone going to the theatre was decked in finery. Eamon supposed that it was not an occasion for just anyone. Not since the ball at the palace had he seen such clothes, or so many servants scurrying along beside their masters and mistresses. Why had Alessia come to him alone – not even attended by Lillabeth?

People stopped to stare at him. He tried to hold his head aloof as he had often seen Cathair do. What right had they to judge him? He had done everything he could have done for the throned. Men, some likely better men than he, had died doing it; the swarming gentry could not say as much.

Alessia led him through the theatre gates. A swathe of steps rose to the doors. Other Hands ascended them, along with lords, ladies, and rich artisans or merchants.

The steps led up to a grand entry hall, with a floor patterned with coloured stones that traced soaring eagles and crowns. There were two tall staircases leading off to each side – Alessia took him to one of them. An attendant bowed to them.

"My lord; Lady Turnholt."

Alessia gave him the markers that denoted their seats. The servant led them to the next floor of the building. There was a hallway in which were a dozen numbered doors. Eamon realized that they led to the separate boxes on the upper balconies of the theatre – they were reserved only for the noblest. Somewhere nearby would be the Eagle's Box, used by the Master and his closest Hands.

The attendant escorted them to a door and opened it, bowing grandly. Alessia thanked him for his service before he left.

Their box was high, with a dazzling view of the theatre. The gentry were beginning to fill the other boxes; those across from them were crammed full of exquisite dresses and cloaks. Each box had a few seats – tall, comfortable, cushioned affairs, red and bearing crowns. The stage was draped with thick red curtains. Casting light from above was a chandelier shaped like a towering golden crown. Candles burned at each point, shining through golden and reddened glass to touch the stage far below. The light picked out paintings on the upper parts of the theatre's dome.

"It's beautiful," he said, turning to look at her. There was no one in the world as beautiful as she!

She sat slowly, the red chair seeming to engulf her. He sat beside her. They could see the stage clearly and could be seen by all below them. Some seemed appalled to see him; women leaned across to their companions and pointed towards him as they muttered behind their fans. He shuffled uncomfortably. He could imagine what they were saying, and knew that rumour was never kind to the truth. How could he dare to show his face at so public a place, and with so distinguished a lady? It was outrageous.

Attendants began dousing some of the lights. The murmur of people rumbled all around them and Eamon felt the building of old excitement in him. His father had sometimes taken him to the theatre when he was younger, though never to the Crown. They had certainly never sat in a box – though sometimes they had stood in the pit, right up against the stage. He vividly remembered his first visit to a small, round theatre in the North Quarter; he could have been no older than seven, scrabbling to sit on his father's knee so that he could drink in every drop of what he saw and heard. It had been a play where two Gauntlet officers duelled over a woman. He could still conjure the clash of the painted swords.

He felt a light touch on his arm. "Eamon," Alessia whispered. Her face seemed pale in the flickering light. Something about her expression worried him.

"Are you all right?" he asked, catching her hand in his own. It was chilled; he covered it with both of his. "You're frozen!" he exclaimed, leaning down to kiss her fingers.

"Eamon, I need to speak with you," she said, her voice strange and urgent.

"Of course," he answered, wondering at her words. "What is it?"

Alessia smiled, seemingly reassured, and drew breath to speak.

Before another word could leave her mouth the door to the box opened. They looked back towards it and then rose swiftly to their feet. Eamon let go of Alessia's trembling hands to bow.

"My lord," he said.

"Lord Goodman; Lady Turnholt," said the Right Hand. He was framed in the doorway by the tall lights beyond and his face chilled Eamon to the very heart. "I hope you will excuse this interruption?"

He wished he could refuse it. "Of course, my lord."

The Right Hand gestured for them to sit. They did not dare. "It is very brave of you, Lord Goodman, to attend a dramatic performance such as this, given your own recent theatrics," he commented. His smile seemed placid, but Eamon calculated intent behind it. It terrified him. What did the Right Hand want?

"It is dramatic that you, my lord, should appear publicly with me."

"If such is shameful to you, my lord, we will leave," said Alessia. Eamon glanced at her – she quivered.

"Oh, you need not take such a departure on my account, Lady Turnholt," the Right Hand told her. "It seems only right that such dramatic souls as ours take company together."

"You will not sit in the Eagle's Box?" She seemed nervous.

The Right Hand offered her a smile. "I will sit here. Besides," he added, "there is no company here more beautiful than your own, lady."

Eamon could only watch as the Right Hand took the seat beside his. He arranged himself comfortably in the chair as he spoke again. "I am the patron of this theatre, Lord Goodman, and I like to attend performances from time to time, to ensure that my name births good things."

"You do rightly, my lord," Eamon answered. Alessia shivered at his side. She could no longer speak to him. What plagued her?

The Right Hand smiled again. "Please, do sit."

Eamon lowered himself into his seat. Alessia sat beside him, still trembling. He reached across the dark to press her hand.

The stage curtains drew back. The Right Hand began to applaud and the rest of the theatre followed suit, an ocean of noise following the first crest. Eamon heard the Right Hand's palms beating strongly together; the noise was deafening. There was no doubting the man's power.

The stage was deep and scenes representing a battlefield had been erected at its back. At the front was a tall pole, on which hung an eagled banner. Three actors, dressed as Gauntlet soldiers, entered from different directions. Each bore an injury and the same eagle as the standard. Stepping to the front of the stage, one called to the audience: "To his glory!"

The whole theatre answered him: "To his glory!"

The soldier stepped back; the drama could now begin. One of the other actors hurried over to him. "What news?" he asked. "The Serpent is fallen and his brood is fled, but I fear for our noble captain!"

"Did you not see? Have you not heard? What a captain! He came alone from the press, badged in the blood of the viper's brood, bearing the standard of the Serpent himself. He will carry it to the Master!"

"Do you know this play, Lord Goodman?"

Eamon started: the Right Hand spoke softly in his ear.

"I do not believe I do, my lord," he answered. He was aware of Alessia watching him.

"Ah! Let me explain it to you!" The Right Hand spoke with relish. "Its historical accuracy is, of course, questionable – as is so often the case with drama – but it is the story of a captain who fought for the Master at the battle of Edesfield. I am reliably informed that it is a town you know well," he added with a small smile, "so I will not describe it to you."

Eamon nodded silently.

"The captain," the Right Hand continued, "a man of lowly birth but promoted for good service, is honoured for capturing the standard of the enemy, and rewarded for his deed by betrothal to the only daughter of a noble family, a woman he has always loved and never dreamed of obtaining. But," he went on, "another loves her and, to spite him, his aspiring rival lays proofs showing her to be of the Serpent's pay. The captain marries the noblewoman, a moment of utter bliss for him, and then finds the false proofs. Deeply grieved, he goes to his rival – once his closest friend – for counsel, dressed still in his wedding robes. His rival encourages him to take the life of his wife and offer it as a gift to the Master."

Eamon wondered at the growing delight with which the Master's closest told the story. He could see the actors moving and speaking on the stage but could not take his attention from the Right Hand.

"The captain, taking his friend's counsel deeply to heart, waits until evening. Then, when he should be consummating his marriage, he murders his wife, despite her pleas, to which he turns deaf and sorry ears. He takes her body before the Master as a witness of his loyalty, and at the moment when he presents it, evidence comes of the falsified proofs.

"He is, of course, overcome with grief, and has heart-rending words to speak over his wife's body. Lord Cathair speaks of it as true poetry, pertaining to the fickleness of love, the duties of power, and the awfulness of treachery." The Right Hand allowed these words to fall heavily on Eamon's ears. "Learning all to be his rival's doing the captain slaughters him, but receives his own death-blow in the fight. He is borne, dying, to the Master, and begs for his estate to be passed to his brother, swearing his family's eternal allegiance. The play ends with the captain's death and the brother's ratification of that oath."

Eamon glanced at the stage. The three soldiers there were speaking about the noble qualities of the captain. As two of the three left the stage, the third – presumably the rival – delivered a terrifying soliloquy, declaring his fear that the captain would obtain the highest prize of all: the lady.

"It's quite the tragedy," the Right Hand observed. "Still, I understand that there are those who hold that tragedy is good for us. I quite enjoy a little tragedy myself. Don't you, Lord Goodman?"

Alessia's grip on his hand grew tighter. What was wrong?

"Yes, my lord."

The drama continued. The play was well written but Eamon was painfully aware of the constant, derogatory claims made against the King, of the brutal language used to describe his death, and the revelatory way in which the Master was set in his place. It churned his stomach. As the play drew to the close of its third act the captain, a man whose voice reached the top-most eaves of the theatre, grimly announced his intention to murder his wife. The curtains fell to applause.

"I wonder that your lady hasn't told you," the Right Hand said, his voice close by Eamon's ear, "but the captain figured here by the dramatist takes his tale from the history of no less than one Tobias Turnholt. The family received their patrimony for capturing the standard of the Serpent. The captain did indeed kill his wife – they say that she merited death for some other betrayal. Is that not the case, Lady Turnholt?"

"My lord," Alessia whispered. She trembled. He wished that he could hold her close – but the Right Hand prevented it.

"Whatever its guise, Lord Goodman," the Right Hand told him, "and whatever excuses are given for it, treachery is a terrible thing. It cannot be forgiven or undone." He looked long at Eamon. Eamon was grateful for the dark in the box, which hid him. What did the Right Hand mean by saying all this?

"And those who betray those they claim to love?" The Right Hand shook his head. "That, Lord Goodman, is most treacherous of all. Death is all that can answer such a betrayal."

Suddenly Alessia snatched her hand from Eamon's and rose, quaking.

"Lady Turnholt, what ails you?" the Right Hand asked pleasantly.

"I humbly crave your indulgence and your pardon, my lord," she answered, "but I am not well."

"I can understand how you might find this play troubling," the Right Hand soothed.

Eamon leapt at the chance to escape. "My lord, may I have your permission to escort Lady Turnholt home?"

"Of course, Lord Goodman, of course," the Right Hand replied. "How uncouth of us it would be to let her go alone! I am only sorry that you will miss the rest of the play."

"As am I, my lord." Alessia shook visibly. Eamon set her cloak over her shoulders. "By your leave, my lord."

The Right Hand nodded as Eamon bowed.

"Do take care, Lady Turnholt!"

Eamon escorted her from the box. Alessia said nothing to him as they left the theatre. She tried to walk swiftly, but her whole body shook, slowing her. The streets were cold and quiet, lit occasionally by lightning far away. No thunder reached their ears.

They walked the Coll in silence. At last, they passed her gates.

It was on the darkest part of the path that Alessia stumbled. Eamon caught her and raised her to her feet with soothing words.

"We are almost home," he told her. "Come, Lillabeth will help you."

She shook her head, resisting his touch. He stopped. Tears streaked her cheeks. He reached out to touch her face. She gave a startled cry, shying back from him with harrowed eyes.

"No!"

Alarmed, Eamon took her hand. "Alessia?"

Suddenly she pressed herself close to him and buried her face against his breast. She began to cry and held him tightly, as though she feared that he might disappear.

Whispering encouragement, Eamon wrapped his arms about her. As she sobbed he held her, resting his head upon hers. He kissed her brow.

"I'm sorry," he said quietly. "If I had known that the play would affect you like this I would never have agreed to go with you."

"Eamon, I wanted to tell you before," she whispered, raising her trembling face towards his. "I should have told you before, but I couldn't…"

Was this all her fear? "Alessia," he whispered, and kissed her. "It's only a play."

Suddenly she pulled away, shaking her head. "You don't understand." She looked at him, haunted. "I love you." Her voice quivered. "I have always loved you and I will always love you."

Eamon looked at her, confused. "And I love you –" What did she mean by such words? "Alessia," he began, reaching out to touch her face again. She pulled away with a shrill gasp. It shook him and angered him. "Why are you so afraid?"

She was ashen. "Eamon, I couldn't… you were at Pinewood… I…" She seemed to be steeling herself against something terrible. Her face was riven with grief. "I can't tell you," she whispered at last.

What could be so terrible? "Do you trust me?"

Alessia nodded silently. "Yes," she said, "but I am afraid."

He stared. "Of me?"

"Yes. Of what you'll do."

"What I'll do? Alessia, I don't understand." Suspicion yawned open inside him. He gripped her hand. "You must tell me."

"My family has always served the throned," she began, "the women no less than the men. The men swore their swords, their lands, and their sons to the banner. The women swore to him what, as women, was allotted to them…"

Jealousy snarled in him. "Alessia, while I was gone did you –?"

"No," Alessia shook her head. "No. They haven't made me give myself…" She swallowed. "Not for a long time."

Relief.

"I am so sorry." He shook as he kissed her brow again. "I'm sorry that they have ever asked you to. Is that what you were afraid of telling me?" He touched his brow against hers. "Alessia! I will not judge you for that." She was his.

For a long moment Alessia stood still in his arms. He pressed her close.

Suddenly she spoke again. "Eamon," she whispered, "on the same day that you arrived in Dunthruik, I was summoned to the palace."

He went cold, stepped back. Her face was pale and her lips trembled.

"You are a lady of Dunthruik," Eamon answered, trying to assuage his troubled thoughts, "and heir of the Turnholts. Why should you not be?"

"They took me before the Right Hand." Her eyes were wide and frightened. Eamon imagined her kneeling on the cold stones of the Hands' Hall. "He gave his orders. I had no choice."

Eamon watched the shadows on her face as she struggled to speak. His heart was seized with fear.

Son of Eben…

"Alessia –"

"He told me about you," she continued. "He told me that you were arriving in the West Quarter College. He told me that you were important to the Master but suspected of being under wayfarer influence. He told me to shun Alben, and pursue you."

He staggered. The words fell like blows on a dying heart.

Nothing but a whore, son of Eben; she defiled you! Defiled you with a whore's designs.

. "No," he choked. Hot tears bit. He tried to drive them away. She had been sent to trap him. Mathaiah had been...

Desperately, wrathfully, he wrung her hands in his. "No!"

"Eamon, let me finish –"

"Finish?" he cried brokenly. "Finish? And what will you say? That all the love I received from you has been under the auspices of the Right Hand?"

"No, Eamon!" She wept freely and grasped his arm. "They wanted me to lure you, capture you, hold you, and learn from you the truth."

He remembered how she had smiled at him and invited him to follow her back to her home, to her chambers, to her very bed. All the long nights that they had spent together, and the laughter and kisses that he had shared with her, passed before his eyes in a moment. The memories cut him like a jagged knife.

"*And those who betray those they claim to love?*" The Right Hand's knowing, mocking words ran through his head, poisoning his thought. "*That, Lord Goodman, is most treacherous of all...*"

A treacherous whore; defiler of your flesh. You will answer her betrayal, son of Eben. You will revile her.

He staggered. The words, the lies, permeated his wounded thought.

"Then this is all we are?" he hissed, glaring at her. "You the seductress, and I your prey!"

"No, Eamon!" she cried. "I never wanted to take you – you frightened me, and the rumours about you frightened me. But when I saw you, dressed in the uniform of a King's man... when we danced at the masque, and I felt something in you far beyond what I could see..." She closed her eyes with the force of the memory. "I saw why they feared you – and I saw that I loved you."

Lies! Nothing but lies!

"Loved me?" Eamon cried. He tried to tear away but her hold on his arm was true. She reached to turn his face towards hers but he wrenched back from her touch: she was venom on his skin.

"Don't touch me!"

"If you ever loved me you will hear me now! Week after week they demanded to know what I knew, and I told them nothing. They scorned me, and called me whore and threatened me. But I knew nothing."

Eamon shook. He had told her everything. Fool – *fool!*

"Even after I learnt the truth, I told them nothing!" Alessia trembled furiously. "I spoke not a word, and I lied to them for you because I loved you, and the man that I loved wasn't a Hand or a lieutenant or even a Gauntlet officer: he was a King's man."

Lies! You are mine!

Eamon cried out as though struck; she held him firmly.

"The night you left for Pinewood, Eamon, they came for me. The Right Hand often came unannounced to my house, demanding information. He came that night."

Eamon remembered the way she had started the first time she had seen him in black. Could she have mistaken him for the Right Hand?

It could be true. Everything that she was telling him could be true…

She deludes you, son of Eben!

"They could have tortured me, Eamon, or violated me in any way they chose, and I would have said no word to betray you. But they did not need to. They took me to the Hands' Hall and breached me." Her voice broke at last, and she collapsed to her knees, clinging to his arm and sobbing at the memory of an ordeal she could not have shared with any other.

"They breached me, Eamon! They tore out everything that I had refused to give them! They had made me a whore, a painted doll to be dressed and undressed at their leisure, but I had borne that, because that was the nature of my service, and who could stop them? The throned demanded it of me. Then they laid me out for you and I glimpsed something in you that they never meant me to see. I followed after it – how could I not? – and betrayed them by loving you. They repaid me for it."

Eamon watched her, wretched on the ground before him, a mask of tears over her face. He almost knelt down by her to assuage her grief: did he not love her? He knew that he did, or at least that he had done so, and that what they had shared should have some hold on him now. Had she not borne him up in the depths of his own grief? Had she not held true to him? His whole heart moved towards her.

She lied to you, defiled you, betrayed you. And you would go to her? It is treachery, son of Eben. You despise her!

It was treachery. Treachery was unforgivable. The voice spoke truly.

He glared at her. Her face grew paler. She pressed his arm.

"Eamon —"

"Let go of me," he demanded. She did not.

"Please," she whispered.

"Let go of me!"

"I took you to the theatre so that we could speak without being heard," she cried. "But then he came…" Suddenly she gasped. "Eamon! They know about – they're going to take him!"

"Take who?"

It was then that Alessia let go of him. She looked up at him and faltered, as though she knew that with her next breath she would lose him forever.

"Forgive me, Eamon. It's Mathaiah. They're taking Mathaiah."

For a moment he could not breathe. Then sense came to him, inflamed by betrayal.

"You treacherous, perfidious bitch!" he roared. She recoiled, falling as though struck; he could not stop himself. He answered her with worse than death – he turned from her.

"No," she called, "please, not like this. Eamon!" It was to no avail. He whirled and ran as fast as he could. She sobbed wretchedly behind him. Rage drove him.

He tore out of the gates. All his thought was on Mathaiah. His ward had been right all along. How could he have been such a fool!

He had exchanged honest friendship for lust and dreams of power. Stricken and furied, he cursed Alessia as he raced into the Brand.

There were torches at the college door and a crowd of cadets on the steps. Waite stood by them, watching as Hands filed down, Cathair at their head, his eyes flashing exultantly.

Eamon stared. Mathaiah walked caged among the Hands. The cadet's jacket had been torn from him and he went in the cold night air dressed only in his shirt and trousers, his hands bound behind him. Yet he held his head high. There was a long, fresh streak of blood down one side of his face.

As Eamon gaped at the scene, enraged and appalled, Mathaiah looked up. A grim cloud passed over his face. It accused him.

Eamon wanted to cry out, to explain everything, to beg Mathaiah's forgiveness, to offer himself in his ward's place if they would only let Mathaiah go – but he could not.

Lord Cathair smiled at him as the procession passed, his green eyes mocking him. There was nothing he could do – because of her.

Thunder broke. He was too late.

CHAPTER XXIV

He watched – he could only watch – the Hands escorting Mathaiah to the palace. Its gates threatened from the distance, lit by streaks of the coming storm. Eamon stared, staggered, his mind a tempest.

They had taken Mathaiah.

"Lord Goodman," Waite acknowledged, paler than ever.

"Captain." He heard the cry of wounded men inside the hall. Had Mathaiah resisted? "What happened?"

"Lord Cathair arrested Cadet Grahaven," the captain answered brusquely, grey eyes pinned on the disappearing escort of Hands. Waite seemed but a shadow of himself. "They say he's a wayfarer. A snake! In my college." He rubbed his scarred hands. "Lord Goodman, I can't quite… Did you know, Lord Goodman?" The question was sudden.

"No."

"He was such a determined cadet." Waite didn't seem to notice the infinitesimally small pause that had preceded Eamon's answer. "Just like all of mine. They're all good lads. You were a good one, better than good…" He shook his head. "If Grahaven was a snake…" Waite glanced over his shoulder at the other cadets and officers. Some were beginning to disperse; others, a group from the Third Banners, still looked on, grey-faced.

"If he was a snake, any of them could be. I will have to have his whole group interviewed. They will get the names of as many other snakes out of him as they can, poor boy. Maybe they'll spin it as an expedient for the culling. Captain Belaal won't let me live this one down, Lord Goodman, when he hears of it," he added grimly. "Still, this college will survive its losses."

"Yes." Eamon felt numb. Mathaiah was... He froze as some part of his brain seized on what Waite had said.

Of course they would try to extract information from Mathaiah. They would torture him and breach him if they could not make him talk. Eamon's mind span. Had he taken Mathaiah for interrogation, what would he be expected to do? Seek the chain of informants through which the cadet had contacted the wayfarers – by any means necessary. Cathair was a master of the art. Whose name would they get first?

He lurched. Lillabeth. The very first name they would draw from Mathaiah's screaming lips would be Lillabeth's.

Thunder cracked.

He had to do something, *now*. He could not be too late again. He was the only one who could save her. As he thought it he felt the hiss of the voice in his mind. It stole his faculties in its vehemence.

You will not, Eben's son.

"Are you well, Lord Goodman?"

The question drew him back to his senses. He could not listen to the voice. If he did not go both Mathaiah and Lillabeth would be lost. He would not pay that price.

"Yes. If you will excuse me, captain, I must attend to some urgent business."

"Of course."

Eamon turned to go.

"Lord Goodman?"

"Captain?"

"He was your ward." There was tangible grief in the man's voice. The captain stared at him in disbelief. "Did you never even suspect?"

Eamon didn't answer. He bade the captain good night and left the Brand. As soon as he was out of sight he channelled all of his anguish into his limbs; he began running as fast as they could carry him.

He had to get Lillabeth out of the city. But how? There was nowhere to go. Where could he take her? He tried desperately to force his mind back to Hughan. Hughan had said something...

You won't remember, the voice spat. *You can't remember, Eben's son.*

He had to remember, he had to... Before leaving the Hidden Hall, Hughan had said...

He swore. He remembered nothing but the falsified events he had presented to Lord Tramist.

You do not remember!

He gave an angry cry; he would not lose Lillabeth on account of a voice in his mind!

"I will remember!" he retaliated. "As I am a King's man, I will!"

The voice sneered. *You are no man of his!*

But his declaration dragged Hughan's face through the mire of memories until it was crystalline before him. He was holding papers and stone, and hearing his friend's voice as clearly as though it spoke beside him: "*There is an inn on Serpentine Avenue in the South Quarter...*"

The Serpentine! The inn was called the South Wall; he remembered Giles showing it to him. That was where he had to go. He would take Lillabeth there and speak to the landlord – somehow he would get her out of the city.

He would go to Alessia's house and get the girl out. But he had to do it discreetly. He trusted some of the servants but knew others would talk at the slightest opportunity. He did not want his name mentioned when the Hands came looking for their snake.

He raced to Turnholt House. What would he do if the whore saw him? How could she have betrayed him as she had done? He had put all his trust in her. For that, Mathaiah would suffer and die.

It was his fault. He had made that exchange. His lusts and ambitions had done it.

He howled and ran on.

The tall windows of the house were mostly dark; only those at the lower levels were lit. So it was only the servants still about.

He did not go to the main doors. Skirting the stables, Eamon moved to the servants' entrance. He drew his cloak tightly about his face and, breathing hard from his long run, pounded on the door.

At length he was answered by the house's elderly matron. As the woman peered into the dark Eamon struggled to remember her name.

"Toriana!"

Seeing the hooded figure at the door she shrank back.

"My lord." Terrified, she curtseyed low. Eamon relaxed – he counted her trustworthy. He let the cloak fall from his face. "Lord Goodman!" she said, surprised.

"Toriana, is Lillabeth here?" She frowned at his haste. "Answer me!" he snapped. "Where is Lillabeth Hollenwell?"

"She's in the kitchen, my lord –"

"Are you alone?"

"Yes, my lord –"

"Then let me in and close the door. Bolt it. Take me to her."

"My lord." She latched and bolted the door behind him, then led him down the narrow kitchen passageway.

A low fire burnt in one corner and Lillabeth stood, setting a cup and jug on a tray. She looked pale, and shook with what seemed fatigue. One hand was pressed across her stomach and she leaned hard against the table.

"Oh, Lilly!" Toriana cried, hurrying to her. She sat the girl down in a chair. "Lilly," she said, pressing her hands. "Lilly, are you well?"

"Yes."

Eamon had forgotten the gentle tone of her voice, and was suddenly struck by her as never before. There was goodness and nobility in her, and unfailing service. How could he have forgotten that? She lived in Dunthruik and served the enemies of her King, and yet she bore it faithfully. How could he not have done as she had done? It shamed him.

"I am well, but Lady Alessia –"

"Lilly, Lord Goodman is here –"

"Lord Goodman!" Lillabeth cried, seeing Eamon for the first time. She tried to climb to her feet but was unsteady. The matron grasped her. "I'm sorry, my lord, I would have risen –"

"Don't be ridiculous," Eamon told her. "I should be standing for you."

Lillabeth stared at him with round, astonished eyes, and glanced at the silent matron before looking back to him. He could not guess her thought. "My lord," she whispered.

"You have to come with me, now."

"How can I trust myself to you?" Lillabeth demanded.

Eamon could only imagine what she thought of him.

There was no time to explain, but he had to try. "I have been a foolish man," he answered, anguished, "and now hope to repent and make amends, at least in part. I can offer you no proof of that intent but my words." He faltered. She watched him in silence. His forehead and palm burnt. "Lillabeth, they've arrested Mathaiah – they'll come for you next. I can't let that happen."

Lillabeth sank down with a shudder. "Mathaiah."

"I am truly sorry, Lillabeth," Eamon told her. He understood her fear: however courageous Mathaiah was, her cover was as good as gone. The Hands would not be gentle with her when they found her.

The matron tried to check her shaking with soothing words. Eamon started forward.

"Please," he said. "Please, Lillabeth; get a cloak and come with me. There isn't time for anything."

Shaking, Lillabeth rose. Toriana rushed to find a cloak. This she draped over Lillabeth's shoulders, doing it up tightly at the front. She kissed the girl's forehead. "Courage, Lilly. You knew it might come to this. Courage!"

"Is she trustworthy, Lillabeth?"

Lillabeth matched his gaze. "As I am."

Eamon turned to the matron. "Toriana, on your very life I charge you to speak nothing of what you have seen tonight. You must not mention my name, and you must not tell Lady Turnholt anything. Do you understand?"

"Yes, my lord."

At Alessia's name Lillabeth started in anguish. "I cannot leave her like this!"

"But you will," Eamon told her vindictively. Lillabeth stared; he realized how fiercely he had spoken.

He drew a deep breath, trying to temper, or at the very least swallow, the anger and urgency that he felt. "We must go now. Keep your charge, Toriana."

"I will, my lord."

The matron quietly unbolted the door. She glanced outside.

"It's safe." She took Lillabeth's hand a moment. "Take care, Lilly."

"Take care of Lady Alessia," Lillabeth answered urgently. "There is some terrible grief on her tonight."

Eamon grabbed Lillabeth's other hand. "Come on."

They went in silence, and far more slowly than Eamon would have liked; Lillabeth seemed weak. He pulled up his hood to disguise himself. As they passed the doors of the house he heard footsteps and weeping on the balcony above.

With a firm hand he pressed Lillabeth back into the shadows of the building. He heard his own heart pounding. Then a call broke the silence:

"Lilly!" it called, shredded with tears. "Lilly!"

The girl gasped. "My lady!"

"No!" Eamon hissed, forcing her back. What if Alessia had guessed his intent and meant to trap them?

"She needs me!" Lillabeth countered angrily, striking him away.

The lady called again. The voice was torn and desperate: "Lilly!"

Lillabeth drew breath to answer – Eamon drove his hand over her mouth.

"I said no!"

She glared at him with angry, suspicious eyes, and shook herself free.

"What did you do to her?" she hissed. Eamon could not comprehend the fierce love in the girl's voice. "What did you do!"

"Lilly?"

Eamon seized the maid's hand. Blocking Alessia's weeping from his ears, he dragged Lillabeth out of the gates.

The moon lit the road. Eamon made sure that Lillabeth's hood covered her face and looped her arm through his. He slowed their pace and hoped that anyone who saw them would not guess the identity of his companion. Lillabeth shuddered angrily. Eamon ignored it.

They followed the Coll to the Four Quarters. There, Eamon bore down Coronet Rise to the south and then onto the Serpentine. The streets were quiet, but he was anxious; he was not a frequent visitor to the quarter.

The Serpentine spanned a crumbling part of the city, showing few traces of former glory in its abandoned stones. The road snaked through the South Quarter, going almost diagonally across it from Coronet Rise to the Blind Gate. The houses were dimly lit and Eamon scanned each one, looking desperately for the sign that would proclaim the presence of the correct inn – the road had several. At each false sign the voice mocked him. He tightened his grip on Lillabeth's hand. It would be there. It had to be.

At last his search was rewarded. A small inn stood halfway down the road, partially collapsed against the neighbouring building. Its sign showed a wall – appropriately, as the city wall was not far away. Eamon saw guards walking the misty parapets.

Keeping Lillabeth close he strode to the inn door. The windows were misted, and in the scant candlelight he could not tell how many people might be inside. Drawing his cloak tightly around him and his hood around his face, he opened the door.

He had no idea what to do. The few clients who sat at tables rose to their feet and bowed as soon as they saw him; he cursed his black robes.

He led Lillabeth to the bar. The innkeeper rose.

"You honour us, my lord."

Eamon fixed all his hope on memory of Hughan's words. Had the King not said that the innkeeper could help him, should he need to escape? Could not that warrant secure Lillabeth's freedom also?

You are a fool, Eben's son.

"Are you the proprietor of this inn?" Eamon deepened his voice to disguise it. He needed to speak to the man in private. But how…?

"Yes, my lord," the innkeeper replied cautiously. "I have that little honour."

The answer came to him. "Good. You will take us to the best of your rooms." He scattered coins indolently across the table. Lillabeth stiffened. Eamon was sorry, but he saw no other way.

"At once, my lord." The innkeeper dashed behind the bar, fumbled for a set of keys, and bade them follow him. Lillabeth was reluctant at Eamon's arm but he made her follow. They delved into the inn's smoky depths.

The man led them up a small staircase to a room. He unlocked the door with trembling hands and bowed again.

"I hope it pleases you, my lord." Eamon saw the man watching Lillabeth pitifully. "You will not be disturbed here."

Will you not do as he expects? The voice goaded him. *Why not take her, son of Eben?*

Eamon pushed Lillabeth roughly through the door. As the innkeeper made to leave, Eamon stopped him. "I require your services a moment more, keeper."

The innkeeper looked petrified, but at the terrible look on Eamon's face he stepped hastily into the room. Eamon snatched the keys from his hand, pressed the door closed, and locked it.

"My lord!" the keeper began. Eamon hissed for silence.

He prowled the room, examining its every part. The keeper and Lillabeth watched him fearfully – he knew it – and as he strode he strove with the voice that preyed on him.

You are angry, Eben's son. Visit it on them. It will relieve you.

Eamon swallowed and focused. The walls seemed sturdy enough; the room's window faced the street. He turned to the innkeeper.

"You are certain nobody will hear us here?"

"My lord, have pity!" the keeper cried, falling to his knees.

Eamon was stunned. What did the keeper think he meant to do? What had other Hands done before him?

"Please," he whispered, stepping up to the keeper, "do not kneel before me." He laid a gentle hand on the man's shoulder.

"You're… you're not going to –?"

"I intend no harm either to you or to the girl. I am sorry if I misled you into thinking otherwise. A man in my position has many battles to fight, I fear, and must sometimes do so by indirect means. Good keeper," he added kindly, "I have need of your service."

"My service?" The keeper stared. "My lord, I don't know what you mean –"

"I understand that this looks strange. Please. I come on behalf of a name higher than my own, and it is service to him that I require."

"A higher name…" The innkeeper glanced at Lillabeth. She stood motionless. Wide-eyed, the keeper looked back to Eamon. "My lord… who are you?"

"I am the First Knight." The words came boldly from his lips.

Lillabeth's silent mouth fell open. The keeper was at a loss for words.

"You… you…"

"This lady serves the King," Eamon continued. "She is now in danger. I would ask you to see her from the city."

"How can you be the First Knight?" the man asked. He gaped at Eamon – and his black robes – incredulously.

"Will you help her?"

With odd dignity, the innkeeper rose to his feet. "Follow me," he said.

He led them silently down the staircase and to the back of the inn, away from watchful eyes. He directed them to a storeroom filled with barrels, kegs, and sacks of grain hoarded against the remaining winter months. The door was closed behind them.

Kneeling down beside a collection of large barrels the keeper laboriously began to move them aside. Eamon helped him. For what seemed an eternity all that could be heard was the sound of wood scraping hard across the stone floor.

The barrels revealed a small trapdoor, wide enough for a man to slip down. The innkeeper ran his hands into a groove in the wood and lifted up the thick board. A wave of air ran up towards them, guttering the torches dying on the wall.

Eamon peered downward. He saw nothing in the darkness. "What is it?"

"Part of the old sewer system, disused for centuries, my lord, and in poor repair." The innkeeper took a torch. "Go to the end of the tunnel. There are a few forks; go straight. There's a dead end topped by another door. Knock. They'll let you out."

Eamon nodded. "Thank you."

At the keeper's direction, Eamon positioned himself in the trapdoor and lowered himself down the ladder that he found beneath his feet. It did not descend far; reaching the ground, he found that the tunnel was barely two hands above his head. The innkeeper passed down the torch, then helped Lillabeth. Eamon steadied her as she climbed down.

"You must go straight, always straight!"

Eamon thanked him again. He was turning when the man called after him: "First Knight!"

Eamon marvelled at the power of this title – his title. Just as a smile from him as Lord Goodman had made cadets and lieutenants beam, this name – a name of his that he had forgotten – seemed to draw out something from deep within him. Something that stirred hope and courage in him and bestowed them on others. He saw both then on the innkeeper's face.

"Keeper?"

"Will I know you, if I see you again?"

Eamon was glad of the hood hiding his face. "Keeper," he said at last, "you will know me when the King deems it time. Until then, treat all of my colour with the same caution you always have."

Awestruck, the innkeeper nodded.

"The King's grace go with you," Lillabeth whispered to him.

"And with you!"

The keeper closed the gap. Eamon heard barrels being replaced over the trapdoor. The torch in his hand spat, threatening extinction; a tinge of claustrophobia gripped him. The floor was slippery and the torch smoke stung their faces.

He held out his hand to Lillabeth. "Come on."

The tunnel was narrow, the air thin and stale. Stonework crumbled overhead and underfoot. Lillabeth stumbled repeatedly.

"Are you well?" he asked, steadying her. She was breathing hard.

"Yes," she answered him. "I'm well. I'm sorry."

"Don't rush," he told her as she struggled to gain her feet. Her face was pale, her eyes reddened by tears and smoke. He made her lean on him. Holding the torch high, they carried on.

They passed bends and gaping forks. Eamon ignored them. At length they reached the end of the tunnel. The straight way, which curved slightly westwards, came to an abrupt end.

The torch was dying in Eamon's hands. Trying not to panic, he held its spattering embers high. Where was the exit?

"There," Lillabeth said suddenly, pointing upwards. Eamon looked. In the darkness above was a trapdoor. The wood was set in a channel in the stones, just out of reach. A plank of wood was below it.

Eamon passed the torch to Lillabeth and grabbed the plank. He lifted and angled it beneath the trapdoor before driving it upwards in three firm knocks.

He kept very still, listening. No sound of movement above. Lillabeth swallowed nervously. He strained and knocked again.

Nothing. Chilled sweat beaded his forehead. What if there was nobody above to hear them?

"The torch!" Lillabeth gasped.

It was sputtering. Hefting the plank he knocked again; the sound echoed the long length of the tunnel.

No answer. Eamon dropped the plank.

The torch died. He took it and cast it down, the last embers spitting and glowering before fizzling out.

Lillabeth shivered. Eamon wrapped his cloak about her.

"I'm sorry." His voice echoed, like the dead knocks.

A faint noise. They both looked up. Something moved overhead. Suddenly the trapdoor ground to one side. Beyond were stars and torchlight.

"Who goes there?"

"Bearers of the King's grace," Lillabeth replied.

A rope ladder fell. Eamon steadied it for Lillabeth. She reached the top without difficulty. Drawing his hood over his face, he followed her. The torchlight was blinding as he emerged. He heard the River. They were beyond the city walls!

Even as he marvelled, blades were drawn and arrows knocked to strings.

"Hand!"

"Kill him!"

"No!" Lillabeth shrieked, throwing herself between them and him. "He is a King's man!"

The men around them were dressed in green and brown, like those Eamon had seen in Hughan's camps. They watched him fiercely.

"If he is a King's man," one growled, "let him show his face."

"He can't –" Lillabeth began.

"It's all right, Lillabeth," Eamon interrupted. Alessia had betrayed him; the Hands would already know everything. Showing his face could not hurt him now. He sternly met the gaze of the leading man. "You and your men will swear never to speak my name to any but the King."

"That depends on your face!"

It was answer enough. "Very well."

He pulled back his hood. He did not know whether they recognized him. He did not care. He had to see to Lillabeth. "Miss

Hollenwell has been compromised," he told them. "You must take her to the King."

"We will." Seemingly satisfied, the man gestured for his men to lower their weapons. He looked Eamon up and down uncertainly. "Are you going, too?"

"No," Eamon replied. "I must return to the city. I have a friend there in grave peril."

Lillabeth turned to him in horror. "If you go back they'll –"

"All the same, I must."

"Then my companions will take you back into the city through the port; you can't return by this way. We will take Miss Hollenwell to safety."

Eamon nodded gratefully. He turned to Lillabeth. "Thank you."

Lillabeth looked surprised. "For what?"

"Your faith in me today. I have never earned it – but I have changed."

Lillabeth took his hand. "He always believed that you would remember."

Eamon frowned. "Who?"

Lillabeth froze. "You don't know," she breathed. But she could not continue – one of the wayfarers took her arm.

"I beg your pardon, Miss," he said. "We have to go, and so does your friend here, or he'll be missed. That's costly in his garb."

"Yes, of course." Lillabeth looked back to him. "Take care, Lord Goodman."

Eamon watched, utterly bemused, as she disappeared. Who had believed he would remember? Who had maintained such hope in him, despite all that he had done?

There was a voice at his ear. "This way." The wayfarer gestured towards the Sea Gate and the port. "We can't take torches or they'll see us from the walls. You'll need to watch your step."

"Of course." Gathering his cloak about him, he followed his guide towards the port.

They waited until the guards were changing and then Eamon made his way through the Sea Gate alone. The streets were silent and he kept his hood drawn close. His heart pounded with exhilaration – and fear.

Surely the throned already knew everything that he had done – why had he not been incarcerated, like Mathaiah? He could not fathom it. There had to be some reason – but what? He felt a dreadful pawn in a game beyond his imagining. Perhaps that was all he was.

It took him very little time to reach the palace. As he passed the threshold of the Hands' Hall a figure rose towards him. His guilty heart leaped.

"Evening, Ratbag!" said a cheery voice.

Eamon grasped his chest; his heart beat so fast he feared it might burst out.

"Ladomer! River's sake, you scared me!"

"You scared me," Ladomer countered. "What are you doing, coming in at this hour?"

"I was with Lady Turnholt…" Eamon began the response then fell grimly silent.

"Lovers' quarrel?"

"No."

"Why didn't you stay with her, then?" His tone was disquieting. Eamon decided to change the subject.

"You're up a little late, aren't you?"

Ladomer shrugged. "Apparently Lord Cathair doesn't sleep. He had some last minute papers that he wanted to send to the Master. Some cadet they arrested, I think. Details of his effects, and so on." He waved his hand – Eamon knew the drill. He was seized with dread. Could the papers be about Mathaiah?

"Well, I hope they let you go to bed sometime soon," he answered, trying a small smile.

"You're right; can't waste my boyish good looks on this kind of work! Sleep well, Ratbag."

"You too."

Chapter XXIV

Eamon quickly made his way to his quarters, trying to drive thoughts of Mathaiah from his mind. He could do nothing until morning. Lord Cathair was of the kind to stay up all night interrogating his prisoners.

He woke early, disturbed by the light. His legs ached and the smell of smoke clung to him. The throned's banner watched him from the wall.

You will pay for what you did. He will pay for what you did, Eben's son. He is already paying...

Eamon lurched across the room to his basin. He splashed water onto his face and let it drip dry. His heart was unsteady and his mind reeled.

What was he doing? What had he done? Would Mathaiah really pay for what he had done? But how could they know? They couldn't know...

His eyes fell to the table by his bed. On it was a ring that Alessia had given him long before. He had given her more than kisses in return. It sickened him. He thought of Mathaiah, bound and led away by the Hands. What tortures had his friend endured in the night?

He opened the trunk by his bed. Inside were his paltry belongings – some papers and coins, a stone from Edesfield. Among these things lay the heart of the King, discarded for so long. It glinted in the half-light. He was the First Knight –

A name you voided long ago! the voice hissed. *Now you bear no name but the one I give you.*

He weighed Alessia's ring in his hand. When she had given it to him, when she had set it in his hand and covered him with pernicious kisses... even then, she had meant to betray him. The desperate cries for Lillabeth that he had heard the previous night had to have been part of that same ruse. It had all been meant to trap him.

How could Lillabeth, a servant of the King, have loved such a woman so devoutly?

How could he have loved her?

He hurled the ring into the trunk and drew out the heart of the King. It was cool. He drew it slowly over his neck and buried it beneath his shirt. Its weight was soothing, as it had been of old. Could he be forgiven and released?

Suddenly there was a knock at his door. Closing the trunk, he rose to answer. Febian stood outside, his face pale.

"Lord Febian."

"Lord Goodman; the Right Hand wants to see you."

A chill ran through him. "Of course. Where is he?"

"The Hands' Gate."

Driving tentacles of the voice from his mind, Eamon hurried to the main hallway.

As the sun was just throwing her early rays onto the yard, he was confronted with an awful sight: a long row of men, many of them members of the militia but a very high number in Gauntlet uniforms. Spaced between them at intervals were nervous-looking knights.

One by one Eamon recognized the faces of men who had followed him to Pinewood. In fact, the line included every man who had survived that expedition. Added to their number were the remaining thirteen Third Banner cadets. All looked anxious.

"Lord Goodman, how good of you to join us."

The Right Hand stood near the end of the line. He had evidently been inspecting it. Eamon noticed a group of belligerent-looking Hands to one side. What was happening?

"You summoned me, my lord?" he asked, bowing.

"Yes, yes I did," the Right Hand answered. "You slept well, I trust?"

Eamon felt uncomfortable beneath his keen stare. "Thank you, my lord, yes."

"Rise, Lord Goodman. Ah, the last man." The Right Hand looked contentedly along the line. "Soon we can begin."

Captain Anderas staggered through the Hands' Gate. He was escorted by two Hands who forced him to join the line near its centre. When he stopped he was breathing heavily with fatigue.

Filled with foreboding, Eamon turned to the Right Hand. "My lord, what is the meaning of this?" he demanded. Why had they brought Anderas from his rest? Over-exertion could still kill him! The captain was not the only injured man who had been forced into the line – there were groups of others, some swathed in bandage or looking unsteady on their feet.

The Right Hand glared. "That is uncivil of you, Lord Goodman." Vengeful wrath was in the man's cold eyes.

Hands closed the gate. Eamon was startled to see the bolts being drawn. The men shuffled and exchanged disconcerted looks. None spoke. The Right Hand turned to face the line.

"Good morning, gentlemen." Each word struck horribly at Eamon's heart. "You are all men who can lay claim to a singularly dubious honour. You have all served under the command of Lord Goodman."

Eamon looked across sharply, but the Right Hand didn't look at him. He was pacing along the line, a smile twisting his face.

"Most of you will know that Lord Goodman is a man of an equally singular reputation. The man who surrendered his sword, who escaped the clutches of the enemy, who became first lieutenant of the West Quarter College in days, and a Hand in mere months.

"But recently, gentlemen, Lord Goodman has suffered a series of debilitating misadventures." Eamon's blood curdled. "Those of you who were with him then, know that what was a routine, regular, simple operation at Pinewood became a massacre due to his incompetence. But Lord Goodman has suffered another indignation, gentlemen. Last night his own ward, a cadet whom he had promised to teach to serve the Master, was arrested. On what charge?" Here, the Right Hand met Eamon's gaze. "Being a snake."

Eamon's breath caught in his throat.

The Right Hand glared at the line. "This charge has been

proven," he said, "and reflects ill on a man whom you have all followed and to whom you have at times pledged your trust. These motley dishonours require atonement – would you not agree, Lord Goodman?" His voice was quiet, deadly, and Eamon feared to answer. More than that, he feared not to answer.

"A fault requires a punishment, my lord," he managed.

The Right Hand smiled. "I am so glad that you agree." He looked back to the line. "These faults need addressing. In the same way as following his commands was allotted to you, Lord Goodman is in agreement with me that his faults should be atoned for by you."

Horror ran through the line. A hundred betrayed men turned to him.

He gaped at the Right Hand. It wasn't true! He had never said such a thing. He had explicitly given that the fault lay with him, and him alone! "My lord –"

Suddenly a cruel voice spoke behind his ear: "If I were you, Lord Goodman, I would hold my tongue." Eamon froze; the voice was Cathair's. "Or he'll make it one in five."

One in…

A decimation. It had to be. They had searched for Lillabeth, and found her gone. They had to know – or guess – that he had removed her. They could not prove it. This was to be the punishment visited upon him for his defiance; one to press him back into their service before he strayed too far.

He had to do something.

"Lord Cathair," he begged.

But it was too late. The Right Hand motioned his Hands forward. "To atone for Lord Goodman's many faults, one in ten of all those who have served under him shall shed his blood."

Stunned silence gripped the line. The Right Hand was undaunted.

"Any man who runs will be slaughtered for cowardice, and the men who flanked him will share his fate." Suddenly he smiled. "Lord Goodman has ratified this course of action and is here to oversee it. Comport yourselves with honour, as befits him."

Cathair grasped Eamon's shoulder. He bit his tongue.

The Right Hand pointed at a man, one of the polemen from Pinewood. An armed Hand surged forward. The chosen man blenched – and the Hand was upon him. The knife was quick.

Horrified silence. The corpse dropped.

The Right Hand counted along the line, and pointed to another man, a cadet. Another Hand went forward, and another body fell.

"No!" Eamon gaped. How could the Right Hand do this?

"Hounds that bite must be punished," Cathair hissed. "A man who would take a flogging for his cadets is best punished when his men pay on his behalf."

Eamon turned cold.

The Right Hand counted again. Another Hand went forward, another man fell. Eamon's chest heaved with rage and anguish. What if the Hand's gesture alighted on Manners or Anderas?

His mind whirled. It was barbaric that men should be punished for his faults. They would not publicly kill a Hand – that was why they had to kill the men. But they knew his weakness. This punishment had been chosen with him in mind: they meant to break him.

They will not kill a Hand, Eamon.

The thought ran through him with startling force. Suddenly, he knew what he had to do.

Another ensign tumbled to the ground, and the Right Hand counted austerely along the line with a wicked smile. But Eamon counted the ashen faces more swiftly than he, then tore across to the line, reached it, wrenched an ensign out of place, and took it.

The Right Hand's count alighted on him, the number ten on his lips.

"Step out of the line, Lord Goodman," he commanded. He voice was very still.

Eamon glared back. The man he had pushed from the line lay on the ground behind him, stunned. Whatever else happened, his men would know that he had not agreed to this scheme.

Defiance, he realized, could not be wrathful. He would not outlive it, otherwise. So thinking, he knelt before the Right Hand.

"I humbly bend my knee before you, my lord. I never ratified this decimation, nor would I ever have done so. This you know well. I will pay for all faults attributed to my name. I alone am responsible for my failings." He felt something warm at his breast – his heart leaped. Could it be the heart of the King, maybe even the blue light? Was it that which gave him strength to defy the Right Hand?

"Curb yourself, Lord Goodman," the Right Hand spat. "Retract your words, and step out of the line."

"No," Eamon answered steadily. "No more of these men, each of them loyal to the Master, will pay for my errors." There was boldness in every limb; it strengthened him to speak again. "I demand to see the Master! Let me atone for my own error in whatever way he deems fit." He looked up. "You will not deny me."

He stunned the yard. The Right Hand glared speechlessly. Eamon feared a hideous reprisal. The smell of spilled blood rose in his nostrils.

At last, the Right Hand moved. "Very well," he said. "I will speak with the Master. Keep them here," he added, calling to the other Hands.

He stalked to the East Wing of the palace, his cloak streaming behind him. Eamon quivered, but he felt a strange exultation. He had pitched himself against the Right Hand, and lived! How many could say as much?

He heard a sound behind him, as of weeping being stifled, and turned. The ensign whose life he had saved shook on the ground. Eamon took hold of the man's arm.

"Courage," he whispered.

"You will keep your place, Lord Goodman!" snarled Cathair.

Eamon did not turn. After holding the ensign's look for a long moment he rose to his feet, the ensign with him.

"I will keep my place, my lord," he said, "and this good man will keep it with me."

Chapter XXIV

The ensign's trembling hand was on his arm. Eamon settled him into the line and nodded encouragement to him. Only then did he turn to Cathair. The green-eyed Hand looked fulminous. Eamon saw his men gaping and wondering at him. Nothing of the like had ever happened in Dunthruik. What Hand would risk his life for mere men? Sun touched his face.

It seemed a long time that the courtyard stood in silence, the armed Hands prowling the line. Blood spread from the fallen men but the line held itself. The bustle of the rising city could be heard beyond the palace walls.

At last a black-clad figure appeared at the far side of the colonnade: the Right Hand was returning. Sudden fear yawned within him. What if the Master really did demand retribution of him?

You are wise to fear me, son of Eben.

The Right Hand halted and surveyed them darkly. "I speak the will of the Master," he said. "Let none oppose me in it." He fixed Eamon sinisterly. "The Master will allot to Lord Goodman a task by which he may redeem his and all your honours. If Lord Goodman is successful, the Master himself will bestow honour on you. If he fails, each of your lives will be forfeit."

The line was crushed; Eamon staggered. How could he propose such a thing?

"Let them leave," the Right Hand commanded crisply. "Lord Goodman will remain."

The gates were opened and the line filed into the street beyond. Only Anderas dared to meet his gaze as he passed; it was fraught with worry.

Eamon reeled. What had he done? Now all their lives rested on him.

The other Hands drew round him. He felt small and afraid.

The Right Hand glowered. "Follow me, Lord Goodman."

Struggling to steady shaking knees, Eamon did as he was commanded.

The Right Hand took him to the throne room. The doors were bound before them. The doorkeeper was there, and bowed low. The Right Hand ignored him. He turned to Eamon.

"You are too bold, Goodman." His voice was thick with ire; even the doorkeeper trembled. "You will not defy me again."

Eamon did not have time to feel afraid. Suddenly the doors to the throne room stood open and the voice of the Master summoned him inside.

CHAPTER XXV

T he doors closed leadenly behind him. There was no escape.

The throne room was struck through with the first light of the day, making the paintings the eerily vivid guardians of a fiery realm. The figures upon the walls watched him; they were but pale reflections of the one who sat upon the throne.

The Master was dressed in black and red, his powerful face framed with fiery hair, tangled in which sat a crown. No painting could ever conjure the full terror and grandeur of the one enthroned in that hall: the unassailable, immovable, grey-eyed Master. Surely very worlds would fall to their knees before him?

"Come forward, Eben's son." The voice brooked no defiance and expected none.

Eamon could barely breathe. Quivering, he crossed to the dais. Every step sounded in the interminable length of the hall.

Reaching the throne, he dropped to his knees.

"Your glory over all things, Master." He felt as though he were dissolving in fear.

At last the Master spoke, his voice filled with a father's indulgence for a wayward child.

"There is an unspeakable, high-minded impetuosity in your blood, Eben's son." The voice cracked down Eamon's spine. The throned laughed – a sound that rocked Eamon to his core. "And to dare my Right Hand! He could have killed you where you stood and left your carcass to glut a raven's brood." The eyes grew as keen as knives. The Master's voice rose with wrath that might part flesh from bone.

"When you defy my Right Hand, Eben's son, you also defy me."

Eamon's tongue clove to the roof of his mouth and neither breath nor word could venture forth. How could he not have seen where his defiance would lead? Now he could only await the Master's fury.

The throned's face was touched by a smile. "It has been long since anyone defied the Right Hand."

Why was he smiling? The Master's eyes glistened.

Receiving that look, Eamon did not know whether to feel relieved or terrified. As he tried to calm his heart he felt memories of Alessia and Lillabeth being tugged to mind. Those thoughts beat wildly about him.

The throned was watching him – was he watching his thoughts? With a desperate effort Eamon forced his churning mind to be still. Being in the presence of the Hands was terrible enough, but to be alone with the throned – as he suddenly realized he was –threatened to shred his very soul. He tried to rally his courage but trembled wretchedly in every limb. He knew the throned could see him shaking.

The Master stood. "Rise, Eben's son."

Eamon glanced up: it felt akin to peering into the heights of the heavens. Meeting the grey eyes, he could only obey. He rose. The Master seemed a giant who had deigned to gaze upon some crawling worm beneath him. His pale face was proud and strong, limitless in power, and the grey eyes showed forth a shrewd and domineering mind.

Any sense of victory that Eamon had felt was torn from him, like a veil from a maiden, as he rose before the Master.

"Good," the Master smiled. "Walk with me."

Eamon stared at him for a moment, utterly incapable of comprehension. The throned stepped down from the dais. The Master never once looked behind to see if his order was obeyed. Eamon stumbled after him.

Whether by arcane powers or hidden hands, the great doors opened before the Master. He was lord of all that surrounded him. It seemed that the stones trembled to bear such mighty feet.

The throned passed through his great hall to the Hands' Hall. Guards, Gauntlet, servants, and Hands dropped to their knees or bowed down before him, falling still in their places with calls of: "Your glory!"

Eamon realized that his name would be on the lips of every man in the palace by the end of the day. First he had defied the Right Hand, then he had walked alone with the Lord of Dunthruik. All eyes watched in horror and awe as he followed the Master. The throned sailed past them all, noticing neither their obeisance nor their homage.

Lord Cathair was in the hall, speaking in agitated tones to one of his servants. As the Master's shadow passed over him the Hand fell suddenly silent.

"Your glory, and an unexpected grace, Master," he said, bowing.

The throned nodded and passed by. Eamon followed, flinching back from the gaze with which Cathair crushed him.

Gradually, Eamon realized where they were going. He remembered the times that Cathair had taken him through those halls, to make him an actor of deeds he had not always wanted to commit. He remembered Clarence's screams of agony, the tortured look on the faces of both father and son. The power of the memory nearly forced him to his knees.

Clarence forgave you, Eamon. A voice spoke clearly in his mind. It was not the voice of the Master. It surprised him, and he faltered.

The throned looked back sharply. Eamon bowed low in terror.

"Your glory, Master."

A smile grew on the throned's face. "Do you know where we are going, Eben's son?"

Eamon nodded – they were going to the Pit.

The smell touched him long before anything else; it had haunted his nightmares. Blood, waste, rotting flesh. How could he have forgotten it? And yet he had done so. It was more terrible than the smell after Pinewood, or the stench of the village that had been destroyed thereafter. It was more terrible than the smell of the blood spilled by the Right Hand but half an hour before. It was the reek of torment and suffering.

The throned led him to one of the rooms adjoining the Pit. Several Hands were there. They bowed with lightning reflexes. Eamon heard raised voices coming from a chamber beyond the room.

"Your glory," spoke the Hands in unison.

"Call them out."

The Hands moved at once. Eamon stood, his limbs trembling. Why had he been brought there?

Men emerged from the chamber. One was Ashway. The Hand wore a look of utter rage and swore vilely. Eamon did not recognize the other Hand, nor did he care to; all he saw was that the second Hand dragged someone roughly forward. The victim was thrust before the throned.

It was Mathaiah.

Eamon stared in horror. His ward had been stripped. Added to the crusting scar on his face the young man bore welts, bruises, cuts, and burns. He seemed injured everywhere, except for his hands and face.

Eamon gaped at the marks of torment. What had they done to Mathaiah? He dared not think on it. And how could the young man have endured so much? Exultant defiance shone in the cadet's eyes. Eamon was awed by it. Mathaiah faced the flame-haired throned without a trace of fear on his quiet face. How could he?

"What have you to tell, Lord Ashway?" demanded the Master.

"But little yet, Master," Ashway answered, glancing at Eamon as though he were dirt. "No more than that of which you are already aware."

The throned turned to Mathaiah. "You will bow down."

Eamon silently willed the young man to obey. Retribution would be unspeakable if he did not!

Mathaiah raised his head. Though he trembled slightly, he did not flinch.

"I will not."

His answer stole Eamon's breath away.

"You will crawl on your knees before the Master, snake!" The Hand holding Mathaiah dealt him a series of blistering blows. Mathaiah staggered, but he did not kneel.

"There is no man here to whom I may bend my knee!" Mathaiah gasped, eyes clenched against the pain.

The Hand hit him again.

"Lord Goodman," commanded the Master, "tell your ward to kneel."

Mathaiah saw him for the first time and drew shocked breath. He quickly averted his eyes, as though the mere sight of him was worse than any torture he had endured. Eamon took it as a blow, but he could not speak. The Master stood by him, his face framed in the hellish mane of red.

Eamon bent to meet Mathaiah's gaze as resolutely as he could. He forced fear from his voice. "Do as the Master bids you, Mr Grahaven." The beating had opened some of his wounds – Eamon saw the Hand's bloodied fist ready to continue, felt Ashway's glare upon him, and the throned's will behind him. He swallowed. "Kneel."

Mathaiah stilled. For a moment his gasping was all that could be heard. Eamon wanted to call him by name, to beg of him to do as he was bidden. Did he want to die? He only needed to kneel…

His ward met his gaze. Without uttering a single word, Mathaiah Grahaven shook his head.

The Master held out one hand. He laid it on Mathaiah's bare shoulder. The boy wrenched back, as though it brought with it intolerable pain. Red light roared about the Master's fingertips – Eamon choked back a cry. Mathaiah howled as the light scoured him, broken sobs from cracked lips.

"I am the Master of the River Realm and the Lord of Dunthruik. You will obey me." The red light, stronger than bands or flames, increased, and suddenly Mathaiah was cast onto his knees. There was a horrid crack as they struck the cold, hard floor.

The throned withdrew his hand. The light vanished. Mathaiah crumpled, writing. As he choked on his agony his eyes found Eamon's; they burned with anger.

"You may break my body, or make it kneel," he gasped, "but you will not have my heart. I am a King's man."

The throned regarded the young man silently, machinations marching behind his grey eyes. None dared to move.

"Eben's son, tell me what you see on the table."

Tearing his eyes from Mathaiah, Eamon forced his gaze to the table. There were some papers and a small bag of coins on it. At least one of the papers appeared to be a letter written in Mathaiah's hand. By it lay a small silver ring.

"There are coins, a ring, and a letter, Master," Eamon answered.

"Bring me the letter."

With shaking hands, Eamon handed the parchment to the throned. The Master turned to the cadet.

"This letter was for your father." His voice had the roar of fire. Mathaiah gasped and squirmed, as though the voice alone hurt him. "He will learn how you have served his name."

The throned held the paper before Mathaiah's reddened eyes. "Parchment can be read. It is pale; it can be burnt and torn." He slowly tore the letter into halves, then quarters, letting the shreds fall before Mathaiah's eyes. "Even so can a woman."

For a moment, Mathaiah gaped, his face riven with horror and despair. His breath quickened, becoming almost uncontrollable as the Master's grey eyes held him; his hands trembled where shreds of the paper had fallen among his fingers.

Suddenly he fell still. He closed his eyes and pressed his hands about the paper. "You do not have her," he answered simply, "and I am not afraid."

Eamon glanced at the ring with terrible foreboding. What did he not know?

"Have you nothing that you would say to Lord Goodman?" the Master asked. "In my name and for my glory he brought you here. All that you suffer – everything that she will suffer – is due to his work."

Mathaiah looked at Eamon with unbearable ire. Eamon steadied himself. Mathaiah would speak and betray him – betray them both!

There was a long silence. They watched each other across the small chamber, Mathaiah still panting. Eamon's heart beat hard.

Slowly, the anger in Mathaiah's eyes turned from scorn to pity, and from pity to regret and sorrow. "I have nothing to say to Lord Goodman," he whispered.

Eamon reeled. Not one word? Was he not worthy even of Mathaiah's anger?

The Lord of Dunthruik cast a withering gaze on the cadet. "Then you have outlasted your purpose. Lord Ashway, send him to the Pit."

Ashway bowed quickly. "Your glory, Master."

The Hands dragged Mathaiah to his feet. The cadet was beaten, gasping and bleeding. Scraps of parchment were pressed between his fingers while the Hands hauled him away. As the doors opened to let them pass, tortured cries issued from the Pit, pain percolating the air. Mathaiah clenched his eyes shut.

The door closed. Again Eamon stood alone with the Master. The torn remains of the letter lay like ashes about their feet.

"Follow me, son of Eben."

Eamon followed. Mathaiah's silver ring glinted in the light. The throned's back was on him – no one would see. Silently, he took the ring. He slipped it into his pouch and followed the Master.

He was led back to the throne room another way. Eamon followed the length of the hall to the throne. The Master sat. Eamon sank at once to his knees before him. He kept his eyes low and tried not to think of Mathaiah.

"Fear not, Eben's son. Your erstwhile ward may be strong now, but he will be broken." It was as though he offered salve to the tormented mind of a child. "Though there may be little use for him other than death, he will glorify me just as you do."

Eamon nodded. Yes. It was right that Mathaiah should be broken for his insolence. No mercy should be shown to such a man.

"Yes, Master."

What was he thinking? Eamon tried to eject the insidious thoughts that masqueraded as his own. The cadet would never glorify the throned. Mathaiah Grahaven was sworn to Hughan, willing to prove that service on his body and with his life. Eamon knew too well what horrors the Pit held – to think of Mathaiah being cast to its torments grieved his whole heart.

Eamon blinked back tears. The young man whose life he had once saved, who had spoken against Alessia and unswervingly kept his oath to Hughan, the young man who was even then being committed to the bloody embraces of the Pit, was a man whom he loved. How could he have forgotten it?

He became horribly aware of the throned's gaze upon him – were his thoughts being sifted? His brow burnt, and his thoughts turned involuntarily from Mathaiah to Lillabeth. Terrified of what might be happening he tried to stop himself remembering the inn on the Serpentine, the tunnel, and the wayfarers to whom he had entrusted Alessia's maid…

Suddenly the burning became an intolerable band of fire. With a gasp he raised his hands to his head – and found that the throned's were already there. His gasps became cries as he struggled to hold his own. The Master watched him.

"Tell me, Eben's son, did you think to strike against me?"

All indulgence was gone and a strange, quiet tone, more deadly than the fiercest poison, took its place. The voice grew darker, the pain greater.

"Did you think that I would permit it? Your little treacheries have been tenderly endured. They will be so no longer."

Panic seared his veins like lightning. He had feared it all along, and now he saw that it was true. The throned knew everything – he had always known it.

"You will serve me, son of Eben. You will glorify me."

There was a flash of red and he cried in alarm. Suddenly the throned towered over him, gripping him with the force of a raging sea.

"Your very heart stands in my power, and it beats or fails at my command."

Eamon froze. He felt the power in the hand upon him. Terrorized, he waited for the obliterating wrath of the red light.

But no light came. Instead, the Master's fingers delved under his robes. They drew out the heart of the King.

The throned brought the cold stone towards him; the chain tightened. Eamon choked for breath.

The throned turned the stone in his hand. He laughed. His steely eyes met Eamon's.

"Please, Master –" Eamon gasped.

"You need not speak to me of this, Eben's son." He pulled on the chain, forcing Eamon to rise to his feet. "From the east it came. I know its making and its history better than he who entrusted it to you – and you would dare to bear it before me."

The throned looked long at the stone, smiling the smile of long remembrance. It remained dead and cold in the hand of the King's enemy.

A tremendous force hit his neck. He collapsed, half-throttled. The chain was broken, the stone clenched in the throned's hand. Red flames appeared in the Master's palm, a torturous, grievous light that burned so fiercely that Eamon could not see. There was an ear-splitting sound – Eamon cried out as it struck him, its intensity forcing him backwards.

The noise died away. Gasping, Eamon dared to open his eyes.

Blue-grey shards lay on the ground. Eamon bit back a cry of grief, but he dared not speak – and he dared not reach for the broken heirloom.

The grey eyes looked down on him. The Master's voice came, gentle and soothing, to his ear.

"You will serve me, redeem your honour, save the lives of your men, and claim your rightful place in this city, Eben's son."

A cold thrill ran through him. How could he refuse? "Yes, Master."

"Bear these shards to the Serpent. You will win his trust. You will seek out the commander in his camp that hails from the east, and you will take his life." The commands had the force of iron bands.

"By sunset of the twenty-seventh, seven days from the next dawn, you will bear that man's head to me. If you do not, your men will lose their lives." Eamon looked up in fear. The Master smiled. "Be sure of this, Eben's son: if they lose their lives they will not lose them to mere knives. Their deaths will be slow, left to the invention of Lord Cathair, and you will witness them."

Eamon stood, dumbstruck. He could not let them die – they were many, so many... Not for his fault. He could not betray the throned.

But how could he betray Hughan again?

He forced his gaze to his Master's. The throned knew his heart – and knew he had no choice.

"The shards, son of Eben." His voice was quiet again, as though he spoke to a child. "Then go, and glorify me."

With trembling hands, Eamon took up the shards of stone and broken chain – emblems of a shattered oath. He rose, bowed low, and left the throne room.

He emerged in a daze, feeling as though he had been rent open, his tortured mind visible to all. Even the breeze chafed him. He heard the city living beyond the palace walls. It could not be more than the third hour. It seemed as though a whole day had passed.

A whole day...

His limbs full of fire, he ran back to the Hands' Hall. In his frenzy he stumbled, nearly dropping the shards. He gripped them tightly. He had to hurry.

He reached his own room. He entered, pressed the door shut, and rested his back firmly against it. The scars over his shoulders burned. The colours over his bed glared at him. He sank down to the floor, the shards of the precious stone crushed in his hands.

Tears streamed down his face.

The choice before him was terrible. It had, he realized, always been terrible. Though he had sworn oaths and been branded and named, it was the choice that he had never made. Now, when so much rode on his staggering heart, he had to.

How could he?

Eagle talons crushed him, constricting his bleeding heart. The eagle pushed him against a serpent, tall, coiled, and venomous on the dark plain. There was a sword in his hand. Again and again the eagle forced him to strike, and his name was screeched like a curse. The serpent endured his every blow, and each grisly strike revealed not stinking flesh but the flanks of a unicorn.

A final blow shed every scale. The unicorn blazed and the eagle was pierced by blue.

With an evil screech the eagle fled. He staggered to his feet, his breast ripped by claws and sorrows. The unicorn came towards him, inclining its head towards his bleeding heart. There was a star above its brow…

He woke, shivering and cold. The sky was darkening. His dreams pounded in his veins like things alive. He felt the talons about him still, their poison coursing through his veins.

The shards of the stone were still in his fingers. He lowered his head against them, pleading for comfort and courage.

He had to leave the city.

He put the shards into a small purse that he wore under his clothes. They felt heavy and dead.

As he passed through the Hands' Hall he met Ladomer. His friend's face was grey.

"I'm to tell you that there are fresh horses at the South Gate. I've sent a message ahead of you, so that when you get there at least one will be ready for you."

"Thank you, Ladomer," Eamon answered. He did not dare to ask who had sent Ladomer with such a message.

The sun was westering under the cover of a grey sky and a strong wind blew in from over the sea. Eamon shivered.

"I've been hearing some terrible rumours about you today, Ratbag."

Overpowering weariness swept over him. What answer could he give? "I suppose you have."

A flush of anger passed over Ladomer's face. He turned Eamon roughly round to face him. "Whatever possessed you to speak to the Right Hand like that?"

Eamon stared. "How do you know?"

"For pity's sake!" Ladomer retorted. "Everyone bloody knows, Eamon! You defied the Right Hand in front of a hundred people. Have you any idea the repercussions it will have for you? What kind of a fool are you?"

Stung, Eamon swallowed. "I'm a brazen fool, Ladomer," he whispered. "I am paying for it."

"I'll say!" Ladomer was explosive with ire at Eamon's folly. "The Right Hand will not forgive you."

"I know."

Ladomer forced himself to calm down. "What happened with the Master?" he asked at last.

"The Right Hand hasn't told you?" Eamon snapped.

"Yes, I have been told," came the harsh reply.

"Then I'm sure you've heard enough."

They stood together for a while. Eamon watched a company of Gauntlet soldiers pass by. He drove his hands over his face. "I'm sorry, Ladomer. I don't want anyone to die."

"That was always your problem." Though his tone was still harsh, his face grew kinder. "Honestly, Eamon! Did you think that this would be easy, that you could saunter around in black and take no responsibility for your command?" He laid his hand on Eamon's shoulder. "We both dreamed of becoming Hands, Eamon. You have been made one. For both our sakes, act like it!"

Eamon stared angrily. "Should the lives of those men mean nothing to me?"

"Despite the Serpent's best efforts, soldiers are still easy to come by, Ratbag." Ladomer offered Eamon a faint smile, and pressed his shoulder. "Men like you – poetic, romantic, chilvalric men – are, I fear, little but a dying breed of quaint curiosities."

The jibe somehow eased the tension that had been growing between them. Eamon shivered once. "I'm sorry, Ladomer."

Ladomer nodded, accepting the apology. "Seven days?"

Eamon breathed deep. "Seven days." There was little else to say.

Beyond readying a horse and gathering some provisions, there were no preparations to make. The Hands knew of his intended absence and he had leave from Cathair to be out of the city – he knew this only because Ladomer delivered the appropriate paperwork to him. Eamon had not been surprised at that. He supposed few of the high-ranking Hands – most of whom he had embarrassed in the last few days – would be in a hurry to see him before he left.

The day went on, and even though he seemed ready he could not bring himself to go. He could not think straight, and found himself nervously pacing and retracing his way through the Hands' Hall. At last he left it, thinking that walking to the Four Quarters and back would clear his mind. He knew that he looked nervous and he was sure that he was watched from every quarter, but he barely cared. The Master's voice was always in his mind. The throned knew everything.

He does not know about the ring, Eamon.

Eamon paused. How could the Master not know? And yet, if the throned had known about the ring would he not have called him to account for it? Would not the voice take back word of it?

Eamon: his voice is but his voice. It is a liar, an oppressor of thought. Nothing more.

Eamon reached into his pouch and drew out the ring. It was like a band of starlight on his palm. He looked at it for a long time – but the Master's voice remained silent.

The sea wind whipped about him, stirring his cloak like ill-omened sails. He saw the Blind Gate and, beyond it, the distant shimmer of the mountains. He stopped and watched mist veil the peaks in a dun haze.

He found himself going on into the East Quarter. He had not gone far when he heard the sound of an approaching horse. A familiar face: Captain Anderas.

The captain drew his steed to a halt. "Lord Goodman."

"Are you well enough to be riding?" Eamon asked, surprised.

"I seem to be well enough to stand in a line," Anderas answered. "The surgeons told me that riding a short distance would be beneficial to me."

"Is it?"

"I've only come from the Ashen," Anderas answered, gesturing over his shoulder towards the East Quarter's principal plaza. "It is a short ride." He looked worriedly at Eamon. "Lord Ashway told me what you're to do."

Did the whole city know of his shame?

Anderas touched Eamon's shoulder. It was a good hand; it would recover to wield a sword again.

"Be careful, Lord Goodman."

Eamon glanced up. "You fear for your life, captain?"

Anderas laughed softly. "No, Lord Goodman," he replied. "My life is but my life. I fear for yours."

Eamon was swept away. "How can you –?"

Anderas smiled. "There is something about you, Lord Goodman, which inspires devotion. It is a fearful gift! I would not see you cast your life away – and I would not lose my friend. My wishes are not entirely selfless. But this city needs you. Thus, I say, take care."

Unable to reply, Eamon nodded. Anderas saluted him and returned to the Ashen.

He drew his cloak about himself in a quandary. How could Dunthruik need him? The city was dense and rotten, ridden with the throned's malice and corruption. It was tangible, and the people of the city bore haunted looks. Even the gentry, he realized, not free. They could laugh and dance, but the women were whored and the men betrayed or pawned in politics and war. The Gauntlet were blind in their service, working for the glory of their Master. The Hands enforced that law and all the while the city, a thing of splendour with eagles and carven crowns on every lintel, was foul and stagnant at its heart. And yet not all was evil. Anderas was there, and Waite, and Manners… Why was it not simple?

Beyond the city walls coils of smoke rose from the pyres. They had been stoked to deal with those taken in the first waves of the culling.

He realized that it was true: the city was founded in blood. The Hands and the Gauntlet were bound to it and in it.

The throned had mastered him. It was the natural consequence of being in Dunthruik. Surely that was the role allotted to him? His place was at the throned's side. Hughan had been wrong about him; there was nothing left in his blood but treachery, and the blood of a traitor could not be offered to the King. The King's grace had abandoned him, disgusted with his service, and the King's heart had been taken from him. Mathaiah was dead.

Eamon brought himself up sharply. Was the throned's influence over him so great that his own thoughts were twisted, even without the interference of the voice? Mathaiah was not dead! He was alive, and Mathaiah had stood against the man who called himself "Master", just as Eamon had stood against the Right Hand. Though they had been punished, neither of them had surrendered. Surely that was worth something?

The silver ring was cool beneath his touch, driving away the heat in his hand and forehead. His mind was still his own.

Anger grew in his heart – but it was not the vile, burning rage that had driven him to attack Giles. This was a fierce, pure anger: it strove against the voice that had so often turned him against himself and all that he held dear.

You would fight me, heir of Eben? Divested of all disguise, the voice openly mocked him. *You have not the skill for that. You are mine. Why do you resist?*

Eamon shut his eyes. The voice penetrated like a hundred incisive blades. The plain shivered blackly around him. He was not alone – something hovered ghoulishly just beyond his ken.

"Get away from me!" he cried. His skin crawled with the sensation of something brushing past him, round him, encircling him.

You are sworn to me. I will not leave at your behest. Your oath is binding.

"Leave me!"

The black cloak seemed grotesquely large on his shoulders. His heart pounded and his whole body shook.

The voice laughed at him.

"Leave me!" he cried again, desperately.

Did you not hear? You swore yourself to me. Your blood is bound to my will. It has always been bound to me. None can free you from that. I command you, Eben's son! Learn it at last, and submit yourself to me. Serve my glory.

Eamon froze. This was it: the moment he feared had come. He tried to hold to Mathaiah's defiance but the memory was blown away by the darkness. All he remembered was the cadet's body writhing on the ground.

Do not delude yourself. You are the traitor's heir. You can have no choice.

There, in flame-bound darkness, Eamon felt his whole heart inclining, submitting all to the voice that had known him longer than he had been made.

Come, Eben's son. You yearn after me; you know where your place lies. Bind yourself to me.

Courage, Eamon!

His will and heart rose to the call. Rising above the insidious, crawling din of the unseen beast that hounded him, he made his choice:

"In the name and grace of the King, get behind me!" Eamon yelled. "Do you hear? Behind me and hence!"

The darkness was gone. His hands met the walls of a building on

Coronet Rise. A cat crouched near him. He steadied himself against the stone. Blood raced in his veins.

The dreadful voice was gone. He tentatively awaited its resurgence but found nothing in his mind but silence. His own thoughts returned to him clearly.

He did not know what would happen when he left Dunthruik or how he could do what had been commanded of him. But he would try. And there was something that he had to do before he left. He might not have another chance.

Go, Eamon.

His heart washed with courage, he returned to the palace. Men fell back before his determined stride. He stopped for none; his will laid clear the road before him. Reaching the Hands' Hall, he passed through the guarded passages without a moment's hesitation.

He went to the Pit.

There was a small antechamber at the foot of the case where trailing torches blackened the walls. The doorway to the Pit stood open, its smell overpowering. Eamon steeled himself against it and strode inside.

The gaping fissure in the cavern stood open. The system of ropes and pulleys suspended over it hung motionless. Two Hands stood guard there, masks drawn over their noses and mouths to lessen the choking stench. As Eamon entered they rose from the table where they sat alone. It was late. Lord Cathair was not there. Eamon knew it at once: none of the doors leading to the smaller chambers were open. Cathair liked others in the Pit to hear the nature of his work.

"Lord Goodman." The Hand seemed uneasy in his presence. Eamon imagined that his name had run before him.

"I come from Lord Cathair," Eamon told him. "I will address Cadet Grahaven."

"Good luck to you, my lord!" the other Hand sniffed, muffled by the mask. "None can get anything from him. Lord Ashway practically hurled the boy back down there this afternoon; he spent three hours trying to break him." Eamon shuddered. The throned had ordered further questioning of Mathaiah?

He laughed grimly. "I have breached this man. He will not elude me."

"Do as you will, Lord Goodman."

Eamon stepped up to the stinking welt in the cavern floor. His stomach pressed at him, but he gagged it and choked it back down. He heard coughs and desperate cries below. One was being quietened by the indistinct words of a firm, gentle voice. Eamon knew it at once: his ward's. He felt a surge of pride.

The Hands seemed uninterested in his doings; they had returned to their table and were engaged in conversation. Eamon heard them laughing together. However uninterested they looked, he resolved not to take any chances.

"Grahaven!" He forced his tone to fury. His hands shook. "Grahaven!"

Silence fell below.

"I am Grahaven," came the reply at last. "To whom do I speak?"

"You will know me well enough when I repay you for your insolence!" Eamon roared.

"You can only repay it to my body, Lord Goodman," Mathaiah answered. "And you shall be no better at that than your so-called Master."

Eamon turned to the Hands. "Bring him up," he commanded.

The Hands looked at each other uncertainly. Eamon heard laughter down below.

"I will not come up!" Mathaiah's voice was clear and bright.

One of the Hands shuffled uncomfortably. "Lord Goodman, he cannot be brought up." The Hand lowered his voice. "The light cannot hold him."

He remembered the red light that had drawn the arching, agonized body of Clarence's screaming son up from the Pit – the way it had crackled and burned like furnace irons. It could not hold Mathaiah? He was astounded.

"Very well – then I will go down."

He said it without thinking. The two Hands glanced at each other in alarm.

"Lord Goodman –"

"I will go down," Eamon repeated forcefully. The Hands did not move. Eamon glowered at them. "Oppose me, and you shall answer to Lord Cathair! Prepare the ropes."

The Hands began to work the ropes, bringing across a strung ladder that could be lowered into the orifice. The contraption looked flimsy; Eamon dreaded how climbing on it would be. But he had to go down; he could not leave the city until he had done so.

As the Hands worked he took off his cloak. He laid it aside and stood, shivering, in his remaining garments. He unbuckled his sword.

The Hands stared at him, but obeyed. They had steadied the ladder and let it hang into the Pit. It was carefully attached to one of the pulley systems so that they would not have to bear his weight as he climbed.

"You will bring him up?"

Eamon set his hands and feet into the first rungs. "If I must," he answered. "But my business can be conducted as well there." One of the Hands shivered at his grisly tone. They knew that he was a breacher, and what that entailed. They would not interfere. He smiled slickly. "I will call you when I have concluded."

He began descending the ladder. The climb was longer than he expected it to be; he remembered Cathair's insinuation that the Pit was much larger below than its narrow entry suggested. Cathair had certainly been truthful in one thing: it was completely dark. Eamon could see nothing as he fumbled down. The sounds of human suffering grew louder. He fought the urge to retch.

Suddenly a voice below burst forth. For a moment Eamon could barely distinguish the sounds, for the darkness and the terrible smell distorted them. But then they reached his ears like the notes of silver trumpets.

> *"I have been hounded into night*
> *By foes that seek to take my life,*
> *But there is light inside of me*
> *Born of a hope they cannot see."*

Eamon's heart soared. How well he knew that voice and how strongly it sang!

More rallied to Mathaiah's song, until all other sounds were drowned by the bounding power of the melody:

> *"Though fires raze and tempests cry*
> *I'll be a King's man 'til I die.*
> *He is my hope, my strength, my shield,*
> *Before him alone I kneel."*

Eamon reached the ground of the Pit. It was slippery with excrement and vomit; the reek threatened him with fainting. He forced himself to breathe. Singing voices surrounded him in the dark. Most were faint, some old, some young. The song reverberated everywhere. None noted him as he descended – he was just one more shadow in a pit of hell. Straining his ears he listened to the voices, trying to pick out Mathaiah's.

> *"I fear no harm, nor darkness drear,*
> *I fear not flame, nor mired mere.*
> *I do not fear the eagle's throne;*
> *I fear my awesome King alone."*

Eamon stumbled towards the cadet's voice. Filth soaked into his breeches; his very boots filled with it. But there was such strength and joy in the song that it drove him forward.

Mathaiah's voice was right before him now, unfettered and resounding. He imagined the cadet standing with his defiant head raised to the unseen reaches of the starry sky.

Suddenly joy was in him and the song was on his lips – though he neither knew it nor clearly heard what he sang in the dark. One voice near him faltered as he lifted his own, for it recognized him and fell silent. He did not care; he sang as though his one voice could break all the darkness in the world:

> *"In iron towers and pits of stone,*
> *'gainst roaring wind or rising foam,*
> *My true vow calls again to me,*
> *And in his service I am free."*

He felt something warm at his breast – and his eyes seemed to see. It was no deception: streams of light, faint but true, escaped from the shards bound in the pouch. Suddenly he saw Mathaiah. His ward stood before him, eyes wide in fear and amazement. The singing was strong around them.

Eamon sank to his knees before his friend. The sludge was thick. He bowed his head to his breast. Fear threatened him: what if his ward would not listen to him? What if, after all he had done, he could not be forgiven?

"Mathaiah," he breathed. He began shaking uncontrollably. "I'm sorry."

Tears broke on Eamon's cheeks. He reached into his pouch. The silver ring came forth on his palm with a glowing shard; he held both towards the young man. It seemed a piteous gesture, but he did not falter.

"I brought this," he whispered, "to return it to you."

Mathaiah gasped. Eamon closed his eyes, feeling his heart upon a precipice. He had laid himself before the young man whom he had held above all other friends; he could only wait.

A hand reached out and clasped his own, its grasp firm. Eamon opened his eyes. Mathaiah knelt with him. His breath died in his throat. The cadet's eyes searched his. Then Mathaiah smiled.

"Eamon!" His voice was washed with joy that went beyond his

frame. Eamon's name had scarcely sounded as dear to him as it did in that moment.

They began to laugh and cry, overcome and overjoyed. They embraced each other, and in their joy their voices rose up again to join the peal of song in every cranny of that darkened place:

> *"Let darkness try me if it can!*
> *I shall burst through every band,*
> *Darkness cowers, for I sing*
> *Of the coming of the King!"*

Light erupted from the pouch at Eamon's breast; startled, he covered his eyes, but when he looked he could see light, blue light, flowing along every wall and rising upwards towards the Pit's opening. It gathered strength from the song, which carried it up with awesome speed.

The walls began to shake and then to rumble. The Hands above cried out in alarm. Suddenly there was a great crack and stones sheered away from the narrow entrance. Then the roof of the mire was shattering to dust, tumbling into the Pit beneath. That dust neither hurt nor blinded, but fell as a gentle rain to cover all the filth and torment that had lain below. Torchlight flooded down from the cavern above. The prisoners cheered and the blue light struck out of the Pit with a startling clarity.

Then it was gone. The song lingered in the air behind it.

There was a long silence. Eamon saw the light at his breast falling still again, and though torchlight reached them it seemed poor compared with the light that had been. He could just make out Mathaiah's awestruck face before him.

Eamon knew it would not be long before the Hands ventured to the lip of the shattered Pit seeking him. He grasped his friend's hand.

"You were right."

"I was right about you," Mathaiah answered, eyes shining with joy. "I knew you would come back. But I was so afraid –"

"I meant that you were right about Alessia."

Mathaiah faltered. "I'm sorry." He seemed genuinely grieved.

"No, I am. You never deserved what I dealt you. I don't have much time," he said suddenly. "I'm going to the King, Mathaiah."

"What?" Mathaiah whispered. "How?"

"My own foolishness – but perhaps it will work to the good." Eamon looked nervously up to the roof of the Pit – were the Hands coming? "The King's grace is with you. Hold fast, Mathaiah. I will come back for you."

"Don't fear for me," Mathaiah answered firmly. "They can do nothing to me. But for you they are still laying traps. They have been trying to break you far longer than me. They will not stop. They have some design for you – something ancient, twisted. Please, Eamon…" He placed his hand on Eamon's shoulder. "Be careful. And hold to the King."

"I will." His promise was given, and he meant to keep it.

A voice came down from above, choked and distressed. "Lord Goodman! Lord Goodman!"

Eamon pressed ring and shard into Mathaiah's hand.

"Where did you –?"

"They are yours."

"I wanted to tell you –" Mathaiah began.

"You will tell me." Eamon raised his voice: "Ropes!" He looked back to Mathaiah. "You will tell me, when I come back for you."

"Yes… sir."

Eamon embraced him, then rose from the sludge and dust. It was in his hair and clothes; his skin was plastered and his boots were filled with filth, but his heart was clear.

"Ropes!"

The shadow of the rope appeared above him. Eamon took hold of it. Then he was hoisted up in fits and starts. As he reached the crumbling lip of the Pit he realized why: the Hands were hauling him up themselves. The pulley system was snapped and hung precariously overhead. As he staggered out into the upper chamber, Eamon still felt the reverberating song. It thrilled him.

"Are you well, Lord Goodman?" The Hand's face wrinkled in distaste at the state of him, an expression that made Eamon want to laugh. Just in time, he remembered to perform a fierce scowl.

"Do I look well to you?"

"What happened?" The Hands shook, and Eamon realized that what they had witnessed – the awesome power of the King's grace – was terrifying.

"I was trying to do my work, and I was interrupted," he snapped. "Report the matter to Lord Cathair," he added tersely, striding away from the lip of the Pit. "I have business to conclude."

"But Lord Goodman, how do we explain –?"

Eamon rounded on them. "It would seem that the singing started it, so I suggest that you do something about the singing. Tell Lord Cathair that I breached the snake to help me with my task and that I bid him a most cordial farewell. He may discuss the matter with me on my return."

The Hands gaped. Eamon treated them to another angry scowl and snatched up his cloak and sword. With song and light echoing in his heart, he left the Pit.

It was nearly the second watch when he reached the South Gate. He barely believed what he had done.

Mathaiah had forgiven him. He did not know what dark roads they would both tread before they next met, but it gave him hope and courage. Perhaps Hughan would forgive him, too.

The guards at the gatehouse were expecting him. They expressed surprise at his state. He did not explain it to them. He was able to exchange his stinking breeches for a pair of standard Gauntlet issue. His black shirt he left as a rag for the gate guard's litter of puppies. The guards happily supplied him with an old, white, officer's shirt, of the kind intended for wear under ceremonial uniforms. It was not practical, but it was clean. He kept his back away from them as he changed, to hide the marks of his flogging.

Chapter XXV

He was brought a horse – a dark creature with a patch of white on its broad nose. It breathed softly and patiently in the darkness. It little guessed where they would go – or that it carried the man who had chosen to be First Knight.

He rode to the gate, a group of men in its shadow. One stepped forward: Manners, jaded with fatigue. A few other Third Banners were with him.

"Shouldn't you be at college, gentlemen?" Eamon asked quietly.

"Yes, sir – my lord," Manners corrected himself. He had a haunted look. "Will you – you will come back, my lord?" he blurted.

Eamon met and held the cadet's gaze. "I will return, Mr Manners. You have my word."

Manners searched his eyes. "Thank you, my lord." The Third Banners saluted. Their drawn swords shimmered, marking Eamon's moonlit passage.

It was early on the twentieth of February. He glanced up at the gate, so tall it seemed to touch the clouded sky. By the twenty-seventh he had to have returned, bearing with him the head of Hughan's ally. It chilled him. It seemed impossible.

He tightened his grip on the reins. He would not fail. There would be a way. He would go to Ashford Ridge – where Hughan's camp had been, where he had breached Giles, and where Dunthruik had lost almost two hundred men. If he rode hard, he might reach the ridge by the next evening. He would reach it. He had to. Hughan would receive him, forgive him, help him.

And if he did not? Or if King and camp were gone – if there was nothing to find but the bodies of the Master's dead… what would he do then?

"Good luck, Lord Goodman!" Manners called.

Eamon grimaced. He needed more than luck.

"Courage," he murmured to himself. "Courage."

He urged his horse into a canter and clattered out of the city gates.

Eamon Goodman's journey continues in Volume II of
The Knight of Eldaran: The King's Hand.

ANNA THAYER

Anyone can deceive. But there's always a price.

THE KING'S HAND